MAIN CHARACTERS AND FAMILIES
IN THE STOCKHOLM SERIES

NILSSON

Henning (b. 1845, d. 1879) and *Lotten* (b. 1848, d. 1889)
have the following children:
August (b. 1868, see Bodin), *Emelie* (b. 1870),
Gertrud (b. 1871, see Lindgren)
Olof (b. 1879, d. 1902).
Olof marries *Jenny* Fält (b. 1881); their daughter is *Maj* (b. 1900).
With the singer Julius Törnberg Jenny has a daughter,
Elisabet Törnberg (b. 1910).

LINDGREN

Thumbs (Ture, b. 1845) and *Matilda* (b. 1845) have three sons:
Rudolf (b. 1868), *Knut* (b. 1870) and *Mikael* (b. 1875). Rudolf
marries Gertrud Nilsson. They have two sons and three daughters.
Knut is married and has a family; Mikael goes to sea.

BODIN

Fredrik (b. 1835, d. 1898) and *Annika* (b. 1846) adopt August
Nilsson as their son; he receives the name Bodin.
August marries *Ida* Wide (b. 1868); their children are:
Karl Henrik (b. 1895), *Charlotta,* (b. 1897), *Anna* (b. 1898),
Fredrik (b. 1900) and *Elisabet* (b. 1904).
With Bärta (see Karlsson) August has a son,
for a long time unbeknownst to him,
Gunnar (b. 1889).

KARLSSON

Johan (b. 1870) and *Bärta* (b. 1868) have the following children:
Tyra (b. 1895), *Beda* (b. 1897), *Erik* (b. 1899) and *Bengt* (b.
1900). With August Bodin, Bärta has a son, Gunnar Karlsson
(see Bodin).

In *City of My Dreams* the years 1860–1880 are depicted. *Children
of Their City* covers 1889–1900, and *Remember the City* spans
1900–1925. Two more novels follow in the Stockholm Series.

STOCKHOLM SERIES: II

CHILDREN OF THEIR CITY

STOCKHOLM SERIES: II

CHILDREN OF THEIR CITY

1882—1900

A novel
by
Pers Anders Fogelström

*Translated from the Swedish
by
Jennifer Brown Bäverstam*

The Stockholm Series:
City of My Dreams
Children of Their City
Do You Remember That City
In a City Transformed
City in the World

Children of Their City originally published in Swedish as *Barn av sin stad*
by Albert Bonniers Förlag, Stockholm, 1962.
Swedish copyright © 1962 Per Anders Fogelström
English translation copyright © 2008 Jennifer Brown Bäverstam
Penfield Books, Iowa City, Iowa
Library of Congress Control Number: 2008936022
ISBN 978-193204348-8

Cover design by Molly Cook/MACook Design
Front cover illustration detail from, "On Kungsbron" by Erik Tryggelin,
October 1898, courtesy of the Stockholm City Museum.
Back cover photograph by Jennifer Brown Bäverstam.

TABLE OF CONTENTS

III

IV

THE AUTHOR

PER ANDERS FOGELSTRÖM is one of the most widely read authors in Sweden today. *City of My Dreams,* the first book in his five-volume Stockholm Series, broke the record for bestsellers. A compelling storyteller known for his narrative sweep, his acute characterization and the poetic qualities of his prose, Fogelström was highly acclaimed even before he wrote the *Stockholm Series.* Ingmar Bergman made one of Fogelström's earlier novels, *Summer with Monika,* into a film that is now a Bergman classic.

Born in 1917, Fogelström grew up in Stockholm and lived there his entire life. He was a vast resource on Stockholm's history with enormous archives on the subject, and published much non-fiction about the city. He spent his early career as a journalist, and in the 1940s he co-founded a literary magazine. His own prolific writing resulted in over fifty books.

Fogelström's *Stockholm Series* has remained a favorite in Swedish literature among readers of all ages, and he continues to be greatly loved and respected as a chronicler of his people. Fogelström died on Midsummer Day, June 20, 1998, two days before the unveiling of a statue of him at the entrance to the hall where the Nobel prizes are awarded in Stockholm.

THE TRANSLATOR

Jennifer Brown Bäverstam has traveled and studied languages all her life. She has translated several books and articles from Swedish and French. She holds a degree in French and economics from Georgetown University and has studied translation at the University of Geneva. She lives in Boston, Massachusetts.

Translator's Note

Swedish place names are generally one compound word with the proper name at the beginning and the kind of place at the end.

Because most of the place names in the book have not been translated, the following terms explain endings for names of streets, hills, bridges, etc.:

backen: hill   **gränd:** alley
berget, bergen: hill, hills   **holm, holmen:** island
bro, bron: bridge   **torg, torget:** square
gatan: street   **viken:** estuary

I

CHILDREN
OF
THEIR CITY

The city had been called the rival of Constantinople in beauty and in squalor. It had been a picturesque yet dirty idyll. And its many poor had accepted life as it was; they had learned that neither weeping nor cursing helped. A person who did not emigrate had to try to adapt and go on living in the society that existed, through the years and in all the quarters of this idyllic misery.

When industry forced its way in, the sky darkened. Smoke rose from the foundries' furnaces and the smiths' fires, from the high factory smokestacks. Hammers pounded and wheels rumbled; tumbledown houses shuddered beneath the heavy breathing of the machinery.

Roaring factories pushed even further into the city, chewing the idyllic countryside and the greenery into a gray mass. It was as if poverty and misery grew out of these machines instead of being checked by them.

More and more workers were tied to the wheels that whirled ever faster. In spite of the stepped-up pace, work shifts were still both eleven and twelve hours long, and there weren't enough places to live for all those who were drawn to the city. Even if a great many new houses were built, numerous people still had to live crowded together in tiny hovels.

The multitudes—who were sometimes called "the working and the wretched"—coughed, went hungry and labored as they always had. Their misery felt more oppressive than before because now they had come to be aware of it, come to feel their degradation and their poverty. At times they felt like hating and mocking the people who incited them to struggle and insurrection, who gave them this new and bitter awareness.

If the rumble of the machinery was turned into song, it was the song of the treadmill they sang. Bitterness and hate grew. But the greater number of them neither had the strength nor the courage to give voice to their protests, they carried a dark heaviness inside them. This feeling of heaviness was there in the force of the sledgehammer when it fell on the anvil, when the sack of coal was hoisted, in the desperate grip on the work tools and levers. It tormented them—but they remained silent.

A twelve-year-old girl hurried down the walk made of wooden boards that hid Stora Badstugatan's runoff. Beneath her the sewer rushed and gurgled. Outside the many farmers' lodgings along the street, the first farmers had already gathered in the early morning. Flies buzzed beneath the carts where pieces of meat and cheeses were barely covered by old sacks and dirty horse blankets. The girl slipped quickly past, taking a few steps out into the mud of the street to avoid a couple of drunken tramps who had come to buy tainted meat, which they would later manage to unload door to door in the poorer neighborhoods. She lifted her long, gray skirt carefully. Her heavy, black boots gleamed, newly brushed.

She was roughly and simply dressed, small and gray with a pale face under the white headscarf. Yet she walked softly and lightly, her blue eyes sparkling with joy and curiosity. The house beside her began to shake: the machines in the mechanics' workshop had started up. And from inside the shed in the neighboring yard, the hammer blows of the wagon makers and coopers answered in reply. She knew the noises of the street, she also knew her way through the city. She was a little cog in the big wheels now, ever since school had ended, and she had found work. She was no longer afraid of the many men in the doorways, and hardly at all of the enormous bulls and oxen who were driven bellowing toward Hälsinge farms along Holländaregatan and Hötorget. She was beginning to get used to everything, could always slip away, move on. And, in any case, she couldn't stop and hide from it all—her way to work was long.

At the entrance to the factory she did stop a moment. High up on the hill at the crown of Trebackarlånggatan, the windmills swung their sails over garden plots and houses as if waving hello. Suddenly she laughed and waved back.

And the sun came out of the morning's gray mist, shining a fiery red between the gables of the houses. The hands of the church clock merged into a vertical line, and the bells began to chime six. It was a cool, early morning in August 1882.

ON THE STREET OF SMELLS

This was one of the roads into the city, from the north tollgate's small, silent houses to Hötorget's marketplace crowds and bustling commerce. Winding like a country road, it descended a spur of the ridge beside the tollgate, and then ran alongside a gray wooden fence bordering a giant sand pile. The houses that at the beginning had stood solitary, like country cottages in green gardens, grew denser, forming city neighborhoods. Breweries, tanneries, small industries, apartment buildings and farmers' lodgings were crammed in together; even the air thickened. A stench arose from the open sewers, from the large vats of the tanneries, from the bone meal factories' windmills and the dung heaps of the slaughterhouses and the stables.

Stora Badstugatan was mainly a street of pungent smells but there were also houses on it that emanated more pleasant odors, such as the many breweries or the large Ljunglöfska snuff company in number 24, and the little cosmetics factory in number 23.

Melinder's cosmetics factory lay on the corner of Trebackarlånggatan. A deep archway opened to a courtyard where carts and barrels stood between the sheds that made up the work areas. Inside the arch, a door led to the office where factory director Melinder and his two office clerks had a room facing the street.

Emelie, the twelve-year-old girl, curtsied to the shadow behind the office door's frosted glass. Most likely it was just the cleaning lady, none of the fine gentlemen were usually here at six in the morning, and actually she was curtsying in jest and not out of politeness. She had noticed that the shadow in there couldn't see anybody who was passing by in the dark archway. Still, she continued to curtsy, while she silently giggled to herself:

"Good morning Director Me-hinder." It was Fat Tilda in perfume bottling who had made up the nickname, and she claimed that there was always something to hinder him whenever the factory director went to fulfill his promise of a pay raise. He was an old woman, Tilda had said. Then Emelie had laughed, much too loudly, but she could imagine Melinder's long, black coat growing out into skirts and him flapping across the courtyard like a large crow with his wings clipped.

It would soon be two months since Emelie had started working in soap packaging, ever since school ended at Malongen, back home on Nytorget. She had had dealings with Melinder for several years, when the factory owner was still a bookkeeper at the big cosmetics factory on Bondegatan. Emelie had taken work home, folding and pasting boxes from the factory. Melinder had praised her work many times. One day, half a year ago, he had been alone in the office when she came to be paid. He had asked if she would be finishing school in the spring and what she would do after that. Then the remarkable thing had happened; he had offered her a permanent job. He knew that she was quick and methodical, though she was only a child. He told her, in a voice low and full of secrecy so that Emelie felt she was conspiring with him, that he was going to take over a little factory and run his own firm.

The day after school ended she had begun at Melinder's factory. The way from her home on Nytorget on Söder to the factory on Stora Badstugatan behind Hötorget on Norrmalm was long; it took almost an hour both morning and evening. The working hours were also long, from six in the morning until seven in the evening, but the pay was good for a beginner and a minor: three kronor per week. The money was needed at home.

Emelie had to leave home by five each morning. She had always woken up easily and, at least now when it was summer and light out, her mother had only to say her name once softly and she would fly out of bed and get ready. Her siblings were still asleep, the one-year-younger Gertrud who still had a year left in school and Olof who was so little that he hadn't started school yet.

After the anxiety-provoking uncertainty of the first few days, Emelie began to learn the most direct route. And learned not to be frightened by so much that was new, variable and unruly. Now the morning walk was her daily adventure, a replacement of the freedom and games of the school recess. In the evening, her mood was heavier, almost melancholy. She preferred dreaming to playing.

She liked her work, even if it was tiring to stand all day long. At times her legs ached so she could hardly fall asleep when she crawled into bed as soon as she had eaten after arriving home. But she liked to work with her hands, to stack up the one pile of attractively packaged soaps she'd done after the other, to see how they disappeared into the large cartons. As if she were playing a game. It was exciting to try to step up her pace, see how fast she could go without doing bad work. She was as quick as the adults—some of them got irritated at times with her speed and adroitness. That pleased Emelie, and she picked up her pace even more. She could be merciless the way children can be in their games.

"Little snip," muttered the defeated Karin who had trouble keeping up. Karin had a fiancé, was expecting a child and beginning to be unwieldy. Both her fiancé and her child were accidents that had burdened her and destroyed her appetite for work. Emelie had to guard her soaps. When the foreman looked away, Karin sometimes took the opportunity to take some of Emelie's finished work to augment her own. She was seldom successful. Emelie didn't want to give in, not even when Karin pinched her or scratched her. But Greta, on Karin's other side, sometimes quickly shoved a few of her soaps over to increase Karin's pile so the foreman wouldn't complain about the pregnant woman.

Shortly before it was time for the morning break, the factory owner made his rounds through the work areas. He arrived in his formal black overcoat, stood carefully a little way from the large packaging table and saw how the deft fingers worked for him. Melinder was proud of his employees, but he couldn't let them know it. To outsiders he would say that they had been carefully selected, people he had observed a long time before he had offered them work. He wanted to show that he had scientifically and meticulously built up his factory. He had had the time over the many years of waiting for the inheritance which would make his plans possible.

The events of the last few years had made him wonder, occasionally, if one should really start a company in times like these. Melinder had his nightmares: from out of the darkness of the night and the city the under-class would rise up. He would warn his employees against the socialist agitators' attempts to stir up rebellion, explaining that he didn't want to give birth to and clothe any followers of that "lame tailor's" heresies. The employees began to be even more interested in what that Master Palm could have to say, since the factory director seemed so anxious.

Emelie was the factory director's youngest employee and Melinder had probably worried that the girl wouldn't be able to keep up. But now he could say that he had done the right thing when he had employed the girl, and took pleasure in his foresight and his sharp eye. Especially if he avoided looking at the increasingly swollen Karin. If he had known that the woman was pregnant, he would never have given her a job. He felt that Karin had deceived him somehow.

But he liked Emelie, and when he stood there and observed her she looked up and smiled. He gave a start and thought of continuing on, but then he just had to smile back. She looked silly—red from eagerness and ambition.

Emelie curtsied quickly and deeply and hoped that the factory direc-tor wouldn't notice that she was about to burst with laughter. But his long coat was really too much like a skirt, and she imagined she could see how his thin nose grew out into a long and sizeable beak.

A shadow fell over that day's work. It had a name: *The Season.*

The factory director had spoken with the foreman about the unex-pectedly large orders that had come in—a good sign, secure work for them all. But some orders were pressing and had to be attended to immediately; it was important to keep the new customers happy. Their space didn't allow for more people to be hired, and so they had to begin working over-time sooner than he had thought they would. Any sort of cash compensation would not be paid out, but the employees would be invited for coffee and buns at the end of regular working hours, and they had to begin that very day, all those who didn't have the most urgent reasons to go home at the regular hour.

The foreman relayed the message, and after a minute, the low-ceilinged room was buzzing with agitated voices. Karin and some others explained that they couldn't work overtime without any warning at all. The foreman complained ill-humoredly that he had no chance of getting off himself so he didn't think anybody else should either. He threatened to "remember" those who made trouble.

But some of them managed to stand their ground and left at seven o'clock, enviously watched by those who had to stay. Emelie didn't feel like she could ask to be allowed to leave even if she feared her mother would worry. She said nothing to the foreman and didn't find out that the factory director had said that naturally the girl could go home if she wanted to.

The packers sat down on boxes and stacks of cartons and drank coffee, the compensation for three hours' extra work. They poured it into their saucers and slurped it slowly; they had to admit that the factory director stinted on neither coffee nor buns. Old Greta massaged her sore legs, and Ellen ran out to the entrance to intercept her husband. He came by from the brewery at this time. Now he was the one who would have to make sure the children at home got fed. And the break was over, the work continued. At ten o'clock they had had enough, according to the foreman, now they should go home and sleep for a few hours.

Emelie wrapped her shawl around herself and hurried out. She stopped a moment in the entryway's arch. The darkness of the street waited, it was like plunging into cold water. Frightened, she stood and looked, thinking about an old woman who had been attacked out here. A terrifying man with a dark, bushy beard had hit the woman in the neck and tried to take her coin purse out of her dress pocket. But she had managed to cry for help and the villain had disappeared, running.

Now it would have been nice to have some company. But out of all the people, Emelie knew that only Fat Tilda from perfume bottling walked the same way, and she had left a long time ago. That department hadn't had to work overtime.

She looked toward Trebackarlånggatan. One of the new, covered streetcars was just being pulled around the corner by two horses, on the way down to the stables on Träsktorget. Emelie had an acquaintance there, a stable boy. They had walked across town together a few times. It had felt safe to walk side by side, and when they talked the way became short, it disappeared without their knowing how it had happened.

But no boy was waiting for her, there was nothing else to do but walk alone.

She pulled the shawl even more tightly around herself, as if she wanted to wrap it so tightly that bearded villains would see how impossible it was to take the empty coin purse she had in her dress pocket. She ran toward Hötorgetsgatan. The darkness seemed full of shadows and sounds. Horses whinnied inside the backyards, drunken farmers and vagabonds quarreled outside cafés and taverns. Horses' hooves clattered and wagons glided past and she thought about the collision she had seen: the gravel cart that had run into a coach and the coachman who had fallen down into the street bleeding from his mouth and nose.

Now the city felt dangerous, threatening. The worst part was around the open market at Hötorget, she thought. Lights gleamed from wagons and stalls; the last shops were in the process of closing. A few boys shoved each other on their way past, yelling, on the prowl for the half-rotten fruit that had been discarded around the stalls.

She ran as fast as she could. She stumbled over a wagon shaft, and felt pain shoot up her leg. She managed to get to her feet, and continued toward Drottninggatan. A sob caught in her throat, but still she didn't want to cry.

On Drottninggatan it was a little quieter, and anyway she didn't have the energy to run any longer. She tried to stay reassuringly close to some fine gentlemen, coming so close that she almost trod on the heels of one when they suddenly stopped at a doorway. They looked at her with annoyance and muttered something about lesser people letting their children run around half the night.

She turned onto Gustav Adolfs torg and continued across Norrbro. People hung over the railing and watched the fishermen seining. A short while ago someone had caught a salmon weighing seventeen pounds, and of course one wanted to be present for such a sensational event.

Habit made her turn onto Gamla Norrbrogatan, which ran behind the royal stables' dark, pungent walls. She regretted it almost immediately. It was like sticking her head in a sack. But she didn't want to lose time turning around and walking through the bazaars, and instead continued on, running across Lilla Norrbro, and heard the tromping of boots on the wooden surface while the water pounded in Stall Canal.

The lights of Västerlånggatan greeted her like a haven. Here she could walk more slowly again, feel the protection of the close walls and the closely spaced lanterns. The clock in Storkyrkan's belfry struck ten-thirty. She had never been out so late before. But she was big now; she was working. And during the fall there would be many late evenings, that was when they would be in the middle of the season.

Now Söder waited with its dark hills, with laughing whores on the benches around the equestrian statue at Slussen, with drunken sailors on the crowded incline of Stora Glasbruksgatan. But in some strange way she was no longer as afraid. She was at home, the rowdies were the rowdies of her own streets and she felt like she had seen them all before—and managed to evade them. Small and gray she glided up the hill, saw the face of the clock shining dimly in the moonlit haze around Katarina Church's tower, was glad it wasn't the witching hour yet. Her brother had told her that Sturen's horse galloped on the wall of the churchyard every night at twelve o'clock.

The small wooden houses along Nytorget lay dark. In one of the windows a curtain moved. Emelie ran a few steps closer, waving excitedly. The curtain moved faster. Mama was awake and waiting. The tension broke and the girl began to sob. Now she felt the pain in the leg she had banged, how her calves had stiffened from standing still all day and then walking rapidly in the evening. She felt so little, not at all like she had grown up and gotten a job. Foolish tears forced their way out, ran down her cheeks. And she ran limping across the square, through the gate in the fence, up the stairs.

NIGHT IN THE MAHOGANY VILLA

Lotten had stood at the window a long time looking out over the pot-holed and weed-covered field called Nytorget. From out of the darkness shone the planks of the walk that crossed the dark square at an angle. Large stones, piles of dirt and garbage heaps, carts pulled up alongside each other between tumbledown houses, it wasn't a beautiful scene being lit by the moonlight and a few gas lamps. But she knew the picture so well, had lived here as a child, and when she was young had stood in the window and waited, seventeen years ago. That was when she had danced in the yard and met Henning. When they got married and moved to Åsöberget, she thought she had left the past forever. Now she was a widow and back in the room and the house of her childhood, beside the square of her childhood, in the "Mahogany Villa," as people called the rotting wooden house.

Lotten was thirty-four years old but looked older. The years had worn her down. Heavy work had made her back bent, hunger and fatigue had made her chest cave in, while her stomach jutted out. Care and worry had carved furrows in her face, her eyes had become dim and almost lifeless, her hands coarse and cracked. She was a draft-animal, a deathly-tired person, an anxious mother. Life was over. Now she lived for her children. She was indifferent to everything else. She envied those who weren't obligated to go on living.

Once she had loved life, even the impoverished life of the poor. Now it frightened her. It gave so little and took so much. As long as Henning had been alive, even when he had been sickest, she had been warmed by his flame and had managed to be happy in spite of everything. She had been able to get over one of their children dying shortly after birth, but when Henning had died, one of consumption's countless victims, a piece of

Lotten had also gone with him. Numbed, she had given her consent for their oldest son to be adopted by some rich people. Of course, she had wanted to prevent it, had wanted to keep him, but it had to happen for the boy's sake.

She heard sighing from out of the darkness behind her: two of her children were sleeping. It was Gertrud, whom she seldom had to worry about; the girl was healthy and able, if still a little too lively. It was harder with the little one, Olof. His stomach had given him trouble ever since he was born; he woke up and cried in the night, and slept fitfully. Often she wondered if the child's agitation was caused by having been conceived by a fatally-ill father and a worn-out mother. The boy was the fruit of poverty and misery, of sickness and anxiety. How would things work out for him?

But when Lotten stood in the window her worry for her oldest daughter had taken hold and overshadowed the other worries. Emelie usually got home at eight o'clock every evening. The girl had a long way to walk and her workday was long, though, of course, they had to rejoice that she had gotten a good job. This evening the hours had passed and darkness arrived. Lotten had walked back and forth from the beds to the window, listened to the sleeping children, looked out for the one she expected, and thought about the boy she hadn't seen for several months now, he who no longer was hers. Now he was at the summerhouse of his new parents; in the fall he would surely be able to come home and see them again as a favor, once a week. Every time she had to wonder: how much longer? August hadn't said anything. Lotten didn't dare guess but sensed that his new mother, Annika Bodin, had regretted her promise about the visits. She probably would want the child for herself and sweep away the tracks that led from his poor home on Söder to the fine house on Skeppsbron. August bore their name now, the Bodin's.

Will everything be taken from me? Her worry over Emelie grew stronger again, what could have happened? Images of horror flashed before her: heavy streetcars rolling along, horses shying, drunken rowdies. The city was big and dangerous, the road long, and the girl was little, but self-assured, perhaps a little too unafraid faced with danger. If Lotten hadn't had to watch Olof she would have hurried out into the city to look for her and meet her. It was bad luck that the children's grandmother was away for the evening.

She pushed away the curtains to see better, thought she saw a shadow and leaned closer toward the pane. Something small and gray flew across the white plank walk down there, a hand waved, seemingly both joyfully and desperately. Lotten hurriedly drew the curtain back and forth in greeting.

She received the girl who threw herself into her arms. Gradually, the child calmed down, dried her tears, tried to tell her story. Actually nothing had happened, said Emelie, who was ashamed of her tears. She had just gotten scared and banged her leg. So nothing else had happened? No, she felt so dumb. Everything was just as usual, except that she had to work a few hours overtime, so it had had time to get dark out.

They had greeted each other in darkness. Lotten lighted the lamp now, turned the flame down low so as not to wake the sleepers. She gave Emelie a piece of bread to chew on and undid the shawl and the newspapers that she had wrapped around the potatoes to keep them warm. Still they had almost had time to grow cold, but it would take too long to light a fire in the fireplace and it was most important to get the girl to bed quickly. Besides, Emelie didn't have the strength to eat much, she was too tired and had stuffed herself with the factory director's good rolls, which sat like a lump in her throat and made it difficult to swallow.

Finally Emelie fell asleep, curled up beside Gertrud on the foldout sofa. Lotten sat where she was beside the lamp and sewed. For a moment, she was able to feel joy and thankfulness, the happiness and calm of at last sitting down. The soft, consoling darkness of the night and the room surrounded her. Now she had her children under her wing, they had found their way home and were safe with her. As if the house's and the room's rotting walls could protect them from a world, from all the evil and dangerous things which lay beyond. But August was still out there.

The boy was so cautious, afraid to say anything that might worry or wound. Sometimes Lotten sensed the barriers that were growing. Her son lived in a world which she didn't know, never would be able to make her way into. He spoke sometimes with new words that she didn't understand. He adopted other habits, knowledge, gained experience. Whether or not he wanted it, he was slowly being transformed into a Bodin. Even if he never forgot where he came from, he would still get used to servants bowing to him and the poor begging him for alms. He would enter the Bodin firm, and his words would be the orders of the workers. When he came to his old home, in some way he had to put on an act, use a language which his real mother and siblings understood, take on some of the customs which were beginning to be foreign to him, unfamiliar. The old world would become more and more of a memory, a dream. The new was everyday and real.

Walls that grew in the darkness. He could still get over them, though Annika Bodin might hold onto his coattails to prevent him.

Lotten became agitated, pulled so hard that the thread snapped and came out of the needle. With fumbling and aching fingers, she tried to coax it back into the small eye of the needle. Olof squirmed and started to whimper. She got up and tucked him in again, hoped that he wouldn't wake up and cry and waken Emelie who had just fallen asleep.

Didn't she have enough, so many people to take care of and worry about? Did she have to begrudge the childless Bodins the chance to take care of August? Shouldn't she rejoice that her son was so well off?

She tried to talk herself into it while she threaded the needle and went on sewing. She tried to feel grateful for what August was receiving and had received. Suddenly she fell asleep on the chair where she was sitting, worn out from the day's labors and the evening's worries. She never dared sit leaning over the table, for then she might knock over the lamp if she fell asleep.

It grew light out and the first rays of the sun fell slanting across the White Hills. The light woke Lotten's neighbor, Washer-Johanna, who had a window facing the courtyard and the hill. The unhealthily fat old woman sat up groaning, and pounded on the wall. According to their agreement, she would wake Lotten. Johanna's husband, who was called Fearsome by his workmates, was jostled awake by the swaying of the bed, broke off a snore midway, and blinked at his wife and the relentless light. Every day was a new torment; he had difficulty keeping up with the dock workers' hard job, he was starting to get too old. Below the bed, on the floor, their eldest son still lay asleep with his wife and two children. The youngest one had woken up and was groping hungrily for his mother. Still sleeping, the young woman arranged herself, her white breasts shone in the rays of the sun.

Everywhere in the mahogany villa's overpopulated hole, people began to get up. For the first time Lotten had to shake Emelie to get the girl to wake up and get ready for a new workday.

FRIENDSHIP POINT

The summer villas gleamed through the foliage, forming a wreath around the island of Stora Essingen's desolate interior. Wooden pinnacles and towers rose above the treetops to claim a view—and to arouse admiration. Steam launches and ships chugged by, plowing quickly disappearing furrows in the blue surface of the water. The Sea Maiden was on her way to Fittja and the island's own small sloop glided past the point called Friendship Point to then continue up toward Sans Soucie on Lilla Essingen island.

The boy who sat perched on the edge of the hill, on the boundary of the wilderness, knew the names of the numerous boats and their routes. He had sat here alone many days, read a book, and now and then checked on what was happening on the water. He fled his peers in the neighboring villas, those who knew his secret: he was the childless Bodins' adopted charity case. Small, refined young ladies would sometimes wrinkle their noses when they saw him, as if they smelled the poverty.

At times he felt as if he had no home—because he really had two. He didn't belong anywhere, was accepted neither by poor nor rich. His old friends stayed away when he came to Söder, or even threatened him with a beating sometimes. They saw him as some kind of a traitor. The children in the neighboring villas avoided this outsider who had made his way into their circle; they had heard their mothers talk about dangerous germs and contagious diseases.

At times he gave in to self-pity, tasting its cloying sweetness. Weren't both the rich and the poor better off than him? At least it was simpler for them, they followed their group codes, they were a *part* of it and not on the outside. They never had to brood, the road was laid out for them. As for himself, he stood on the sidelines, confronted by the constant need to make his own choices. To choose also meant to give something up. Actually even worse than that: it also meant to betray something. Wasn't he obliged to pretend the whole time? Pretend he was the way he always was when he visited his mother on Söder, not make her sad by revealing that he had become somebody else and that he could like his new parents too. Around the new parents he had to pretend he had almost forgotten everything old, silence his homesickness, hide his love for his real mother. The two mothers were jealous of each other, he understood that. They kept watch, spied on each other when they asked him seemingly innocent questions.

On Söder he had Mama, in his house he had the one he called Mother. Mama and Mother. Mother was the most difficult, the most dangerous. Because she was the one closest to him, she was the one who made decisions, and because she was the one who demanded the most. She had a constant need to conquer him, to turn him into her child completely. Sometimes he felt like she was devouring him.

Still he felt a kinship with Mother. They had both made it over that difficult to cross and well-guarded border. Both of them in disguise, they had tried to avoid being unmasked and excluded. They hid a secret and because of this were imposters of sorts, were bound to each other by the solidarity required of partners in crime.

August Bodin was fourteen years old. Without being especially tall for his age he looked older. He seldom played, but often read. His schoolmates of the same age seemed strangely young to him when they were unruly and mischievous and got into fights. He would barely miss them. The spring had ended with his high school entrance exam, and in the fall he was going to begin studying classics at Stockholm's High School for Complete Secondary Education on Södermalm. He savored the long name of the little school on Sankt Paulsgatan; it sounded so dignified that he even hoped his classmates there would be more grown-up in their behavior and appearance,

He closed the book, and climbed down from the rock. He thought he might sit a little while on the dock below, watch the steamboat Tessin pass by on its way to Drottningholm.

It wasn't until it was too late that he noticed someone on the way to the dock ahead of him, a girl. He didn't recognize her; she didn't belong to any of the neighboring houses beside the Bodins. Well, he wouldn't disturb her, he'd just sit on the opposite side of the dock from the one she chose.

But she stayed right in the middle, so he took his time on the shore, broke the head off a blade of tall grass and cleaned the shaft between his fingers.

She looked at him, and he lowered his eyes, afraid to meet her gaze and be beset by the usual thought: everyone knows, everyone can see I don't belong here. But at the same time, he tried to guess her age and where she lived. She was probably a few years older than him, fifteen or sixteen, possibly seventeen. If she wasn't a visitor, she probably belonged to one of the houses north of the dock, perhaps Augustenborg, which lay closest.

He couldn't just stand here like a bashful kid pulling at reeds. He had to make up his mind. He walked out to the end of the dock and scanned the horizon, as if he were waiting for a boat. But he couldn't stand there and pretend much longer, so then he sat down and let his feet dangle in the water. He heard her footsteps on the dock, the rustle of her skirts. Then her clear voice sounded and he gave a start and sat up.

"Has Tessin gone by?" she asked.

He rose politely to answer: No, not yet. He had been sitting and waiting on the hill up above, so he knew.

Did he live here?

Yes but farther south from here, near Värdshus dock.

She lived up almost as far as Stenbrottets dock, had been taking a walk. There was absolutely no one her age up there, no one she really liked being with.

Her light-colored cotton dress flapped in the wind. Laughing, she tried to tuck in some stray locks of hair the breeze was playing with.

"Here it comes!" he shouted. He had caught sight of Tessin, which had appeared beside the rocks of Långholmen.

They walked down to the grassy strip beside the water, saw the boat arrive, grow larger, pass by. Then the wake came rolling in, almost before they noticed it. Suddenly the first crest of waves broke over the grass, and they had to hurry to get out of the way. The girl tripped over her long skirts, and August had to grab hold of her so she wouldn't fall. He felt her nearness, how her hair tickled his cheek, and the scent of her perfume. Carefully he supported her, led her out of the path of the waves.

"Thank you " she said and laughed. "What's your name?"

He answered, and dared use the familiar form when he asked her name. Her name was Ida Wide and her father was a building contractor. What was his father?

A dead dock worker, he thought, but he answered, "A wholesale dealer." He blushed, a little disconcerted. He didn't know if he was lying or not. But if it was a lie, the lie was going to be the truth from now on. In any case it was easiest.

"Maybe we'll see each other again," said Ida. "I usually come down and watch Tessin."

He stood there a moment on the dock and watched her go. There was a warmth in her voice, something he was lacking: the joy of youth, and the confidence he knew one should have and exhibit in this class of society he now belonged to.

The light-colored dress fluttered amid the dark green of the trees while he stood there and longed to meet the girl again. Not because she was a girl and he had held her for a moment and felt her hair against his cheek, but because she was someone his age who might become his friend. Yes, just because she was friendly.

"Maybe we'll see each other again," she had said. She usually walked down to Friendship Point and watched Tessin pass by, and if he dared come down at the same time he might run into her again.

He lingered a little longer on the dock, to stay there in the evening glow. When he walked up the path a white handkerchief lay there shining against the brown pine needles. It must be hers, it hadn't been here when he came. Carefully he lifted the small lace-trimmed piece of cloth, and brushed away some pine needles that clung to it. He looked around nervously, but there weren't any people nearby. Then he sniffed the handkerchief and caught the scent of eau de cologne.

Now he had to meet her to give back what he had found. He didn't dare place the handkerchief in his pocket, it might get wrinkled and dirty. Instead, he carried it in his hand, felt the light, strange caress of the silk against his fingers and palm.

In the garden at Somarro, a worker was propping up the fruit-laden boughs of the apple trees. The man lifted his cap politely to "the young master," and August bowed a little clumsily and tried to hide the handkerchief behind his back. He sneaked into the house and managed to reach his room unseen. Once there he sat at the desk and looked at the message he had received, followed the curlicues of the lace, and anxiously made sure that the delightful scent hadn't disappeared. But when he heard footsteps on the stairs, he shoved his secret hastily into one of the desk drawers and pulled out a book. He seemed deep in his reading when Mother came in.

Annika Bodin made a little grimace of annoyance and small wrinkles flitted across her forehead and nose. He read constantly. That was good and of course he did well in school, but a young boy in a good and rather well-off family should look happier. His seriousness turned into a reproach, as if he were lacking something. Once again she had to anxiously wonder: did he long to be away from her, with *her*?

"Where have you been?" she asked.

"Over at Friendship Point."

"You should go see your friends instead," she said, and he heard how her voice sounded reproachful. She grew irritated that he always walked around alone and didn't want to keep company with the children from the neighboring houses. As if he didn't want to enter into the milieu that was and would continue to be his own, and instead bashfully and stubbornly keeping aloof.

"They are such nice children, of course," she continued in a friendlier tone. "It must be a lot more fun to get together with them than to go and wander around alone."

He wanted to answer what he believed to be the truth: they don't like me, don't want me around. But then he knew that Mother would try to "fix it," arrange something, invite people over, force them together, and he didn't want that.

"I want to read," he answered.

I hope he never decides to become a clergyman, she thought. It was surely a fine and honorable profession, but she wouldn't like having a minister so close, inside the family. Besides, he was going to take care of the company, succeed Fredrik when the time came.

"Father is coming from town on the three o'clock boat," she said and walked toward the door. "He has a guest with him. You can go meet them, I have to get changed."

Dusk came early in August. The kerosene lamps were lighted on the glassed-in porch. They spread their soft yellow light over the group around the table: the two dark-haired men and the stately, fair women, the boy who was curled up in a wicker chair and once again reading the letter he had received from his sister.

Annika Bodin bent forward to bring her coffee cup to her lips. She quickly squeezed one eye shut in reaction to the pain she felt when her corset cut mercilessly into her waist and ribcage. She had grown spoiled over the summer, worn a "home corset" everyday, which was hardly more than a camisole. Autumn awaited her now with its stringent demands and tight lacings. The dress that her seamstress was sewing required the body to be severely tortured and disciplined. The body was to shoot up like a slender stalk from the wide vase of her hips, with her breasts pushed out and lifted as high as possible,

She smiled at the lovely torments that awaited, the privileges and pastimes. Meanwhile the host and his guest, a tavernkeeper, who was among the Bodin firm's more important customers, were conversing about the events of the day that they could touch on when a woman and child were listening. The new bridge, Vasabron, had collapsed again after months of repair work. As soon as the authorities closed off a street or bridge they could be sure that the site would lie deserted, despite the fact that there was no shortage of workers. The bridge had stood for weeks without anyone doing anything to it and people had to spend two öre and put up with the inconvenience of taking a dilapidated old steam launch.

Scandalous, that's what it was. That troublemaker Palm could try to get those imbeciles who were working on Vasabron moving, thought Fredrik Bodin.

The tavernkeeper had passed by Lill-Jans Park where the lame tailor was holding one of his seditious meetings, he told them. A few hundred people, mostly boys, had stood and listened. The tailor had told them that everything wrong with society would be fixed if his listeners organized on his side.

The gentlemen laughed and lifted their glasses. The tailor was a crazy utopian that they didn't have to take seriously. Though of course there were great inequities in society, admitted Fredrik Bodin. He had seen his share first hand—the firm was located right on the harbor. A while back an unmarried mother with three children had tried and succeeded in drowning her youngest just below Last Farthing Stairs. She hadn't been able to find housing for herself and her children. Nobody wanted to take in a crying baby, so she had killed the youngest in order to take care of herself and the other two.

"August, can you go see if the girls remembered to bring in the embroidered tablecloth from the arbor," interrupted Annika. Fredrik looked at his wife, a little annoyed. The boy could certainly handle hearing this, as big as he was.

August stuffed the letter he had received into his pocket and left. Of course he had listened, felt something of the black, sinking feeling that always came when someone talked about the poor and the harbor. He wondered if he had ever met that mother, the one who had killed one child to save two others. Why had his own mother given him away? For his sake, or for the sake of the others, the ones who got to stay with her? For their sake, he thought in the twilight. It felt best to think that way, to feel himself sacrificed, deserted. It felt so close now when he had a letter from home. Though Emelie only said that everything was the same as usual, except that she had to work overtime, till ten every evening.

As for himself, he was on summer break, free. He had it the best of all the siblings. Still, at times he wanted to change places. He wondered how Emelie would like it here if she could come here and walk around dressed as nicely as the girl he had met that morning.

That led his thoughts in other directions, and the flowers along the path smelled like eau de cologne and he no longer felt sacrificed and abandoned.

The next day he went back to Friendship Point, getting there in plenty of time, and he sat on the dock and tried to read. That didn't work: he had to continually turn his head to see if the girl was in sight. She came and got her handkerchief, it seemed as if she had hardly noticed she had dropped it.

"We're moving back to town tomorrow," she said.

So he didn't see her any more that summer. Their meeting never had a chance to grow into a friendship, but he had felt some sort of friendliness and welcoming warmth; she had treated him like an equal. August felt the temptation to forget his old life, to stop the balancing act in between and move into the new.

Betray? Was it necessary in order to live happily? He could remember the tone and the expression on the face of Thumbs, Papa's friend, who had warned him: they will want to turn you into a traitor. Resist. Never forget where you come from, never forget the injustices and the outrage.

But both Mama and Mother thought Thumbs was a man with strange ideas. Mother even said that prison was the right place for such agitators and that Thumbs would certainly end up there someday. She inquired at times to be sure that August never met that dangerous man when he visited his old home at Nytorget.

A TIME OF GROWTH

The city grew with amazing energy. Avenues were laid out over previously bare fields, while previously developed areas turned into deserted expanses with half-wrecked buildings jutting up over blasted rocky outcroppings, dug-up streets and demolished gardens.

It had taken six centuries for the city to reach a population of one hundred thousand; only thirty years had been necessary to double that amount. Now the inhabitants were living in a gigantic construction site. They watched with regret and pride at how their city was transformed. It would never again be the way it had been before. Much of what they liked would disappear, but it would be better and cleaner, straighter and grander.

The people from the countryside arrived in a steady stream. Many of the new ones had to begin with building up the city that would become their own. Workers' housing was constructed on the mainland, palatial buildings in the new city center that extended farther and farther north of the old city. Wires were extended to the buildings where the latest wonder was to be installed—the telephone.

All land inside the tollgates rose in value without cease. A man who had owned a couple of shabby wooden houses and, after arguments and threats, had managed to extract a few kronor from his obstinate tenants, could now find that he owned a gold mine—centrally located plots of land. Many hurried to buy land from those who had not yet become aware of their new opportunities. Mysterious figures with strange nicknames presented themselves as building contractors: Brawler, Loudmouth-Kalle, Calamity-Pelle. Often these so-called building contractors were only fronts. They hired some knowledgeable underling to be in charge of the work and cashed in on the profits themselves.

Some started with only a fifty-kronor bill in their pockets. That sum was enough for a down payment on a parcel of land, and then they could take out a bank loan for the construction. If the architect was too expensive, an apprentice draughtsman could draw up the building plans needed. Many suppliers gave generous and long-term credit. A general contractor wasn't even under any obligation to keep accounts, a duty which otherwise affected the smallest grocer. Some of the building contractors lived like they were in the middle of a gold rush; they tossed around large sums, made enormous profits and losses and partied as if each day might be their last.

They liked to gather at Bähr's Café on Riddarhustorget, which was conveniently near the Hantverkar Bank on Storkyrkobrinken. Bills of exchange and securities were passed around along with cakes filled with meat and cheese, and ice buckets with bottles. Sometimes a grim-faced and silent group of workers stalked through the locale in search of foremen and builders who had cleared out without paying the weekly wages. The workers always came in a group, well aware that superior force was necessary if they were to get their money and not a punch in the face. Many work teams might wait until eleven or twelve o'clock in the evening on paydays before the foremen came with the money. Sometimes they had to take the law into their own hands. One team had made their way into their employer's house and, despite the protests of the contractor's wife, had hauled the house piano to the pawnshop.

Herring wholesaler Fredrik Bodin was one of those who suddenly found himself sitting on a gold mine. His father had invested a fair amount in land—idiotic speculation, the son had thought many times. The properties had yielded a lot more trouble than income over the years. Even if it went against his grain, Fredrik had to admit that it was due to luck more than skill that he still owned the properties. If anybody other than that notoriously miserly goldsmith had come to him with the first offer, who knew how it might have gone. He had come close to being fooled by Troberg's proposition: two thousand kronor for a few shacks ready to be torn down alongside Stora Träskgatan and Smalagränd. But because it was Troberg, he had realized in time that the offer must mean that there was more money to be made.

It was after a good dinner at the Bodin home by Skeppsbron that his friend Troberg had put out his hook. Fredrik had to smile when he recalled the conversation, how eager Annika had become, how close a call it was. It had felt good to explain things to her afterward, felt good for his self-esteem. It was so seldom that he got to show himself cleverer than Annika, she always wanted to know best.

Naturally, she couldn't be gotten the better of. She had changed her mind about the whole affair so he was wrong in any case. He should have looked into the prospects earlier; they had skimped and gone without and been on the verge of ruin and bankruptcy with a fortune hidden in his pocket. He sold herring while shrewd men made huge transactions in property and construction.

Sometimes he felt like tormenting her. Make her feel small and afraid, so small that she would be able to love him. But it was a dream without hope and he knew that his presence filled her with disgust. He went less and less often to her bed now. That route was closed, and he was looking for a path away from her.

At his office, he had a map that he had bought the day after Troberg had made his offer. On the map, he could trace the brown shading, which indicated built-up areas. It created an image of a woman's figure he thought: the head was the new buildings around Drottningbroviken, the bust extended between Central Station and Nybroviken, the arms were stretched out toward the old houses on Kungsholmen and Ladugårdslandet's stately esplanade. The waist was slender as a reed, and Slussen and Södermalm were a wantonly short and full-fringed skirt. In the evening dusk the figure of the woman became an indeterminate shadow. Still, he could see how the woman danced and heard her promises. She was soft and weak and waited for his strength; she admired his power. She was a dream without the flaws of reality.

But reality had been good also. Fredrik Bodin had become one of the city's new "building developers." One good apartment building was soon to be ready for occupancy, on Kammargatan near Adolf Fredrik's Church. An even grander house had been started on Drottninggatan; he had a lot of speculators on that one. Eventually he would also begin to plan what would happen on the property that Troberg had tried to swindle him out of: on the future boulevard that would run the length of Stora Träskgatan, all the way down to Nybro Harbor.

Fredrik could give himself credit for being cautious; he hadn't thrown himself into any foolhardy transactions. And he had an old builder, one of his father's surviving friends, as advisor. As the foundation for the new business there was the old, and at times utterly despised, herring firm. Often he longed to get away from it to a less foul-smelling operation. That was why he liked to put on his hat and coat and take up his cane and set off to inspect his building sites.

The September day was sunny and fine, and Fredrik strolled along slowly among the harbor's motley and ever changing working life, past the construction of the elevator alongside Mosebacke. They had just raised the last roof truss on the building at the foot of the large elevator. The flags flapped from the scaffolding, and the names of the builder and the construction company stood in letters forming a large wreath. The elevator was one of the many signs of the new era, an innovation. As one of the city's building contractors, Fredrik Bodin felt himself a participant. He was one of the ones creating the new city, the new world.

He walked past the locks at Slussen and quickened his pace when he saw a trolley car standing there on the other side of the bridge. The powerful draft horses were munching in their feedbags while the driver and conductor had locked their fingers in a tug of war. Fredrik climbed onto the car with the ring line's green sign, and a couple of minutes later the trolley car was shaking and rumbling along Lilla Nygatan on its way to Vasabron. At the double tracks of the passing point, it had to wait while trolley cars going the opposite direction passed. His route continued past Central Station and onto Barnhusgatan along toward Stora Bastugatan, where Fredrik got off. Now there were just a few steps to the building on Kammargatan.

That day Fredrik had arranged a meeting with the builder who had put up his own first building. In a week or so, by the first of October, it would be ready for occupancy. Fredrik himself would take the best apartment, a corner apartment one flight up. Annika wasn't really pleased with the building's location; it was a little too far out, and the area was a little too middle class. She would have preferred to live down in the Klara or Jacob areas, or most of all up along the new esplanade, where so many upper class people were trying to move.

But the house was well situated, in Fredrik's opinion, close to Adolf Fredrik's cemetery. The apartment on the second floor would give a fine view of green trees, and the location was quiet with a one-block buffer from the stench and noise of Stora Badstugatan. At the rate the city was growing, it would soon be very centrally located. August would not have so far to go to his new school. The boy would of course have to transfer from Södra Latin to Norra. As for Fredrik himself, he would have farther to go, as long had he kept his firm down at Stadsgården. They were talking about new demolition and blasting to widen the harbor even more, and in that case he would have to move the firm anyway. He wasn't sure he would continue selling herring. This new business with construction and property was more appealing.

The building contractor, Granat, came out and shook his hand. Granat's giant fist gave away the fact that it hadn't been so long since he was a bricklayer.

"Be glad that I used an anchoring iron," he shouted over the din. " A stairway on Söder collapsed last night, the builder had saved money on iron... there... You can't be too stingy, see."

It was Granat who had spoken in favor of saving money this time, but Fredrik had stuck to the advice of his father's old friend concerning an anchoring iron in the stairway. The building contractor had forgotten this now. Fredrik didn't remind him, Granat became quarrelsome and difficult easily, but was known as reasonably good at his profession.

"Everything is rented out," he said instead.

"Damn right," the big man answered with confidence. "Anything you can build you can fill with people too. Actually you should start building a lot of small apartments now. A number people have started doing that."

"Is it really profitable?" asked Fredrik.

"Of course," the builder assured him. Calculated according to square or cubic meters, the apartments become more expensive the smaller they are. He could tell wholesaler Bodin that the city itself was the worst when it came squeezing rent out of people. Up on Södra Tullportsgatan, they had housed eight women with their twenty-two children in one room. The fathers of the families couldn't live there. Each family had to pay five kronor per month. That amounted to forty kronor in monthly rent for a single room in a hovel with broken windows. There wasn't a luxury apartment where they had to pay the same price per square meter.

"They must be living in cramped conditions, those people..."

"Well, I suppose," the builder acknowledged. "Their closest neighbor is a branch of the Dihlström Institution with sixty men in bunks on top of each other all in the same room. It all depends on what you get used to. Men are waiting in line to get in there. If you're poor you can get used to a lot."

Workers passed by and bowed to their building's proprietor, and Fredrik touched his hat brim and smiled in a friendly manner. He felt himself to be a good employer; no one had to hunt him down at the taverns. For a moment he wondered how those who were constructing his new building might be living. Maybe one of them had a wife and children in one of those barracks Granat had told him about. Maybe one had been part of that group of homeless people the police had rounded up down in an alleyway at the harbor the other night. He didn't know. But Granat was probably right about it being profitable to build small apartments. It was a good deed, too. He would discuss the matter with his father's old friend.

His dead brother's widow, Margareta, had, of course, inherited some of the old man's lots also. A few were on Söder, a "suitable" neighborhood for workers' housing. He would have to speak with his sister-in-law about those properties, warn her against selling to anyone else and maybe being cheated. He couldn't pay too much if there was to be any sort of deal for him—but still: honorable. Though he wouldn't be able to tell Annika about it, she hated Margareta and would think that any price was too high. Once Annika had pressured him into giving his sister-in-law the least possible compensation. That was when the firm had been threatened with bankruptcy, and he had bought out Margareta for a paltry sum. Once had been enough, he couldn't manage carrying more shame.

When he got home to the house on Skeppsbron he had to eat dinner alone. Annika was indisposed and lying down, and August had eaten earlier and was now out visiting his mother and siblings on Söder. The building developer, with all his great plans, sat feeling alone, unease gnawing at him. No one to talk to, no one who cared about him or wanted to listen to everything he had to say. He wondered if he should go out and meet August. He didn't want to look like he was spying on the boy or trying to hurry him up. It was only to keep him company on the way home, only to have someone to talk to, and then he could pass by those properties that Margareta owned and see what could be done with them.

He drank a few glasses of cognac with his coffee and felt the way he usually did—the drink affected him a little. It would probably be good for him to take a walk. If he sat at home he would drink more. He looked at the map before he left. It had been a long time since he had climbed the hills on Söder. He had not actually been there since they had settled August's adoption three years ago.

August had come home to Nytorget with news of his moving and changing schools. The distance between them would increase, the way home would be longer, but he could naturally ride the streetcar to and from Slussen and from there he wouldn't have any farther to walk than before. No streetcar horses would ever have the strength to make it up the hills of Söder; people would always have to walk in that part of town. But he would take the elevator to Mosebacke when it was finished he said. Then his old grandmother shook her head and said it was way too dangerous, God hadn't intended people to glide through the air like birds. If people had not comprehended that before, they should now that Ricardo the high-wire artist had fallen from his high wire at Mosebacke vaudeville and been taken to the hospital. It was a sign the head of the elevator construction should take to heart.

They sat at the scrubbed white wooden table by the window, and Lotten had put out coffee. She sat between the guest of honor, August, and ten-year-old Gertrud, while old, pain-wracked Washer-Malin sat on the bed diagonally behind them. On the kitchen sofa, along the other long wall slept the little boy. The fold-out bed that the girls used at night stood folded so that there was an open passage between the table and the window, and the stove and the door at the other end of the room. Lotten urged August to take another slice of coffee bread. She, herself, didn't want anything, partly because the slices were so few and expensive, but also because she couldn't make any bread go down just now. Anxiety sat like a lump in her throat. She wasn't worried about his moving; he had promised to come visit anyway. But she was searching for something new and strange in him, which in a way other than physical distance separated him from her. It felt as if she didn't really dare put her arms around him like before, she was afraid of imposing on him. And she had to wonder if he would be ashamed of her if they ever met each other out on the street where strangers could see.

He asked how things were with Emelie. Gertrud was the one who answered. She told him laughingly about the little, self-important factory owner who looked like a crow. Lotten quieted the girl down: you should-n't say such things about the man who gave Emelie work and bread. What would August think? Maybe he thought they spoke with as little respect about his foster father.

But August only smiled, and told about a stingy goldsmith who tried to swindle the Bodins out of some properties but who, to be sure, didn't succeed at all with his dastardly plans. They were building there themselves instead, large and fine buildings.

"Just think if August could build a house for his mama when he grows up," said Grandmother. And Lotten hurriedly hushed them again.

Grandmother shouldn't put such ideas into the boy's head, it was his new parents he was obligated to and to whom he had to think of first. But August thought he would, no doubt, build if there was any space left to build on.

Lotten looked for something else to talk about, something that couldn't be perceived as an attempt to intrude, to demand advantages from one who didn't have the right or position to give and promise. She never had the opportunity because someone was knocking at the door.

It was Fredrik Bodin, who had been wandering about among the houses and asked his way there. Lotten curtsied and drew back carefully to leave him room. He explained that he neither wanted to disturb them nor to hurry them. He only wanted to say that August should wait for him so they could go home together. He would take a walk until it was time, but wanted to be sure that August didn't leave alone.

Lotten felt she ought to ask him in and pressed him until what she wished for least of all did happen: the gentleman entered and sat down where Gertrud had hastily vacated her seat at the table with the coffee.

They were out of bread Lotten was forced to admit with embarrassment. If they had only known.... But Fredrik Bodin assured her that he had come straight from the dinner table and wanted absolutely nothing more than a cup of coffee. Luckily, there was enough left in the pan that sat over the glowing coals in the fireplace. Lotten served him and lighted the kerosene lamp. It was beginning to grow dark. Old Malin pulled herself back as carefully as possible. She had on her everyday dress and was afraid their visitor might notice all the spatters on it.

The conversation moved forward with difficulty. Fredrik would ask and Lotten or August answer. Yes, the oldest girl was working and returned home late, it was *the season*... The little boy was three years old and a good boy, although he had a delicate stomach. Gertrud was still in school. It was very close by, just diagonally across the square. August had also gone there at one time.

Fredrik leaned forward and looked out across the trash-strewn square, over to the schoolhouse. Even though he felt the women's shyness and discomfort, he was enjoying himself. Everyone was considerate and kind and sat here together in the crowded room and talked in the dusk. There was a warm friendliness that he was lacking at home, although it certainly was cramped. Where did they all have room to sleep? Where did they have a quiet corner? He had to look around, and Washer-Malin huddled even more in the shadows.

He was in a very good mood as he walked homeward with August. He had gotten to talk about his plans, about empty lots and construction, and they had sat nodding in agreement and admiration. They were sensible people, not pushy in the least or importuning. Now after talking with them he was determined to buy those lots from Margareta and build good, cheap housing for poor people.

August walked along silently. He had a feeling that Mother wouldn't have liked Father paying this visit. He was afraid that Father would say too much, but in that respect he was reassured. Father explained that he hadn't intended at all to come and disturb them, and that they didn't have to say anything to Mother other than that he had met up with August.

They walked the route that August usually took, Stadsträdgårdsgatan toward Storaglasbruksgatan. Miserable shacks, warped fences and a low stone house here and there lined the street. A few simple stalls where people sold used clothing and rags were still open and small lanterns shone over piles of cheap goods. It was lively as always around the tavern on Kocksgatan, Masis Knosis. They could hear bellowing and shouting. Suddenly a man came flying out of a doorway; he staggered up the street pursued by a screaming and threatening mob. At the street corner, the man who fled was caught by the faster and perhaps more sober pursuers, then knocked down and kicked. A miller jouneyman pulled off his belt and began to flog the prostrate man. Fredrik pulled August closer to him, horrified, and hurried away, but people who heard the beaten man's shrieks and cries of distress came and helped him up while the perpetrators escaped.

No, the world of the poor was certainly not so pleasant. Fredrik walked on anxiously, holding August tightly by the hand. Someone really had needed to come and get the boy, he could be attacked here. Hadn't some newspaper written that this was a highly dangerous part of town to walk through after dark? How could they let that girl, who was a couple years younger than August, walk home in the middle of the night? It was probably necessary for August to take the carriage there and back if he was going to visit his old home again.

Could it really be profitable to build houses for people who behaved the way those fellows had? Wouldn't they immediately destroy the apartments? Fredrik had to think the matter over; one shouldn't be hasty. But the building sites he had seen seemed to be good, solid bedrock so they could avoid expensive pilings. The decision would have to depend on how much Margareta demanded. Any larger sum was out of the question when it came to these godforsaken outskirts. And they hadn't seen a single carriage....

The boy walked along silent and bitter, felt ashamed of his old neighborhood in front of his new father.

EMELIE LISTENS

The first snow arrived, the waters began to freeze over and the pontoon bridges were put out. Closer to Christmas there was a thaw, and the streets became almost impassable. Icicles fell from the roofs, dirty water formed large puddles and sprayed out from under the wheels of vehicles. Emelie's long, wet skirts slapped heavily against her legs as she hurried to and from work. Now both her morning and evening walks took place in darkness.

Inside the cosmetic factory's workers' sheds, the kerosene lamps flickered in the drafts. The season had stretched all the way to Christmas, and the employees were overworked and irritable, working mechanically without even having the energy to talk to each other. Normally they would talk and joke, and during breaks things could get really congenial when they sat around one of the worktables and pulled out their lunches. But during the season they ate quickly and silently and threw themselves into their work as quickly as possible; they had to get it over with, see it through to the end, and then finally get a little relief.

Just when there was the greatest rush, the soap packaging team lost two of its regular workers. Karin had her long-awaited baby; the delivery was difficult, and she couldn't return for a few weeks at the earliest. One of the oldest packers had been gored by a bull on her way to work. A drunken cattle handler had let the animal out, and old Rosa hadn't moved out of the way in time. After a few days in the hospital, she had died, and her workmates took up a collection for a funeral wreath. The foreman saw it as his chance to escape for a few hours and represent the factory at the funeral. It annoyed the others who knew that he and Rosa had never gotten along.

In January the ice stopped steam-launch traffic between the shores of Lake Mälar, and some of the employees had to walk a longer route. The railroad put in an extra local train between Liljeholmen and the city, with many stops along the way. But riding the train was a luxury that few could afford. Consequently Emelie and Fat Tilda often kept company with the old packer, Greta, who lived on Hornskroken and now took the route across the locks at Slussen. Whenever they met or parted, there they had to look up at the enormous elevator to Mosebacke. High up under the dark sky small lights were glowing, allowing work to continue round the clock. One of the lights was something new and strange; it was electric and run completely by machinery.

"My brother is going to ride in the elevator when it's finished," Emelie had told them. But Tilda was a little tired of hearing about the wonderful brother, and said that anybody could ride the elevator, at least if they could afford the three öre that the ride down would cost.

One evening they met people streaming down the stairs from Mosebacke where some strange fanatics were holding meetings. The gatherings had become a big entertainment, a greater success than high-wire artists and other performers. Greta had heard that the Salvation Army was running wild on the hills of Söder. This repulsive and repugnant troop of religious clowns, founded in England, had sent five missionaries to Sweden, and the soap packers caught a glimpse of some bizarrely dressed Salvation Army soldiers hurrying across Slussen toward the town, followed by a gang of street urchins.

"Do you think that might be Palm?" Emelie asked Greta. But the senior soap packer shook her head.

"No, that was someone else, probably a pietist." Then Emelie told her how on Sunday she was going to visit a man who was a follower of Palm's.

Greta looked around anxiously and hushed her, warning Emelie against saying anything about this at work. She knew, of course, what factory director Melinder said about the tailor and his followers. Anything could leak out... if you weren't careful. That their foreman was a gossip was common knowledge. But Tilda didn't take it so seriously, it wasn't as if Palm was a leper, she said.

The road from Nybrotorget to Åsöberget wasn't long, perhaps six hundred meters. Still, it led into another world—that which was past and gone. Lotten felt both longing and fear at the thought of their destination; the memories became so palpable, the loss so great. Lotten had lived her life with Henning in the house where Thumbs and Matilda lived with their children. Signs of his handiwork were still there: the walls he had repaired, the flowerbeds he had laid out. When she opened the gate, it almost felt as if he was waiting for her in there, but a harbor worker and his family now lived in the room in the attic that had been theirs.

Lotten and the children came out onto Nytorget to the sound of sleigh bells; two horse-drawn sleighs flew past in the direction of the winter tollgate. Gertrud grew excited and forgot how slippery her boots were and landed on all fours in a snowdrift. She had gotten boots through charity at school, stiff and heavy gear with wooden soles and iron heels. Everyone could hear and see that they were shoes for the poor, but Gertrud had a sweet and easy-going disposition and would laugh and say that she had the same boots as the guys at the Dihlström workhouse.

Lotten had to carry Olof there and back; he had nothing to put on his feet, only homemade slippers. The boy had begun to get too big to lug around like this, and she regretted not borrowing a sled. But it was too late now. Their friends were waiting for them at Thumbs'.

She forced herself to walk up the steep incline to the White Hills without stopping and resting. The girls trudged after her; Gertrud slipped and stumbled and sat down wailing in a snowdrift, but Emelie pulled her sister up and hurried her along. She had noticed some of the tired and hard resolution in her mother and was worried.

It got easier once they had passed the Bible ladies' mission and reached the windmill named the "Hat," spreading its sails between snow-covered barns filled with tobacco. Now the downhill stretch began, and Gertrud ran into a classmate with a sled and whirled off down the hill. When the rest of the family had come down to the crossing at Tjärhovsgatan, Gertrud was waiting on the corner and brushing off her clothes. The vehicle had tipped over at a convenient place, right where they were going to turn off.

Matilda was waiting at the gate. Lotten was happy to see her; Matilda's presence softened her encounter with the past. And when they opened the door to the house, a smell of meat cooking wafted out in welcome and even made Lotten pleasantly hungry. A genuine gentleman's roast beef dinner was being prepared. Thumbs had been working for a butcher for a while and received some of his salary in meat.

He stood in front of the stove and basted the roast; yellow flames licked the bottom of the iron pan. He turned around and saluted her with the ladle. He had never quite grown up Lotten thought. His black bangs hung over his pointy nose beneath a baker's cap that was cocked to one side. The cap was a souvenir from his time as a worker in a bakery. Thumbs was a man who tried his hand at all professions, but could never settle at one.

He wiped his fingers on a rag and smoothed his moustache, then he lifted the child out of Lotten's arms, up to the ceiling rafters. Olof shrieked delightedly, and felt dizzy as he sped back down to the floor where Thumbs carefully placed the boy before turning and welcoming Lotten. If it had been any other man who had hugged her so tightly, Lotten would have protested angrily. But Thumbs was Thumbs and an old friend, Henning's friend. A moment later he had his arms around the little girls and was assuring them that they became prettier every day. They giggled and blushed, they were unused to such attention. But Matilda wanted Thumbs to watch the roast, and he was standing by the stove again making grand gestures with the basting ladle. Could they smell the aroma? They were really hungry, weren't they?

He put them all in a good mood. He made Lotten and Matilda sit down, then organized the group of children. Emelie and Gertrud were to set the table, thirteen-year-old Knutte and eight-year-old Mikael were sent to bring in a board and sawhorses from the shed. Olof stood by the stove and admired the funny man's way of cooking. And when they sat down at the table everyone was happily, almost ceremoniously, looking forward to tasting the beautiful brown roast enthroned in the middle of the table. This was truly a feast for those who seldom had more than a piece of salt herring with their potatoes. Others would have stinted and saved the meat over a long period, but Thumbs invited them for a party. Lotten had to smile and felt how unused she was to straining the corners of her mouth like that. She wondered for a moment if she was about to cry, to smile was to open up something on her everyday hard shell—was there anything but crying inside?

The small windows didn't let in much light; dusk came early to people in wooden houses. The mist from the snow spread across the water below, creating a gray expanse without beginning or end.

Full, a little bloated from so much food, the adults stayed sitting in the room. Emelie lingered with them. The other children made a hubbub in the kitchen talking to the three girls from the spinning factory who lived there. They had just returned from the mission and were tasting the leftovers. They were going to a dance hall that evening, despite all the preacher's warnings against sin and retribution.

Emelie heard the gay voices, the laughter. Normally she would have been drawn to it, left the grown-ups and looked for the children and the other young people, but now she had been captivated by another tone, another world. It happened suddenly: like standing in a darkened doorway and peering into a sunlit yard. A yard which was always there, which one had passed countless times, but never seen because houses and fences hid it. Now it revealed its secrets.

The unveiling was something of a shock, the light which illuminated the picture merciless. And there were the answers to the questions, questions it is true she had never asked, but still knew about.

Thumbs, who so recently had made them all laugh, now became serious. His words no longer flowed as quickly, his gestures were not as lively. As if in a short time, he had become older, and with a tired and disillusioned look in his eye observed himself, the carefree boy he had just been. He said, "When Henning was sick, I promised him he would see the revolution, but then it didn't happen. Now I wonder if any of us will get to see it."

"Doesn't something have to happen soon? If we are going to have the strength?"

Astonished, Emelie heard that it was her mother who had asked this—
the mother who always encouraged them to be thankful and content, obey
God and those in authority. Who didn't even want Emelie to joke about
factory director Melinder.

Maybe Lotten herself was amazed at her question. It had slipped out,
had bypassed her self-censor. A small cry of despair: who would dare
believe, who would be able to hope if not even Thumbs did any longer.
When he spoke of insurrection and class struggle, she had to protest, she
believed it was against the order of God and nature. But when he
despaired it was even harder, then she had to cry out at what she dreaded
and suspected.

"You believed that Palm would be able to stir up the workers...,"
Matilda reminded him. "That something would happen when he arrived."

"Of course Palm deserves a lot of credit," Thumbs admitted. "He has
scared the big guys for sure and isn't bashful. But what became of all his
work? Last year, when Palm held his first meeting, the one at Lill-Jans
Park the day after Christmas, they formed a committee to continue the
work while the tailor traveled on, but Dr. Nyström and some other liberals emphatically quashed it at a meeting after Palm left. No one on the
committee, except for Cederborg the carpenter, stuck with socialism, so
that committee was finished. Palm came back and held three meetings,
but nothing more came of it. Not even a new committee."

Palm was good at talking, said Thumbs, but there was nobody else who
could organize. He himself had spoken with a few friends, but didn't meet
with any sympathy. Alcohol was the only thing that interested them. Most
of them just complained about the state liquor store and lined up at
Smith's boats at Stadsgården to ride out to the Fjäderholm Islands and buy
cheap aquavit at Smith's store there. Others organized temperance asso-
ciations. Cederborg was one of those organizers. Now he devoted himself
to fighting alcohol instead of organizing workers for socialism.

Of course, temperance societies were important, too, put in Matilda.
The workers had to be weaned off alcohol before they were mature enough
to organize themselves politically.

They had always heard this kind of talk. Morality and sobriety, but no strikes, those were the slogans of the liberal workers' unions. At the Workers' Institute they gave lectures on "inventions of the middle ages," and "freezing mixtures and steam cooking," but didn't say a word about social opposition. On Mosebacke, hundreds of people gathered time after time to laugh at the Salvation Army soldiers, and down on Ålandsgatan a horde of people had smashed all the tavern windows in Number Two because they could no longer buy alcohol without food there on holidays. Didn't people act as if they were blind? They were robbed of all their human worth, and protested by knocking out tavern windows and spitting on Salvation Army soldiers.

But wasn't it due to alcohol?

Thumbs wasn't willing to go along with that. He had a glass himself from time to time. Palm did, too, he had also heard. Though, of course, there were many drunkards. At the harbor, he had really gotten to see how bad it was. At least one worker a day went on a drinking binge down there. Many of the stevedores paid the wages at the tavern; they encouraged drinking, of course.

The workers were indeed kept down in alcohol and misery. Inhumane working hours and worthless salaries, and unemployment in between times. How could they become anything other than passive, drunken, willing victims? Who had the strength to resist? After twelve hours of work, maybe fourteen including breaks and travel time. No one sat in any meetings, and then the workers were supposedly coarse and uneducated, not mature enough for any voting rights. When would they actually get the time and energy to educate themselves?

Now Lotten recognized the Thumbs she had gotten exasperated with so many times, the one who tried to draw Henning along with him. And now her resistance was aroused. Anyone who has time and money for drinking ought to have time and money for getting an education, she said sternly.

No, there Lotten was wrong, Thumbs said. The poor didn't drink because they had time and could afford it. They drank because they didn't have the strength for anything else. What they most lacked was strength. To have strength you had to have hope, but how many had that?

Maybe there would be better times eventually. There was so much construction going on right now, there weren't many people who had to go unemployed. Weren't most people living under better conditions compared with how things had been before?

You couldn't make such comparisons was Thumbs' viewpoint. They didn't show anything. Naturally, nicer scraps fell from the tables of the rich when times were better, but it was no more than that. The comparison should be made within society at that moment: *how do things look right now?* How large are the gaps? How are conditions for the workers in comparison with the other classes?

He had passed by Bähr's Café at Riddarhustorget the other day. They were putting up a gas lantern with rotating signs over the entrance, as it happened. Beneath the lantern a poor wretch stood crying because he hadn't received his pay from a building contractor who sat on the inside of the glass window eating from the large smorgasbord. The building contractor couldn't afford to pay him, of course, so the brick carrier's children would have to starve for a few more days. There was nothing to be done about it.

That's how things looked. The building contractor was surely educated and upper class enough to vote and discuss politics, while the worker would be rebuked if he drank in his misery. In fact, he wasn't good enough even if he was sober. A giant crack ran through the whole of Swedish society. It didn't help to try to patch and improve things; at the first hard year, all the patchwork would come apart. In times of unemployment, the labor unions would stand powerless, striking would do nothing. The workers wouldn't be able to bring about any actual changes as long as they lacked political influence.

Did he mean that revolution was the only possibility?

Thumbs waited with his answer. Didn't he have the strength to believe in an uprising any longer? Or was it only that he was getting older and wiser and wanted to first try less risky solutions?

"There may be another possibility," he said. "The labor unions can, in spite of everything, be a beginning. Strikes and threats to strike have led to certain improvements, at least during good times. One could use the same means to reach political goals." But organization, solidarity and patience were required.

If Palm returned, if the tailor went to the fore and spoke, and enough people followed in his footsteps and organized, then they could succeed, even if it took time. There were socialist parties in other countries. Palm had translated and printed up the manifesto of the German socialists. If they took the long road they didn't run the same risk of being destroyed by violence. They had seen that when the ones who had power grew afraid, they would call on the military for help, as they had done in Sundsvall almost four years ago. The main thing was to frighten them just enough so they gave in, but not so much that they took up weapons—at least while the workers didn't have enough to respond in kind.

"If we only have the strength to hope," he said. "Then it will all work out." At last Thumbs laughed. "Maybe the tailor can give us some steam. He had just the right kind of anger, and a way with words, too."

"Is he going to come back here soon?"

"Maybe in the summer."

But it was winter now, summer was a long way away, and lately Lotten had been gripped by an even greater worry. Time sped by so fast, and she was so terribly worn out and felt so alone. When she didn't have the energy any longer, there would be no one there to take care of the children, only the one she had lost had been saved. Emelie was already on the treadmill; she had become thin and pale from all the long working days of "the season." In the spring it would be Gertrude's turn to look for work. They needed someone to help them. And Olof was still so little, only three and a half years old. Something had to happen, she felt like she couldn't drag herself along any more.

She felt her eyes fill with tears. She had almost believed that they had dried up. She turned her head away and wiped them on the sleeve of her dress. She looked at Emelie, who sat quiet and pale in the dusk, and wondered if it was so healthy for the girl to be listening.

"Will you go see how the children are doing..."

Emelie nodded and left.

Without daring to lift her eyes to her friends, Lotten turned to them and said quietly, "If I can't manage... if something should happen... could you help the children? Could they come to you?"

They looked at her silently, then looked at each other. That was a big and difficult thing to promise, and yet so simple, there really was only one answer.

Matilda nodded. "We've always stuck together," she said. "If anything happens to any of us... of course we will help."

Strangely solemn, they sat there in the stillness. The promise lay in the twilight between them. Even though it grew out of a feeling that was close to hopelessness, it gave them some sort of hope. They would help each other, at least, try to carry the children across the threshold into new and better times.

"Development...," said Thumbs. "Progress.... The children's world must be better than ours."

Maybe the words were only old magic spells, dead superstitions. Still, he had to murmur them again, quietly, to himself. He had to make use of the power they could give him, the hope he couldn't live without.

"Development, progess...."

Someone pounded on the door in the kitchen. There was a stomping of snow and wet off boots. A low, male, adolescent voice blended in with the higher voices of the girls. Rudolf, the birthday boy who turned fifteen today but couldn't make it to the party, had returned home. Rudolf was a stable boy for the streetcar company, and had the Sunday shift at the stable over by Träsktorget on Norrmalm.

He came in and greeted everybody, followed by Emelie who reported that Olof had fallen asleep on the kitchen sofa. Rudolf wasn't especially like his father, he was already bigger and taller than Thumbs. The restlessness of his early boyhood years had disappeared, now he had more of his mother's fair-haired calm rather than his father's dark looks and excitability. He was strong, and his strength had given him a certain heaviness. Lotten felt like she hardly recognized him, she remembered the restless little boy who had led August off on wild adventures.

Now Rudolf was no longer an adventurer, but a steady young worker. Emelie looked at him admiringly. Whenever Rudolf accompanied her on her way to work, she always felt safe. Unfortunately, it didn't happen very often; they seldom had the same hours.

Lotten, too, felt some of the security that the boy radiated. Rudolf would manage to go far, make his way without asking for any hope for the future, take each day as it came with with calm and assurance. If he were around her daughters, Lotten could feel calm too.

Gertrud and the little boys from their hosts' family played in the kitchen; the spinning mill girls had left again. Rudolf and Emelie drank their coffee together with the adults. They sat quietly and listened to the conversation. Once in a while, Rudolf interjected a word, an acknowledgement of something that had been said. Otherwise he sat silently and ate his food.

But it was time for Lotten and her children to go home, get ready for their workday.

They walked between rows of oddly built temporary housing, sagging wooden cottages and small, stone houses with crumbling plaster. The frozen, deeply rutted wheel tracks made their going uneven and halting, and Olof swayed on Lotten's arm and whimpered in his sleep. Gertrude clomped along as best she could in her slippery boots, a little more subdued than when she had left home. She began to get sleepy. But Emelie felt as if it would be impossible to fall asleep this evening. Her head was too filled with new ideas. Development and progress... and Master Palm would be at the head of the demonstration with Uncle Thumbs on his heels, the strikers who could be beaten down by the military, the men who smashed the windows of the taverns instead of... what?

"Can't we go listen to him, Master Palm, when he comes back to Stockholm?" she asked her mother.

Lotten had been walking along immersed in her own thoughts, and had to ask the girl to repeat her question. Go hear Palm? Was that appropriate? "Maybe we could do it," she said after a minute. "One should listen in any case."

They continued silently down the hill in the direction of Nytorget and home, listening for sounds and voices in the darkness.

THE APPRENTICE CHIMNEY SWEEP

A reeling, howling mob tore down Stora Badstugatan, bringing carts and carriages to a halt, and forcing women to take shelter in doorways. The journeymen chimney sweeps were celebrating payday, and their apprentices formed a train behind them.

The chimney sweeps were a part of the population that set its stamp on street life, the living quarters of the chimney sweeps' first district lay very close to Melinder's cosmetics factory off Kammargatan. Emelie saw the black procession in time and managed to make it into the factory doorway with the milk she had bought from the cowman's sister—it was her job to buy for the packers' breakfast. From her protective niche, she could peek at the blackened men and boys. Last of all, bringing up the rear, came a sniveling and pitiful little figure who trudged along in a coat way too long and wide for him, the youngest apprentice.

The newest apprentice was a whipping boy for all the others, the youngest and most ignorant, who always got the worst job—and the beatings because he still hadn't learned how to carry out orders. He lived farthest down in the chimney sweep hierarchy's blackest hell, and had reason to wish every day that he had never been born.

Emelie stuck her head out. She had to look more closely at the new sweep. Didn't she know him? Of course. It was Johan who had grown up as a foster child at their neighbors' on Åsöberget. Johan had also recognized her. He stopped, glancing anxiously at his workmates and tormentors. Then he ran up to Emelie and asked her breathlessly, "Where can I get hold of an eel skin?"

"An eel skin?"

Yes, he needed it to patch the seat and knees of his pants. Only eel skin could withstand the heat in the chimney flues. He had to get it for the journeyman who would put it on his work clothes.

"Ask at the outdoor market at Hötorget," suggested Emelie. "Maybe you can get some skins at the fish stand there. Or in some tavern."

He waved cautiously and ran away. She stood there for a moment and watched him go. Johan had always been fearful, always had reason to be. She remembered how he used to run away crying behind the fences of Garbage Lane when his stepfather, the coachman everyone called Dad, was drunk and beating all his foster children. And now Dad had sold Johan to the master chimney sweep, getting twelve or fifteen kronor so the boy would spend a year in training without pay, and then maybe earn a twenty-five-öre piece or two per week.

She saw Johan now and then on the street. When he was accompanied by journeymen or older apprentices, he barely dared nod to her. Sometimes he came alone, sneaking out to get advice or help with something. At first they kept him busy, mostly in the rooms where the journeymen and apprentices lived and kept their work tools. He had to carry buckets of water and urine, mop the floor and light the fire in the iron stove. Every day he brushed rows of shoes for the master and his wife and kids. Actually, all this was supposed to happen outside of work, during working hours he was supposed to train for his profession. The first one up and the last one in bed was the rule for the newest apprentice. When the journeymen needed aquavit and money to buy it with, they might wake him up in the middle of the night and send him out; if he didn't come back with something drinkable, he would be treated to a good beating. He might be obliged himself to wake up some kind tavern maid. As a rule, tavern keepers gave credit. They knew that even if journeymen were disorderly rowdies, they still paid their debts honorably.

One evening in March, Johan stood shivering, waiting for Emelie outside the factory entrance. He was thinly dressed; any sort of undershirt was not included in the work clothes the master supplied him with. He was on an errand to Söder for the master and wondered if he could walk with Emelie.

They had to sneak along the back streets in the beginning. Johan was afraid some workmate would see him with a girl. The journeymen educated their apprentices; the other night when a "youngster" had been found with a girl they had coated his genitals with shoe polish "so he wouldn't get into any trouble."

When they got farther away from his workplace, Johan grew braver, and the fast walk had gotten him warmed up. Now he began to brag to Emelie about his job and his workmates. And then about his clothes: the climbing pants, the shirt, and the cap sewn like a sack so you could pull it down over you eyes and protect yourself from soot when you climbed up or slid down the chimneys. Did she see the fine crease he had made in it? If he didn't get it right, he got a beating, though he didn't tell her this. And look at his socks too! He pointed to them. But you couldn't wear socks and boots when you climbed the chimneystacks. You had to climb barefoot. He limped because he had burns on his toes. He had gotten scraped too, of course, though not on his elbows. He was proud of that. You couldn't use them when you climbed up inside the chimneys. That wouldn't leave your arms free to work with the scraper and the brush.

Emelie felt oddly grownup beside the scrawny and insecure Johan. She observed him a little when he wasn't looking, and smiled when she heard him bungle the chimney sweep slang, a dialect in itself, and when he tried to take greater strides than her own. He wanted to be really skillful, a real journeyman chimney sweep, even though he was still a new apprentice. At the same time, he was afraid. She noticed it when he talked about the hot and narrow chimneystacks, about the young sweeps that got stuck. Sometimes they had to smash a hole in the wall of the chimney in order to get them out, he had heard.

One of Johan's friends, an apprentice, had been sitting in a flue flirting with the maids in the kitchen of some gentry, when an older apprentice out of sheer deviltry decided to close the main flue down in the cellar. At the same time, he told the maids in the kitchen it was time to light the fire. The younger apprentice had had to use all his might to climb up the chimney to escape the smoke.

Little brother, Emelie thought. A frightened little friend. She remembered what she had heard at Thumbs' house, the words about solidarity and comradeship. People whose situation was bad had to stick together. She had thought of this often since that Sunday. She would have liked to help Johan, get him to be a little less afraid and manage to hold out. But he was horribly dirty, she thought, always so black with soot. Didn't he ever get to wash? She had to ask.

There wasn't much of that, admitted Johan. As the newest apprentice, it was his job to get and heat the water for everyone in the chimney sweeps' sleeping quarters, but then they washed in order of seniority: first the journeymen, then the apprentices. When it got to be Johan's turn, the water was both black and cold.

Couldn't he go get fresh water and set it up himself?

Was she crazy! What would the others say if a new apprentice got better bath water than his superiors! No, the newest apprentice should come last and take the worst, that was his lot.

If she were to ask her mother.... Maybe Johan could wash in the woodshed at home in the yard. Emelie could heat the water for him. Though it was cold in the shed, of course.

The water froze in the pails overnight in the chimney sweeps' sleeping quarters sometimes. He wasn't afraid of cold, but maybe he was afraid of showing up freshly washed in front of his comrades in their quarters. That might annoy someone. Actually, he was rather proud of his blackened hide, the blackness showed that he went down the chimneys now—was a professional. It felt like Emelie wanted to wash away a little of his dearly bought experience, the sign of his profession and his honor.

She was stubborn, had to rescue him. Couldn't he go do his errand, and then come to their house on Nytorget? Reluctantly he gave in, he had such a hard time saying no; he was so used to obeying.

A half hour later he was standing outside her door with the package he had gone to get for the master. Emelie opened the door and let him in. Her mother came out and greeted him.

Lotten didn't recognize the boy, there had been so many children in the small houses around Åsöberget. Maybe she was a little irritated at Emelie's idea, wasting fuel, soap and water on a completely unknown boy. Lotten was too tired to have the energy for more than her own children, but Emelie had promised to take care of everything, had gone for the water herself. And the boy really did need to be washed.

She looked at Emelie, could feel how the beginning of a smile grew and warmed up inside her—the memory of how she herself had bathed two little girls visiting in the house on Åsöberget. On her mother's side Emelie was undeniably of the purest washerwoman's lineage. Mother, grandmother and great-grandmother had all, at least from time to time, supported themselves in that profession. It was certainly a good sign that the girl couldn't tolerate dirt, that she definitely wanted the little chimney sweep boy to bathe.

Johan glowered at the pot on the open fire. Steam rose from it. Were they planning on scalding him? He had to carry the pot out to the shed himself and mix it to comfortably warm water in an old wooden tub. Before he had had time to do more than that, the door opened and Emelie's mother stepped in.

"It's only me," she said. "Perhaps Johan needs a little help." He didn't have to put on airs for her. She was just going to help him wash his back.

The black water ran down around him. Gradually his skin emerged, amazingly white, quickly reddening. Pimples and sores appeared everywhere: scrapes, cuts and burns, and red welts from the most sadistic journeyman's belt. Her hand trembled when she tried to rub his skinny back even more carefully. If she had had the energy she would have wept. That people could treat people this way, that a child should be subjected to such treatment. Was there no mercy?

Johan was younger and smaller than August. It could have been August in his place. If he had stayed with her, if he had been obliged to take whatever work he could get. No matter how difficult it felt many times, she had saved August from this. Thanks to the Bodins, August wouldn't have to risk having his skin become one enormous scab. She had to remember this; she had to learn to be thankful. Still, it didn't feel like it was enough for August to have escaped it. Not even if her remaining children escaped it. As long as someone was left suffering in misery, as long as someone was being treated like this boy was being treated, as long as it continued... someone had to fight against it, had to protest.

She would go and listen to Master Palm, find out if he had a solution. When she looked at Johan's back, she felt like she could accept all of Thumbs' talk about revolution and upheaval. Anything but this. Things should not be this way, a child should not be treated like this.

But it wasn't the rich people, not even the master chimney sweeps who abused Johan and exposed him to all the risks of the profession. It was his colleagues, workers like himself. Destitution and drudgery could make people this way, and there were people on all levels of society who enjoyed making others suffer. She would like to go down to those chimney sweep quarters and teach those journeymen a thing or two. Still, she knew they could really be kind and decent people, they were known for taking care of their young boys and defending them from criticism and attack from outsiders. Most of the sores on the boy came with the profession. Gradually his skin would become more resilient, thicker, and protect him from heat and scrapes.

It was like becoming an adult, growing tough. She could see it on her own hands—the cracks, the calluses. Life was like that, but it was hard to bear when the devastation was visited on the youngest ones. She watched while he carefully washed his knees. They were the worst affected. The boys slid by their knees when they descended, and they pushed themselves up by their knees when they ascended. The leather patches on their pants didn't offer enough protection, all chimney sweeps were at risk for water on the knee as well.

Johan thanked her and left with his package for the master, half running so he wouldn't be way too late. He hoped his black clothes would leave soot on his body so that he didn't appear too obviously white when he undressed and crawled into his three-man bed. People were so kind, but Emelie's mama hadn't really understood that a chimney sweep should be black. He would have to be careful about running into Emelie. Just so long as everything turned out all right this time, then he wouldn't take such risks again.

Lotten lit the kerosene lamp and pulled out the wooden sofa bed that she made up for the girls. They were having trouble with lice again. No matter how much they scrubbed, the lice made their way from room to room in the rotting house, and carried out continual new attacks. For this reason, she placed the legs of all the beds in jars of water, causing her extra work each morning and evening. It didn't really help either, the malevolent creatures crawled up to the ceiling and dropped down on the beds when they couldn't crawl up the legs. Mechanically she positioned the jars and filled them with water. The girls undressed until they were standing in their long, white shifts, and each pulled on a sweater. Lotten looked at Emelie, a hint of breasts gave her two bulges under the tight sweater.

It was too early for Emelie to start going out with boys. How well did she know that little chimney sweep? Wasn't the girl a little too self-confident?

After the grandmother and the two youngest children had fallen asleep, Emelie still lay awake. Lotten tucked her in again and stroked her hair. She said, "You're still a little too young to start going out with a boy...."

Emelie looked at her mother, surprised, not quite comprehending. "But we have to help each other," she whispered. "The poor have to stick together. That's what Thumbs said."

"That's good," said Lotten. "You're so right. Of course Johan can wash here if he wants." She sat by the lamp and did her mending. She could hear the sleeping children breathing. A horse galloped by on Nya gatan, a few drunken revelers were out on the street now that the tavern had closed.

Of course there was a lot that was hard. Still, things couldn't be completely hopeless as long as some people thought the way Emelie did. As long as they didn't get too tired out and hardened. When the chimney sweep boys' skin grew thick and protective, they became journeymen and tormented new boys.

You had to be strong, but also strong enough to feel. Now she was grateful for Emelie's words.

THE AQUAVIT KING

The snow melted and the White Hills stood bare and dirty, revealing all their poverty. A jumble of crooked and patched shacks clung to the ledges and was crammed into the hollows. Many of the buildings were so dilapidated it seemed like a miracle they could withstand the trials of winter and could experience yet another spring.

Meltwater ran down the hillsides, carrying filth along with it and penetrating the houses. Toadstools and mud puddles formed, while the first coltsfoot of spring stood shining yellow on the southern slopes down toward Barnäng's crossroad.

This was the city's poorest area, its meanest shantytown. People lived here like cavemen. The Bible ladies in the mission station at the foot of the mountain struggled desperately to assist those in the greatest need, but all their work could appear useless. Whatever they managed to accomplish ended up amounting to so little—drowned in a sea of poverty and ruin. Were these people too far out on the fringe, too continually broken? The mission station's superintendent might lie sleepless and feel powerless; the faith that could move mountains could not free the people of the White Hills. Here was where want and aquavit reigned.

Still, springtime teemed with hope and life; it rose like a defiant song from the mud and the dirt. The budding branches of the trees gave out shoots, the grassy slopes turned a light green. The hill bloomed, small children laughed, and sparrows with ruffled feathers chirped among the bushes. Old ladies, bent over, searched for slender shoots of stinging nettles to make into soup, and thin boys with glue-coated switches tried to lure the first birds of flight that arrived.

Everything happened that spring, but nothing anyone had expected, thought Thumbs. He couldn't do more than gape and wonder what had gotten hold of people. Were they all, including the teetotallers, drunk from the alcoholic fumes of the Fjäderholm Islands?

Launches departed from Stadsgården and shuttled people to and from the islands that lay outside the jurisdiction of the Stockholm authorities and the liquor licensing board. The boat trip was free and out there was sold the country's cheapest aquavit. One krona ninety for a jug of the best, that came to about seventy-five öre for a liter of ten double distilled. Nine policemen had been required to keep the lines in order at the harbor on Easter, the day Thumbs rode over to buy a jug. People crowded around the old tavern that had become a sales point. They climbed up onto barriers and screamed and shouted and reached out with the containers they had brought to fill. Many children had been sent to buy; some of them tasted the wares a little to conscientiously. Children and women screamed and cried out when they got trampled on in the unruly lines.

Then there were the people—and often the same people—who bought alcohol and showed an equally great enthusiasm for creating a society called the Anti-Tavern League. A doorman from Södra Station was the chairman for the chapter on Söder, which in a few weeks' time had admitted several thousand members. A number of these were total abstainers who abhorred everything that went by the name of alcohol and taverns. Others were old regulars at the taverns who hoped that this action against the hated state liquor distributors would result in cheaper aquavit and in getting their old, pleasant watering holes back.

Numerous meetings were held all over town; some outdoor meetings had attracted almost ten thousand participants who listened when doorman Forsberg and carpenter Fjällbäck laid out the gospel. Thumbs couldn't quite get a grip on what the message of the new preaching was: whether it was that people drank too much or whether what they drank cost too much. By preventing free competition, they were bleeding people dry, one speaker said. The big competitor of the state distribution system who was being thwarted by it was, as everyone knew, the aquavit king, L. O. Smith.

Most likely it was the aquavit king who lay behind the new people's and workers' movement, thought Thumbs. "A private individual" had announced that newly formed chapters of tavern opponents could obtain economic support for their effort. Could it be anyone other than Smith?

Thumbs had gone down to see Lotten to tell her that he had found employment for Gertrud, who was to finish school that spring. The widow of Baker Sundberg, whom Thumbs had once worked for, was going to open a bread shop on Västerlånggatan and needed a girl to assist her, just to run errands and keep the place clean to begin with, eventually she could learn to wait on customers. The baker's widow was strict and set in her ways, but she was neither cruel nor stingy, said Thumbs. Even if the pay was low in the beginning, it was not a bad position for Gertrud.

While Lotten was rejoicing over things working out for her youngest daughter, Thumbs began to talk about meetings of the people and the discussions regarding aquavit. He had to hear if Lotten thought he had made a fool of himself. He hadn't been able to remain silent, and had leaped onto the speaker's platform at the workers' union headquarters. It was a place where he usually didn't go, not believing in that kind of lame organization, but when the tavern opponents had extended an invitation to a meeting there, he had wanted to hear what it was really about. A carpenter had opened the meeting and said that they should initiate purchasing societies too, to get goods cheaper. Then a paperhanger had taken hold of the chairman's gavel and declared the floor open. Thumbs had sat there and grown angry, and before he knew it he had demanded the floor. Somehow they were keeping something hidden. One speaker warned workers to fight against capital. Another supported the idea of purchasing societies, as long as it didn't hurt the dealers' interests. But the taverns and the state liquor distributors should be abhorred, that was most important, and everyone agreed on that point.

Then it was Thumbs' turn, but he was unused to talking to so many people. He could only come out with one pointed, blistering question: who were these people who had organized the meeting? Why didn't they dare give their names?

Some members of the audience booed.

"I want to know who's behind this!" Thumbs shouted. "If it's Smith, then the whole damned thing's a trick!"

Then everything went to pieces. Apparently he had said exactly what no one was supposed to say. The hall became a seething mass of people talking furiously with each other while the chairman pounded his gavel. Some shouted "Take the speaker down!"

"Smith...!" he shouted again.

But it was no longer possible to be heard. The chairman shook the gavel at him and some people in the audience had risen to their feet—it seemed they intended to storm the podium. The outcome of the whole thing ended with a motion to approve a purchasing society. A committee of fifteen had been set up. Following the chairman's suggestion, it had been decided that the committee could nominate appropriate people. At this point, Thumbs left, wholly convinced that Smith was the "appropriate person" intended.

Yes, there was something strange about these societies, Lotten agreed. But of course, they had to abhor the taverns. Surely it was good for people to become members?

Members of a society run by the aquavit king?

No, he couldn't figure that one out. They would have to see how it all went. It would be strange for an aquavit magnate to give money to a temperance society. That was certainly undermining his own position.

Was Lotten coming to the party in the White Hills? Thumbs went on to ask. He and his family had been invited despite the fact that they didn't live there.

Actually she didn't want to go, was Lotten's reply. But the children had begged and cajoled, all of the children from the area around the hill would be there, and she knew, too, that people resented it if somebody held him or herself apart. She would just have to go home with the children when it got too wild.

Thumbs nodded and left. She could hear him whistling, first on the stairs, then out in the street. She stood in the window and watched him go, saw how he sauntered off with his hands in his pants pockets. Then he turned and waved.

He carried himself like a boy. That was surely why he always called up memories of her own youth, the happy years before Henning got sick. Lotten stood there a little while, squinting into the last rays of the evening sun. But when some drunken apprentice boys began shouting obscenities, she withdrew hastily into the room's shadow, to the tasks that waited.

High above the low wooden houses rose four-story-high stone buildings. The people in the tall buildings had invited the people from the shanties to an enormous potluck dinner. The Bible ladies, who had experienced similar parties in the neighborhood before, tried to protect their lambs from these attacks of Satan, but it was difficult to do anything, almost meaningless to try. A couple of the fallen girls ran away in plenty of time. The listeners at the meetings became fewer and deafer to their pleas and prayers. No one thought of giving up the party. Remorse and regret came afterward, and then it might feel good to pay a visit to the mission and hear if they could receive forgiveness for their sins. Maybe they could get a ticket to the soup kitchen too.

The Bible ladies probably hoped that the Almighty would protect his strays with a storm, but Whitsun's Eve turned out warm and beautiful and invited acts of folly. The inhabitants of the hill streamed out of their holes with bottles and bundles of food. Families and unmarried mothers with ten or twelve children in tow clambered over crevices on the ridge, balanced on boards laid across mud puddles, stumbled onward between fences along the potholed lanes. Young people, who had already taken a few swigs from their bottles, shrieked among the bushes, while grim-faced old folks stumped past determinedly in order to get there while there were still some planks left to sit on.

The gate to the courtyard of the tall building stood open in welcome. The guests suddenly grew a little shy and made way for each other obsequiously, which repeatedly caused crowds of people to back up into the narrow lane of Renstjärnsgränd. Then someone would screw up the courage to go first, and the rest would immediately start shoving in order to be next.

The hosts stood in the gravel yard and bid everyone welcome. The notary, who had once been an office clerk, knew how to organize a party. He had even organized a drinking society, "The Turkish Sunflower," a few years back. Now he made sure the guests had really brought food with them as they were supposed to, and called out to the cigar-maker girls and the girls from the spinning mills to take the supplies of food. The guests got to keep their bottles; trying to combine and then divide up the liquor that had been bought during countless trips to the Fjäderholm Islands would only lead to fights and quarrels.

The Rosenstjärts, two redheaded cigar-maker sisters, hurried over to get the baskets and bundles of food. Sturdy girls, who could tolerate being grabbed and who could down a shot as quickly as any guy. Playfully they pushed away some adolescents with cracking voices who were too interested in the good food. A rock blaster who wanted to feel if the roses had thorns got an elbow in the stomach from Ida, while her sister Hulda gave her fussy, teething baby a rag that had been dipped in aquavit and sugar.

Fair-haired Gullpippi laid out the goodies on the table. Since all the plates were too small for a party of this size, they had borrowed and pieced together the trays they could get hold of. The spinning mill worker liked everything that was pretty: patterned cloths, beautifully laid tables. All day long she had broken off lilac branches and set the table as attractively as she could. Now she was trying to assemble decorative hors d'oeuvres, the kind that fine restaurants offered on their smorgasbords. It wasn't that easy with the materials she had at hand, and the Rosenstjärts had no sense of beauty either. They carped over how long it took—what kind of silly idea was it to decorate with food that way? Besides, it was just going to be eaten up. Who cared how it looked, the main thing was how it tasted.

Gullpippi was the local beauty. Her father sat beneath a budding lilac bush and watched over the girl gloomily. He was going to have a work-filled evening and night. Jealous and angry, he glared at the young upstarts who circled around the girl. He chewed his twist of tobacco, spat and cursed his fate. The man who was poor and owned something beautiful lived in constant fear that everyone wanted to steal his beautiful thing.

Not to keep it, just to sully it. He couldn't count the number of scoundrels he had punched in the jaw. Now, of course, they would be taking liberties again. Tired, he got up, pushed his way over to the table.

"This looks really nice," he said, and tried to sound friendly.

"Isn't it pretty?" She looked at her work and smiled. But the older Rosenstjärt made her way over and threw new bundles of food on the table.

"Just dump it out," panted Hulda. "We don't have time to play with the food now. The notary is about to announce it's ready."

Gullpippi's father helped his daughter gather up the bundles. He stood and watched while she worked, how easily and well she laid everything out, how nice it looked. But all his appetite had vanished. He looked around angrily, as if looking for a face to place his balled-up fist in. Actually, he should beat up every guy who was here. He knew what they wanted, every one of them. Grimly he took a swig from the flask that stuck out of his back pocket.

Lotten and her children stayed together with Thumbs' family, it felt safest. Their neighbor from Nytorget, Fearsome, sat at the same table. Somewhere in the crowd Fearsome's son and daughter-in-law had disappeared, but Grandfather was taking care of their five-year-old. With large and clumsy hands he place the little one on the plank beside the table. He shifted him closer to Lotten who nodded a welcome to Fearsome; it felt safer with more real men in their party.

Emelie was sitting beside Rudolf, and she was proud of it, he was so big and strong and impressive. It maybe annoyed her a bit, too, that Gertrude, who sat on the other side of Rudolf, talked nonstop, forcing him to respond. She would have liked to have Rudolf to herself, but she pretended not to, naturally, just the opposite: she teased him and got him all confused. He wasn't one for lively banter.

Thumbs placed a bottle on the table and tackled the food. Lotten and Matilda each had to be coaxed into taking a shot from the bottle. They made faces, didn't like the aquavit. Fearsome had his own bottle, but didn't dare drink much either, not while he was responsible for the child. He looked around. Wasn't his daughter-in-law going to come and take care of the boy so an old man could drink in peace? But she was probably making sure to stay away. The young people thought they could let go this evening and figured an old grandfather had had his fun and could babysit.

Calm and assured, Rudolf picked up his father's bottle and took an enormous swig. But when the younger Knutte reached out his hand, he was elbowed away; he had to wait until he finished school. That was what Rudolf had had to do.

Lotten saw the quick glance Matilda directed at her sons, but Matilda said nothing. Thumbs had given his approval for Rudolf to take a drink from time to time, and the boy was certainly old enough. Besides, he could hold his liquor, better than many full-grown men.

They ate and drank and sang; a buzz of voices rose from the courtyard. At times there was a spell of silence when all the voices died away, then they could hear hymn singing from the Bible ladies' home. The buzz would rise again as if to overpower them, and the songs from the mission were drowned out.

The dancing began. Thumbs tried to entice Lotten, but she absolutely did not want to, so then he asked Matilda. And Lotten sat and watched them as they walked away, and she didn't notice that Emelie disappeared at the same time with Rudolf. All four came back red and happy, and Emelie assured them that she had never had so much fun before. It was so lively, and the little Rosenstjärt had sat down right in the middle of the gravel yard and screeched furiously at Beefy-Fredrik for knocking her over when they danced.

In spite of the notary's attempts to stand guard, a few uninvited guests had succeeded in sneaking in. Among them were the girls who had run away from the home for prostitutes. They could certainly be considered as inhabitants of the White Hills, but still they didn't really count, they were more like temporary guests. However, once they made their way into the courtyard they disappeared into the crowd where there were a lot of people who wanted to hide them.

The lanterns hanging between the trees were lit, and shed flickering light over the couples whirling past and illuminated the faces around the tables. But in amidst the passageways and the bushes, the blackness deepened, and from the darkness came the sound of giggles and hoarse whispers. Some boys came along carrying a drunken ten-year-old who had fallen asleep in all too dangerous proximity to the heavy boots of the dancers. They threw him in the grass alongside the fence where he rolled over completely and went on sleeping with his head under a currant bush.

Time to leave, thought Lotten, if only she could catch Emelie. She could see her dancing by with Rudolf, but the girl didn't look in her mother's direction, and Lotten didn't want to get up before it was necessary since Fearsome's grandchild was asleep with his head on her knee. Matilda had been asked to dance by a workmate from the spinning mill, and Thumbs was dancing with Gullpippi, of course. Matilda and Thumbs' younger boys were playing tag by the outhouses.

But more and more people were getting completely drunk. Children staggered around the tables, more couples fell over dancing, some older women were pulling each other's hair. The Rosenstjärt sisters made out with the longshoremen who lived in the house. This was nothing for Lotten's girls to take part in. Lotten carefully lifted the boy who was asleep on her lap, and leaned him toward his grandfather. Then she went to get her daughters, and they came, unwillingly but obediently. Thumbs and Matilda returned, too, and the two families left together. There weren't many who noticed they left, and many others had actually gone earlier. But the courtyard was still crowded, and those who remained would certainly need more and more space.

The whole way home Lotten could hear the shrieks and the music. She could even imagine that the noise could be heard all the way to the police station on Tjärhovsgatan. But no policeman ever came out this way; these parts might be too dangerous. Had she ever seen a policeman in the White Hills? She thought about it, couldn't recall having done so. This was the wilderness, and the only strangers who dared penetrate it were the Bible ladies.

The aquavit king's subjects danced and drank, reeled over the hedges, fell underneath the tables. Hoarse cries and piercing shrieks echoed between the hillsides. The younger Rosenstjärt lay dead drunk on the floor of the courtyard's rotting pavilion; someone had pulled her skirts over her head. The notary had fallen asleep on the steps beside her, even in his sleep he held tightly onto his bottle to preserve the last drops. Someone was shaking and pulling on him. The notary woke up blinking and looked up reproachfully.

No... no, he hadn't seen Gullpippi. Had the girl disappeared? Heh-heh... you know youth... best to look in the bushes.

He received a shove that knocked him over and most of the contents of his bottle ran out over the younger Rosenstjärt's white legs. The girl didn't budge. Fumbling, the notary rose to his feet and staggered off to get a bucket of water to pour over her. In the Turkish Sunflower they usually threw water on the new members who would then flounder about. The younger Rosenstjärt was ready and worthy of becoming a sister in the order.

But the man who was looking for his daughter continued searching. For one second his watchfulness had lapsed—and the girl disappeared. He had finally gotten hungry and gone to see if anything edible was left. At that point Gullpippi had been sitting and talking with some other girls.

He went through woodsheds and outhouses, surprised couples making love, and woke up people sound asleep to ask them. He ran up to the room they lived in, knocked on all the doors in the house. Was she out on the hill? Why had she left when he had so plainly forbidden it?

Gangs of youths were standing around on the hillsides, half-grown oafs and sluts, who laughed at him and shouted obscenities. In a clump of bushes he found some boys standing around a girl who was down in a heap. He shoved aside the boy who stood closest, pulled up the one who lay on top of the girl. But the girl was one of the whores from the Hills, and she spat at him for interrupting her business. If he wanted to have her, he had to wait his turn. Besides, she had heard that he was a creep who preferred to sleep with his own daughter.

He didn't have the strength to get upset about such gossip and slander; it only mattered to find the girl. They could believe what they wanted, scream their lies at him. He ran through the park calling her name aloud, but she was nowhere to be found. He was forced to return to the court-yard and hope that she had returned.

He found her in the dark stone stairwell of the building. She was sit-ting there with torn clothing, crying. Five or six, or maybe more, boys had been waiting on the stairs when she ran up to get a sweater. They had stopped her, and before she could scream they had dragged her into one of the rooms. They had thrown her down on the floor, and stuffed a piece of apron into her mouth. Someone had held her down; she hadn't been able to stop them.

"Which ones were they?"

She just went on crying. He shook her.

"Which ones?"

He led her up to the room, letting her collapse onto the pile of rags inside the door. He sat there in the darkness and felt that everything was over. What had he imagined? What had he believed he could save her from? And for what? What kind of a life could a rock blaster offer his daughter? Could he have prevented this if he had managed to lay off the bottle?

The blast came while they were still bellowing and shrieking in the yard, a boom that caused the windows and the walls to rattle. Broken panes tin-kled, a rain of slivered glass fell in the courtyard.

The notary let go of the soaking wet, screaming Ida, and ran toward the house. Some of the more sober men followed him. A moment later they carried the bloody and unconscious Gullpippi down the stairs of the building, out into the lane, and down to the wagon someone had gone for that was waiting on Nya gatan. The rock blaster's headless body was left to lie where it was until the police arrived.

Onlookers, pale and stone-drunk hung around the house all the next day, Whitsunday, discussing what had happened in low voices. Someone thought the man had raped his daughter and then tried to take both their lives. They'd seen what the girl's clothing looked like hadn't they? Horrifying. But it was dangerous for a man alone to have such a beautiful daughter. He had been like a crazy man over his Gullpippi. No, on this day they all needed something to fortify themselves with. If everything had been drunk up someone had to be sent over to the Fjäderholm Islands. They began to band together to collect their last coins.

Resigned and silent, they bowed their heads to king aquavit, tyrant and comforter.

PLEASURE OUTINGS

With the music corps of the second guard in the lead, the Latin School boys marched to Ladugård Field. A forest of wooden rifles swayed through the narrow streets, and the echo of the marching band rattled the windowpanes. They were on their way to do battalion exercises.

From the headquarters of the first chimney sweep district came a group of sweeps with lines and plumbs, brooms and scrapers. The apprentice boys carried their ladders, which they used to reach the chimney tops. The music made the journeymen pick up their pace, and the smaller boys had to struggle to keep up.

Emelie, who was out on an errand, pushed forward in order to see: row after row of marching schoolboys with solemnly frozen expressions. Suddenly in the ranks, one face which she knew so well. Emelie waved excitedly. But August stared decidedly straight ahead. Hadn't he seen her? Or was he perhaps ashamed of her? She looked down at her dress.

When she turned to go back to the factory, she almost ran straight into the gang of chimney sweeps, but this time she was careful not to wave. Johan turned his head the other way when he caught sight of her anyway. Rudolf would have said hello to whomever he ran into, she thought as she hurried along. Rudolf neither felt ashamed nor afraid. Though it was different for him naturally, he didn't risk anything. No one ever gave him any trouble. He was strong too.

In the packaging room the dust hung in the air and played in the sunbeams that streamed through the open door. Emelie placed the milk jug in the middle of the table and took out the bread she had brought from home. She chewed and imagined she could still hear the music blaring in her ears, and when she closed her eyes, she could see August's pale, anxious face bobbing along under a forest of wooden pipes.

He came to Nytorget one evening that same week, in a hired coach which would return two hours later to get him. It was his last visit of the spring; the next morning he was going to move out to their summerhouse on Stora Essingen. Fredrik Bodin had come along to go to his construction sites on Söder. He had bought his sister-in-law's lots and begun to build.

Emelie felt like she wanted to apologize to August somehow for her intrusion when she waved at him. A little tentatively she said that she had seen him the other day when he marched by with his school. August answered that he hadn't seen her but he blushed slightly, and she could sense that he was lying. This disappointed her. She would have preferred a tacit but honorable understanding. Now she didn't really know if she dared say hello to him on the street or not.

But he avoided the subject, and took out the money he had saved, wanted to give it to Lotten. Lotten hesitated, of course, she needed the money—but did Mrs. Bodin know about it?

To be honest, he thought Mama should understand that he couldn't talk about something like that with Mother.

Yes, he lied, she knew.

Everything got so entangled and difficult. Almost to the point where he wished he could go out to the carriage again, before he had to lie anymore. It only got worse instead of better. His schoolmates must surely wonder why he never wanted to go to Stora Badsugatan; they couldn't have any idea that he had a sister who was a factory worker there. Mother grew sulky every time he went to Söder; it was she who insisted that he ride in a coach. The hired coach attracted all the kids around Nytorget. They stood with their mouths open, yelling at him as he passed. Everything and everyone made it more difficult for him. It would feel great to disappear out to the country. Escape.

Lotten stroked his cheek, a thanks for the money he had saved and given her. The hand was rough, he could see the ugly cracks, the nails scraped and broken. He took it, held it against his cheek and felt the longing to stay and the wish to flee.

On the way home he sat silently in the shaking coach, despising himself. He couldn't clear it up. Different rules applied in the two incompatible worlds he called home. He knew no one in the same situation. Mother had been there once, he knew, but she had cut all ties. He couldn't talk about it with her. Although he could understand her—and although she perhaps could understand him.

The coach stopped. He was home again. The coachman wound the reins around the horse's front legs and went inside with him to get the time put down on his monthly bill, and to find out what time he should drive them to the boat in the morning.

During the winter August had wondered many times if he would run into the girl from Friendship Point again. He could bend his arm and imagine he felt the weight of her body against it. Now he was almost afraid to meet her again. He had used her wrongfully in his fantasies at times. Would he dare look her in the eye now? Would she be able to see through him?

On the very first day he went in the direction of Friendship Point and looked for an image, a memory: her fluttering, light-colored dress among the dark trees. She didn't come. Maybe she wasn't living on the island this summer.

One week later Ida and her parents were invited to dinner at the Bodins. August's and Ida's fathers had traveled together on the boat a few times and discovered that they had a common interest in the construction industry. And Fredrik Bodin who had tired of his screaming general contractor, Granat, thought that getting to know Wide could be useful. It turned out that the Wides were pleasant and easy to get along with. Nouveaux riches perhaps, simple souls beneath their polished surface, thought Fredrik. But already from the first instant, Annika Bodin and Signe Wide took to each other. The children seemed to enjoy each other's company, too. It had been a long time since they had seen August so lively and happy. The very first evening the young people went out in the garden and swung on the large swing. It wasn't quite proper, perhaps, but it was really the girl's mother who should think of things like that. Besides, you could see the swing from the glass veranda so the young people were clearly visible. August stood between the seats and worked them up to a good speed. When they were going fast enough he sat down opposite the girl. August was fifteen, Ida sixteen. There was no risk that the boy would seduce her, as shy as he was.

Fredrik began to have more and more trouble finding the time to come out to the country. After a while, he came only for Saturdays and Sundays. Annika believed what she wanted about this work which suddenly descended on him, but she didn't say very much, thought it was nice to have him stay away. Wide didn't come out to see his wife so often either. The gentlemen had their business together. But on Saturdays they arrived laden with news.

It was still the actions of L.O. Smith that everybody talked about. Palm, whom everybody had heard so much about previously, had been completely upstaged by the aquavit king. If one hundred came to Palm's meeting out at Lill-Jans Park, then several hundred gathered at Smith's events. Smith got the workers all whipped up. They learned that they paid more in taxes on their aquavit than the taxes property owners paid on income and capital combined. The lowest quality aquavit, the one the people drank, was the one taxed most highly. One had to admire Smith's fearless fight against the authorities, but his bold flirtation with the lower class was a concern.

The Anti-Tavern League had sisters and brothers now. Smith had spawned new popular movements. The Workers' Ring, the purchasing society planned earlier, had now been created, and the Workers' Bank. But their pursuit of the alcohol distribution system and the taverns it owned was still most important for Smith and what interested people most.

Tavern hygiene had been stringently monitored and criticized, and enormous popular gatherings had pronounced their condemnation of it. Then came the deathblow. The Anti-Tavern League made sample purchases of aquavit at the taverns. The purchased quantities were poured into bottles that were sealed in the presence of witnesses. The measurements showed that most of the glasses used by the alcohol distribution company's taverns were too small. The customers were being cheated.

That Smith was clever.... If nothing else, at least he provided them with a subject for evening conversation around the lighted lamps on their glassed-in verandas. Almost to the point where they forgot to keep an eye on the young people. Where could they be? It was beginning to grow dark.... Ah yes, they had walked down to meet the other youngsters who had gathered on the dock at Värdshuset.

"August is with them," said Annika. "The boy is so quiet, I don't think we need to worry. Besides, there are such nice, well brought up young people on this island."

But now the gentlemen wanted to have something to drink, and the ladies wanted to move into the parlor; it was a little more comfortably furnished than the veranda. The ladies got up, and their bustles bobbed up and down like giant peacock tails as they glided away. The gentlemen stayed sitting where they were to "talk business."

"I have arranged two little tidbits for us at the Stallmästergården Restaurant on Monday evening," said Wide.

Fredrik looked anxiously toward the door, but they were talking at full speed in there.

Wide picked up his glass, stretched his long legs in the light gray suit, and unbuttoned the top button of the high-buttoned jacket. He laughed long and contentedly to himself.

It was not especially lively down at Värdshus meadow by the inn since one of the island families was having a summer party at their house, and a lot of people had been invited. Those who were left out were in bad humor and felt passed over. August, on the other hand, felt more confident when those who were considered more highborn were absent. He sat down on the slope and took off his jacket. Ida sat beside him, pulled off her large white cuffs and laid them on top of his coat. They were ready for the games.

They danced singing games, swinging around so the girls' skirts whirled out and their cotton stockings showed almost up to their knees, where their red and blue garters shone like flowers. But after a while the couples grew tired, one by one, they didn't really feel like playing when they could hear the party music over there at the Bergs' house.

"Shall we go look at the view?" asked Ida.

August nodded and handed her cuffs to her, then pulled on his coat. They followed the road between the garden fences until a path turned off higher up toward the hill. It was steep and narrow, and Ida had a little trouble making her way through the pine branches. When they had gotten past the hardest part and houses and gardens were hidden in the greenery beneath them, she stopped and let out her breath. Whew! She pretended to collapse from fatigue. Then he knew she was playing, and he played along too. He had to take her by the waist to hold her up, but she just slid down farther with her backside sticking out and her arms hanging. Then he took hold of her under her arms, and suddenly when he made a quick movement he found something round where his hands stopped: her breasts that were hidden somewhere in the swell of clothes and lace. He felt how she grew rigid and still. He didn't know if he should let her go or not, but loosened his grip, and found, afraid and happy, how she seemed to fill his cupped hands, pressed herself into them. Then she shook herself, and shook him off.

She began to walk again. He followed her silently, afraid of anything serious, and of the hunger which had been awakened. Now nothing would be like it was, he thought. Now he knew something he hadn't known about earlier, something about delight and lust.

From the hill they looked out over the water that was colored a light red by the evening sun: some white sails gleamed, and a sloop was heading toward town. Green woods along the gray rocks, some houses that could be glimpsed from the green foliage at Ekersberg and from the vicinity of the tile factory at Smedslätten. And over on Långholmen where he was pointing, they could just make out a villa between the trees in which lived a very famous figure. Could she guess who?

No. Would she have to forfeit something?

Yes.

He had to help her a little. Was it a prince?

Higher. A king.

King Oscar himself?

Quickly he took the handkerchief that peeked out of her skirt pocket. Wrong, he said. She had to pay a forfeit.

What did she have to do to get it back?

He didn't really know what you were supposed to do, he mumbled.

Quickly she leaned forward, grabbing the handkerchief at the same time as she kissed him on the cheek. Then she got up.

"Maybe they're waiting for us, " she said, and began to walk.

A little dazed, he followed her, felt how the evening breeze played across his cheek and tickled the damp imprint of her lips.

When they got down to the road, he tried to place his arm around her waist, but she quickly took it away.

Sommarro lay just at the bottom of the hill. He opened the gate for her, and they took the garden path up to the house. Marigolds and daisies shone in the grass, from the shadows beneath the trees. Where the archway formed by the trees was densest he drew her into the shadow and stood there, questioning.

"You may," she said, and offered her cheek.

Carefully he came closer. Then his mouth brushed hastily against hers, before she had time to pull back.

"But August, *that's* not what I meant!"

She was smiling anyway, he thought proudly.

They arrived home in plenty of time. Evening sandwiches were waiting before the party was to break up.

The next morning he walked up to the hill alone, sat at the place where they had been sitting the previous evening. He felt it with his hands, as if he believed there was a hollowed out place left on the rock. He sat where he had been, wet two fingers and pressed them against his cheek. The wind tickled a greeting from her.

He looked out over the water, what was that music? A whole flotilla was steaming along down there. He had to count: twelve festively decorated boats. The orchestras played, the pennants fluttered.

Three thousand five hundred members of the Anti-Tavern League were on a pleasure outing to Mariefred.

Bodin and Wide had even more work in the city. Fredrik had had some troubles with his construction projects on the Söder properties. Granat, who was supervising the construction there, was truly difficult to deal with. Now they decided that Wide would build the remaining building, so the men had a lot to discuss.

Pale and partied-out, they arrived unwillingly on Saturday evenings. They consoled themselves with the fact that their wives got along so well. Annika and Signe met daily, going down to the bathhouse or sitting in the garden to read and sew. During the day, they preferred to be at Sommarro where it was most comfortable; the villa the Wides had rented was small and not especially nice.

August and Ida had many opportunities to meet, often under the eyes of their mothers, but even then they could keep up careful physical contact. While he looked as if he were reading, he could let his hand play along her foot, stroke her ankle, even stroke her leg all the way up to the pleated garter beneath her knee. And Ida had a funny way of pretending that she didn't notice his hand, as if she were completely occupied with her handwork.

Sometimes they walked down to the beach. When no one saw them, they grew shyer, could be frightened at finding they were left alone together. If he tried to hold her, she would hastily free herself. Someone might see. Only in the dark would she dare anything more, sometimes a kiss.

She understood how men lived, she said one evening. It wasn't hard to figure out what her father and August's father were up to when they were alone in town. They were out with, yes, with *those kinds* of girls. All men were, according to what she understood from Mama. No, Ida would never get married, that much was certain. Instead she was going to study the woman's question thoroughly. He must have read about it in the papers?

Stunned, he answered that he hadn't. He knew nothing about the woman's question, not much about how men lived either. He had heard something in school, of course. Two boys had been expelled when they were discovered with some of those girls at a restaurant outside of town. Master Personne had said it was that August Strindberg who led youth astray.

There, that went to show you! Even boys were all alike.

They sat on the glassed-in veranda with a game of Fox and Geese between them. Dusk had fallen. Somehow August had to change Ida's mind. She had to take it back. He placed a hand on her back. A row of small buttons tickled the palm of his hand; he let his hand glide over them. They slipped so easily out of their buttonholes; his hand slid under the dress material, slowed down on the stiff embroidery of her camisole, spread across her soft skin, felt the little wing of her shoulder blade.

"You're choking me," she whispered.

He pulled his hand out, looked at her, concerned. A tear ran down her nose.

"You mustn't say that," he whispered. "You shouldn't believe that is so."

No more actually happened between them that summer. But what had already happened was enormous, and it was filled with joy and terror.

The debates continued to rage in the city. The Workers' Ring had begun to be organized, and in a short time gotten almost twenty thousand members who were interested in purchasing alcohol together to get lower prices. Five officials had been employed to oversee the project; they were paid by Smith. One of them was paperhanger Johansson who had chaired the meeting Thumbs had participated in. Johansson now functioned as Smith's stalking horse as well.

By fall the opposition had matured. Doktor Nyström refused to loan out the workers' union's headquarters for the ring's meetings, and temperance advocates who had previously supported the Anti-Tavern League became its enemies. They felt the tavern boycott only increased drinking at home, and it was wrong of Smith to campaign for cheaper aquavit. Lower alcohol prices led to more drunkenness, the rings should be opposed by any means.

At the same time, opposition within the ring movement increased. The gossip spread that Smith had promised the king that he would keep the workers away from socialism, but some of the leaders of the ring movement organized a debate that ended in pure socialist propaganda.

On the Fjäderholm Islands there was also a backlash against Smith. Frightened local authorities on Lidingö nearby gave in to pressure from Stockholm and refused to renew liquor licenses.

Smith, the workers' pope, sent out half-a-million printed copies of a letter on yellow paper, "the saffron bun," and offered several attractive suggestions. The state should provide paid retirement for all citizens, the ring movement should open employment agencies, steam-powered kitchens in every town should replace the work of housewives.

But the ring movement and the Workers' Bank got into a dispute over who would pay for the first steam cooking experiment, and more men in the ring movement were interested in opening cooperative liquor stores. Smith didn't want any competition with the businessmen who bought and sold his aquavit; he wanted the ring's purchases to go through the dealers. Against his will, a few small liquor stores for ring members were opened.

A few years later everything was to disappear; the whole pleasure fleet of organizations and lofty schemes blown away across the water of the bays. On the same day that paperhanger Johansson would go to America—wanted for embezzling funds from liquor store cash boxes—Master Palm would relocate his workers' movement to Stockholm.

One thing was already clear: the new movement had stagnated, the mighty flames had been reduced to small glowing embers. Not much more than ashes remained.

After the Bodins and the Wides moved back into the city, they continued to socialize, though not quite as intensively as before. For Ida and August, the change was the greatest; they were seldom alone together anymore. But he knew there was a fire within him that could easily flare up and carry her with him. He counted the years until what was now so forbidden could be allowed.

Ten years? More? What would be left of the fire and the intensity then? Life was harder in many ways than he had guessed before, and there was no one he could talk to, no one he dared confess to.

Could Ida feel the same? Sometimes it was as if she suddenly gave up all resistance, as if she would consent to everything. But his fear checked him and later, when his courage returned, she prevented him.

In the autumn darkness, he longed for a new summer with its pleasure outings, and he tried to convince himself that they would only bring him joy, that no threatening, unfathomable depths lay beneath the shining, enticing surface of the waters.

HEAVEN AND EARTH

The days when Lotten went out to wash she had to leave home by two in the morning. Anxiously she would look at the sleeping children, hoping the girls would leave on time for work, and that they would dress Olof properly before they left him with Sofi.

Sofi, Washer-Johanna's son's wife, was at home during the day and took care of her own children and some of the neighbors'. One of her duties was to wake Lotten's girls, but it was difficult to rely on Sofi, she was sloppy. Luckily Emelie woke up easily, often it was she who woke Sofi instead. It was worse to know that Olof was entirely dependent on the neighboring woman.

Johanna panted and groaned, displeased with her daughter-in-law, when the three washerwomen left with their handcart early in the morning. An uneven trio, the large and unwieldy Johanna, the shrunken little Malin, and Lotten, who followed in the tracks of the older women, pushing the cart.

You couldn't depend on that person, Johanna said. The other day she bought a bun on credit and stuffed the whole thing in her mouth. Messy and sloppy, that's what she was, not a real working person. Like most of the others who were home during the day, she went down to the cotton-spinning mill at Barnängen and fetched old balls of bast to use to braid doormats. Though, truth to tell, she didn't get many done during the week. Otherwise, it could have meant a little money. They got one krona per mat in the stores. Johanna wondered at times if Sofi didn't make more mats than she said. Where else did the woman get the money for her liquor?

Children only give you troubles, thought Johanna. She and Fearsome had borne and raised six, four were still alive. Did anyone believe that four children could support their old parents? Oh no, just the opposite. Bengt and Sofi had lived with them for what would soon be three years, and hardly paid for their food. The others had their families and were seldom ever heard from. Johanna began to be worried about the future, her obesity made everything all the harder for her. And Fearsome with his back pain couldn't hold out so much longer at the harbor. What would they do then?

Malin felt obliged to give due credit to Lotten. Yes, Lotten was of course the exception. Johanna agreed with that, but the exception didn't listen to the chatter of the older women, she struggled with her heavy cart, and didn't hear much more than the crunch of the gravel and the grating of the wheels.

Emelie awoke and hurriedly got up, looking quickly at the large zinc pocket watch her mother had bought in installments. It was after four-thirty, and Sofi should have already woken them. Emelie shook her sister. It was time to get up! Gertrud wanted to roll over and go on sleeping, but Emelie pulled her blanket off. Finally her sister sat up, yawned and looked around. Mama had put out a cup of skim milk for each of them, and a few slices of limpa bread.

Their clothing hung ready and waiting—new darning on Gertrud's stockings and a freshly ironed blouse for Emelie. How long had Mama worked last night? Emelie didn't understand how her mother had the energy to stay awake, she got so sleepy in the evenings herself. She had asked Mama not to bother with the blouse, but here it hung anyway, clean and nice. Mama was so terribly stubborn—neat and clean, neat and clean.

The girls pulled on the pantaloons Mama had sewn, a novelty that fall. Before, they had had to make do with layers of skirts. But Mama, who took in washing, knew that finer folk used such articles of clothing, and that they were also beginning to be used by ordinary people. They were made of white linen and had large slits in the middle of the front and back. On top of the long camisole, they had their two petticoats, sewn from old dresses, then the undershirt, blouse, stockings fastened with elastic under the knee, and boots. The scarf and shawl for over their shoulders would stay put on the chair for now. Emelie would get Olof dressed first.

After they ate their morning meal, Emelie took the boy by the hand and knocked on the neighbor's door. She heard the older children carrying on in there, and Sofi's sleepy reply to the knocking. Sofi still lay on the mattress on the floor.

"So it's already that time," she said, and scratched her scalp. "Let the kid play out in the yard for now."

"Mama doesn't want that," Emelie ventured cautiously. It was raining and Olof didn't have any real boots.

"Let 'im stay then," said Sofi, yawning. She might as well wait with driving the kids outside till the stubborn girl had left.

Emelie hurried off. Gertrud was waiting in the yard. They cut across Nytorget via the footbridge and continued down Stadsträdgårdsgatan between the shops that were still closed. A drizzling rain still hung in the air, the October morning was gray and cold.

Sweaty and flushed from their exertions and the heat, the laundresses came out of the washhouse dragging their loaded carts. They pulled them down to the beating dock, feeling how the wind cooled their so recently warm bodies. They beat with the wooden paddles, rubbed and rinsed and sweated, and got chilled all over again.

On the way home from her day's work, Malin complained of being cold and feeling worn out. But it was probably only the nasty weather, they felt wet and miserable, all three. Johanna believed that Fearsome had a nip of something strong at home which they could all take for medicinal purposes. But when they got home, it turned out that the nip had been drunken up. Johanna glared angrily at Sofi, who was quite clearly not sober, but her daughter-in-law didn't let it bother her.

Lotten asked about Olof. The whole group of kids was down at the outhouses playing, answered Sofi. You couldn't have them spending the whole day inside. Lotten hurried down there and found the boy among the firewood and refuse, streaming with dirt and rain. It was going to be a real job to get him and his clothes clean—and then there was the worry over his being cold and wet and surely getting sick, delicate as he was.

The girls came back from work. They too had damp clothes that had to be hung up to dry. The entire little room was filled with wet garments while the fire crackled in the fireplace. Malin lay in her bed and froze, despite the warmth; Olof had fallen asleep after the day's adventures. Despairingly, Lotten looked around. How would she manage? How would everything have time to dry by the next day? How would she dare leave Olof in Sofi's care in the future?

She heard them arguing in the apartment next door. It was Johanna and Sofi who were angrily screaming at each other, while the men apparently tried to intervene. A moment later someone was knocking at the door, and Fearsome walked in. His son had brought a bottle home with him, and Fearsome had asked him for a sip for the frozen women. Malin forced a few drops between her lips and wrinkled her nose at the unpleasant taste, but it helped against a cold. With distaste she drank it down and crawled as deeply under the patchwork quilt as she could. But Lotten refused politely, she would only get sleepy from drinking. She had to stay awake to take care of everything.

It was unfortunate that Sofi didn't take better care of the boy, said Fearsome. But she was a little out of sorts, it would surely get better, Lotten would see.

But it didn't get better. Soon Lotten found that it was just as worrisome to have the boy at Sofi's as to leave him alone. But he really couldn't be left alone, so it had to be with Sofi. Every day Lotten had to feel the same terror, every evening encounter the same bad situation. It wasn't only the worry about the boy, it was about her mother, too, Washer-Malin didn't get better. She grew worse, coughing, fever rising. Lotten wanted to send for a doctor, but Malin said no, she would certainly get better again.

One afternoon when Lotten came home, her mother lay dead. Sofi had, of course, looked in from time to time, but she said that she thought the old woman was sleeping. The doctor who came to write out the death certificate informed her it had been pneumonia. He consoled the distraught Lotten by saying there wasn't much he could have done, even if he had come earlier. When old people got that illness they died, and there wasn't much anyone could do other than alleviate their discomfort a little.

Malin was buried out by Skanstull on a Saturday at the end of October. Yellow leaves rained down over the dug-out hole, and Lotten and Johanna stood and watched the coffin disappear down into the moist sand. The coffin seemed too large for the little woman inside.

More than ever Lotten felt the mortality of all things. Everything is so soon gone, nothing remains to hold onto—as if she were aging herself, had moved into her mother's place, become *the old one.*

Malin's death had to bring more changes. As long as the girls were earning so little, they couldn't keep the room just for themselves. They were forced to take in boarders. Some workers from the tobacco factory who knew that a bed stood empty had already come to inquire about it, but Lotten couldn't imagine having male boarders.

Matilda came up with a suggestion. She still worked at the spinning mill at Barnängen and knew two young working girls who were having trouble with living arrangements. One was a fifteen-year-old whom Lotten hadn't seen earlier; the other was Gullpippi, the rock blaster's daughter. She was in the hospital but would soon be released.

Bärta came and moved in with them with her few belongings. There probably wouldn't be any problems with her, thought Lotten, the girl seemed nice. Though she was a little more forward than Lotten's daughters, talking freely first thing with the boys in the house. There wasn't anything directly provocative in her manner, only that unsuspicious and unselfconscious manner which often led girls to trouble.

At the cosmetics factory, factory director Melinder came into the packaging room to see how far they had gotten. He stood silent and off to the side, away from the noise and the drudgery. He felt shy in front of all the energetic women, who were red with their exertions. He was a little frightened by their activity and camaraderie.

He frowned when he saw Emelie. The girl looked tired, was really too little to work overtime so assiduously. Was she even allowed to do that if one followed the laws and regulations strictly? He waved for the girl to come over.

"Emelie seems tired," he said. "Go home now."

She thanked him and curtsied.

How would she actually get home? Did she still live on Söder?

Yes, on Nytorget.

Then all she had to do was take the streetcar to Slussen.

No, she didn't ride it. That was way too expensive. She walked.

He imagined he could see her trudging along through darkened streets. A lot of drifters out these days. What were her parents thinking of? But her father was dead, if he remembered correctly.

He pulled out his coin purse and looked until he found a ten-öre piece. "Take the streetcar home now," he said. "It's getting late and Emelie needs to sleep in order to keep up her strength."

She thanked him again and couldn't fathom what had come over the factory director. But of course she would leave and go home if that was what he wanted, and ride too. She was certainly tired if she thought about it. A minute later she was standing on the street and looking out for the streetcar. There it was, disappearing into the distance. It would be a long while before the next one came. She had time to walk a way. It was better than to stand still and risk being approached by someone.

She hurried along with the ten-öre piece in her grip. She stopped from time to time and looked, but no streetcar was in sight. Then she continued, and thought how the ten öring was actually her own, and that she could probably do something a lot more fun with it. But the factory director might ask her if she had gotten a ride, and she didn't want to lie.

Ride.... How many times had she thought: if I had money I would ride, not the streetcar, but something more exciting: the new elevator. It was surely not so dangerous; thousands of people had ridden it without falling down.

She would take the elevator, then she would have ridden like the factory director said she should, and gained time, also, which he had intended. She quickened her pace, her shawl fluttering in the wind. When she arrived at Slussen, she saw the dimly-lit boxes that rose and sank inside the openwork iron column. Soon she would travel up there, between heaven and earth. Did she really dare? She had to dare, she had dreamt of it so often.

She joined the line of people on their way up to the amusements at Mosebacke and the hills of Söder. People waiting impatiently behind her jostled her.

She pushed her way into the elevator and handed over her token that had cost five öre. She managed to make her way over to the glass windowpane so she could see out. Suddenly the elevator rose with the aid of the steam machinery. Now it was too late for regrets. She felt a thrill, the coolness of fear. Oh, she was gliding through the air, high over all the buildings around Slussen: the triangle with taverns and shops, the fishhouses, and the statue on its grassy plot and the bushes stripped of their leaves. There were the small cargo boats at Kornhamn, the grain harbor, and small fishing boats at Fiskhamn or Pelikan, the fishing harbor. And now the whole city glittered faintly in the darkness: gas lanterns following the shoreline, and a puffing locomotive chugging its way out of the tunnel at Järnvägen, releasing a fireworks display of sparks and steam.

The elevator stopped with a little jolt, and she looked around anxiously. What if they got stuck, if the elevator fell straight down? But the door opened and a footbridge stretched out before her. She took a quick jump over the narrow gap between the elevator car and the bridge. Now she was safe. Or was she? The bridge seemed so narrow and unsteady, it extended high over the roofs of Glasbruksgatan. Down below, the street ran like a dark sewer, narrow and undulating, dimly lit by a few sparse lanterns. She hurried across the bridge, half running to get home quickly and be able to tell about the fantastic adventure she had had.

THE BIG
COLLECTION

In the beginning of December the journeyman chimney sweeps and their apprentices launched "the big collection," the drive to get Christmas money. They suddenly became very polite, became very careful not to dirty people's apartments, and tried in every way to be on their best behavior. They hoped as recompense for their efforts to get a lot of Christmas tips in their collection box.

The smallest boys received the largest tips, everyone knew that they appealed to the maternal instincts of the women and the young girls. For this reason, the apprentice boys took care of the collecting, but the boys were aware they would get little or nothing when the box was emptied. It would be the journeymen who divided up the spoils. So the boys tried to put away a few coins and came up with the most ingenious hiding places. The journeymen, who themselves had tried to hide coins as apprentices however, knew most of the tricks.

Johan, who was no longer a new boy, but was now called "little," was sliding down flues in a fairly new house on Stora Gråbergsgatan. He worked together with a "medium-sized" and under the supervision of the journeyman Finn-Olle. Finn-Olle was good to work for, he willingly allowed the boys to descend rather than ascend. Climbing up was a lot more work than simply putting your feet against the side and sliding down. But some of the journeymen believed the boys were toughened by ascending. They had to shimmy up with their backs against one wall of the chimney, and their knees against the other. If the chimney flue was too narrow so that one leg had to be held straight the whole time, or too wide so they had to make their way up with their shoulders against one side and their feet against another, ascending could be quite an effort.

Finn-Olle let them descend, could even turn a blind eye if, once in a while, they shot down like rockets through the chimney flue with the brush between their legs and used the scraper to regulate their speed.

Johan branched off from the large chimney stack, the main one, made his way into the extension, the sling, climbed out through the steam hatch and stood on the hearth where the maid had very neatly placed a newspaper. The boy was scrupulous about not getting anything dirty.

"I'm all done here," he said, and wondered how he could hide the coin he would certainly receive.

One of the girls of the family peeked into the kitchen; she had heard the scraping in the chimney and wanted to see the chimney sweep boy. She went in to her mother and said that the boy had crawled into the kitchen. He would of course get a Christmas tip?

He received a whole krona, and his face lit up beneath the black grime. But why he suddenly looked so worried the girl couldn't understand. The kitchen maid offered him a bun, and the boy bowed and thanked her. He was given a cup of coffee too and drank it standing up. He was still holding the bun in his hand when he left.

"Funny boy," said the young girl and the maid agreed, laughing. But outside the door, Johan shoved the krona inside the bun.

"The maid offered me some dishwater to drink with this," he said and broke off a little over half the bun to give to Finn-Olle. The journeyman chuckled, sensing something was up. But in good time the boys would be properly frisked once they got home, and usually whatever was hidden would appear.

Work continued, and Johan was lucky. As they passed by Stora Badstugagatan on their way home, he ran into Emelie, and without saying anything he quickly slipped the piece of bun into her hand. She watched him go, puzzled. The bun was a little sooty, but she wiped it off and ate it. It was lovely, newly baked wheat bread. Then she noticed something hard in it and looked at the coin with surprise, a whole krona. Had he meant for her to have it... was it a thank you for her having helped him from time to time? She didn't really believe that, the amount was too large. It was best to put it aside until she found out what Johan intended.

In the chimney sweeps' quarters the journeymen were calling everyone to account. They turned the little boys upside down and one hidden coin after another fell to the floor. The men felt every fold in their clothing; it was common trick to open a seam and hide some money in a pleat. Every cranny imaginable was examined, and those who had been too inventive got a taste of the whip. Crying and disappointed they curled up in a corner, but perhaps some, despite all the searching, could console themselves with having managed to hide a few coins.

Johan had avoided being hit this time; only one single five-öre piece had fallen out of a trouser pleat. If only Emelie didn't say anything now in front of the others—or keep the money—but he hoped he could depend on her.

The day before Christmas Eve, August came to Söder, as usual in a hired coach. This time he was abundantly laden with a little Christmas tree and presents for his mother and siblings. Along with it, Annika Bodin had put together a basket of food.

August's siblings and Bärta gathered around Lotten while she unpacked everything. August had to press close too, he didn't really know what Mother had packed.

Lotten had placed the basket on the table by the window, but it was hard to see anything since Bärta had squeezed herself in between and blocked his view. At first he got a little annoyed and tried to shove her aside. His knee pressed against her leg, but she didn't give in. She pressed back instead and it was as if she radiated warmth from the point where their legs made contact. She was probably one of those girls his friends called "easy," it suddenly occurred to him, and he began to get excited.

"Oh, does August think I could have a taste too?"

"Of course," he said, disconcerted. "Of course."

"Oh, you're so nice!" she cried and threw her arms around his neck. Lotten looked at her severely. What would August think? Bärta ought to realize that she and August were way too big for such carrying on.

Look! Candles and candleholders for the Christmas tree! Shouldn't they light it for just a little, tiny bit, just enough so August could see it too, since he wouldn't be there for Christmas?

Lotten placed the tree in a pot, and Gertrud ran down to the yard and got some stones, which they wedged in around it. The four candles were put in place, and then Lotten lit them carefully, worried that the flames might come too near the ceiling. It was the first time they had had a tree for Christmas.

Oh, it was so beautiful! Bärta had sunk down on the sofa and sat with clasped hands.

August stared into the small, sparkling candle flames. He could smell the fresh scent of the girl beside him, and at the same time, he felt slightly ashamed of himself. Wasn't he betraying Ida by being attracted to Bärta this way? But Ida was so far away, he saw her so seldom. Bärta was different from Ida, it was as if she knew and acknowledged that she was one of the easy girls. Or was she just behaving naturally? He felt like his old surroundings had already become strange to him.

But the coach was waiting, he had to go. Gertrud and Bärta went down with him; they wanted to ride a little way so badly. Of course, they could he said, and sat like a pasha between his sister and Bärta. He told the coachman to drive a couple of times around the square.

The girls pretended they were gentry. Bärta sat leaning against August and exclaimed she would like to ride this way all night, but she couldn't do that, it was time to let the girls off and go home. He sat and felt grown up and perhaps a little important too—a favorite among the girls—Ida in the country during the summer, Bärta here on Söder, the maid who stared so adoringly at him in the kitchen at home.

The next morning Johan was standing waiting for Emelie outside the factory. It was regarding his krona, he wanted it tomorrow when he would be free for a few hours and could stash the money away in great secrecy. She had hidden the coin at home. He could surely come home with her tomorrow and get a bath at the same time, it seemed he needed one.

No, he really didn't have time for that.

But he surely always needed a bath for Christmas.

He couldn't convince her otherwise, she was too stubborn. In order to get his krona, he would have to have a bath. He swore in anger and kicked at some small stones that flew across the street. The silly girl didn't understand that a chimney sweep had to be black as much as a baker had to be white. That obstinate, annoying girl!

Johan returned to Finn-Olle. The journeyman looked at his apprentice and said this chimney has some obstruction. You'd better go down and then climb back up. To go down and climb up.... That meant that he would first slide down the chimney to the obstructed part and then climb to the roof again. And then take care of the part below the obstruction from underneath.

He went down slowly and carefully. The chimney was old and bumpy and still warm, apparently the fire had been lit recently despite the sweeping. He thought his clothes smelled like they were smouldering, but it must have been his imagination. He increased his speed a little to get out of there faster. His rake scraped against hard soot and stone. With his right hand he swept energetically with the brush, and soot rose up through the chimney, seeping through the cap he had pulled down over his face and mouth. Suddenly he stopped. He seemed to have come to the obstructed part. It was much too narrow, there wasn't a chance of his getting through. He would be obliged to climb up again as Finn-Olle had said.

He tried to prize himself upward, but he couldn't grab onto anything, he was wedged in too tightly. The more he struggled, the more he seemed to be caught. Was he moving now? No, he was still stuck. It was hot inside the chimney and he was sweating. He grunted with his efforts, saliva and sweat soaked through the band of his cap; soot clung to it and made it even harder to breathe through the pulled-down material. He was bordering on panic, he thought he was going to suffocate. He tore and tugged at the cap and managed to free his mouth. He yelled with all his might. No one answered. Finn-Olle was probably checking on the middle-sized sweep.

He would stay here and die in the chimney. He understood this now. They couldn't tear down the whole house for his sake. He yelled again until he no longer had the strength. Then, finally, he got an answer.

It was the middle-sized one, and he wondered if he should toss down the plummet and try to knock Johan loose. No, he screamed, beside himself. The plummet would only kill him. He couldn't go down. It was too narrow, he had to go upward.

How much the boy up there heard and comprehended he didn't know, but after an eternity had passed a plummet came gliding down slowly on a line, and he heard Finn-Olle's calm, calming voice.

He grabbed hold of the plummet, sniffling with joy, and shouted. Maybe they could rescue him now, if he wasn't too hopelessly stuck.

"Ready to haul."

They gave a tug up there, and he wondered if they were going to tear him apart. He felt how the plummet began to glide out of his sweaty, slippery hands; he had to shout that he didn't have the strength to hold on. If he let go without giving warning they could lose their balance up there and one disaster lead to another. They had to try again.

His shirt was hiked up under his armpits, his pants were being pulled off him. Small, glowing sparks scorched and burned him, but he hardly felt them. Rough stones jutted out and scraped against his chest and back. He tried to hold on as tightly as he could, and suddenly he felt the narrow chimney release its hold on him. He was free.

He shouted again. Now they could pull up the plummet, now he could climb up by himself. Slowly he crawled out of the chimney, felt the cold and delightful fresh winter air surround him. But when he went to walk over to the roof hatch, he was so weak that he collapsed and glided on his back down the roof that was as slippery as ice.

"Now Johan's going to be smashed on the courtyard!" shouted the middle-sized sweep. But Johan had managed to dig in with his heels on the gutter and lay on his back.

"Now that had better be it," hissed Finn-Olle. If Johan wanted to be hauled up once more, he would have to pay them fifty öre for all the trouble he had caused them. Otherwise they would close the hatch and leave him.

"All right," whimpered Johan. He would find the money, they'd get it.

"Lower the line," Olle said to the apprentice.

He didn't have the strength to go to Söder to pick up his money, so managed to avoid the bath. But he had to pay the fifty öre as soon as he got the krona from Emelie. In spite of all his efforts, his earnings from the big collection were not more than fifty öre.

FROM GULLPIPPI TO FEARSOME

Gullpippi got out of the hospital, moved into Lotten's room and the bed that Bärta had had to herself up to now. But down at Barnängen there had been less work, and they had been forced to lay off some spinning girls. Gullpippi couldn't go back there.

It was as if it didn't bother Gullpippi that she was out of work, she seemed apathetic to whatever happened to her. She crawled into bed and hid or sat in the darkest corner and just stared. Lotten looked at her new tenant worriedly, wondering how things would turn out. But Gullpippi paid her rent. She still had a few kronor left from the money her father's workmates had collected.

An accountant from the spinning mill had heard about the girl and was moved by her plight. He succeeded in arranging work for her to do at home for one of the factory's customers. She would get to paint hangings, trace different designs on the fabric, and apply the paint. In fact it was work for more slightly refined, better-off women who one could assume would have the knack, but Gullpippi would still be allowed to give it a try.

Lotten had nothing against the girl sitting at home and working during the day. Finally it seemed as if Gullpippi was beginning to awaken from her numbness, and, along with this Lotten was also released from some of her worry regarding Olof. She could stop leaving Olof at Sofi's; Gullpippi would watch him since she was home anyway.

Gullpippi was still pale and silent, but Lotten could see that the worst of the crisis was over, the girl's eyes had begun to shine again. She was kind to Olof, the first smile returned when she was speaking with him.

Every morning Gullpippi lay out her paints and fabrics on the table. Carefully she traced the patterns provided. Olof climbed up onto the wooden kitchen sofa to watch while she worked. Would the picture appear on the cloth now? He pressed his nose flat against the table to be there and see as soon as she lifted the first corner of the dark blue tracing paper. Yes, there was the picture, as if by magic. And now she began with the paints, which she had in small cups, stroking, shading, carefully following the drawn outlines. The gray piece of cloth came to life: flowers and figures emerged, dazzled, shone. Even if he knew what they were going to become—she did many hangings with the same motif—it was equally exciting each time.

Gullpippi worked swiftly and confidently, and with time received more demanding designs. Olof got to see her conjure up whole landscapes with streams and meadows and people dressed in colorful costumes. They danced around maypoles or stood at a fence and watched the red sun setting into the lake. The lake was called Siljan, Gullpippi said.

When Olof got tired of sitting still and watching, he went to visit Fearsome. Fearsome had become so crippled with rheumatism that he could no longer work at the harbor. Instead he had to remain at home. He tried knotting doormats, but not much got done. His fingers just didn't want to, he declared. Olof thought this sounded so strange; fingers couldn't disobey all by themselves. Who would believe Olof if he said it was only his fingers when he was disobedient? But it was different with Fearsome, or perhaps the thing with the fingers was one of Fearsome's many tales.

The rugs that Fearsome made were not as exciting as Gullpippi's cloth paintings. They were the same old doormats that Sofi used to make, before she began to go to Masis Knosis and wash dishes. No, there was something else enticing about Fearsome. All the funny faces he knew how to make, and the stories he told in his booming voice.

Fearsome could tell about boats that had come into the harbor with mysterious foreigners, or about adventures he had had as a boy. Then, a long time ago, everything had been much poorer than it was now, but much more exciting, too. The wilderness had been closer, the islands not so built up. Fearsome had taken a raft across Fabursjön Lake, which no longer existed, and climbed over the fence to the Bavarian Garden. A brewer had a carnival there with fireworks and Bengal lights. Everything had happened during the time of the old king, King Johan.

When the spring sun began to grow warm Fearsome moved outside to the courtyard, he thought it was getting too stuffy inside. Olof went with him and played at the old man's feet.

Sometimes Fearsome talked to Olof about his father. They had been workmates, after all, for many years. Olof knew Papa had traveled far away and was never coming back. He had left so long ago that Olof no longer remembered him. Mormor had also traveled to the same place. You went there when you were dead. Olof had found a dead house sparrow under a bush and carried it to Fearsome. He couldn't understand why it hadn't gone too. It would probably do it as soon as it woke up, Fearsome said.

But this time the old man was surely wrong. When Olof told Gullpippi about the sleeping bird, she went with him down to the courtyard and looked at it.

"It's dead," she said. "We have to bury it."

And she dug a hole, a dark little hole in the earth in the light green weeds of the hillside. Questioningly, Olof looked at her. They weren't going to stuff the bird in there, were they? Then it would be closed in and wouldn't be able to fly when it woke up. But Gullpippi explained to him that the bird would never wake up again, never fly again. What had flown was something that had been inside the bird and couldn't be seen. If it hadn't been a house sparrow that sang so badly, you could have called this thing its song, its twitter, or its breath. While the bird was sick and sleeping, what had been life itself had flown out of it, and the bird never woke again, it was dead.

"Is it the same with people too?" he asked.

"Yes," answered Gullpippi.

He didn't dare ask any more, he saw the tears in her eyes. But in the evenings when he was going to sleep, he shut his mouth tightly, afraid that his life would fly out of his mouth while he slept.

Gullpippi and Fearsome left these impressions on his days, gave them tone and color. He was equally fond of them both.

One evening at the dinner table, the girls began to bicker over what was the most beautiful thing in the world. Maybe a flower or the sky? They found more and more examples and giggled and laughed so that Lotten had to become stern, quiet them down and remind them that they were sitting and eating.

Gullpippi and Fearsome were the most beautiful, Olof suddenly let out.

With that the girls exploded, despite their recent admonishment. They had never heard anything so ridiculous.... Gullpippi, yes—but Fearsome! Where did the boy get all his notions?

Olof felt offended and laughed at. A sob caught in his throat, but Lotten consoled him, he hadn't said anything foolish, just the opposite. It was only that the girls hadn't thought of it before. It was lovely. With that Olof felt better again, very satisfied at being the first to come up with the truth: Gullpippi and Fearsome were the most beautiful things in existence. One day he would paint as beautifully as Gullpippi and tell as exciting stories as Fearsome. They were his gods, his security and his adventures.

II

THE YEARS OF STRUGGLE

Want grew and fed hatred.

It was like a violently swollen abcess among the unemployed who roamed the streets. Many were poisoned, would always hate, hate themselves as well as their closest kin.

My final wish is to see the vampires' blood running in the gutters, said a letter written to Master Palm.

When there were many fighting over work opportunities, salaries went down. Every year forty thousand people fled the country that couldn't feed them. Those who left were often the strongest, the proudest, those who found it hardest to beg.

Many turned to the socialist workers' movement that had quickly evolved, but still hadn't organized itself as a party. After several unsuccessful attempts, after inside fighting and power struggles, it had begun to take shape and stabilize itself. With that, it became dangerous, hated by the ones who felt they had reason to fear it. The time for ridiculing it was past, the battle had begun.

August Palm had been easy to smile at—his gibberish, the eternal gestures and the halting gait. Everything had been taken note of by cartoonists and journalists. Now new men came forward and took in hand the tasks the tailor had not been powerful enough for: gathering together the splintered factions, organizing.

Gradually, with both wonder and admiration, the workers watched a young man take more and more charge of the new movement. The man, not yet thirty, with the big beard and the cropped hair, had given up every bourgeois opportunity for a career, and devoted himself to the socialists. Now he made the voice of the workers heard, both in the newspaper that Palm had founded, and at the meetings. The newspaper had moved its editorial staff from Palm's apartment on Stora Glasbruksgatan to Number Ten Hötorget where the young man from the upper class occupied the position as editor in a room above Paul U. Bergström's newly opened dry goods store.

The newspaper was owned by and read by people who lacked the means to influence public life. Not much more than six percent of the population had voting rights. The rest were under the authority of others. Now there were new tariffs on pork and grain, and they affected the poor most of all. The struggle for voting rights and against the tariffs became the slogans. At the meetings they sang the song a journeyman cork cutter had written to a well-known melody:

> *Human dignity is what we reclaim*
> *Struggle for justice, freedom, and bread.*

It was a song that was ridiculously unrealistic. Who could dare believe that such dreams and demands could ever come true? Could even the young Branting do that, he who had asserted a few years earlier in a student essay that today's utopias would be tomorrow's reality?

THE WINTER OF
THE WOLVES

Gray steam rose from the waters of Norrström. The cold held the city in its grip, froze it solid. Streetcar drivers' noses and cheeks were frostbitten and tramps were found frozen to death in sheds and cubbyholes. Wolves had been sighted in the southern and central regions of the country—it was reported—something that hadn't happened for many years.

For several days the thermometer hadn't risen above twenty below. At the stations the drivers built snow huts to crawl into. Many people went without work and froze and starved during the winter. Some were employed breaking up macadam, but the supply of emergency jobs was far from enough for everybody. At the stock exchange a list was posted urging the public to pledge amounts of money for supplying firewood for the needy.

August Bodin stepped out of the doorway on Drottninggatan where the family business had moved. The old building at Stadsgården was going to be torn down when they expanded the harbor. In conjunction with the move, the herring concern had been liquidated. It had never really yielded a large profit. Fredrik Bodin now devoted himself wholly to the real estate business: buying lots, building, renting out, selling. August had gotten a job at a general contractor's office for a few summers and had even put in a year at business school after finishing his degree. Now he had begun working at his foster father's office.

Work and studies had prevented him from paying visits home to Söder as often as before. There was much else that tempted him too, socializing with old schoolmates and young people from the Bodin's circle of acquaintances. When it wasn't too cold, they liked to get together on the ice at Nybroviken. But he hadn't seen Ida Wide for a long time, the families no longer spent time together since Wide had gone bankrupt and caused

Fredrik Bodin to suffer some losses as well.

The hired sleigh August had telephoned for stood and waited. The coachman sat concealed in a gigantic fur coat, hoar frost glittered around the horse's muzzle. August pulled his coat around him and huddled up inside the carriage. He heard the clang of the bells and the soft thud of the hooves against the snow. When they reached Slussen, he melted an opening in the windowpane with his breath to take a look at the steam-powered streetcar. It had just pulled onto the turntable and let out a cloud of steam when it stopped. With its help, Söder's hills had finally been conquered. It steamed its way straight up over the summit of Hornsgatan without any trouble at all. But horses had been spooked by it and bolted, and several dogs had been run over by the trolley during snowplowing. In spite of all this, property on Söder was going to increase in value since the streetcar system had been expanded.

The sleigh glided on. August sat and felt uncomfortable about the approaching meeting, had a guilty conscience. He should miss home and Mama, but the knowledge that he couldn't help her irritated him. He didn't have any income and his pocket money was never enough. He saw how she was worn out, and he couldn't do anything about it. It was no use speaking to Father or Mother about it. He couldn't impose his whole family on them, he should be more than grateful for what they had already done—for him, him alone.

Someone stood pressed against the side of the house, as if not to be seen from the upper windows. It was Bärta. She seemed completely frozen and he wondered why she was standing there.

He gave the coachman the order to return at eight-thirty. Bärta drew back into the courtyard, and he stopped to say hello to her. He felt that little tingling sensation that always came when he saw her. He took her arm; it was slippery in the courtyard where the water for the fire hydrant had to constantly run so the pipes wouldn't freeze. They made their way, balancing across the ice banks. Before he had time to open the door to the stairway, she paused, holding him back.

"There's something I have to talk to you about," she said quickly. "But not now. Afterward, when you go home. Can I come along and ride with you a little way?"

"Yes... I suppose."

"Then I'll go ahead and wait just beyond the grocer's on Stadsträdgården."

She used the old name. The street was one of the ones that had been renamed a few years ago. Now it was called Nytorgsgatan, but he knew so well what she meant, the store that had a metal sugar lid for a sign.

What could Bärta want from him? The coachman would certainly think one thing or another. But of course she could ride along a little way, and she wouldn't protest if he gave her a hug in the darkness of the carriage. He opened the door, went to help her in before him. But she stayed where she was.

"Pretend we haven't met. I'll come up soon."

She disappeared across the courtyard, in the direction of the outhouses. And he walked pensively up the stairs.

Lotten stood by the fireplace; she had had trouble with the fire going out. The damp ends of boards Olof had gathered burned poorly. They hadn't been able to afford to buy wood the past few weeks. Bärta hadn't been able to pay her rent for a while. She had been forced to stop at the spinning mill when the budget had been cut. And Gertrud was also without work.

It was best if August kept his coat on, said Lotten. It was cold in the room and since he wasn't used to it he could catch a cold.

He looked at the silent, fair-haired girl who sat hidden in the corner. Gullpippi was so shy and fearful, he thought. Didn't she know how good-looking she was? He knew her story. He had tried to speak to her a few times, but had only gotten one-word replies.

Lotten excused herself. They had so little to go with coffee, hadn't had time to buy anything. But he knew it wasn't time they were lacking. Gertrud was at home. He would slip a few kronor to Mama before he left. But he had to have enough left so he could get by tomorrow. No matter how much he wanted to help, he couldn't show up then without money.

They stood a little on ceremony with him. He had to sit down, be served first. Wasn't this good coffee? Emelie asked. Gullpippi had been allowed to take the grounds from a charity bazaar she had worked at. Good-quality grounds that had only been boiled once.

Emelie and Gertrud chattered on. Bärta came in, but was more silent than usual. Olof had gone over to the neighboring family for a little while, and Mama sat, tired and pale, and looked mostly at August. He felt out of place in his fine suit, not at home here anymore. He wanted to get close to them again, but he couldn't. They tried to hide as much as they could of their poverty, somehow they were lying to him. So that he wouldn't feel sorry for them and felt obligated to help? Or because they were ashamed and didn't want him to see their wretchedness? He didn't know.

It was a relief to know that the coachman was coming by eight-thirty. It wouldn't be such a long visit. They had to get up early and needed their sleep.

Bärta stood up and said good-bye to August. Lotten watched her go but didn't ask any questions. Bärta was only a boarder and didn't have to report where she went. But Lotten would have to speak to the girl soon, couldn't let her stay without paying. She would have really liked to help her, but how when there wasn't even enough for her own?

"How do things look?" she asked August. "Are there really going to be better times soon?"

August shook his head. Things looked bad. Businesses were having a lot of trouble, there were more and more unemployed.

If August heard of anything.... Both Gertrud and Bärta were out of work.

Was that why Bärta wanted to talk to him? Did she believe he could get her a job?

He would let her know if he found out about anything. Just now he knew nothing. He pressed two kronor into Mama's hand before he left. She wondered worriedly if he could spare the money, and he felt ashamed—he had a large bill in his wallet.

It had taken him a little while to leave, he had almost forgotten that Bärta was standing out in the cold. She walked quickly toward the carriage. He opened the door and pulled her in. The girl was completely stiff with cold, but also strangely rejecting when he held her.

There was something she wanted to say first.

At Gustaf Adolfs torg he told the coachman to stop. He was going to accompany the lady a little way on foot. The coachman grinned knowingly and noted the time on his slip. The coach disappeared into the sleet and August took Bärta by the arm and led her in the direction of Drottninggatan.

But she didn't need to... he said. She could borrow some money from him instead.

Bärta shook her head firmly. No, she didn't want to borrow. She didn't think she could pay him back. But maybe he didn't want to...

Her voice dropped. It was the first time she had offered herself. Of course, she had lain with a few boys, but this was something different. If she hadn't liked August so much she would never have dared ask, but because she did like him, it was actually more difficult. Still, she didn't see any other way out. If August wanted her... and paid her. If she could have four kronor, though, that was a lot of money.

But he didn't want it to be like that—that it had happened for money. She understood that surely?

And if it hadn't been for the money?

Then, of course, it would have been different. If she had really wanted to.... But this... she wasn't that kind of girl.

She knew what she was, she said.

Bärta's suggestion was undeniably the solution to a difficult problem. He had walked under the windows of the brothels, followed the "street nymphs." Came this close to going with some of his friends to an attic room where a prostitute was waiting. He was an adult now, would turn twenty before the year was out. Everyone his age had done it. He felt like he was the only virgin, and virginity weighed on him and worried him.

Was it really true that she wanted to?

Bärta nodded, didn't dare answer with words; he might be scared by the sobs in her voice.

They had arrived at Drottninggatan. He looked up at the windows. Dark and silent. Quickly he led her across the street and opened the outer door. Had he planned this when he stepped out of the coach, so close to the office? Yes and no, he couldn't answer that himself.

"Walk quietly," he whispered. "We can't risk turning on the light."

Cautiously, like a thief, he unlocked the door.

The next morning August hurried to the office ahead of his father. He walked straight into the director's room. Normally he sat in a smaller room outside his father's. He stood for a long time and looked at the new velvet sofa, picked off a few hairs, found two hairpins. He stuffed them in his pocket, would make sure that Bärta got them back at the next chance. Now he wouldn't be found out, now there surely wouldn't be any more traces.

What had happened the previous evening seemed so unreal when the room was filled with the light of day. The fire crackled behind the doors of the ceramic stove. The office boy came early every morning and laid the fires. August had to lean forward and stroke the soft cushions with his hand. This is what it had felt like in the dark, this is how it had been beneath Bärta's skin.

What would happen now? How would it be in the future? Once Bärta had gotten over her initial shyness, it was she who had guided him, and he had willingly let himself be guided. But what would it lead to? He knew that Mother would never accept Bärta. He wouldn't either, in the light of day. It felt good to come to her in the dark, like sinking into a soft and warm wave. But she wasn't beautiful, was already missing two front teeth. He could never love her. She had helped him, he had helped her. Could it be that easy?

He suspected that he would meet with her several times, in the same way as last night. This would be difficult so long as he had no income. He had just handed her a whole five kronor, four for her and one for the coach. But he guessed that she had walked home despite the cold, since she had been adamant about his not accompanying her to the cabstand at Brunkebergstorg.

He was obliged to get money for the coming evening. And soon, too, for more meetings with Bärta. He had to ask his father for a salary, had been a schoolboy long enough. Now he was no longer a child.

Justus Ek was the organizer among the old classmates and their friends. He had organized a sleighing party, and they were to gather at Brunkebergstorg. Their goal was a distant one: Nackanäs Inn.

They arrived wrapped in furs, full of expectation. Young ladies in elegant sporting costumes with swaying bustles stood and stamped their feet in slender, elegant, high-heeled boots. Couple by couple they packed themselves into the sleighs.

August got Linda Sjöfält as his partner, a sister of one of his classmates. He tried to behave as courteously as possible, holding out his hand to help her up into the sleigh, tucking the fur rug protectively around her. A little shyly he looked at her, had to admire the sight. The little curving hat, the tight-fitting blue jacket with embroidered braid and fur edging which came up high around her throat. The jacket narrowed unbelievably at the waist, before it billowed out over the hips. And such small hands she had, clad in tight-fitting gloves. Could that little muff provide any warmth?

The couple across from them in the sleigh spoke in whispers, sitting tightly together. August hoped they weren't going to begin any flirtation in the sleigh, that might make Linda feel uncomfortable. And himself too.

He looked for innocent topics of conversation. When the long row of sleighs traveled down Folkungagatan, called Pilgatan when he had lived there, he told them about the area. And look... they had a streetcar all the way out here at the edge of town. Small cars, but they had to be pulled by two horses since the streets were so bad and pot-holed. If people wanted to ride here from Slussen, they had to first take the steam-powered streetcar up Hornsgatan hill and then change; the horses couldn't handle the worst hills.

His fellow travelers listened distractedly. They had to ask how August came to know so much about this out-of-the-way part of town. He hadn't anticipated this question, and he got a little flustered before he found the right answer: when you're in real estate development you get to know the whole city. This response gave him the right to show off all his knowledge, and he pointed out things and talked and noticed that Linda seemed to admire him for his wealth of information.

Some shacks were being torn down, and a flock of children had gathered there. They had been sent out to find firewood. One of them might be Olof. August pulled himself back, horrified, grew silent. What if Olof were there, caught sight of him and called his name?

But no boy came over. The children were completely occupied with guarding the pieces of boards they had found and with chasing rats that attacked them from time to time in order to defend their holes.

Linda whispered something, he bent down over her. Her hands were so terribly cold, could he rub them a little? He placed one of her hands between both of his. It was stiff with cold. Couldn't she take off her glove, it impeded her circulation. She demurred, a little embarrassed. But it would certainly be good to get a little life back into her hand, he ventured. She pulled at the narrow fingers of the glove. They fit as tightly as sausage casings, and he had to help her. He hid her hand under the fur rug, massaged it, felt at last how it got a little life back into it.

By this time, they had reached the tollgate. Here the sleigh made a sudden turn off the road and out onto the ice of Hammarby Lake. Fourteen dark sleighs glided like shadows across the wide, white surface. From far away they could see the lights of the inn glittering between the trees. At Nacka Sound, they made a turn off the lake and up toward the broad drive in front of the inn. The restaurant keeper stood on the steps and received them. Flickering torches lit up his pale, corpulent features.

They gathered in the large hall. On an alcohol stove the glögg steamed in an enormous pot. The restaurant keeper himself took a large silver ladle and filled the circle of tumblers round the pot. Then with some courage, he climbed up onto a chair, raised his cup and wished them welcome.

The party had begun, the food awaited. And soon the dancing began, and August invited his evening's partner to dance. Some of the more advanced couples disappeared into the smaller rooms, but August and Linda were careful to stay in the large hall. They participated a little while in the dancing, but he soon realized that her feet hurt. Then they sat by the fire, and he got her some refreshments. The drink enveloped them like a mist; they spoke more and more freely and were suddenly sitting hand in hand. She leaned toward him, laughing so heartily, not at all like the cautious girl who had climbed into the sleigh.

He wished the evening would never end, but it had already begun to grow light a little, and the sleighs had been waiting out in front. Couple after couple returned, those who dragged behind were hurried along by eager companions.

Finally the row of sleighs wound its way out on the ice again. Linda half lay against August's shoulder. He cupped his hand over hers—so close and yet so out of reach, hidden under quantities of clothes and conventions. He thought of Bärta, who wasn't protected by anything, who only craved a couple of kronor for herself. If he could choose, he would give up Bärta for Linda, never go to Bärta again. But at the same time, he knew, he couldn't come to Linda like he could to Bärta, only if they were married. It would be many years before he could think of anything like marriage.

The city closed around them once more. A few homeless people dragged through the streets, afraid to sit down and fall asleep in the cold. The first workers appeared, on their way to the workplace. Someone was bellowing from the sleigh behind them.

They were alone in their sleigh, and Linda sank down against August, less cautious now. He held her around the waist, could feel the tight corset. He felt he had experienced the secrets of woman, but tried to drive away thoughts of Bärta. They said nothing but he pressed his cheek against hers and felt her nose rub against his. This meant that they were almost going together he thought. And still he didn't feel really happy; the memory of Bärta's all-too-soft, waiting body lay between them.

BANNERS IN
THE WIND

The winter slowly and unwillingly released its grip. Half-blinded by the spring's piercing sunlight, people stood and watched the miracle. The earth came to life again. Green shoots made their way out from the cracks in the walls and from among the cobblestones in the streets, bushes and tree-tops shone violet and green alongside fences.

The foliage was still fragile and conditions rough, the night frost claimed anything sprouting too early. Men who were lured by the sun's warmth and the possibilities afforded by spring had fled the overpopulated rooms of the workhouses, and looked for night shelter in rocky clefts and the woods. They were hunted down by the police and large numbers of captives were reported.

Work opportunities seemed hardly to increase, despite the spring. Many of the unemployed walked down to the harbor at Stadsgården. They clustered on the wooden docks alongside the dilapidated and doomed stone hovels by Last Farthing Stairs and looked out over the now open water, where wintering coal barges floated like toads, glistening black in the glitter of the sun. The ice still remained on the sounds and inlets— spotted and gray, but stubbornly holding fast.

It was the first of May before the navigation route to the city could be opened. But when Hermes put in at Strömmen, followed in its wake by five more vessels with flags and pennants fluttering, the tired and frozen men at Last Farthing's dock felt like hope had arrived. Suddenly someone laughed and the laugh was contagious. They slapped each other on the back and joked around like children. When Stevedore Lundström came out with his spyglass he was greeted with cries of hurrah, and he swung his large hat proudly.

Although the spring was late, it came as a surprise to many. At the end of April, drivers were still coming from the country to the city in sleighs and found to their dismay that sleigh driving was over for the season. They were forced to place their sleighs on wagons to get through.

Such a rig managed to tip over at Stora Badstugatan, and a barrel of molasses fell off the load and was smashed on the street. As if someone had given the signal, women and children suddenly swarmed out of the houses. Equipped with containers and tubs of all kinds, they tried to scoop up the molasses which ran through the filth in the street. Most of them worked silently and efficiently, but a few ended up in fistfights and soon full chaos reigned.

Emelie had to take a wide detour out into the street so she could get by. Something was being given out for free here, though not on such a large scale as at Hornsgatan where a crate had fallen off a load and three hundred rabbits scampered out and been chased by screaming hordes of people. But she didn't have time to stop and try and get some of what was being offered. Anyone who was lucky enough to have a job had to take care of it and not get there late.

Emelie was still at Melinder's cosmetics factory. During recent years, she had occupied a more demanding position; she was in charge of luxury packaging. To put together gift boxes with soaps and bottles was like furnishing little dollhouses. In the beginning, it had been difficult, it took time to make everything perfect, but now she worked like a machine, and knew every movement of her hands by heart.

Factory director Melinder came and stood beside her a while every day, as if fascinated by her handwork. The factory director had aged quickly, his hair turned white, his body bent inside his large, black coat. The factory's success hadn't caused its owner to puff up. He only grew thinner and more silent. He stood there alone, at her side. At times Emelie thought he might want to speak to her, but didn't dare. From time to time, she had tried to say a few words. But she knew she shouldn't unless spoken to. Think how horrified her mother would be if she heard how Emelie tried to open a conversation with the factory director himself. Still, he seemed grateful that she had said anything, reddening and clearing his throat and searching for a few friendly words—grateful and embarrassed.

Others were less shy. The new foreman came to check her work. He held up a carton and looked at the different corners, finding an excuse to criticize. He liked to tease, and Emelie didn't have anything against teasing. When he tried to hold her, she was less pleased. If she was going to work effectively, she couldn't be defending herself and keeping an eye on him the whole time. She snapped at him even though she was conscious of the foreman being an important man whom she should treat courteously. Luckily, or even worse, it seemed as if her anger pleased him. She was so pretty when she got mad he declared—and worked better too.

There wasn't a lot she could do. But she was careful not to work overtime alone, and took every opportunity to remind him he was married.

Within a few years, she had grown up and left the child she was behind. This spring she would turn eighteen. Her mother had been the same age when she had met Emelie's father. She sometimes wondered: had she also met the one who would be hers? No words were spoken, but they got along well together, keeping each other company to and from work sometimes, going out together from time to time. Rudolf had always been the boy she looked up to, placed before all others. He was her rock, her security. She felt a thrill of joy when she saw him stand at the very front of the streetcar and salute her with his whip. He was a driver now. The girls at the factory were so impressed when they saw Rudolf in full uniform, stately in his long coat, with the glistening buttons and the cap with the polished visor. But like the rock he was, Rudolf could not be stirred, moved. He was still shy despite all his self-confidence. Or possibly just principled: no entanglements with girls before he had the means and the ability to bear the consequences such actions might have.

Even though Emelie knew it wasn't the right way to deal with Rudolf, she couldn't resist teasing him. He had a hard time sticking up for himself once she got started, couldn't find any answers, didn't like to speak unnecessarily. He let Emelie know that he had heard way too much talk—had a father who never stopped. For this reason, all the others in his family had gotten used to doing without chatter, all except for Mikael, the youngest. It would certainly be he who would go on talking when Papa Thumbs no longer had the energy.

Most of the boys Emelie knew were not especially good at the art of conversation. Like August... he said so little when he came home. The apprentice chimney sweep, Johan, had an easier time talking, but he couldn't win an argument. He'd swear a blue streak, but that was about it. Actually she was displeased with Johan, he wasn't nice to the other chimney sweep boys. Johan who had had such a difficult time himself ought to understand. But you couldn't talk to him, he only answered that he had had his turn and now it was the new ones' turns. He had been tormented, now he would inflict torment, that was his view on justice. Johan had no power to break the evil circle. She wanted to pound some sense into him, but she had to satisfy herself with arguing and upbraiding, and knowing that it didn't do any good.

Sometimes it had seemed as if Johan wanted Emelie to be his girl, but how could she think about Johan when she dreamed of Rudolf? She understood that Johan had given up on her, turned to others. She had seen him together with a filthy little café girl. That would probably be Johan's fate: that kind of girl and a trail of half-starving children.

Life was so terrible—not for everyone, but for many. They were too weak, didn't have the strength to defend themselves. They starved and conceived, the children fell like lice around the ramshackle hovels. At times she felt an impoverished pride, a dangerous arrogance, a desire to cry out, "Not me, never me!" Rather than slave like most, she would remain unmarried. Rather than create such misery, she would refrain from creating any life at all.

She could be hard, could want to be hard. She could feel a kind of bitter satisfaction in driving Johan to sniveling remorse. Or see Rudolf squirming anxiously and groping for the answers he never could find. She could walk along and hope she would run into August on the street, hopefully when he was out with his friends and wouldn't know how to act as if he didn't see her.

She thought she had seen how life required a hard shell. The soft and the good were destroyed so fast. She remembered her father, his friendly voice and smile. He hadn't reached more than thirty-five, he had been worn down so quickly, so totally. He had lacked protection and armor, but she had loved him more than any other person, more than her mother, more than Rudolf. Maybe because he was so soft, so weak?

Can you love anyone who is hard? And yet you have to become hard, still life demands it.

She twisted the tissue paper, made the little bed for the perfume bottle that looked like a rococo shepherdess. She laid the shepherdess between her rustling sheets. Picked up the next one. She felt the hand that reached for her hip, took a step to one side.

"How can I work when you won't leave me alone?"

"You don't work with your rump. Is the order ready?"

She nodded toward the pile of boxes, not giving herself the time to point.

"This is the last."

"Good girl!"

"Put your fingers on the boxes instead!"

"Now, now... Who is the one who gives orders here?" But the foreman acted nice, laughed at the silly girl who got so mad when he was friendly to her.

Emelie swept up the scraps, took the big dustpan and threw the trash into a crate. She shook off her workday, wrapped her shawl around herself, knotted her scarf under her chin. She would have liked to have a mirror somewhere. Rudolf had promised to come and pick her up.

He was waiting in the archway by the entrance. The girls from the factory passed by, giggling. Some stopped at a short distance and stared. He seemed not to notice them, but when Emelie came he saluted her, and the sudden flush of pride turned her a blushing red.

She stood there a moment, as if she didn't really know which way they should walk. And then the foreman came by, as she had expected, caught sight of Rudolf, and drifted silently away. Happy, Emelie pulled at her beau's coat. Now they could go. They walked past the churchyard's dense barberry hedge, beneath the linden trees' branching, budding limbs. Between the as yet bare trees shone Adolf Fredrik Church, white and lantern-shaped. Out on the street a few youths rode past on high bicycles, and Rudolf stopped for a moment, pensive. If those wobbly contraptions became too prevalent, it could be bad news for streetcars. So many new things were coming; it made the future feel insecure.

The evening breeze swept through the light blue dusk, caught hold of the girl's shawl as they strolled across Vasabron, and turned it into a fluttering banner lit from behind by the setting sun. The windowpanes of the cottages on Helgeandsholmen Island glittered, small rowboats bobbed up and down alongside the numerous dilapidated piers, and between the magnificently ornamented columns of the bathhouses hung flapping white laundry.

Emelie stepped so lightly beside the heavier Rudolf, she almost danced along despite the many hours of her long workday.

At Järntorget they ran into Rudolf's father; he came half-running through the lane at Slussen. He was in a hurry, but still stopped to talk. He was on his way to Café International on Svartmangatan, to "visit a friend" as one said, at the "Nest."

Was he, a married man going to the nests? laughed Emelie.

"Don't try," he said. Emelie certainly knew what he meant. He was going to the premises adjoining the café where the Union met. It would be interesting this evening. Palm was imprisoned at Långholmen, and Branting might end up there as well, now that he had printed that article that Lennstrand, the atheist, had written. All the labor leaders usually came to the "Nest," a lot of other famous people too. Even women came, though the workers weren't as numerous as they should have been.

The workers weren't very big on speeches, according to Thumbs. He couldn't fathom what was so great about talking so much that you ended up in the prison at Långholmen. What did words mean? Nothing.

It was good that Branting spoke out clearly against the pietists, thought Thumbs. Religion was a poison for the people. Marx had said that. And they had always known that priests were among the worst enemies of the people.

Look! There was one of those types who tried to distract people's interest from what was really important. A female Salvation Army soldier came marching in time as if to the strains of a military band. Her massive red hair glistened, her blue dress billowed. Across her chest she had embroidered in garish yellow letters: I SHALL SAVE SOULS.

"What a loony!" screamed Thumbs. But the soldier passed by unperturbed, without letting herself be annoyed by Thumbs' heckling.

Emelie walked the last part of the way alone; they each had to go home to their own lives. Between the piles of earth on Nytorget, a group of children was playing. Olof was with them. Fearsome had helped them make a kite. It rose up over the square in the spring wind—all the way up to the last rays of the sun, which had now sunk behind house and hill. The children screamed with delight, but Olof looked pale and thin, he had trouble keeping up. Worriedly, Emelie looked at him. Didn't he want to go up with her, rest for a minute before they ate? He shook his head, wouldn't acknowledge his tiredness. Mama hadn't come yet, he said. If Emelie heated the food, she could call him when it was ready.

She went through the gate into the dim light of the courtyard. She felt some of the perilous chill of the spring evening, a fear for their lives, which so recently had been so far away, crept closer. How was Olof, really? How long would Mama manage?

Only Gullpippi was home. Gertrud and Bärta had eaten ahead of time and gone out. Gullpippi sat alone in the twilight, had been playing with a brush on a scrap of cloth. Emelie had to ask to see it and almost ashamedly Gullpippi showed what she had accomplished. A boy's pale face looking out from among newly opened green leaves. Silently Emelie looked at the picture, both admiring and afraid. That was just the way

Olof looked, so pale and thin and that look in his eye—something of defiance, something of suffering.

"It didn't turn out so well," said Gullpippi. "But I think there's something right about it, somehow."

Of course Emelie could have it, if she really wanted it. But it was only for fun, nothing to keep. Gullpippi put away her pots of paint and her brushes silently and helped Emelie heat the food. Emelie carefully wrapped the picture in a piece of paper and placed it in the drawer where she kept her belongings. There was a rustle of paper, she had a memento there from before: the handkerchief she had received from her father on her eighth birthday. She showed Gullpippi. Forget-me-nots.... Wasn't it beautiful?

Gullpippi nodded seriously. "I wish I had something left too," she said in a low voice. "Anything.... Not just the memory of what happened that day."

Olof's step was heard on the stairs, and Gullpippi hurriedly dried her tears.

COMMON TIES

The summer was dry and hot. Many fires had wrought devastation. Two cities in Norrland, Sundsvall and Umeå, burned down almost completely. But the Stockholmers delighted in the beautiful weather and spent their free time in the city's parks and green surroundings.

One Sunday, in the beginning of July, the workers held demonstrations for universal voting rights. The police had forbidden all processions through the streets. People had to be satisfied with gathering at Lill-Jans Wood.

Lotten stood and watched the girls get ready. Emelie and Gertrud were going together with Bärta. Gullpippi was staying at home as usual, afraid of crowds. Olof would have liked to go along, too, but Lotten didn't dare let him go on such a long walk, he would get too tired. And since Olof had to stay home, she didn't want to go either. She also had other things to do; she didn't know how she would have the time and energy.

Many times she had thought she should go to one of the meetings that were being organized. But it had never materialized to more than plans, everyday tasks always prevented her. She had many people to think about. The girls had such long workdays that she couldn't even wish they would help her more than they did. Now Gertrud had work again, and that was naturally a relief, even if it increased Lotten's workload. Bärta had found a job, too, if only temporarily. In this way, everybody in the crowded room was in a good situation, they were better off than most. It was always easier during the summer when there were more work opportunities.

Lotten watched the three girls go. She felt some pride over her daughters. If only Olof would grow a little stronger, what more could she ask for? She forgot her own weakness. She felt how her joy over her children held her up, gave her the strength to go on.

From the window, she looked out over the square in its Sunday repose and waved. The girls took the walkway, made of planks, diagonally across the square toward the youngster who waited for them at the other end.

It felt safe to know that Rudolf was with them, then they were in good hands.

Emelie and Gertrud felt they had prior rights to Rudolf. They placed themselves on either side of him and Bärta found herself on the fringe. Rudolf became the center of the group—the only rooster in the chicken coop. But since Gertrud was in such a lively mood, most of the attention was gradually focused on her, and then Bärta, who was at Gertrud's side, could also join in the conversation. It was Emelie instead who got a little left out. She didn't think about it especially much. She was so happy to walk by Rudolf's side that she walked along quietly in her happiness.

Gertrud had a different way about her from Emelie. She never teased, never said anything that could irritate anybody. She was easygoing and cheerful. She was able to make the otherwise taciturn Rudolf talk, too, even laugh. And Bärta helped her along—improving on her stories. Those two could be so childish sometimes, thought Emelie.

The streets began to fill with crowds on their way. When the four young people from Söder came out from Norrlandsgatan and out onto Stora Träskogränd, they could see all of Engelbrektsgatan seething with people. In among the dark masses, the spiked helmets of the policemen glinted in the sunshine. They had been ordered out to prevent any attempts to take charge and form a demonstration march.

Rudolf led the girls through Humlegården Park. It was a long way round, but they avoided colliding with the police. After that it wasn't long before they were able to take their places at Lill-Jans Wood and try to push as close to the speaker's platform as they could get.

There were undoubtedly ten thousand people assembled when the speakers slowly wended their way through the audience. Rudolf recognized them. The heavy-set man with the large beard and bushy hair, that was Branting. He was going to speak for voting rights. And the one with the black moustache and the round face was Axel Danielsson who had come up from Malmö to speak for social democracy. The snobbish one in the light suit was the salesman, Sterky. His objective was revolution. And the one who walked last, with the turned-up nose and the wavy hairstyle, was the cooper, Engström, who was going to speak against the police. Engström, slight and boyish, was the oldest, Rudolf knew. He was thirty-nine, none of the other speakers had turned thirty yet. The movement was young. They stood beneath the pines, whose tops reached up to the deep blue sky, and heard one speaker after another present his text and fling their red-hot words at the pinnacles of society.

Solidarity, community. The words carried in the wind. At times they frightened Emelie. Community demanded so much, bound so tightly. You could bind yourself so that you yourself sank.

They needed another girl at work, and she had summoned up the courage and asked if Bärta could have the job, since she didn't have any. Factory director Melinder had nodded yes: if Emelie recommended her she must be a good girl.

But Bärta wasn't especially handy. She had trouble keeping up. Instead of trying, she occupied herself with endless small time wasters, and was both slovenly and careless, Emelie thought. She gave herself airs with the foreman, joked with the boys who built crates in the shed outside the packaging room, found endless reasons to steal away from the worktable. Things couldn't go on like this, but Bärta didn't want to listen when Emelie admonished her.

"Of course you...," she said, almost accusingly. "You work more than you have to so you make us all have to work more than we need to. You think everything is moving too slowly, but the foreman isn't complaining."

No, not the foreman. He was indulgent with Bärta. But Emelie could see and feel that the factory director was dissatisfied. Not only with Bärta, but also with Emelie who had recommended her. The factory director looked sullen whenever he came by, showed his annoyance so clearly that Emelie would never again dare utter a word without being addressed first. As if Emelie's work performance had gone down in worth since Bärta's was so low. Bärta would not be allowed to continue on, Emelie understood that. But even after she left some of Melinder's faith in Emelie would be gone, forever.

That's what solidarity had cost her. Alone she had been strong; ties of community had entangled her.

But this was the day of solidarity. Anxiously she wondered, was she disloyal to her comrades in thinking this way, in working the way she worked? But shouldn't one do one's best?

She looked around, as if to ask someone, get advice. Her gaze fell on some youths who had taken their seats under a tree. She nodded, knew a few of them by name and by sight. One of them she was very familiar with: Johan.

Johan came over and said hello, he had seen that the three girls only had one male escort. This tall, ungainly streetcar driver certainly didn't have use for so many. The tavern waitress Johan had been seeing for a while seldom had Sundays off, and, besides, he had grown tired of her.

He accompanied them after the meeting, and suggested they take a little walk on Djurgården since they were on this side of town anyway. But once they got there, he disappeared with Bärta, and the others waited a long time, looking among the groves of trees before taking a ferry over to Söder. It had grown later before Bärta returned. She claimed she and Johan had looked for the others but hadn't found them. Johan had walked with her to Slussen, then he had to go back to the chimney sweeps' lodgings.

Bärta knew she was careless, felt that Emelie was dissatisfied with her, and understood that she wouldn't be able to keep her job. Still it was as if she didn't have the energy to change, everything was too completely meaningless.

Life was bewildering. Whatever she did was wrong. August had helped her, and she had probably helped him as well. But it wasn't just a question of helping each other. If she dared use the word, she would say she loved August. He didn't feel the same for her, she understood, accepted. She herself knew that she was too simple, wasn't good-looking. But still, she had been both surprised and saddened when he showed up with the two hairpins he thought she had lost in his father's office. He ought to have understood she wouldn't have such fine hairpins. They must have belonged to someone else, someone who had lain on that sofa before her. August had seemed so inexperienced that she didn't believe he had had any girl before her, but apparently he had.

He lived near the cosmetics factory. A few times she had seen him, once with another girl. She had slipped away to avoid greeting him. It was an upper-class girl August had been with, a fine lady. And it was only natural that he would choose someone from the class he belonged to. He had only needed Bärta while he waited, and she had certainly been paid, like a.... The word was difficult to spit out at herself, she had recoiled from it. She hadn't felt like one, despite the money. She had just offered help and received help.

Still, even though she had seen the refined girl, she had come to their arranged meetings, accepted money even though she had a job now. This had been going on for four months. Now suddenly everything had become different, soon she would have to decide. Or hadn't she already decided today?

She had let Johan have his way. They had lain among the bushes in the woods of Djurgården. He had been sooty and handled her roughly, but she wasn't a fool. Now she hoped perhaps the child she was expecting would have Johan's features and feel like Johan's. She mustn't burden August with this; his helping her shouldn't become his misfortune. She had to bear it herself, maybe with someone equal to herself, like Johan. He hadn't had to pay anything—hadn't helped her. Therefore, he could shoulder the burden.

August could remain only a dream. Johan was the poor reality. She had known this as soon as he approached them. Suddenly she grew calmer. She thought: I'll do better at work. I have to be able to stay. August would have to wait in vain next Saturday, even though they had arranged a meeting. She wasn't going to come, had decided to meet Johan instead.

August waited almost an hour after the agreed time. He wondered if she had gotten sick or had to work late. In a way he was glad she hadn't come, then he would be spared the guilty feeling when he met Linda the next day.

Surely some of his friends would be sitting at Bern's Café. He could look in on them there. He was alone in town since he had invited some friends out to Sommarro on Sunday and wanted to go with them then. A little foolishly jealous, he didn't want Linda going with the others unless he went along. But Father and Mother had gone, leaving him behind with many cautious warnings. They had taken the maid with them. Were they afraid that she would seduce him?

They couldn't suspect, knew nothing about Bärta. Now he was actually glad that she hadn't come, it made it easier to meet his parents, too. He thought, it has to end now. He had to have character. Had to pretend as if nothing had happened—turn it into something not done. Still, he waited a few more minutes, and looked around time after time before he went off to find his friends.

They were his age, old classmates. In March they had enlisted together at Johannes fire station. Now forty-two days of military service awaited them, twenty-one that summer and as many the following summer. They were a little nervous; it would no doubt be a long and difficult time without freedom. Naturally they would be gentleman conscripts, Justus Ek had said. They had to order or rent uniforms well ahead of time. He had already ordered tents for them at the sailmaker Östberg on Skeppsbron: three tents for eight of them. Now they could plan what they were going to take with them.

August listened a little distractedly, he had received permission to order a uniform for himself—everything would work out. But why hadn't Bärta come? Could she be sick? He fingered the kronor he had in his pocket, the money she would have gotten. His glass would certainly be empty soon. Since he had the money, he could stand for half a bottle of arak liqueur—or a whole one even.

She didn't come. He was released from the ties, the complicated and dangerous ties which had ensnared him, threatening his relationship with Linda. What would Linda's parents have said if they had any inkling of his involvement with Bärta? He had met them, met with approval. But they didn't know the truth about him, not even Linda knew it yet. Soon he would have to tell her, admit that he was only adopted. Would it change anything between them? What if she had regrets then? What if the intended engagement didn't go through? For a moment it felt as if he would be released then as well.

Applause. He realized suddenly that he was sitting there clapping his hands. Of course, the orchestra had stopped playing. Maestro Meissner was bowing over and over—the last piece for the evening. Soon time to go home, sleep in the empty apartment, and wake up early, get Linda, meet the usual friends and their girls on the boat. Mother would certainly arrange something nice for them tomorrow. At some opportunity he would have to try to be alone with Linda, to tell what had to be told. Maybe they could walk up on the hill above the house. He had sat there with Ida once, long ago.

Where was Ida now? What could have happened with Bärta? What would Linda say when he told her the truth about his origins? And why did he always have to feel like a traitor, an imposter?

FIRE AT THE HAT

The tent city spread out beneath Kastellet, the little red brick citadel. In the middle stood the large cloth tents where the privates were crowded in with their corporals, close to twenty in every tent. The "gentlemen conscripts" had placed their tents as far out on the edges as possible, making coming back easier after leave was over.

August Bodin shared a tent with Justus Ek and Linda's brother, Edvin. They each had their own iron bed and straw mattress that the corporal had helped them stuff. In one corner stood a bureau, in the other a washstand. Justus had also brought along a card table, but that had to stay folded according to the rule to take up as little space as possible. The tent had a floor, in the middle of it was a trapdoor. Beneath it they had dug a cellar, a hole where arak liqueur, cognac, beer and soda water were kept. A brewer replenished their supply of beer and water twice a week.

The corporal was the young gentlemen's manservant. Since he only earned six öre per day from the crown toward his snuff, the fifty-öre piece from the young gentlemen conscripts meant a lot. That was the sum they put together daily for him to tidy up and make the beds, care for their uniforms and brush their shoes. For a cognac now and then, he could also step in and cover an inconvenient guard duty or fatigue duty.

The privates in the cloth tents lived simply, lying in a tight ring with feet toward the tentpole and heads toward the cloth sides. There was no floor in the tent, and air holes gaped along the ground. Often a sleeping head would be sticking out, and soldiers sneaking back at dawn from "French leave" had a hard time resisting sticking a blade of grass into its nostrils.

At five o'clock in the morning three drummer boys came marching through the camp, beating on their drums with all their might. The first few mornings, the conscripts had flown out of bed terrified and wondered if war had broken out. But gradually they grew accustomed to it, and the gentlemen conscripts soon had to promise their corporal an extra glass if he would shake them to consciousness after reveille.

After morning coffee and goose giblet soup, hours of hopeless exercises awaited on the enormous grass fields. Some corporals managed, however, to always advance with their small troops until they were out of sight of the officers. Then they would throw themselves down on the ground, offer each other cigarettes, and wave over some old woman selling doughnuts or an old man with buttermilk.

Brown herds of cows grazed on the green slopes. Between Fågelbacken and Hackberget, the country road wound toward the tollgate. Longingly they looked in that direction—if only the clock would strike twelve for their break.

Finally the signal. Gentlemen conscripts rushed into the tents, and cleaned themselves up, dressed in their own uniforms, and left the military service of the crown in the corporal's care. They pulled on white gloves, and hurried out to try and find a coach: preferably a cheap "gypsy cab," one unregistered and illegal.

After eating at home or in a restaurant, they usually gathered at Bern's Café for the afternoon concert and coffee. But today August announced to his comrades that they shouldn't wait for him, he had some errands to attend to. He hopped out of the carriage and waved good-bye. Waited while an open-sided wagon with barrels rolled past, on its way to Porter brewery with its belching smokestacks.

How was he going to do this? Why could he never be free of worries like the others?

This evening he would have to take "French leave." Mama was turning forty and was certainly expecting him to come home to Söder. He might have been able to ask permission, but in that case, he would have had to give the reason for his request. In which case, he would rather take the risk of being caught.

Thoughts of this evening were joined by worry over what Linda's parents would say when he—soon—would have to tell them the truth. Linda knew now. She said that it didn't change anything between them, but hadn't she seemed disappointed, unhappy? Her brother, Edvin, his tent-mate, hadn't been told anything. Sometimes, August thought that his unmasking was dangerously close. Rudolf had been drafted at the same time. Luckily Rudolf was in the Göta guard, a red tail, while August and his friends were in the Svea guard, saffron braids. But the red-collared and the yellow-collared camps didn't lie far from each other. He had seen Rulle and they had nodded to each other. Rulle went about like a constant threat of danger.

After the evening's last boring hour of exercises, he took off once again toward the town. He reminded himself to be happy and content. Everything had worked out. During dinner break he had spoken with Father and gotten money, both for a present and his many daily expenses. Now he didn't have to feel like he used Mama's birthday as an excuse to get money for his own use. She would get every öre he had received for her present.

In spite of this, he has self reproaches: he sits in a tavern while they starve. He pays to avoid having to clean his shoes while Mama has to toil for strangers. He could understand that self-reproaches were the price he would have to pay. He couldn't break away from his friends, he had to adopt their habits, good and bad. For all too many years, he had stood apart. It had cost him much in overcoming his own self and forcing himself to have the courage to draw closer to them, to become one of them. He wanted to be like the others, one of many in the social class he now belonged to.

Otherwise he would be alone again. He could not return to his child-hood friends, they would not acknowledge him. Rulle had nodded, but not stopped, not extended his hand. And he no longer heard from Bärta. Would he see her tonight? The thought frightened and tempted him. One day, when Mama no longer existed... Would he regret it all then? Or feel release? He didn't dare search for the answer.

The questions pricked and plagued him, made the journey to Söder unbearably long. Finally the coach rolled up to Nytorget. He smoothed the paper that protected the flowers, dried the perspiration from his forehead. The coachman pulled on the reins and the carriage stopped. When August stepped out, he saw that someone was hanging out of the window. It was Gertrud waving. Then she turned back into the room and yelled, "Agge's coming! He's alone!"

Who had she thought he would come with? Yes, of course, Rudolf! But he hadn't even seen Rudolf today and wouldn't probably have thought to ask him either if he wanted to ride together.

Lotten sat and felt alone in the middle of the activity, as if the buzz of voices shut her out from the others, prevented her from reaching them. The dizziness which she sometimes suffered from had come back. She worked too much, slept too little. She didn't have energy for more than the daily routine; a gathering like this one became a burden which she could hardly bear.

August had given her way too much money, a whole ten kronor. He outdid himself. But, of course, she was happy and grateful, and proud. He looked so handsome in his uniform. Rudolf, who had arrived red and sweaty a little while ago, looked mostly like a typical private in his, but August had gotten a uniform made to order. Rudolf had to take what he could get.

Lotten tried to see through the fog, and guard, protect. Here were her children around her. Three of them soon grown, but still they needed her, not just Olof. Even August perhaps. She had to step in, get Thumbs to stop. Couldn't he see that he was embarrassing the boy? Why did he have to go on and push his socialist propaganda just now? He certainly had to understand that August was obliged to show solidarity with his new parents.

She stood up, hoped that no one would see how she faltered. "Now let's have some coffee," she said. "And only talk about pleasant things."

She urged Fearsome and Johanna and Thumbs and Matilda to sit on the beds closest to the window; the young people had to sit where they could further inside the room. In this way she shielded August from Thumbs, built a little barrier between them. And August was almost pushed into Rudolf and had to begin talking about the military.

Rudolf detested his master sergeant. Every day huge amounts of porridge and peas and other food had to be prepared. Whole cauldrons full were dragged from the cooking pits and poured into barrels for swine fodder. With pitchers and bottles, the poor came from the outskirts around Ladugårdsland to try to get a little of the food that was left over. But the master sergeant profited from selling to the pig farms. He placed guards around the barrels so that no one would get too close to what by right belonged to the pigs. Rudolf had let some old women fill their containers, and that had cost him two days detention. But those who had been placed in the "cage" had trained in a special squad during their punishment, so Rudolf didn't think he ought to eat any humble pie afterward. He was going to be released at the same time as the others.

The young people gathered tightly together, there wasn't much space left over for them. Rulle sat down with his legs apart and took Emelie on one knee and Gertrud on the other. August wondered if he should try and get Gullpippi to sit on his knee, but she sidled down beside him and pulled Olof over to her.

Where was Bärta then? asked Rulle.

August gave a start.

She had gone to meet Johan answered Emelie.

Had he seen correctly—was she in the family way? asked Rulle.

August almost jumped to his feet and cried out. But he kept control of himself, sat and felt the blush mount and couldn't stop it.

Yes, she was expecting, said Emelie. It was distressing, Johan didn't have any salary to speak of, it would be a few years before he became a journeyman.

Gradually August understood the child was Johan's. Now he also grasped why Bärta hadn't come, and he felt thankfulness, liberation. He was without guilt, and the chapter was closed, what had happened between him and Bärta was as if it had been obliterated from reality. Still there was a little aftertaste of jealously, of bitterness. Was he himself not capable? Or had they really been careful enough, even though they thought they had failed so many times?

He had to get up. It was unbelievably hot.

The window was open. The little room couldn't be any cooler when so many people were gathered. Also, the air outside had felt oppressive. He had been sweating on the way here.

"I'm going to cool off in the yard a minute," he said.

"The landlord doesn't want you to stand under the apple tree like before," said Gertrud. "You have to go way over to the fence if you...."

He walked down the dark staircase, entered the twilight. The air felt just as close, as repugnant to inhale. Odors wafted from the row of outhouses and from the stone-lined gutter where garbage and dirty water ran. He heard whining from the other side of the fence and claws scratching. The dog man had moved into the shack next door. He rented out watchdogs and cooked dog meat which he sold from his stand in the square.

Suddenly the darkness erupted. A bluish light flickered. A moment later there was a giant clap of thunder. The dogs whimpered nervously. Then one began to howl and the others joined in. He felt like howling with them, from sorrow and release. But he satisfied himself with going over to the gate that opened onto the street, and looking out on the square. They had hurried to close the window up there, a pale yellow light streamed out. Their voices were just audible, like a soft purring.

Rulle sat there snug and secure with a girl on each knee. August thought of his friends; they were probably sitting at Bern's Café again. If he could only slip away to join them..., but then Mama would be upset. They had surely arranged for leave and would take a cab back, but he would sneak across the field and risk being caught.

A new flash and in the same instant an even louder crash. The thunder was apparently right overhead. And now they heard heavy raindrops start falling through the trees.

The thunder continued, but the rain didn't. The guests thought it best to try and leave before the clouds burst for real. The girls hung out the windows and watched their friends leaving. The boys stood there waving, but

Matilda had almost made it to the street corner. Thumbs sniffed the air and said, "Smoke!"

And Matilda could see a glow when she reached the corner, somewhere in the vicinity of the mission station.

The girls threw on their shawls and hurried out, despite Lotten's wanting them to stay inside. But they had to see what had happened, and would come right back.

From the dark and silence of the night, the light and the noise grew. Now they could hear the shrill siren of the fire brigade and the clatter of horses' hooves. They began to run, had to see if some danger threatened the houses on Nytorget.

It was the windmill, "The Hat," that was burning. It stood there with crackling sails aflame on the spur of the White Hills, at the head of Skånegatan. Lightning had struck.

The birthday guests ran up the steep hill, past the mission station where the anxious bible ladies and their wards were clustered together behind the windowpanes. And now the steam fire engine was arriving, it had driven up Bondegatan. Smoke billowed out of the wagon's smoke stack, black and greasy. The two horses in front reared, wet with the strain and fear. The smoke spread, almost hiding the street with its gray veil. Firemen in shiny helmets hurriedly laid out the hose; the engine's gleaming brass pistons moved up and down. But before the water had had time to spray out, the two topsails of the windmill fell to the ground with a giant roar.

They stood and watched, fascinated by the drama, Rudolf safe and secure between August's two sisters. Thumbs discussed it with Matilda. He had definite views on how the job of extinguishing the flames should be carried out. He grew agitated, and Matilda had to do what she could to make him refrain from instructing the fire captain. August felt alone once again. But then he thought how there must be yet another who felt alone here: Gullpippi. He went over to her and touched her arm. The girl jumped, startled. But when she saw who it was, she stood quietly at his side, and gave a sob.

"Let me..." he fumbled, had spoken so little with her, didn't know how he should address her.

"Permit me to take you home," he said to her politely. "You'll be upset from seeing all this."

But it took a while for him to convince her. Without wanting to see, she stayed standing where she was. Finally, he led her down the street. She was crying softly and stumbled along. He tried to place his arm around her waist to support her a couple of times, but she evaded him. Finally, it was as if she submitted. Carefully he guided her along, felt how her thin body trembled.

"Don't worry now," he entreated her. "It was only an old windmill that was burning."

It wasn't until they reached Nytorget, away from the uproar, that she grew calm again.

"Yes, it was only an old windmill," she said. "Please forgive me for being so silly."

He accompanied her up the stairs. He felt like being friendly toward her, comforting. But it was as if there was no way for him to express what he wanted to say, everything could be misinterpreted, he knew. It could be misunderstood and misused even by himself. And he felt his hands grow numb, words evaded him.

When they entered the room Olof had been awakened by the noise and sat up tired and coughing in his bed. August heard Gullpippi's gentle, low voice. She didn't need any consoling now; she had Olof's arms around her neck, the child's eyes on hers.

He sat there a little while and talked with Mama, figuring Rudolf would return and they could keep each other company back to the camp. But Rudolf didn't come and finally August left alone, nodding farewell to Gullpippi who was still sitting by Olof's bed.

The early morning sun filtered through the clouds across the enormous field, exposing those who were carefully sneaking back to their tents. August had gotten out of the cab at the tollgate for safety's sake, carriages were always noticed. The sun reflected off the buttons of his uniform and the brim of his hat, turning him into a glittering target for the sentries' spying eyes. He ducked down in a ditch and changed his clothing around as he heard he should: turning the jacket inside out and the hat so the bill faced backwards.

A few of his fellow adventurers hid behind knolls and bushes close by, likewise engaged. From various directions, via roads and over fields, the soldiers on French leave tried to sneak into the camp. Cautiously, cautiously. Closer and closer. And then: the last bit at top running speed, straight into the passageways between the tents, shielded by the tents, straight to the right one.

He had a sentry behind him but managed to make a few sudden turns and threw himself into the tent. He dove into bed, fully dressed, and pulled the blanket up to his ears.

Saved.

Reveille sounded a few hours later. By then the sun had disappeared, and rain was streaming down on the canvas tents.

GROW HARD,
GROW TOUGH

Children streamed out of the big, new elementary school that had been built on Nytorget. Their wooden charity relief clogs clattered over the cobblestones.

Olof was eager to get home, driven by anxiety. With angry cries, he urged Ludde, who preferred to stick his head into every cluster of kids and see what was happening, to hurry up. Didn't Ludde understand that every delay lessened their chances?

Fearsome had given them the idea. He had told them about the harbor, about everything that could fall out of split sacks and broken crates. Sometimes even sacks of coffee split open.

So: quickly home and drop off the schoolbooks, grab the baskets. Out again between Nytorget's mounds of dirt and piles of stones and water-filled holes, and they were off, down Renstjärnasgränden. What mattered was to be among the first and get there before it grew completely dark.

Willpower drove Olof onward, he refused to let fatigue rear its head. And when Ludde had gotten away from the area around the school, he, too, became excited. Ludde was one year older than Olof and had more strength. He picked up the pace, with Olof panting to keep up on his trail. The hills sapped them of their energy, but at the summit of Stigberget the wind came up, carrying the scents from the harbor and the water. Now it was all downhill, with the long stairs ahead of them.

Ludde had a two-öre piece and wanted to buy candies from the "countess in the gilded chicken coop," old woman Granberg. She had a stand right where the stairs on Söderberg began. Ludde offered one to Olof, and they sat on the wooden stair railing catching their breath and sucking on sweets. Beneath them lay the harbor, and before them spread the gray water toward the dark trees of Kastellholmen and the clustered buildings of the city.

The boys slid down the railing, and took a few spins around the railroad's turnstile at the bottom. Then they made their way in among the bales and heaps, ready to flee if any authority were to appear. They found a few pieces of coal, a couple of potatoes, but there were many people fighting over the finds and they didn't see any coffee.

Ludde had his own technique. He kicked thoughtfully at the tarpaulins. Suddenly he crouched down, crept under them. Olof watched him curiously. After a short time, his comrade came back, stuffing his knife into his pants pocket with a sly smile. He parted the newspapers he'd laid over the basket: it was full of yellow coffee beans.

Olof looked around. No one was in sight. He crawled into the darkness, feeling his way forward more than seeing it. He found the sack, which had a good-sized slash down the middle. The beans that had fallen out crunched under him. He positioned his basket, heard the light rustling. Then the boys ran as fast as they could, carrying the heavy baskets. It wasn't until they had gotten back up the stairs that they dared rest a moment. They huddled together in the shadow of the "chicken coop," peeked under the paper covering the baskets, and were filled with pride. Now that the lamps had begun to be lit down in the city, one little yellow flame after another flaring up and beginning to glow, they could follow the lamplighter's path.

And Ludde's eyes lit up as well. He would demand a whole five öre from his mama. He was almost sure to get it, so much coffee he was coming with. She wouldn't ask, she herself took whatever she could come across. One day she had come home from washing dishes at Masis Knosis with a big piece of sausage between her breasts. Then Olof had to wonder what his mother would say. Now he was practically sure she wouldn't like it. He was only allowed to pick up whatever lay on the ground.

I didn't split open the sack, he said to himself in defense. I only took what had spilled out out, I only squeezed it a tiny little bit.

The November evening was cool. Just recently they had been sweating, now they were cold. They couldn't sit any longer. They plodded uphill on Renstjärnsgränden, grunting and lugging their baskets, trying to get a better grip on them as they grew ever heavier. A spiked helmet gleamed at Tjärhovsgatan, and for safety's sake, they rushed off in the direction of the tollgate, in a completely different direction from where they were going. They snuck carefully across Folkungagatan, where a streetcar was bumping along behind two big horses, then they turned onto the dark and narrow Kocksgatan, back toward Renstjärnasgränden.

Finally they were back at Nytorget. Ludde rushed ahead on the stairs. But Olof was no longer in a hurry.

Only Gullpippi was home. He wanted to ask her advice, but it was hard, he was mad at her, though perhaps she didn't know it. But she came up to him and gave him a hug, he must have overstrained himself. He should be careful, his mother had said. And such a heavy basket he was carrying!

Why did it have so much coffee in it? She ran the beans through her fingers—totally clean, no dirt from the street.

"But Olof... what have you done? How did you get this?"
He had to tell her. The confession came out sullenly. And she tried to come up with a solution. They couldn't put back the stolen goods, they couldn't throw away something so fine and expensive. Olof's mother would be upset and worried, she didn't have the strength for this. How could he, who was a whole nine years old, be so lacking in judgment?

He would never do it again, he answered her. If only she could help him, if they could arrange it so Mama wouldn't be upset.

Then he had to do something he would never do again: hide the truth from Mama. Gullpippi would take care of the beans and roast a few at a time, place a few in the can now and then.

He cried a little over his mistake, and over the fact that he was soon going to lose Gullpippi who had always been able to rescue him. Why wouldn't she stay with them?

But he didn't ask her, jealous pride prevented him.

Gullpippi might also have questions to ask herself. She could hardly comprehend what had happened.

Was it August who had helped her back to life? Nothing had happened between them that time when the Hat burned down and still it was after that evening that she felt the change. He had been so stubborn in his desire to help her. And suddenly she had found that she was no longer afraid, that not all men needed to be harsh and demanding, that kindness existed. And she had begun to exchange a few words with the paint dealer that she left some of her hangings with, he had always been so friendly toward her.

So one thing had led to another: after a time, he had asked if she wanted to marry him, despite the fact that he was fifteen years older than her. More than that: did she want to emigrate? He didn't believe he had any future in Sweden. He had a brother in America who wanted to help him make a new start.

In the dark stockroom of his store, she had told him the truth about herself, the events that had marked her. And he thought that she, too, would benefit from leaving the land that had given her such experiences. She, too, could start afresh in a new and young land. He didn't have to convince her, she would gladly go with him. She was happy and grateful, and she loved him. Something of a father, but more of a husband.

But she would miss Olof, and he would miss her. Though he was young, had experienced so much, new experiences would make him forget. If only he lived. For his sake she still might want to stay to watch over him, make sure he got dried off when his shirt was wet with sweat, help him deal with his situation. May he not be too badly damaged by life, may he manage without her.

"You can have my paints when I leave," she said. "All my paints. I have to go, you know, because I like Uncle Carl so much that I can't leave him. But I like you so much too. It is the same as if you had to choose between going with me and staying here with your mama. Sometimes things are that difficult, you see."

It would be hard to choose between Mama and Gullpippi, he knew that. Still, it felt as if Gullpippi had betrayed him, pushed him away.

Gullpippi and the paint dealer got married in a very simple ceremony on the day they were going to leave.

Their friends from Söder walked down to Central Station to wave them off. And Olof almost forgot the pain of farewell with all the new and exciting things he saw. Carriages for hire stood in long lines outside the station, and a carriage dispatcher walked around authoritatively with a bundle of number chits in his hand. The streetcars rattled past on Vasagatan and rang their bells continuously. Inside the large station, people hurried by in all directions; the enormous doorman organized lines and told off people who were disorderly. Porters streamed in, hauling their burdens. At the counter for "OVERWEIGHT AND DOGS," anxious travelers hoisted their heavy suitcases to the incessant barking of dogs.

It was as if Gullpippi was already a stranger, so splendid was she in her gray traveling costume. Had she really belonged to their impoverished world? Olof handed her the flowers they had bought in the gardener's greenhouse on Värmdögatan. And Gullpippi hugged him tightly, and promised to write as soon as she came to the new land.

It was time to depart. The conductor closed the iron gate, the stationmaster swung his lantern, the locomotive let out a giant belch of coal smoke, and the steam whistle gave a shrill signal. Slowly the giant wheels began to move, screeching and shaking, the train started up. They cheered and waved their handkerchiefs, and the train glided out from under the enormous glass dome, away toward the crossing at Kungsholmsbrogatan where the guards shut the gates in plenty of time, and out toward the railway bridge.

He waved, the tears coming to his eyes. He heard the throbbing of the wheels: never more, never more, never more.

Gullpippi had left, was gone.

New days came and Olof carried his basket, pushed his way in at the harbor around the fish stands and restaurant kitchens. Competition was tough. Some adults also found pleasure in cheating the children. The hawkers at the fishing harbor filled Olof's basket with rotten fish one day. He struggled up the many hills carrying it back, and shone with pride when he handed his stinking load over to Lotten. But he learned, he wasn't fooled the same way twice. He developed sharp elbows, learned to beg and grew tough. He clenched his teeth, fought, carried.

One day he came up with the idea of going out to the slaughterhouses at Fredriksdal outside Skanstull gate. He marched off together with Ludde. They stopped outside the open door of a shed where steam was escaping into the darkness of the December afternoon.

Inside it was hell. Smoke from blood and clouds of water vapor rose up from the stone floor. Shrieks of terror from traumatized and dying animals built a fantastic chorus of pain. Three huge giants appeared from out of the steam; one got down on his knees and sliced open a pig's stomach, lifted it up and yanked it out while the animal still was kicking. Clubs swung and beat down mercilessly, animals fell, screaming like children, rattled, and died floundering in blood and waste.

"Drink up so you'll grow strong," said one of the slaughter hands and laughingly held out a scoop full of blood to Olof.

The boy didn't dare say no, drank the still warm blood. He got the bottle he had with him filled. The giant was friendly, nodded, singing to himself. He was brown with coagulated blood.

Outside the shed Olof threw up. And together with Ludde he walked home, quiet and shaking. Small candles flickered in the windows of the cottages on Gallows Hill, some drunken farmhands bellowed in Silverling's pasture, and in a doorway on seedy Hammarbygatan a homeless girl sat and wept.

Drink and grow strong. Drink their blood.

He came back home. Felt that he had grown stronger, that he had the strength to endure more.

Now he was prepared for life, hardened for resistance and the ability to survive. Now he had been destroyed.

THE DARK DAY

The two washerwomen pulled their little sled out onto Hammarby Lake. From out of the downy, gray winter fog rose the great stone slabs of Klippan, but the large windmill on the top of the hill was only visible as a black shadow against a wall of gray endlessness. Out by the candle factory, clouds of steam rolled upward from the "warm stream," a dangerous opening that the warm water from the sewage drain thawed in the ice of the lake.

The two women were also black shadows in their dark clothing as they shuffled with their loads over the snow banks. The ice hole they were looking for had been covered over with a thin film of ice, and the younger woman broke it up with the point of the gaff they had brought with them. They chopped hard at the ice all around them to be sure it would hold, laid out the board they were going to lie on. Rinse and wring, feel their hands go numb from the cold. Lotten didn't dare think about the many hours that waited. Of course she was glad to get such a large wash load, of course she needed the money. Still, it was with some despair that she viewed the fully loaded sled.

She stood motionless a moment, just staring straight ahead. But the fat, old Johanna puffed and blew and adjusted the sled and cheered herself with the thought that she had arranged a coffee break for them with an old lady in one of the nearby cottages.

The work began. They took hold of one item of clothing after another, rinsed it, beat it with the paddle, wrung it out. They saw through the mist how some sleds glided by on the other side of the lake: farmers from the archipelago on their way into town. They disappeared out by the miller's and Danviken. The factories at the tollgate belched out their billows of smoke. At the dye-works a watchdog barked, and from Seniorberget the Dihlström workers could be heard breaking up macadam.

Lotten was barely conscious of the sounds, they drifted together into one tone that was as gray and everyday as the picture she saw before her. As she so often did when she worked, she let her thoughts wander, seeking comfort. The girls would be able to take care of themselves soon, they were turning out well. Emelie, nineteen this year, and Gertrud, eighteen, grown up and capable. Both had work, that meant a lot. Maybe they wouldn't need to take on any more boarders after Gullpippi, keep only Bärta. However things turned out for Bärta—she was still at the asylum where her son was born. The girl was foolish, she should have held back. It would be a while yet before that skinny apprentice chimney sweep could support a child.

But Lotten's own daughters brought her joy. The children had come into their own, so independent, sometimes she felt something missing. Such a relief that they could take care of themselves, and still a little painful. Like August. Of course, she was glad for his sake, yet it was still hard at times.

When she searched inwardly for comfort, she sometimes encountered anxiety instead. Olof's face shone through the mist, so pale, much too pale. She felt she could see flickers of eagerness and trouble on his face. The boy was always searching for something, constantly straining to do more than he should. He would arrive with his baskets, panting under his load. But nothing helped, he was so stubborn, she couldn't keep him in check.

If for nothing else, for Olof's sake she had to go on. But one day, one terrible and happy day, she wouldn't have to have the strength any longer. That day Olof would also be able to take care of himself. Then she would have the right to be tired, have the right to die. That day. May it come soon, may it never come.

The hours passed by while they worked. They froze and sweated, their hands lost sensation, as if dead. They had taken a few breaks, gotten warmed up and drunk coffee in the old woman's cottage. The gray mist darkened to twilight and evening. They really should have finished for the day, but it was good to get it all done, not have to start over again in the morning. So they continued, working breathlessly without even having the energy to talk to each other any more.

Lotten stood up to straighten her back a minute, but maybe she did it too quickly, her feeling of dizziness increased. She wondered if she was going to faint, looked for something to hold on to, but didn't reach anything, only fell. And while she fell, she felt the icy cold and the terror. She didn't know if it was she herself or Johanna who screamed.

Time after time, the girls and Olof looked out the window. They pressed their noses to the glass, trying to force their gazes to penetrate the darkness out there.

But no one came, no sled squealed on the sand outside the gates.

"A horse," reported Olof, "and a sleigh."

The girls hurried over even though they didn't have any great hope that it was their mother coming, she never got a ride with anyone.

From the gray bottom of the sleigh shone a white sheet, suddenly becoming visible in the light of the streetlamp. A sled loaded with washing was farthest forward on the sleigh, and leaning against the sled was a dark, shapeless figure, Johanna.

Two men walked beside the horse. They stopped right beneath the window.

The three upstairs didn't understand anything at first. Then Emelie felt horror grip her, the sureness that something awful had happened. And she ran down the stairs, out into the yard, over to the gate that was now opening.

Gradually Johanna was able to speak.

She had made desperate attempts to help Lotten up but not succeeded. The ice had given way, the gaff disappeared under the edge of the ice. Finally she had had to leave Lotten to run for help.

When she got back with two men, only the empty, black hole in the ice was there staring at them. Lotten lay a little inside the hole, pressed against the ice.

Johanna had a message to bring to Emelie: *Take care of Olof.*

AFTERWARD

Then the world became empty and cold, and in this desert there was only despair. The days slipped by, unreal. What had to be done was done, as if in sleep.

Without wondering at or being frightened by her boldness, Emelie climbed the broad stairway inside the fine house on Kammakaregatan. August received the news and bowed under its weight. Sorrow and regret cut him. Now he would never be able to make up for anything, always have to live with the feeling of a debt that has not been paid.

But he didn't cry, not as long as Emelie was there. He forced himself to say a few words, ask what he could do.

Annika Bodin came out into the hall. August had to explain and Annika asked Emelie to come in. She closed the door so the maid wouldn't hear anything, and went in to Fredrik. Somehow they had to help, for August's sake.

Fredrik twisted a little uncomfortably. Naturally he wanted to help, even if it was difficult just now. He had invested such large sums in his building purchases. They had to talk to August's sister, see what she had in mind, what was needed.

The reply calmed them. Emelie said that their mother would surely want to rest beside their grandmother in the south cemetery that used to be called the paupers' graveyard. Their father also lay buried there, but his grave had already been leveled, destroyed. During recent years, the place had been fixed up. In spite of it still being spoken of as Gallows Hill and cholera or paupers' graveyard, it had really been put in order, given proper graves and simple landscaping.

August had no objections. It was appropriate, and how it had to be, his real parents belonged in a paupers' graveyard. They would have felt at home there, he thought.

Emelie left with the promise that Fredrik Bodin would speak with the graveyard contractor. It would be an "honorable burial" with carriages.

During the week that followed, the coffin stood out by the row of out-houses and sheds, visible to the children playing in the yard. On the day of the funeral, it would be carried up to their room for a final farewell. Olof, who had just come back from school stayed irresolutely in the yard. To go up and get the basket seemed so meaningless when Mama wasn't there to show his finds to. He couldn't really understand that Mama lay there, that she existed yet didn't exist. She was so alone, and it was so cold, wasn't she cold? Did she really not feel anything any longer? And he was so alone. Why couldn't he talk to Mama? But Fearsome opened his window and called Olof to come up.

Mama had died, Gullpippi gone away. Fearsome and his sisters were left. Fearsome was always there, it felt good to go to him. Gertrud just cried and couldn't speak. Emelie had become so strict and serious, admonishing him and checking up on him. Fearsome didn't ask for anything, not even to talk to him. He was just there, and if you didn't say anything he talked on anyway.

Johanna lay there scrubbing the stairs. When she caught sight of Olof, she began to cry so that her whole enormous body shook. He hurried past, her crying frightened him. But when she had finished scrubbing, he still had to go out and watch while she took a sharp stone and drew loops and patterns on the large stone slab outside their door. She always had her fixed pattern which she followed and repeated; the pointed stone had worn deep tracks into the stone slab over the years. Now she formed her loops especially carefully before the funeral, in honor of her dead friend.

The work, the act of creating calmed Johanna a little; she wasn't crying now. She was so completely immersed in her work, groaning and toiling. When she was done, she spread some old sacks over the stone so it would-n't get dirty.

Should they put out the pine branches now? Olof wondered. Together with Ludde, he had walked across the ice on Hammarby Lake and broken off branches in the woods by Sickla, dragging home two sacks full that stood in the shed next to the coffin.

No, not yet, not before early tomorrow morning.

"Oh God..." she said, and began to cry again.

Fearsome stood in the yard and waited with his hat in hand as they carried the coffin away, he didn't have the clothes nor the strength to go with them to the graveyard so he said good-bye here. Olof looked back at him, he would have liked to stay with the old man. But Emelie didn't let go of his hand. He had to go with her, out through the gate to the street, among the onlookers who had gathered there.

Once they were up inside the coaches, it felt a little easier. It was the first time Olof had ridden in a hired coach, and he had to lean forward and watch the driver and see as much as possible.

The carriages swung out onto Götgatan, heading south. White snow covered the old brickworks with its collapsing kilns and barns for drying. On the more built-up side of the street, women and children formed lines at the grocer's, which was allowed to be open before Sunday services.

The horses struggled slowly up the incline on Fyllbacken with its many breweries and taverns, past the large Wideqvistska estate, and on past the Holländska windmill spreading its sails over rope makers' sheds and greenhouses. And out on the point at Skanstull gate were more hills on up to Gallows Hill and the graveyard.

The outskirts' hungry dogs roamed around the slaughterhouses at Fredriksdal, and Olof looked to see if any of the slaughter hands were there even though it was Sunday. But the sheds quickly disappeared behind the hill, and the fine coaches glided strangely onward among the ramshackle and colorless shacks by the graveyard. They had arrived.

The sawhorses that the coffin had been resting on were still in the room when the siblings returned home. Rudolf carried them down to the shed, while Emelie lit a fire. August wasn't there; he had gone home with the Bodins who had followed the funeral procession at a distance. He would come some evening very soon.

But Rudolf and his parents came with them, and even if Matilda said that it was entirely unnecessary, Emelie still wanted to put something out to eat.

Matilda repeated what she had once promised Lotten: if anything happened, they would help each other. The girls couldn't afford to keep the
room on Nytorget now. Besides, they might need a little help with Olof.
Thumbs and she had talked it over. At the moment, they had two girls living in their kitchen, but one was going to move out soon. Then the three
siblings could move in instead. Of course it would be crowded, but it
would surely work. However, they couldn't put up Bärta and her child. It
was tough, but Bärta herself had to find a solution.

Emelie would have liked to keep the room. But wanting was one thing
and being able to another. If they kept the room, they would have to take
in more boarders and risk getting some who didn't pay the rent regularly.
Bärta would have a hard time working now and had already been unde-
pendable with the rent earlier. And, of course, it would be good to have
help with Olof. Matilda worked, it was true, but would still be supportive
in a lot of ways.

For Olof it would be better to live in the kitchen at Thumbs' and
Matilda's than to live among perhaps not very savory boarders. Emelie did-
n't really like him being together with Ludde so much either. Or with
Fearsome either, the old man put so many strange ideas in the boy's head.

She was worried about Olof. He was only nine years old but still so
independent, and weak at the same time. He needed proper food, and it
would probably be better if they lived together with Thumbs. Someone
would always have money to buy the absolute necessities, and Matilda
surely would have an easier time getting credit in the shops.

And there were Mama's words: ask Emelie to take care of Olof.

Emelie knew that it was up to her to come to a resolution now. Gertrud
would go along with her decision. Her sister somehow pushed away the
responsibility. And Emelie? Did she grab hold of it? She didn't know, all
she knew was that she was one of the people who made decisions.

While Emelie talked with Matilda and Thumbs, Gertrud stood with
Rudolf at the window and looked out over Nytorget's dirty field of snow.
Gertrud was still swollen and red in the face from crying, but she had
calmed down a little now, consoled by Rudolf's comforting voice. When

she heard that they were going to move, she suddenly gave a faint but grateful smile. It felt safe and good that they were going to go away from here. Away from the room where the coffin had stood, from the increased responsibility that she too would have if the siblings remained here. She had been troubled by Emelie's hard determination and forcefulness during these difficult days, had felt how she didn't have the strength to obey her sister. Now she wouldn't have to, kind Matilda would be there in her mother's place, and they would have life and activity around them with the three boys and their parents. She felt relieved.

But Olof, who sat and drew on a paper bag, was frightened by the changes. Would he lose Fearsome now too? He understood that he couldn't protest, it would be as Emelie decided. But he thought: everyday after school I will go see Fearsome. They can't forbid my going there. They can't take Fearsome away from me too.

THE BREAKUP

Spring was coming; the people in the city knew the signs. The tugboats broke up the ice covering the bays, the pontoon bridges were taken in, steamboats chugged between the shores once more. But the bridges on the outskirts by the tollgates were still weighed down with ice and snow, some had sunk so that people and horses had to wade through ice-cold water half a meter deep to get to the other side. The streets of the city were almost unnavigable, there were deep, gaping water-filled holes. And at the old swamp by the new railway station, all the garbage that had been lying out began to ferment; the foul gasses were carried by the wind all the way to the exclusive Esplanade.

On the footbridge from the elevator on Mosebacke they had begun to put up new and higher railings. During the few years the elevator had existed, seven people had already thrown themselves off the bridge.

The dock workers leaving work looked up at the scaffolding, made coarse jokes about the high leap taken by those who were tired of living. It was Saturday evening and many of the longshoremen intended to celebrate their time off at one of the taverns before continuing on home. Several went into Fläskoset tavern; a lot of bricklayers and carpenters from the construction site at the customs house also went there.

Thumbs arrived and sat down beside some bricklayers he knew. After many years of moving around among the different trades, he had returned to the harbor. There was more freedom there than at the other workplaces. And apparently old events had been forgotten, he had gotten work on one of the stevedore teams, despite the stevedore once forbidding Thumbs from ever showing himself at the harbor again—but that would soon be twenty years ago.

Something remarkable had happened that spring—the workers' party had been formed. It had happened during a congress at Easter in Stockholm with representatives from Sundsvall in the north to Ystad in the south. Thumbs had been there to elect Palm and Sterky as the Social

Democratic Party's representatives. Now he wanted to discuss politics with the bricklayers. Their union had also sent a representative to the congress. But they were busy with their own problems, discussng a strike.

Relations within the construction union had been difficult for many years: economic crashes, buildings that collapsed, great risks of accidents during work, "percentage bosses" who confiscated wages. The new system that had been implemented the previous year brought complete misery. It amounted to the workers not getting a large portion of their income until the building was done—at which point many building contractors took the opportunity to go bankrupt. Now the bricklayers were talking about striking against the new system, and the carpenters at the next table said they would demand forty öre in hourly wages and eleven-hour workdays. But times were bad for making demands, unemployment was only rising.

Thumbs' second oldest son was in training to be a bricklayer. Try to get him into another line of work, advised the bricklayers. No employers could be worse than the building contractors.

He left worrying if there was better work for Knutte, but it was surely as bad in all lines of work, and a bricklayer was still a real tradesman. The boys should learn a trade. He still believed that—because he had never been able to do it himself.

The party had put shorter working days and fair wages as their first demand, he tried to console himself.

They were having a party in the house on Åsöberget. There was no special occasion, only that Emelie was turning nineteen. But since it was Saturday, they took the opportunity to get together and put on the coffee pot. Rudolf had the evening off, and August had come to visit and had some dress material with him as a present.

He had only visited his siblings one time earlier since they had moved. That time Thumbs hadn't been home, and August half hoped not to see him this time either. It had been so convenient to go this evening, Linda was in bed with a cold, and he hadn't arranged any meeting with his friends. Besides, it was Emelie's birthday.

Once he got there, he regretted it. He felt like a stranger and an outsider, they treated him differently from the way they treated each other. He found it hard to talk, couldn't find anything to talk about. Rudolf was gruffly taciturn, and Knuttè sat heavy and silent after a hard day's work. Emelie seemed tired and sad, was probably worried about Olof. The boy had gone down to Fearsome's on Nytorget—had taken a slice of white bread to the old man.

"He has such a hard time chewing," laughed Gertrud. She chattered on, was the easiest to talk to. But when she became too loud Emelie looked almost accusingly at her sister. Then Gertrud grew quiet and blushed.

Gertrud had cried the most at the funeral but gotten over her sorrow fastest, he thought. Living was so easy for her. And forgetting. But Emelie remembered, grieved without tears for a long time. And clung to her duty, her worry about Olof. Could he help her in any way? Maybe get the boy to a good doctor? August was a dependent himself, had only his allowance that was for clothing and pocket money.

Thumbs arrived. Saw through the window that they had a guest and went out to the woodshed where he washed and put on his Sunday suit. In front of such a fine gentleman as August, he should be fine himself. He spat and sputtered at the unnecessary trouble.

When they had drunk the coffee, they sat at the table and talked, gathered around the circle of light cast by the kerosene lamp. Thumbs interrogated August: how were things really going in the construction business? August tried to explain: Bodin's didn't actually do the construction, but rather made use of different building contractors. Many were hard to deal with, it was a difficult business where a lot of scandals occurred. The Craftsman's Bank crash a few years earlier had uncovered a whole lot, a giant construction swindle. Afterward it had gotten somewhat better, many of the worst building contractors had gone under. After the crash almost every other construction site had to shut down and stand there half finished and boarded up. Now they had recovered somewhat, but there was still less construction than before. The numerous speculation projects had saturated the market, there was plenty of housing now.

August grew silent and thought about the building contractor Wide, Ida's father, one of the victims of the bank crash. Father had lost a lot of money through Wide. How were things for Ida now?

But Thumbs continued to examine him. That new system—could it be justified?

August was ignorant of his motives, didn't know enough. Naturally, a number of building contractors had trouble getting the money together, he said, it was no longer as easy to get credit. Perhaps that was why....

And then they went bankrupt and the workers were swindled out of their wages?

Some had done that, had gone bankrupt. But then they had lost a lot themselves, August assumed.

But someone made a profit?

Yes, someone must have done that.

Maybe someone who didn't do the building himself?

August didn't know. He reddened and grew silent, he certainly knew that Father had done some business with construction bankruptcies.

Knutte had been on such a construction site before, Thumbs said. After the crash, the building had, of course, been bought up cheaply by one Director Bodin.

Matilda wanted them to talk about something else, but Thumbs obstinately wanted a response.

That was possible, answered August, he didn't know all the firm's business. They bought one building or another that was for sale. Naturally, it was desirable to get them as cheaply as possible, they had to sell the buildings themselves afterward.

And make money on the workers not getting their salaries?

Bodin's couldn't do anything about that, they hadn't been the employers. They had only bought some buildings that were for sale.

Thumbs grew angry. The boy was slippery, tried to talk himself out of any responsibility. Of course, they were playing under the blankets together—bankrupt building contractors and those who bought up bankrupt buildings. Bodin's firm was made up of capitalists and bloodsuckers too, just like the others. Lived well off the sweat of their fellow human beings. Wasn't August just bragging that they lived off other people's misfortunes? The building contractor went bankrupt and the workers starved—but Bodin's, they took the opportunity to buy the buildings cheaply.

"One day we will put a stop to such swindling," hissed Thumbs. "Then people like you will learn to work honestly instead of being parasites."

"I think I should go," said August and got up. Out, out, he thought. Never back here again.

"Are you afraid of hearing the truth?"

"No, but...."

"Quiet now," pleaded Matilda. "You can't behave like this toward August."

"He needs to hear the truth some time," said Thumbs. "Before the fine gentleman's family destroys him completely. Sit down and I'll...."

"It's best that he leave," interrupted Rudolf.

"Yes, I'm leaving," said August.

Emelie had gotten up, stood pale and upset behind her brother. What should she say? She lived here, was a dependent. But that didn't matter, nothing mattered—if only she could find the words, could turn things around.

August extended his hand to say good-bye, and not leave as an enemy. But Thumbs wouldn't take it. He wanted August to sit down again.

"It's best that you go," repeated Rudolf.

He left without saying anything more, not even to his siblings. They had betrayed him, he thought. Not said anything in his defense, not asked him to stay. But out in the yard Emelie caught up with him.

"You can't leave like this," she whispered.

"It's probably best this way," he answered bitterly. "I can hardly go in again and maybe get thrown out."

"Are you never coming back?" She cried softly.

He took her hand, squeezed it hard and quickly.

"If there is ever anything, if you need help.... You know where to find me." The gate slammed behind him. She hurried forward and opened it, looked out. He walked down the street, stumbled on the deep wheel ruts, disappeared in the shadow.

She stood there a moment in the darkness. When she had calmed herself she went into the kitchen. Gertrud and Rudolf stood silently, waiting for her.

"August is never coming back," she said. "Why did this have to happen?"

"It's best it happened," said Rudolf curtly and looked out the window.

"But he is our brother. He can't help what Bodin does. He has to side with those who are his parents now, doesn't he?"

Rudolf said nothing and stared out the window. But Gertrud suddenly drew in air, as if she was inflating herself in defense.

"It's good that he left," Gertrud said quickly. "He's not one of us any more."

Emelie looked at her sister. What did Gertrud mean? Wasn't he one of them? Their own brother. She felt how anger began to seethe, how it stuck in her throat. Gertrud and Rudolf went out into the yard. They fled, she thought, didn't dare stand up for what they said. They wouldn't get off this easily.

Then Matilda came out to the kitchen, cried and wondered how they would be able to make everything right again. Behind her stood Thumbs, muttering. The women were crying, and he was the villain. But he had only said what had to be said. Besides, he hadn't driven August out, quite the opposite. He had asked him to sit down again.

Still, maybe what had happened was best, he said. You make your bed, you lie in it. And no one can be a friend and an enemy at the same time. If Thumbs bore any guilt, it was from long ago in the past: he had not tried forcefully enough to prevent August from coming under the custody and power of the Bodins. The boy was lost, as completely as if he had died of hardship. Now they had one more enemy. Nothing was improved by pulling solitary individuals out of poverty to live the good life. If improvements did not take place within and with the classes, then they were not improvements. He was glad that no one had wanted to pay for school for his boys and give them ideas.

What had happened was best, he had nothing to reproach himself for. Yet still, he was a little afraid of Emelie, he didn't dare look at her except when she wasn't looking. Right now she looked like Lotten, the Lotten who had once flared up and boxed his ear. He shook off the unpleasant memory, he hadn't had any defense that time he was about to hop into bed with the slut who was living here.

But it was beautiful anger, with force and earnestness in it. As long as it was directed in another direction, the right direction.

Of course, he felt sorry for the girl, about her birthday and her brother. He did like him, of course... and actually there was nothing really wrong with the boy. He was made of good material, but it had fallen into the wrong hands. It was too late to do anything about it now. If only the boy hadn't run away, if only he had been able to finally talk to him, make him understand.

But in spite of everything Thumbs had gotten to say one word of truth, it might stay inside August and germinate. Today Emelie was crying, one day she would understand. Of course Thumbs knew that August wouldn't say hello to his sisters if he saw them when he was out with his friends. Gertrud had told him that. Was that kind of sibling relationship worth so much? If only Emelie would calm down now. And Matilda stop crying. Then everything would be fine again. But you had to be able to say what you think and believe.

August half ran between the wooden houses that stood there lopsided and sagging like grotesque shadows in the dusk of the spring evening. Everything was ugly, poor and rundown. He had come from this, he had grown up among this. Now he had also outgrown it. Before he used to think he was coming home when he came to Söder, now he had no home here anymore, they had kicked him out. So he no longer needed to feel any solidarity, no guilt or shame. He was free to go his own way.

For a moment August may have felt that Emelie had betrayed him. She hadn't said anything in his defense. But when he calmed down a little, he had to ask himself: what could she have done? She couldn't go with him and she had Olof to take care of. Maybe it would be very difficult for Emelie to stay on after what had happened.

But just now he didn't have the strength to feel any sympathy for anybody other than himself. She will reconcile with them, he thought, she will also start to hate me. He agreed with Rudolf. She could stay, they all could stay. But if Emelie needed his help he would do what he could.

Weren't there any coaches here? He couldn't see any streetcars either. And no police were in sight. He ran, glaring fiercely at some half-drunken rowdies.

Never again, never go back there.

For the first time he felt total solidarity with his new social class.

Emelie would remember her nineteenth birthday as the day of the breakup. When August disappeared. And when she understood that she had lost Rudolf.

Without anything decisive happening or being said between them, she had always assumed that she and Rudolf would be together.

Now he was pulling away from her. He was perhaps ashamed of what had happened with August or suspicious because she had taken her brother's side. It might also be because he had tired of her ways, thought she had become boring or depressing. She knew she was boring, worry about Olof weighed on her. She always had to go straight home and was completely occupied with keeping the boy healthy and clean, making sure he got to bed, disciplining and raising him. She had so little time left over.

No, Emelie didn't have many chances for competing, and that was certainly what was needed now. She had noticed how Gertrud had taken advantage of the situation, how her sister had hurried to place herself on Thumbs' and Rudolf's side, against August. The truth was that Gertrud and Rudolf had always gotten along and talked easily together. It wasn't until Gertrud was there that Rudolf grew happy and talkative. She acted childish and dumb and asked for help, clung to Rudolf.

It was Gertrud he went out with now, Gertrud who asked him to pick her up at work so she wouldn't have to walk alone through the dark streets. Emelie had never asked him, didn't want to beg. And it was always possible for Gertrud to go out when she was free; she had only herself to think about.

Of course Emelie would have liked to compete. But she didn't dare. Everything became so meaningless after her mother's death, everything except for the responsibility she had inherited. She had to satisfy herself with only watching, watching how Rudolf went over to Gertrud more and more.

She felt tired and alone. Only saw her one-year-younger sister laugh and have fun, become prettier from love and happiness. While she herself sat there, boring, complaining and admonishing.

Thumbs tried to cheer her up sometimes—would come and joke with her. But he didn't get many words in reply, she couldn't forgive what he had said to August.

One evening Matilda told Thumbs to leave Emelie alone. He couldn't make it up to her, could only wait and hope time would heal the wound he had torn open.

Then he grew indignant and read aloud from *The Social-Democrat.* The building contractors had created a confederation to fight their workers. The workers' appointed representatives would be made to go breadless, working days kept to more than twelve hours, police had promised their support. "The flagrant insolence of the workers had made itself known in all its nakedness during negotiations with this worthy organization," they wrote. Now they thought the workers should get a taste of the whip.

Did it say that August and his stepfather were a part of it also? No, there you have it.

Come on, she surely understood that they were part of it, that all building contractors were cut of the same cloth.

"Women!" he growled. Disagreeable and impossible, without class consciousness. August belonged to the others now. Eventually they had to be able to realize that.

WAITING FOR AUTUMN

Like the fruit to come in the flower, there were foreshadowings of autumn's darkness in the midst of summer's light. The first sign was the lamplighters' preparations; they came carrying their ladders, climbed up to the lights, carefully polished the glass and cleaned the gas pipes with kerosene. After having been extinguished for two months, the streetlamps were lighted anew one evening at the end of July. A week later the café at Strömparterren tried out its new lighting: a whole temple façade reflected in the whirling waters of Strömmen.

People began to get ready for fall everywhere. Three boatloads of floatable walkways were unloaded in Mälar harbor. They were perforated sheets of iron that were to replace some of the usual wooden gangways.

But summer was still there and autumn's slush was only a distant threat. August turned out warm and beautiful. Many of the city dwellers went and sat with picnic baskets in the meadowed hillsides and woods surrounding the city. Every Sunday the police made raids among the illegal beer sellers who were also drawn there. In the park at Kungsträdgården a new attraction drew the city dwellers who stayed within the city gates: the opening of the Swedish waxworks.

They came through the dark lanes of the Old Town, out across the open square at Slussen. Before them stood the forest of masts at Kornhamn and the equestrian statue suspended over the busy green stretch of Karl Johanstorg.

She carried a child in her arms, and he had a sack over his shoulder. Johan had picked up Bärta at the Asylum for Women in Confinement and Their Children.

One of the benches under the statue stood empty and they sat down. While they were resting, he was able to explain to her in a little more detail his attempts and failures; at the asylum it had been difficult to talk about these things that didn't concern others. As he had promised, he had tried to persuade the master chimney sweep to give him money weekly so he wouldn't have to eat and live in the room there. He had had a little hope of succeeding, thought it might be in his favor that he had stayed with the master when the chimney sweep district was divided up last spring, and the journeyman Klarino became master in the new district. But the master's saying no was really not a surprise, not even all the journeymen could manage to get such wishes fulfilled. Johan was still just an apprentice.

So then he had quit. Not quit the trade, of course. To advance more rapidly he had to experience conditions under different masters out in the countryside as well. He had to tramp about for a few years; most of them did that. That didn't solve his and Bärta's problem—when you traveled your income wasn't big.

Wouldn't it still be best to leave the child with someone?

No, she didn't want to do that. Johan, who had been a foster child himself, could understand that?

You had to learn how to mind your manners, that was surely a good thing. He had managed.

But Bärta didn't want to. She would look for work. And he had already arranged lodging for her and the child.

Of course, but it wasn't really a good solution, he didn't want her to believe that it was better than it was. She would surely regret it.

His foster father had died a few years ago. But his foster mother still had a mob of kids and boarders. In truth, the whole house was a rat's nest. People were crawling all over each other. Johan had talked to the old lady, and Bärta and their kid would get a corner and get use of the stove. One of the half-grown girls who were home during the day would certainly watch the boy for a small sum. But that wasn't so good.

Anything was better than the asylum, said Bärta.

By the way, he had bought a mattress—used but not so bad. He had been able to store it with Emelie and Gertrud. If he had put it at the old lady's, it might have disappeared before Gertrud got there.

It'll be nice to end up near their old friends, thought Bärta, if Emelie could still arrange it so that Bärta got to return to the cosmetics factory. But she couldn't hope for that.

It was best they continue on now. Johan didn't have many hours free.

From time to time Bärta went to visit Gertrud and Emelie. She was thankful for the moments she could slip away from the bedlam in Mom's overstuffed cottage.

She didn't get any work the first weeks, and her situation began to be critical. If Mom didn't get any money, she would throw Johan's woman and child out without mercy. Bärta understood that. She knew now that she wouldn't get to return to Melinder's factory. It was full, too, at the spinning mill where she had been earlier. It was the same everywhere.

One day Knutte told how the police had come and taken away one of the mortar girls at his construction site. She was a girl who had stayed at the treatment clinic and now had been taken in as an unregistered whore, despite the fact that she had screamed and cried that she was innocent. She had been raped by an infected bricklayer, she said. But what did the police care about that? The mortar girls had a reputation that worked against them.

The mortar girl's misfortune might create an opportunity for Bärta. She went with Knutte the next morning. The construction site lay out on Kungsholmen, a rapidly growing part of the city. The streetcar rails shone through the dust and gravel of Folkungagatan, but the cars hadn't begun this early in the morning. The steam launches had not begun for the day either; there was no other option but to walk. In any case, it cost way too much to ride.

Well before six-thirty, when the whistle for work was to blow, Bärta stood and waited for the boss. He arrived, looked at her thoughtfully and wondered if she could really manage it. She wasn't used to carrying things, hadn't had that kind of work—and soft, fine hide here, there and everywhere. But that was her affair. His job was to make sure people kept up and did their job right. She could give it a try.

The salary was twelve öre per hour, for uninterrupted carrying of rolls of thread, as the buckets with their yokes were called.

The mortar girls stood by themselves in a corner by the platform, waiting for the whistle to blow. She walked over to them, said hello and got to hear more about her sensitive hide. A little anxiously she looked at their hands. Hers were going to get like that and it was going to be worst in the beginning. The lime corroded, the rough handles of the pails scraped.

The signal went off, everybody was in motion. The bricklayers walked up the gangways to their work places, the brick carriers began to organize their piles. The first wheelbarrows with mortar arrived and were emptied onto the large platform.

Bärta got to begin by carrying two buckets between two stories, one of the easier tasks. The worst was going around and pouring mortar in for the bricklayers. They destroyed their hands the most this way and only got abuse in return.

She hooked on the handles, lifted them up, carried them up the ramp, put them down and unhooked them, returned for a new load while the next mortar girl carried the buckets on to the next story above—over and over, an eternal cycle. The lime sprayed on her when she swayed, the yoke pressed on her shoulders.

After endless hours, it was break. The construction site was situated quite far from any place to eat, so many brought food with them. But Bärta and a few others rushed off to the café, gulped down some food and ran back again. Ten minutes to eat, twenty minutes of running—that was their break. Panting, she made it back to her place just before the whistle blew again. She bent over to lift the yoke, but didn't have time to do more before the undigested food came up. She threw up as discreetly as possible in the corner and began walking. They were already shouting impatiently for her up there.

Then a lucky interval: a short rest when the mortar ran out on the platform. It didn't matter that the bricklayers swore and the boss vowed to geld that hauler when he finally arrived with more mortar from the works.

Bärta got a little help from one of the mortar girls, the yoke had chafed her shoulders open. They managed to find some rags that her comrade tore up and placed under the yoke, hoping it would help somewhat.

The building contractor came to visit, looking questioningly at the idle women. Rough women, much the worse for wear. He hurried on.

"Gentleman caller," said one of them and sneered.

"Don't stand there grinning, get going and work you damned whores!" screamed the boss.

"We have to get the mortar here first," said one. "Or is it good enough if we shit in the buckets?"

"Whores for that one—sure!" snarled another.

They grumbled and quarreled until the delayed hauler arrived.

In the beginning Bärta had to go around with "puppets" on almost all her fingers to protect the many open sores. Eventually the skin was toughened till it was hard. But of course, it smarted and was painful. Her back felt broken, her legs heavy and numb. The way home through the city became unbearably long.

In the "rat's nest" screaming and strife waited: arguments over pieces of food, places in the beds and whose turn it was at the stove. And children's dirty clothing that had to be washed, everything she had to find the time to do.

Dead tired and sniffling, she sat down and held the boy, fed him with thin gruel; she had had to wean him in order to work. She lay him down as protected as she could in the corner, afraid that someone would trample him.

In the beginning she thought: I give up. I'll go to August and tell him the situation, he has to help me. But still she stuck it out, forced herself to view the little one as Johan's child. August had nothing to do with this. Eventually Johan would come home and become a journeyman, everything would get better. It was only a question of managing until then.

Despite the hard labor and the cold that waited, gradually the autumn could no longer scare her. She had gotten a job, passed the test. And despite everything, she liked the construction site better than the factory or the spinning mill. Most of her work colleagues here were men and she

liked their swears and raw language better than the giggles and tittle-tat-
tle of the women. She could answer them, could hit them if they got too
forward and comfort them, too, when they were tired and down. They
liked her with her awkward and abrupt ways; she felt this and was content.

The wind swept ever colder through the open site, and the brick carriers said it was time for her to wear two pairs of underpants. The brick
carriers were full of beans and her favorites. One of them had taken her
brooch as a trophy—he used it to fasten the sack he carried over his shoulders. But they drank ferociously. That was no surprise, said the older
mortar girls who knew—the brick dust completely destroyed their lungs.

Johan was far away, working in Eskilstuna. He couldn't send any
money, but she would manage for herself and the child, now she knew she
could manage.

DRAWING CLOSER, PULLING AWAY

August was on his way to the office—a Monday morning, the last week in October. As usual he was out early. Checked his pocket watch against the Linderoth watchmaker's window where a clock gave the "correct time." He cut diagonally across the street to see the novelty underwear that was on display at Berendt the shirtmaker's. It was beginning to get cold out. August had heard that Doctor Lahman's cotton underwear was both warm and healthy. What if he tried them this fall instead of Jaeger's wool ones?

While he stood and thought about it, he heard horses' hooves. Six hired coaches came driving up the street, unusual this early in the morning. He looked a little curiously at the turnout. A man who stood on the street corner began to wave and the coaches stopped a moment, a gentleman with a large moustache looked out. Suddenly August recognized the moustache: Hjalmar Branting. There was something in the paper about the socialist chief being released from Långholmen Prison today. He had been there over three months for blasphemy. Apparently he had been fetched by his loyal followers.

There, so close to him, was the man who was going to wipe out the Bodin firm and force August to take "an honest job." According to what Thumbs said, he didn't look especially dangerous. A traitor was what August had heard someone say. But traitor was what Thumbs had called August, or hadn't he?

August had felt out of balance for a long time. First, his mother's death and fear that his sorrow would be taken as a reproach against his new parents. He grew so lonely, there was no one to share his grief with.

Then this affair with his siblings. It had had a greater effect on him than he wanted to admit. He should be proud, unperturbed—if he does-n't fit in, so what! But strangely enough, if anything, he felt shame. As if Thumbs was right about him. Before, he had been able to joke about his origins, now he was ashamed that those he had sprung from disowned him.

And something that only grew more and more irritating, that gnawing doubt: did he really love Linda? She was very beautiful, a beautiful picture. That wasn't enough, he realized that now. He couldn't talk with her about what was really was important to him. Not about his mother, not about his siblings. If he tried she would say some friendly, comforting words. But she wouldn't understand him, what he said wouldn't concern her. Perhaps she would be unpleasantly affected. These were issues he should avoid broaching.

But wasn't it precisely difficulties, shame and suffering that they should be able to talk about? People who loved each other should give each other consolation and strength. Maybe the strong could manage with a beauti-ful picture. August wasn't strong. This made him almost afraid of the beautiful, cold face. He looked for someone who existed faceless in the darkness and who understood, accepted him.

Ida had been there that way when he had told her about his real par-ents and siblings. She had understood, asked, but not too much. Answered—and not too simply—but fully feeling how difficult it was. That was a long time ago now. But in some way, he still benefited from it. Once somebody had understood. It could be understood, he wasn't a hopeless case.

Bärta had also been there in the darkness without a face. He had not talked to her, with her he had looked for a wordless comfort.

When he had told Linda about his real parents, he had been walking with her in a cold light, and she had almost seemed vexed at receiving his confidences. She had hurried to say that it didn't change anything between them, then had shaken it off as something disagreeable, begun to talk about something else. She didn't want to know more than necessary—neither asked nor answered.

He had long felt ill at ease. But life surely had to be accepted, he had thought, it wasn't perfect. Nothing could be changed any longer. To break up with Linda would mean breaking up with his old friends, Linda's brother Edvin was one of their circle. Besides, this wasn't what you did: go out with a girl for two years without marrying her. He may have monopolized her best years, prevented her from getting other and better offers. Still, sometimes he felt like overturning everything.

He would like to calm down, push away all his questioning and accept his life such as it was. If he hadn't seen Ida again. But since that day, everything had become harder.

She worked in an office on Drottninggatan. That she was working was a sign that the Wide family was still in poor circumstances after the crash. August had greeted her only from a distance just as she was stepping onto a horse-drawn omnibus that was traveling up Drottninggatan. But he had seen which doorway she had come out of, and a couple of times afterward thought he had seen her in a window above the doorway.

He knew where she was. He would be able to stand outside the doorway and wait for her when she came out. Maybe she was engaged. But she had looked so happy when she had seen him from the omnibus, as if she had thought of coming over to him. He had not dared stay, only waved and left. It was only after a moment that he turned around and watched the omnibus disappear up the steep incline of Kungsbacken, where the white extra horses were waiting.

Annika Bodin wondered how things were really going for August. During the past few years, she herself had begun to calm down, didn't feel the same hectic agitation as before. She could ask herself: had she become resigned? But it felt good to become inured, grow a little plump, not drive herself so hard. When some of her own restlessness let up, she had time to see her surroundings. She felt responsibility for August. At one time, they had yanked him out of his environment. A dangerous experiment, maybe, but it looked like it had been successful. He had become a support for Fredrik as far as business went, was a fine and well-behaved young man whom everyone liked, and had met a beautiful girl from a good family.

But he didn't seem happy. Had he ever been really happy? She remembered how he had walked around alone out at Sommarro, always with his face in a book.

Yes, for a few years he had been happy in that youthful way—had made friends, gone out and had fun. But lately he had seemed depressed, looked tired. He hadn't gotten over his mother's death apparently, and he didn't go see his siblings anymore. Wasn't it ever since his last visit that he had become so melancholy?

As so often was the case, they had eaten alone together. Fredrik was out with business acquaintances. Out in the pantry, the new, strong gas lamp burned, a fishtail burner with a flat flame. They had gas lighting in the kitchen, the hall and the pantry, but in the dining room and the other rooms, they still had the more homey kerosene lamps.

The maid asked if she should turn off the lights in the pantry, she was finished out there now. Annika nodded. It felt good to sit in the soft kerosene lamplight together with August—an intimate glow.

"Are you unhappy?" she said.

He looked up quickly, but averted his gaze. Didn't know what to answer.

"Even if I can't do anything, you can still tell me what is weighing on you."

He felt the temptation to speak, spill it out, and at the same time he felt ashamed; it was his siblings it was about. He couldn't leave them out.

"You have been unhappy since... that's right, since the last time you were on Söder," she said in a low voice.

He looked at her, surprised. Did she know? Was it so visible on him? And he thought he hid his worries so well.

It was easier to talk than he had believed. The dusk gave him courage. He defended his siblings, they hadn't been a part of it after all. Just the opposite, Emelie had said.... He might have exaggerated her role a little. To Annika it sounded like Emelie had defended August to Thumbs. But Emelie was together with Rudolf, the son of the house. They were engaged or something, according to what she had understood. It wasn't so easy for his siblings to say anything, they were so dependent.

Thumbs. Annika could see him before her, the way he had looked when he was young, younger than August was now: that roguish smile, the long, narrow nose, the shock of hair hanging over his forehead. At one time, she had liked Thumbs a lot. Later she had hated him. Because he had so quickly let her go to Fredrik?

No, it wasn't easy to help August—too late to do anything now. His sisters were grown, were going their own ways, were tied to an environment that was hostile to August. It was probably the same with the little boy, Olof. Annika didn't think she had the energy to take the boy, with all the responsibility. Besides, that wouldn't help August much; the sisters probably meant more to him, especially Emelie.

She had to satisfy herself with trying to comfort him. It wasn't he who had brought about the rupture. On the contrary, he had shown such consideration the whole time. He was blameless, she could assure him of that.

Even if he knew that Mother wasn't right about everything she said, her words gave him a certain solace. It wasn't my fault, he repeated to himself. I reached out my hand in spite of everything. He nodded to her—things felt better now. She was right, it was good to talk. And now he would take a walk before he went to sleep.

But his seeing Ida and doubting his love for Linda, he said nothing of this to Mother—not this time.

He walked down Drottninggatan, past where Ida worked, on down to his office. He saw the lamp shining through a window and wondered if someone had forgotten to turn out the light. It was probably best if he went up and looked.

He opened the door, heard some voices from inside his father's room. A laughing female voice, his father's darker tone. He sneaked out, closing the door quietly behind him. There were more than he who used the velvet sofa.

August wasn't especially surprised but still felt unpleasantly affected. Ida had declared several years ago that both her father and August's father met with "girls like that," when they stayed in the city during the summer.

He had believed her and disbelieved her—Father, an old man of fifty, Father who had Mother.

Mother was often alone. He had never thought about that before—that he could also feel sorry for Mother. Feeling sorry for Mama was something he had always felt, but Mother who was so self-confident and beautiful and could get anything she wanted.... Now he should be the one to comfort her. He couldn't say anything about what he had just seen and heard, but he could still be kind to her, talk to her a little, show her he liked her.

On the way home he stopped again and looked at the building where Ida worked.

A few weeks later, he sat alone once again with his mother in the dining room. It was snowing outside, the grass and the graves of the churchyard had been covered with a white blanket, one window in the churchwarden's house shone like a lantern made of snow.

"I broke up with Linda," he said.

She gave a start and stared at him anxiously. "But why?"

He tried to explain. He knew himself that he was hiding a name under his words.

Was there someone else?

Yes, there was. They had met her, a long time ago. Ida Wide. But he had to hurry and say that he had broken up with Linda before he had even spoken to Ida Wide. He didn't know yet if Ida had somebody else.

Why had he broken up with Linda then, hadn't he acted a little hastily?

He didn't think it was right to have Linda as some kind of reserve. And he wanted to be free when he came to Ida.

And what had Linda said, how had she taken it?

He thought she had been more angry than sad, that she had actually been rather relieved that it had ended this way. Ever since she had learned that he was adopted, she had acted a little differently from before. At least he thought so.

But Ida... that it was Ida. Her father had gone bankrupt, been involved in business affairs that weren't entirely honorable. In any case Ida was honorable, and he felt that what he did was right. Finally everything was real; he didn't have to pretend anything that wasn't true.

Annika might have wanted to protest. But still she thought that what August had done probably was right and admired his strength. She had never had this strength herself—been all too drawn to anything "refined"—and failed? Not outwardly, she was in a good situation, living well above the environment of her impoverished childhood. But inwardly?

It would be wrong to restrain him, and perhaps it wouldn't work either. She would only lose in the attempt—lose his confidence that she felt she had just recently won.

"I hope you're doing the right thing," she said. "At least I think you're thinking right. Father and I…"

But she refrained from saying anything, even though she felt the urge to talk about her own failure. Maybe he had understood this anyway; he was beginning to be an adult, had eyes to see with.

He was waiting. She knew that.

"We won't oppose this," she said. I'll talk to Father. He will understand."

"Thank you," he answered.

"Besides, I have missed Signe Wide," said Annika. "We used to have a lot of fun together."

August stood up, pushed in his chair.

"Are you leaving?"

"Yes. I'm going to hear my verdict," he said, but smiled.

Of course, he was anxious when he left, anxious that Ida wouldn't want to keep on seeing him, and maybe, too, that he had let himself be fooled by a romantic childhood memory. Still, he was pleased with himself. Finally he got to stop feeling like a traitor. Thumbs could say and think what he wanted.

Ida had gone down to the doorway, was waiting behind the frosted plate glass. As soon as he saw her, he felt his worry retreat, he didn't need to feel anxious. They belonged together.

MAY FIRST

There was a big day of drinking to celebrate the arrival of spring. Most employees got to finish work in the middle of the day. It had been this way as long as they could remember.

The workers lay down their tools and their loads, hurried home to change clothes. Everyone who had a nice Sunday suit put it on. The bosses watched the crowds of people, thoughtfully—didn't really know what to think. It was hard to say no to the time-honored holiday, even though they guessed what it was going to be used for this year. They weren't going to drink, they were going to demonstrate.

In cities throughout Europe, even as far away as America, everywhere, the workers were going to demonstrate that May first for an eight-hour working day. It had been decided at an international congress in Paris the previous year.

It was unusually warm for the time of year. The sun was shining from a practically cloudless sky when the people from all the corners of the city made their way up to the eastern part of town. The gathering was going to take place by the circus locale on Karlavägen, as the Esplanade was now called.

Actually, they would have liked to march with music and banners throughout the whole city, but the authorities didn't allow any demonstrations on the streets of the city. The workers complained: were they going to be denied walking on the streets they had paved with stones, among the buildings they had built? The protests brought about no changes, the demonstrators had to satisfy themselves with starting fifty meters inside Ladugårdsland's tollgate, almost out in the country.

They gathered silent and serious, even ceremonious. For many it was the first time in the new and distant part of the city; they observed curiously the rows of fine buildings. Karlavägen's wide thoroughfare, which usually gaped empty and desolate, was filled with throngs of people pressing forward against the circus building with its onion cupolas. There were traffic jams in the narrow lanes beside old ruins of houses still standing on steep hillsides. Policemen in spiked helmets tried to contain the onlookers, the sun shone playfully on their shiny badges and the brass knobs of their hats. The workers' patrols hurried through the lines, trying to help arrange everyone among the different standards and banners. The organization of the demonstration had been advertised in *The Social-Democrat* in red ink in honor of the day.

Banners and standards were unfurled, blazing with their violently utopian slogans: *Eight hours work. Eight hours rest. Eight hours free time.*

The dream, to all appearances unattainable. One union, the bookbinders', had refrained from participating since the slogans seemed to them much too unrealistic. They had considered walking under their own banner with a demand for a ten-hour workday, but had let the matter go.

But a group of bakery workers participated. Otherwise, the journeyman bakers' best effort was to put together a written proposal to their masters, a demand for a maximum of twelve hours work per twenty-four hour period. That would be granted them a few weeks later, provided— said the masters—that the workers worked hard and didn't fritter away the work hours.

This was indeed the day of dreams when the goal was set so high. Bargaining over the demands, adjustments and small attempts at improvement had to be saved for everyday.

They came pouring out of streets and alleys. They pulled up short for a moment when they reached the broad esplanade and saw the sea of people, impressed with their own assembled multitudes. This unheard of support was not something those who made the decisions could escape noticing. Now they had to understand that the people were on the move. Everyone was in a hurry to push his or her way in—be a part of it.

It took a while to organize the lines; people were to walk six by six. Then the parade finally got underway, the drums beat, the band tuned up for the Souvenir March. Those who were just recently murmuring in expectation grew quiet, those who felt they were standing alone and weak were filled with the strength of community. As if a giant wave lifted them up and carried them forward, the wind took hold of the banners that were fluttering, their standards were swollen to sails. All were on their way, together with their comrades in many lands. They imagined they could hear the rumble of all the workers of the world marching together. The red banners shone in the sun with their mottos and work emblems—the shoemakers' shoes and the brass and metal workers' laurel-enwreathed scissors and hammer.

Thumbs walked as if in a trance, felt how his eyes filled with tears and wiped them away, embarrassed, with the sleeve of his jacket. He had had a little difficulty deciding where in the demonstration he should walk. He would have preferred to appear under the red flag of the party with the two fingers held upwards. The party walked first in the parade. The Katarina Workers' Club, which he had helped form and still belonged to, walked third in the parade. But he walked in between the two organizations, among the "social outcasts," as *The Social-Democrat* called them.

The dock workers had finally gotten a union going. The meetings were held every other Sunday morning in a locale on Brännkyrkagatan. The organization had already been able to show results. Thumbs had been part of the delegation that oversaw the stevedores. Working hours from six to six were their demands, with two hours free for breakfast, lunch and an evening meal and increased pay.

Lundström had looked at Thumbs thoughtfully, must have remembered how an earlier effort at organizing had been suppressed, but the stevedore had given in to a certain degree. He had crossed out the evening meal and not given forty öre per hour, but still given thirty. Even if their demands had been bargained down, it had meant a reduction of work time from twelve hours to ten and a half, and an increase of wages by five öre per hour.

It was a victory, and it had brought many of the dock workers to the union. Lundström was one of the bigger stevedores, when he went along with things the smaller stevedores would surely follow suit. Now Thumbs had to walk in the demonstration among the outcasts, among those he had been part of leading to a first victory.

He hadn't been able to get Matilda to come along; she had a pain in one knee, but Rudolf was there beside him. The streetcar personnel had no group of their own even though they were organized. They had also won benefits, thanks to their union. Rudolf now had a monthly salary of eighty kronor in addition to the öre he received as a percentage of the amount he brought in.

Knutte was back with the bricklayers. They were walking somewhere behind the society for temperance, *The Times*, but ahead of the coopers and the cork cutters. Both of Thumbs' full-grown sons were there in the parade—the music and the banners, the rumble of thousands of feet.

He felt sorry for those who didn't get to experience it, who didn't get to be carried forward toward better and brighter times. Wasn't this what he had once promised Henning—the revolution, the wave that couldn't be stopped? If only Henning could have been there, been able to feel this.

The gigantic human serpent moved up toward the two speakers' chairs on Fågelbacken. Close to fifty thousand people had gathered, but very few of the many who had come had voters' rights. They were declared legally unauthorized to manage their own affairs, were called and called themselves "minors." Many felt they should be silent and obey like children.

Now they protested.

Gertrud and Emelie had taken Olof and Mikael along and gone on ahead up to Fågelbacken to try and get close to the speakers' chairs. The girls belonged to professions that hadn't organized. They watched the dark parade come over the softly arching, light green slopes, and saw how the hill turned black. The banners were grouped together; the chorus placed itself opposite the two speakers' chairs. "Welcome Beautiful May," it sang. "The Marseillaise," "Springtime and Freedom" and then "Sons of Labor:"

The struggle was mounted
Against the ravaging gold calf,
With feelings and courage aglow!

The first speakers climbed up to the two speakers' chairs, shouted out their words over the enormous sea of people. Only those who stood closest could hear everything, then the words were whirled away on the wind, disappeared. Four deliveries were given from each speaker's chair, Palm and Branting ended it. The resolution was accepted with loud shouts of "aye." The band played. All around on the hillsides vendors had set up small stands.

That day, one of the speakers had said, would come to be viewed in the future as the dawning spring morning of the workers—rich with promise.

The friends from Söder had decided to meet afterward at Djurgårdsbron, but they managed to find each other at the foot of Fågelbacken. Slowly they walked toward the tollgate, and then continued on to Djurgården. Thumbs, between Knutte and Mikael, was already deep in discussion. Emelie with Olof, who must have been tired out by the long walk and all the speeches. And a little way behind them, Gertrud on Rudolf's arm, happy and excited and a little round in the middle—she was in her fourth month.

Rich with promise, spring dawning.... Still, Emelie felt tired and melancholy, as if the spring lacked meaning.

III

THE TURNING POINT

The spring they prophesied was a long time in coming. Unemployment and famine increased instead. Tired, desperate bands of people dragged through the streets.

Class hatred swelled, fed by the famine.

Those who had a few öre to pay lined up outside the Salvation Army's soup kitchen and other meal provision centers. For the poorest children, charities had organized meals in schools.

Should they fear a revolution? Anxiously, those in power watched how something called The People's Parliament was elected by one hundred fifty thousand who were otherwise unentitled to vote. Their representative had an audience with the king, but was not allowed in to see the prime minister. His Excellency Boström said he would not recognize any other representatives than those chosen according to the laws of the realm.

Was violence the only solution? More and more asked themselves that. Agitators whipped up emotions. The unemployed tried to organize their own union. They paraded up to Stortorget to demonstrate outside the Stock Exchange, where those authorized by the state assembled. Police on horseback intervened and dispersed the demonstrators; some of their leaders were charged with vagrancy.

"We will infuse ourselves with the poison called hate so we will be ripe for any kind of violence," Hinke Bergren had declaimed. The Social Democratic Party had chosen him as their representative at the party's second congress. Branting, who had spoken out against violence, got only one vote.

"As long as a pulse beats in the body, fiery hate will not die," wrote the bard, Gabrielsson.

The workers' newspapers printed statistics that claimed the average life span of a priest was sixty-seven, of a factory worker thirty-two.

Soon, very soon, something had to happen.

During Whitsuntide 1891, the second Social Democratic Congress was held, meeting in Norrköping. The most important question at the time was violence, revolution. Branting had come to the congress as a representative from his province.

As its main resolution, the congress recognized that the party was revolutionary and had to take into consideration that organized violence could be the proletariat's ultimate emancipator. But—so long as peaceful means for attaining voters' rights had not yet been tried, they stated their emphatic disapproval of any kind of agitation that made use of dynamite. Agitators who incited violent actions against individuals were stamped as traitors to the principles of the party.

By twenty-nine votes to nineteen, the congress confirmed an earlier pronouncement against violence as a means of fighting in the social struggles. The minority voted in favor of Berggren's suggestion that the organizations should discuss what form of violence could be viewed as the most practical.

Despite the fact that the darkness was just as large, despite increased unemployment and famine—they had reached the turning point. The bloody revolution was written off. The fight that waited would be carried out by peaceful means.

For some this decision meant defeat—capitulation. They didn't have the strength to wait any longer, were tired of talking about the voters' rights they would probably never receive. Was there any reason to sacrifice time and money working for an organization when those with the highest supremacy in the movement betrayed the revolution in this way?

The dock worker, Thumbs, was among those who gave up. He stopped going to party meetings, didn't do anything either to keep the new dock workers' union active. During times of unemployment, the harbor was always filled with people looking for odd jobs who took the wages they could get, it was impossible to come with any demands. Interest in the unions faded away. Finally they stopped calling meetings, and the unions were left to die out on their own.

But the older and better-organized unions held out. When the need for help was large but incomes small, they tried to stretch their cash by holding parties and bazaars. The factory workers' union advertised a dance on Gallows Hill.

Thumbs, who had a hard time sitting calmly at home, went there one spring evening, directly from the tavern. He received a red paper rose as a ticket to enter; it was to be fastened onto the pleasure outing's most beautiful girl. A bottle washer from Götgatan got the most votes, but not much joy from the recognition, only the nickname the Rose of Drunkard's Hill. Drunk, angry and tired, Thumbs headed toward home. The red rose still lay in his pocket. He threw it, trampled it in the mud. Red roses, red banners—stuff and nonsense, wrinkled paper and cloth rags. He hoped that he would meet some fat and impudent bourgeois on the way home; he longed to hit someone hard.

What was it Marx had said? Should the ruling classes tremble? That was laughable in any case. They had nothing to be afraid of; Branting and his hangers on had guaranteed that. He knew he was being unwise and unfair.

But still, still.

ON THE PRECIPICE

A blast rang out and the little house on the hill shook so the windowpanes rattled. Gertrud flew up from the chair where she was sitting and sewing, looked out the window. A gray cloud rose up the steep precipice below. She stayed at the window a moment, saw how the men crept out of the crevices and crannies where they had taken cover from the explosion.

They were blasting for the new railroad that would soon make its way here, from Stadsgården through the hill, Erstaberget, and past Danvik's tollgate. The train was to go through long tunnels, across bridges and viaducts and along ledges carved out of the hillside, out to the new and fine neighborhood called Saltsjöbaden. The track between the new area and the tollgate was already finished, but from the tollgate passengers were still transported via steamer to the center of town. The track didn't lie far from their window. It would be fun when the trains came, Gertrud thought—livelier. As long as they didn't rumble so much that the children got upset.

Gertrud had not yet turned twenty-three. She still felt like a child in many ways, a little girl who needed help from the adults. But she was a mother herself now, had two daughters of her own—the three-year-old who was playing in the road and the one-year-old who was sleeping in the bed by the stove.

The children gave Gertrud the right to be at home, to be the last one in the house who needed to run from workplace to workplace and beg for a job. This right brought with it obligations. They probably expected her to have time for more than she did. Since you're at home... you maybe have time for this—and this—and this. But she didn't have time, and knew that she was almost worn out. And then she longed for her own home, a room where only she and Rudolf and the children lived, and where no one other than themselves could demand anything of her.

Otherwise, Gertrud liked having a lot of people around her. In her own home she would surely feel lonely at times, and unsure and anxious. Now she could ask Rudolf's mother for advice regarding raising the little girls. Olof and Mikael ran errands for her when they didn't have any work, and Emelie helped her with preparing the food and the cleaning.

Actually it was Emelie she would have liked to move away from. Of course Gertrud liked her sister. But Emelie was so capable, managed to get so much done, didn't understand that not everyone was as quick on his or her feet. Gertrud could stand there and just watch Emelie, it was hopeless to try and do anything herself when Emelie did everything twice as quickly and well. Sometimes it even happened that Emelie redid something Gertrud had already done. Such as the patches on Olof's clothing that Gertrud made so ugly—Emelie could put them on so they were hardly visible. And then there was no reason for Gertrud to even try.

The hours passed by so fast, the days just disappeared. Sometimes Bärta didn't have any work, so she came with her little boy and sat and chatted. Then Olof and Mikael would come and want coffee, and they would sit there another while. Then suddenly it was evening, and a whole lot of things that had to be done weren't even begun yet. Then Gertrud felt like moving, preferably before Emelie got there.

Although Gertrud and Rudolf had two children together, they hadn't gotten married yet, not even moved in together. Times were bad, Rudolf said, even if there was housing to move into now. There were always some of them out of work, and they had to economize. It was easier when they lived as they did and could put together the money they earned.

Thumbs had a very irregular income at the harbor. Everything depended on how closely together the boats arrived, and if his team was lucky and got good boats. One week he might earn seven kronor, another thirty. Matilda got a little over ten kronor a week. The spinners were always poorly paid, and the women there naturally had it worst. Rudolf got close to twenty kronor a week; his money was more secure. Knutte, as a trained bricklayer, earned the most—when he had work—a whole forty öre per hour. But he often had to go without work and for a long time, especially in the winter. Emelie got twelve kronor a week. Olof and Mikael had not had steady work for a long time; they got a few kronor now and then for different odd jobs.

If one compared them to others, their life wasn't bad; they were many people of working age. They could earn upwards of ninety kronor in a good week. But ten people had to live on that, including the small children, and the ones who worked had to have warm clothes and proper shoes. Sometimes they were forced to buy wood and it was expensive—seventy öre a sack. And kerosene and soap and the newspaper that Thumbs absolutely had to keep up with. And the rent, of course—twenty kronor a month for a room and a kitchen.

You had to save. Gertrud still lived in the kitchen with her siblings and her two children. Rudolf slept with his parents and two brothers in the main room. As soon as times got a little better they were going to move and have a place of their own, Rudolf had said. If he said something, that was the way it would be. He knew everything, she had only to ask him. Gertrud would never have to take responsibility herself, that felt good. She wouldn't have to worry so much and become a tiresome nag like Emelie. It was Olof Emelie was so worried about. Gertrud, too, could certainly see that Olof was pale and not well. But she had her own children to think of first. Luckily they were healthy and strong.

One day Rudolf would come and say "Now we're moving!" Then they would have their own place, and she would have to manage without Matilda and Emelie. Until then things were good the way they were.

At the end of October, conditions grew harder. During unloading at the harbor Thumbs slipped on a plank, fell down into the hold and hurt his back. He got a few kronor in assistance from the stevedore while he lay at home. Knutte was completely without work; the youngest boys were doing what they had done all fall. And Matilda's knee was in such bad shape that for a few weeks she couldn't even get down to the spinning mill.

Their communal weekly income sank catastrophically to around forty

kronor. A few kilos of horse meat and smoked sausage, a little herring—
they didn't get more in the way of meat in those weeks. But Thumbs read
aloud to them from the newspaper that he wouldn't give up even now, it
said better times were expected. The business cycle was going upward—
whatever that was. But when weeks passed and they didn't see any
improvement, Mikael decided that whatever was going upward had disappeared so far up that the workers would never see any of it. He guessed
that it was up in the upper class, and that they had hidden it there very
carefully.

Times were really difficult when they even had to try to cut down on
skim milk. Gertrud now bought them four liters a day instead of six. Still
they managed, and soon both Thumbs and Matilda would be able to work
again, and Knutte had gotten a half promise of work from a bricklayer
boss.

For Bärta, things were worse. She was alone. When she had no work
she completely lacked income. Johan could send a couple of kronor from
time to time, she knew that he had it tough himself. From the women in
Mom's apartment, she could expect neither help nor mercy. They were
like a group of hungry dogs who fought over what bones they could find.
Gertrud helped her a little sometimes, as if in secrecy. She might shove a
few potatoes toward the boy, give him a cup of skim milk, offer Bärta a
slice of bread. But it was never enough. Gertrud didn't dare and couldn't
give that much.

Bärta came into the kitchen one Sunday evening when Gertrud was
out with Rudolf, and Olof was out too. Emelie was at home, had promised
to watch the children. Bärta was beside herself. No work, the boy was
starving. If he, at least, had been big enough to go to school, at least there
they got one meal a day. Every other day Bärta had gone to the soup
kitchen and gotten one portion; it cost twenty-two öre. The past few days
she hadn't been able to afford it. She had stood in line to get a few porridge
tickets, but the line had been long, and the tickets had run out before she
got to the front of the line.

Emelie didn't have much with to give. But she dug out her last twenty-five öre piece from the slim coin purse. And Bärta rushed off to a stand on Nytorgsgatan where you could buy used coffee grounds and rotten food cheap.

Emelie hadn't seen August for a couple of years, despite the fact that she worked in the area next to the building where he lived. They kept different hours; she arrived much earlier than he left. And when he was on his way home from the office, he took Drottninggatan while she found that the most direct route was across Brunkebergstorg.

Then suddenly one day he came to Stora Badstugatan when she was out for her lunch break. And he didn't just say hello, but stopped and took her hand and wanted to know how things were with her and their siblings.

Emelie looked around, a little embarrassed. People would wonder what such a fine gentleman as August would have to say to a working woman. But she told him: she still had her job, Olof had temporary work now and then, but there was such terrible unemployment. Getrud was married, she said—though that wasn't exactly true.

She was married?

Yes, to Rudolf. They had two children, both girls.

August felt a little confused, wasn't it Emelie that Rudolf had been interested in? But it was probably best not to touch on that subject.

How were they managing?

She painted a somewhat brighter picture when she answered. August got the impression that his siblings were living rather well, even if Olof was frail. His bother wasn't exactly sick, and he had always been frail. August evidently didn't need to have a bad conscience regarding his siblings. They were getting by and still living at Thumbs'.

And how were things with him?

Just fine. He was working in the Bodin firm, of course, and was engaged to a girl named Ida. Emelie had never seen her. How were all the others? Thumbs—and the girl who was living with them before, Bärta?

Emelie told him about Thumbs' back and Matilda's knee, but it didn't seem as if August was particularly interested. But when she told how Bärta and her child were half-starving, August looked extremely anxious.

Hadn't she gotten married? Couldn't her husband support her?

Johan was an apprentice chimney sweep and was out traveling and working so he could eventually get better pay for his work, he found out. Right now Johan didn't have much to help her with.

That was a pity about Bärta. But there was his streetcar coming, August was meeting someone and had to run.

A few days later one of the gentlemen from his office left a letter for Emelie, it had come with a message. She looked at the envelope with the firm's name printed on it, wondering. What could Bodin's want from her?

A few lines on a piece of paper: August couldn't forget what Emelie had told him about Bärta. Could she kindly deliver the money he had placed in the envelope; he naturally didn't know Bärta's present address. It was fifty kronor.

On the way home Emelie went into the house where Bärta was living. She recoiled at all the noise, mess and foul smells. Bärta's son stood by the stove with his nose running and stared at one of the women, who was frying a rancid piece of bacon. He wasn't going to get any of it, just the smell. He looked up shyly when Emelie spoke to him, cautiously backing off as if he expected her to strike him, but he ran off obediently to get his mother.

Emelie waited in the yard. Bärta came out and walked with her out to the street. In the dusk the softly rounded rock slabs shone white from beneath the street's filling of macadam and gravel. Then the road shrank to a path up the hill, winding among yellowing weeds and bushes. It led them to the precipice and to the stairs down to Kvastmakerebacken. Here it was quiet and still now. The blasters were finished with their work, and the rail layers were done for the day.

Low houses looked up from between the crags, gray-black in the October dusk—like a fishing village far out in the archipelago. But from the giant sea of mist beneath them glittered small lights, as if a sunken Atlantis were down there in the deep.

Emelie, who had walked the whole way home, was tired. She sat down on the edge of a rock and Bärta sat down, mystified, beside her. What could Emelie have to tell her? She seemed so strange, almost ceremonious. They sat silent in the unearthly gray silence, as if everything around them had died away, no cart wheels crunched on the gravel, no machinery thumped, no horses' hooves pounded.

Finally Emelie spoke. She described her meeting with August, repeated his questions. Anxiously Bärta asked what it was Emelie was getting at. Emelie handed her the envelope with the money in it. The note was still in it, and Bärta read it slowly, spelling her way through the words. Then she pulled out the money, looked at it incredulously. Did Emelie mean it was for her? The whole thing?

Emelie nodded. And Bärta cried.

When she had finally calmed down, she looked timidly at Emelie. What could August have said? Had he felt he had to explain why he gave Bärta so much money?

"Did you know?" she asked.

And Emelie had to promise to not tell anyone. Not even August. Absolutely not August.

"The boy, Gunnar, is not Johan's."

"Do you mean that August is the father of the boy?"

Bärta crumpled in the twilight, became one with the rock. Sat huddled with her face hidden in her knees, but Emelie could still see that she nodded a silent yes.

"But why didn't you say anything?"

Bärta just continued to shake her head. When she finally got some words out, it was the same entreaty: Emelie couldn't tell anybody. August must not find out. What had Emelie said – that he was engaged?

Yes, she had said that.

Then Emelie understood how important it was that he not find out. August didn't owe Bärta anything, he knew nothing and was innocent.

August's son. That meant Emelie was Gunnar's aunt. But the boy would never get to find out. Not find out. Still, Emelie would feel responsibility toward him, would have to try and make sure he didn't have it too hard.

For the next few weeks, things would be all right. Now that Bärta had money, both she and the boy could eat their fill. Did August really not guess anything? Was it really just that he had that much money?

BOULEVARD BESIDE THE MARSH

A light snow powdered the streets and the roofs of the houses white. Suddenly the city seemed clean and new, but the waters lay dark, had not yet frozen over.

"Everybody" met on the splendid, new boulevard. So many knew each other, greeted each other, stopped and chatted. To an observer from afar, it looked as if a ballet was in progress with a giant mobilization of elegant walk-ons.

Heavy, magnificent buildings created the backdrop. They raised their masses of stone where tumbledown wooden houses had lain close together just a few years earlier. Part of the large boulevard had been finished; it followed the valley of the marshy river that had once flowed there. The jeweler, Hammer, who had owned the shed next to Nybroplan's plaza, had finally given in and allowed the boulevard to pass through. Now people could walk like big city inhabitants in this modern metropolis.

But you couldn't cast too many glances to the side if you wanted to maintain the illusion of a well-planned large city. At Nybro harbor rows of gray, wooden cargo boats lay docked. Bent over old women in rags scavenged for leftover pieces of bark at the unloading places. The rickety shacks of Lutternsgatan still climbed the ridge above the new palatial building at Stureplan. Fall and spring saw mud from higher up run down into the valley. Pools and streams had now frozen solid and become dangerously slippery sheets of ice. At Engelbrektsplan they were doing their best to tear down the Lambyska factory; gaping black holes yawned between the white-coated roofs and collapsed planks.

Still, there was no statelier street than this boulevard that had been named after the city founder. A statue of the jarl himself stood on the large office building that had been built on the corner of Smålandsgatan. An entire building dedicated to business, the first of its kind. It was a sign that pointed to new and brighter times.

August felt like he was floating along at Ida's side. They liked to go down to the boulevard when they walked. They ran into acquaintances, there were fine shop windows to look in, and the Thörnblad tearoom where they could eat pastries and drink coffee to the accompaniment of a player piano.

He liked to show Ida off, was proud of her. He didn't have to be afraid of running into Linda, she had gotten married and moved to a garrison town. She had hurried to reclaim lost time, he thought. But the thought was without bitterness, it just felt good that Linda's fate didn't have to bother him.

August himself was going to marry Ida as soon as times got a little better. Calm, security, and the dream of the future, everything gave him the enthusiasm and a reason to become interested in the firm more than ever. He had slowly but surely begun to penetrate the secrets of business. He plowed through all the papers, studied city plans and building regulations, went out to inspect the buildings and properties they owned.

Something must have happened to the firm about two years ago. From that point in time, it was as if roads once staked out suddenly disappeared. He lost his orientation on the map, couldn't understand the actions recorded.

He wanted to solve the mystery himself, without asking father. Suddenly, he thought, what passed for a picture puzzle would reveal the simple and natural solution.

August knew that building contractors and property owners had been complaining about the hard times. They had built too much during the big boom years of the eighties. Now there were maybe three thousand apartments standing empty and rents were falling. The crisis gave rise to a lot of shady deals. It might happen that a building owner would fill his building with people who neither could nor intended to pay their rents—and then sold the property as "fully occupied."

The buildings had sunk in value because of the lowered rents. But at the same time, there was one thing that had gone up the whole time: land prices. For this reason, he ought to start buying up a lot of cheap ramshackle houses, August thought. That's what that Hammer had done and surely many others with him. But not Bodin's.

He went through the cashbooks: they were losing money on some of their buildings. The ones that had been built during the boom years were often bad; people spoke disparagingly of "the country barn style." The criticism was not directed at appearance only. He had seen some of these buildings. Luckily they didn't own more than one. The filling materials were taken from old lice-infested hovels: half rotten beams, poorly applied plaster. Father had talked about buying one more that was on auction, but it didn't seem like a good proposition. If Thumbs only knew how bad....

And all these middlemen—there were those who farmed out their work second and even third hand. People set up acquisitions using decoys and earned money without actually doing any work. It was no wonder that it was getting expensive to build.

August had sat many days and evenings at the firm and searched for the pattern. He looked for the reasons they utilized more expensive services and materials than necessary, why they sold buildings they were making good money on while they kept others that were only showing a loss. He had tried to learn the game and its rules. Now he was comparing the reality with the teachings of business school and his student years at different business offices. A lot of things didn't add up.

Then he figured out what had happened two years ago. The old building contractor Eriksson had died suddenly. For years Eriksson had been Fredrik Bodin's advisor.

That evening August felt despair. He had promenaded proud and happy, dreamed of the future—without knowing that he was walking across a quagmire. He felt bitterness toward a father who had embezzled away opportunities and a secure future. Did Father understand that the firm's existence was threatened?

August forced himself to sit there and look at more. Gradually the picture grew brighter. Unbelievable amounts had been wasted. But there were still hope and resources, if he found a quick and decisive remedy and made a recovery in time.

He didn't speak about it to his father, wanted to put it off. If Father didn't sense anything, August's discoveries would only make him upset, maybe also angry. Before August said anything, he wanted to have a plan. And he had to be completely sure that he hadn't allowed himself to be deceived—that what he saw really was the truth.

While August looked for opportunities, he felt how he was growing. Without yet admitting it, this made him prepared to take on part of the responsibility. He wasn't afraid of that burden now. On the contrary: he was concerned that he wouldn't be allowed to take it on.

He told Ida some of what he had discovered. She, who had grown up in a building contractor's home and worked in a building contractor's office, could grasp the problems. He supposed they had strange discussions for two young people newly in love. What would Linda have said if he had come to her and talked about bankruptcy custody, protested bills of exchange, wage lists, and the price of drainpipes? He had to smile as he sat there among the heavy, serious cashbooks.

Influenza was raging throughout the city and claimed many victims. When Fredrik Bodin felt he was coming down with a cold, he grew worried about his health and quickly took to his to bed.

His father's illness gave August the chance to devote himself even more intensely to his sleuthing. He could sit undisturbed in the director's room for days at a time with all the papers readily available, could let everything lie out while he hurried home for a quick supper. And he dared ask Ida if she wanted to accompany him to the office one evening and help him.

It was, perhaps, not entirely proper for the two of them to sit there alone together, but to Ida it seemed only natural. Of course they would help each other. Though they didn't tell their parents about it. August wasn't sure if Father would like Wide's daughter gaining insight into their company, and Ida suspected that her parents wouldn't find it so natural that she and August sat alone in the office.

She would leave home on Hantverkaregatan, taking the southbound Kungsholm line, the one with the gray signs. She would tell the driver to stop at the corner of Drottninggatan and Strömgatan. August arrived in plenty of time, he wanted to be sure that Ida wouldn't have to stand alone in the darkness along the quay. He heard the water rushing down below in the deep channel, saw it flow under Norrbro where the large, new gas lamps shed their strong light onto the swirling waters. Helgeandsholmen with its naked smokestacks and broken house gables looked like a war-torn town; they were in the process of tearing down the royal stables and the pile of hovels. The wreckage stood black and ghostly in the light of the bridge's lanterns.

Then the rattle of a vehicle came from the curve up by Vasabron, the kerosene lantern shone like a red eye, the wagon came gliding out of the mist. The coachman pulled on the reins, the wheels stopped. August hurried forward to help Ida when she went to step down. She reached out one hand to him and held up her dragging skirt with the other.

Ida was chilled after the ride in the cold wagon. It didn't help much that they placed reindeer hides on the floor and cushions on the benches; the travelers still got thoroughly chilled.

She and August quickly went into the warm office where the fire was still glowing in the tile stove. She looked around the beautiful and well-furnished director's room, so much grander than the simple building contractor's office her father had had at one time. The Bodin firm gave the impression of calmly distinguished, rock-solid stability. Still she knew that the foundation was quite weak, and August very worried. The piles of papers and cashbooks spread out on the table right under the lamp diverged from the slightly severe and formal orderliness. Somehow, the fine room didn't seem intended for work.

He dictated figures from the cashbooks, which she arranged in different columns. Gradually an image of the Bodin firm emerged, which was quite different from the one the director's room projected. Surprised, Ida began to see the results of their work, the revelation.

Time passed quickly, they wouldn't be able to get through in one evening everything that August had prepared. He pushed the books aside, explained his intentions. She had seen a piece of the whole, where money was being thrown away and where it was accruing. Naturally, some losses would have to be taken in the hope that the general crisis would soon be over; there were signs of it lifting, in which case, it would be foolish to cut back and sell off things in a panic. His idea was to present all the material to his father, together with a plan for reorganization.

While Ida did the figures and read the results, she felt some of the anxiety August had had when he learned the truth. Now, when she heard what could be done, she knew that August had seen the possibilities, and she too sensed the way out of the darkness and into the light of the future. Impatience and joy—the wish to be allowed to take this road together with him—and eagerness beat inside her.

While August put the books away, Ida stood up, opened the door to the "big office" and went out into the darkness between the high desks. It was cool out there, and she felt like she had to cool down her excitement. She shivered a little when she returned, and pulled the door shut behind her against the darkness. The well-appointed director's room gave a feeling of home—their home. So close to each other and only the two of them, shielded from outside eyes. Now the warmth simply felt secure. She felt like she and August had always known each other, were one.

The sofa looked comfortable. She curled up on it, pulled her legs up under her. Half-reclining against the stuffed armrest, she stared into the fire. August was scraping together the embers and the last of the remaining wood.

He turned around. A moment of shame—that was where Bärta had lain, in the darkness. It would soon be six years; he could almost feel it was forgiven by now. Ida hadn't existed then, and during all those years he hadn't lain with another girl. Of course, he had been on the way many times, but he had always been driven back by his shame and the fear of being infected. Somewhere in a drawer at home he still had a gonorrhea syringe. Julius Ek had foisted it on him: too risky to live without one, everyone had one. Perhaps it was the syringe that made him do without. He didn't want it to be that revolting, then there would be no desire left. He had thought of Bärta many times, wanted to go to her. But she was married now, had a child with the apprentice chimney sweep.

Now, when he saw Ida half-reclining on the sofa, he felt the hunger, stronger than before. Still he wanted to wait, not come to her in the shadow of the disaster that the evening's work had shown them. Actually, he didn't want her to sit on that sofa either, with the memories of Bärta, of his father and his father's mistress.

Fredrik Bodin, who found that he had successfully avoided both the influenza and death, got up after a few days in bed. On his second day back at work, August asked if they could go through some things he had been thinking about. Fredrik was expecting a few simple questions, and promised broad-mindedly to be of service.

With the slightly bantering assurance of an adult who is well-informed, he began to answer and explain. But when he understood how much August knew, he felt less confident, and the answers became more evasive, nebulous. Gradually Fredrik switched to haphazard retractions, replying with complaints about hard times and unforeseen difficulties.

He himself heard how pitiable it sounded. And discovered that he almost liked this piteousness. He had always been afraid of deciding and leading, had never really had that ability. First, his father had taken care of everything, then his older brother. After his brother's sudden death, Fredrik had sat there with all the responsibility. Then the old herring firm had slid into bankruptcy. He had been saved by the properties that his old man had bought once, and by the construction industry, and old Eriksson who was luckily on hand. They had sailed through the good years, but when Eriksson was gone and the wind had slackened the firm had run aground. Fredrik had known this for a while, not as clearly as the tables of numbers August had set out concluded, but still....

Bewildered, upset, he sat and listened to his son. Yes, yes, it was bad, they had sustained great losses. He knew they couldn't go on this way, but what could they do?

The numbers buzzed about liked blowflies. Fredrik would have most liked to shoo them away—flee the whole mess, go out to some nice tavern, away to his happy companions, home to his mistress. He only heard the buzzing, felt the irritation. Didn't comprehend what August was saying. Didn't have the strength to carry out even a fraction of what August said had to be done. It sounded like it must be good, but: impossible, too hard, too late, too heavy.

August felt that his father wasn't really with him, didn't understand the significance of the measures he was suggesting. When he now saw his father sitting there red in the face, swollen, with a wandering gaze, he felt like he saw him for the first time as he really was. Before he had seen him with the eyes of a child. And suddenly he understood that it was meaningless to try and save the firm. Fredrik Bodin was not the man who could run it. There was no one with enough experience, they were doomed to fail.

They returned to the office after dinner at Fredrik's suggestion, and August followed him without asking or hoping for anything. He lighted the lamp, placed some pieces of wood on the embers, pulled out some books and papers. Everything routinely as if he were numb. August's thoughts flitted around Ida. In vain, he thought bitterly. He had to set her free, had no future to offer her. She should avoid living through one more bankruptcy.

His father had sunk down in the armchair by the desk, sat and looked out the window, at the darkness, and didn't turn his head when August spoke.

"August," said Fredrik, "I'm only a damned herring dealer. I have never understood this business, but I understand that it is going completely out of control."

August remained silent, didn't have the energy to begin again, knew that his father didn't have the strength and ability to comprehend. Suddenly Fredrik turned to him, and August saw the despair, the tears,

the shame. Bewildered, the son felt how this disaster could be an opportunity, perhaps a prerequisite for something for something new and better.
He didn't know how or why, only that he saw his father's tears with shame
but also with relief.

"Do you think you can? That you understand enough?"

"What do you mean, Father?"

"If you dare and you have the strength, then take on the responsibility.
Maybe you can clear this up. I can't."

August sat down at the table, wanted to try and explain the numbers
once more. But Fredrik only shook his head, didn't have it in him to listen. If August thought he could handle the responsibility he would give
it to him. He could think about it for a few days if he liked.

Then August felt his strength, grew calm and confident. He could
manage it. "Yes," he said. "I want to try. I think it can work."

"Good," sighed Fredrik. "Then we'll go and get something to drink. I
have to wash this down—and wish you success."

Of course he understood his father, the shame and self-reprobation,
the need to flee. For the first time August went to a tavern with his father.

August had been lucky, had managed to step in before it was too late. Now
they were expecting better times. It had been decided that in a few years
the city was going to host a giant exposition; that was a sign. Everything
that had lain silent and dead began to come to life again. New buildings
were being constructed, unemployment was going down. The Bodin firm
that had thrown off a lot of ballast began to slowly make its way to solid
ground. Good times arrived as if carried on a wave.

The beginning of this new leg of the voyage had to be taken with caution. By his tables August could see all the more clearly that the crisis was
over, they would get by this time too. It gave him increased confidence.
Still, he was clearly conscious that he wasn't producing any miracles. He
had just carried out what had to be done within all reasonably well-run
companies. A simple, ordinary efficiency control.

But to Fredrik Bodin, it was as if August was performing magic, and he felt both admiration and fear. He padded quietly out of his director's room, didn't want to disturb the genius at work. He found more and more pretexts to stay away from the office, where he felt like the personnel smiled scornfully, and from home, where he felt like his wife openly showed her contempt.

During the day, he began to spend more time at his mistress's; she took in work for a copy bureau. Their relationship that had lasted for many years, no longer contained the attraction of the unknown, but rather simulated a somewhat less than happy marriage. Fredrik sat in a corner and sipped on a drink and read the paper, while the girl wrote clean copy of the minutes the courthouse copyists refused to copy out since the minutes revealed such vile things. There was an actuary who whipped children and arranged sadistic orgies—and the young woman wrote and sighed over the world's evils while Fredrik napped in his easy chair and dropped his newspaper.

Actually he wasn't comfortable in that small room, which she rented together with another girl. And he could go there only during the day while the other girl worked. They used to have the red sofa at the office as a place for their trysts, but now Fredrik never knew when August was still there working. He felt bound, shut out. The girl grew whiny and nasty, since he never left her alone, and she threatened to leave him. He tried to hold on to her with the promise that she would inherit something from him. He sat in her armchair and felt his wretchedness, went over and over his misfortune. Sometimes she had to leave the confessions of the sadistic actuary and take the sobbing Fredrik in her arms and comfort him. But she derived no pleasure from his closeness, only force of habit and promises kept her there.

He had to leave in plenty of time before the other girl came home. He would walk over to the office, try to look harried and completely preoccupied with business, and knew that August guessed where he had been. He went home and met Annika's contempt.

Everyone knows. Still, he had to pretend and lie to himself. In spite of his being glad that August had taken responsibility for the firm. Now he could be spared it, become nothing to it as he always suspected he was.

He remembered his father's admonishments, his brother's harsh criticism, his advisor's head-shaking, August's incomprehensible figures. He sucked up self-contempt, washed it down with liquor, sobbed it out in the arms of the girl who, repulsed and irritated, tried to free herself from him.

SEPARATE WAYS

In one respect even the most revolutionary city dwellers were conservative. They kept to the most familiar parts of the city. There were families who had lived on Söder for generations, because those who had migrated to the city had stopped there, close to the tollgates they had entered through.

But Rudolf wasn't like the others. He appeared good-humored and calm, but beneath the surface there was a stubborn strength that never let the comfortable and accustomed prevail over the practical and economical. Since he had been a driver for the northern streetcar line—which was larger than the southern and therefore he considered it more secure—he thought he should live close to the stables on Norr, the north side. But not in one of the hovels of Träsktorget, or Roslagstorg as it was now called; it was both unhealthy and unpleasant there. He wanted to go to a real stone building with indoor water and plumbing. At the same time, the apartments couldn't be too expensive; they didn't want to have more than one boarder, preferably none.

Eventually, he decided that one of the buildings in the area called Siberia would suit him and Gertrud best. It was on the outskirts of town, but it still wouldn't take him more than ten minutes to get to the stables. The site was open and healthy, next to the undeveloped hills called Vanadislunden on the map. The roads were slushy it was true; at times they were more like rivers than streets. But it was like that everywhere on the outskirts. Eventually the city would have to do something for all the people living there.

Rudolf told Gertrud about his plans. She thought it would be exciting to move, almost like emigrating.

He rented a room and kitchen in a backyard house on the Geten block on Tulegatan. Despite the fact that it wasn't completely finished, more than three thousand people were already living in the one-hundred-meter-wide and two-hundred-meter-long block. The population of an entire small town found rooms in the cluster of workers' barracks. In addition, there was space for some small industries and workshops in the middle of the block. Gertrud didn't see the apartment before she moved in. It was hard for her to leave the children and it was a long way away.

The impending move gave rise to many discussions and a lot of sorting out. What should Gertrud take of the small amount the siblings had inherited? Emelie understood that her sister wanted to take the dresser which, without question, was their most valuable possession. Their mother had received it from their grandmother as a wedding gift. It was sturdy and heavy, with thick round blocks for legs and three good-sized drawers. It was certainly Gertrud who needed the dresser most, so she should have it. And the fold-out sofa that turned into the bed Emelie and Gertrud had slept in for so many years, and that Gertrud's little girls now used. Olof slept on the wooden sofa; that would stay. Dishes, silverware and household items they would divide up. Gertrud could take the larger of the rag rugs.

While Emelie helped her sister pack, she felt like moving too, getting a place of her own. Their relationships had, of course, changed since they moved into Thumbs'. At that time, the orphaned siblings had been young and needed help. Now they were grown and should be able to take care of themselves. Emelie had a secure position; Olof had been working for a few months at the Bölmark lamp factory on Högberggatan. And even if unemployment was still high, everyone talked about the good times that were expected to come.

Emelie toyed with the thought—a place of her own. But it had to be close so she wouldn't be too far from Bärta. Now Emelie could watch Bärta's—and August's—son, sometimes. More and more she felt responsible for Gunnar. It just happened, without her wanting it that way. Besides, maybe she would be obliged to move. Knutte was seeing a girl and Emelie suspected they were expecting a child. In that case, they would need the kitchen to live in.

But now they were concerned with Rudolf and Gertrud. Emelie had to put away her own worries and hopes to share those of her sister. They had arranged for a horse and sleigh on a Sunday morning. Rudolf and Thumbs carried out the few pieces of furniture together. Gertrud and Emelie took the small items; the coachman piled these up and made them fast. A light snow fell, and Emelie was glad they had wrapped the dresser carefully in old newspapers and rags. Gertrud had seemed to think it was a little unnecessary.

When the load was ready, Thumbs invited his son and the coachman for a moving-day schnapps. Gertrud was going to go with the load, but it was too cold for the little girls. Emelie had promised to take them by streetcar up to "Siberia."

Everybody who was staying home stood out on the street and waved when the sleigh began to glide down the hill. Bärta came running from Mom's cottage, and children peered from doorways and holes in fences to see what was happening. They saw the vehicle disappearing away toward Erstagatan—how it rocked and swayed.

A moment later, Emelie left with the little girls. Matilda cried when she hugged them. She would see them so seldom now. It was like losing them. She couldn't understand why Gertrud and Rudolf had to move out to Norr, so far away. But when Rudolf got something in his head, there was no stopping him.

Emelie held the three-year-old by the hand, carried the not yet two-year-old in her arms—Rudolf's children. And Gertrud's. Emelie didn't know if she was happy or sad at the parting. It had been hard to have Rudolf so close. But it was also hard to separate, to no longer hear the heavy, sure steps, to not get to see him everyday. She couldn't admit it, but knew that he still meant too much to her, that she couldn't pull her thoughts away from him.

Erstagatan went down between low, wooden houses and ramshackle stone hovels, down toward Folkungagatan's valley. The factory smokestack next to the washhouse stood without smoke, cold on a Sunday. The large pile of coal that stuck up over the edge of the nearby fence had been covered by snow, but here and there black crystals glinted from within. Beside the small triangle formed where the streets met down below, the streetcar waited. Emelie tried to hurry the three-year-old along so they wouldn't miss the streetcar.

The journey was long and difficult, with many transfers. Still, it wasn't so much longer to Siberia than to Stora Badstugatan where Emelie went every day. But the streetcars took a lot of long ways around, not least on hilly Söder. The horse-drawn cars took them all the way down Folkungagatan to Götgatan and from there through the narrow streets up to Adolf Fredrikstorg. Since they could change for free here, they waited for the steam streetcar and rode down to Slussen on it. They had to walk across the bridge to take the ring line on the other side of the canal at the locks. It carried them through the Old Town, past Central Station and along Barnhusgatan to the corner of Stora Badstugatan where Emelie's workplace lay. Then they changed to the churchyard line and traveled on to Surbrunnsgatan.

Emelie stood still, looking around, a little unsure of which road they should take. The city ended here. A deserted country road led across a white field, away toward bare cliffs and slopes with wintry black-twigged trees and bushes. A few low cattle sheds stood there, broken and empty. They would surely be torn down soon to clear for new construction. Emelie could guess now where her destination was; a group of high barracks stood strangely alone and created the city's outermost flank against the countryside.

That must be it. They came in on Tulegatan, a potholed road alongside the tall buildings. The road continued on up toward "the grove," where it trailed off and disappeared amidst snow-covered mounds of dirt.

An entryway led through the building on the street to a narrow courtyard that formed a small chasm between the building facing the street and the one facing the courtyard. Outside the block, the expanses stretched empty and deserted; here land had suddenly become expensive and utilized to the utmost. A long row of wooden houses had been squeezed into the barely fifteen-meter-wide space between apartment buildings. They were outhouses, door to door.

There was a rustling behind some of the grated windows; in an open doorway a group of kids was hanging out, around the trashcans the garbage lay in heaps. Emelie looked up at window after window, as if the chasm was filled with faces and voices. She felt oppressed, felt like it was hard to breathe—everything crowded so close together, impossible to escape. There was none of the calm and seclusion of their hill at home, no view, and surely not a patch of earth or blade of grass under the snow. Everything had been beaten down to stone, filled with life yet still so dead. Where could the people who lived here hide their secrets?

Another archway led to yet another courtyard beside the tightly packed, long, narrow workshops and storage sheds. In the center of the block, in the middle of the cluster of apartment houses, was an industrial area. The apartment was two stories up in the building facing the street, and had windows that looked onto the courtyard closest to the street. A passageway led to a cloakroom where three of the walls were made up of doors from the passage, to the room and to the kitchen. On the fourth wall, there were some hooks to hang clothes on.

The kitchen was also very small, hardly more than four square meters. Rudolf had bought an old wooden sofa that they carried in, then there was no more space. In a corner, was a cupboard they called the pantry. There was no ventilation, but there was a real wood stove and a relatively long counter.

The room was nice and large. They had placed everything from the moving van in it: a fairly wide bed Rudolf had been able to bring from home, the dresser, a table and four chairs. There was still room left over, and Emelie understood her sister's pride when she showed off the large space. From the room's window they could see into the apartment opposite—or down onto the outhouse roofs.

They helped each other unpack the boxes and put everything in order. Eventually it was evening and time for the little girls to sleep. Gertrud carried the kerosene lamp out of the room; the circle of light was moved into the kitchen. There Rudolf and the two sisters could sit on the wooden sofa and drink the coffee they had set out on the counter on the other long wall. The space between the sofa and the counter was so narrow that they only had to lean forward to reach it.

Gertrud had gotten a nice apartment, large and practical. A brass water reservoir shone beside the stove—you only had to open the tap to get hot water, if the stove was lit. And Gertrud wouldn't have to carry any heavy buckets; there was indoor water and plumbing. A miracle: only turn the faucet, you could waste as much as you wanted.

Still, Emelie felt like she didn't want to live here. She almost felt like it would feel good to leave and go home. Would Gertrud ever like it in this Siberia? Emelie doubted it.

Before she left the new tenants, Emelie looked in once more on the little girls. They lay on the foldout bed in the large, new room, seemed to be sleeping well. The window, that as yet had no curtain, shone black above them. Emelie looked out. The curtain was poorly drawn in the apartment opposite. A big, fat man with a naked upper body was walking through the room, pulling at his belt. His swaying belly glistened in the light of the kerosene lamp.

She left the window hastily, bumping into the made-up bed beside the foldout one. Tonight and all the nights in the future, Gertrud would lie there, in Rudolf's bed. Emelie pushed away the thought, was ashamed that she could think such things.

Rudolf was stubborn and insisted on giving her the streetcar fare for her trip home. When Emelie walked across the courtyard, the windows in the walls of the chasm shone everywhere. It's like walking inside a lantern, she thought. Gertrud waved from behind a closed window, they had already managed to seal it off against the draft so they wouldn't be able to open the window anymore this winter.

The kitchen on Åsöberget seemed cold and deserted now that Gertrud and her daughters and so much of the furniture was gone. Emelie lifted the lid of the wooden sofa so the bed would be ready when Olof arrived. He was out as usual. Emelie knew that she nagged, but he was weak and tired, should go to bed earlier, still hadn't turned fifteen. He wouldn't accept Emelie's attempts to be like a mother, he thought he was old enough to decide for himself.

She made up the bed she used to share with Gertrud. There was plenty of room now. She felt a moment's contentment: to avoid living in that dreary Siberia, to have a whole bed to herself and be able to stretch out. But when she stretched out, she grew cold. She curled up, didn't take up more space than she usually did. She knew she wouldn't be able to go to sleep before Olof got home. She lay there silently and felt alone, longed to be able to cry, to give up.

Perhaps Bärta's imagination got started when she heard them talk about Gertrud's new apartment. Gertrud and Rudolf had shown that it was possible to break away; whoever dared could succeed.

Bärta had gotten a job as a mortar girl again, on a large construction project that would last a long time. Johann had won his sought-after journeyman status and sent some money from time to time. He was going to find a way to come back to the city. And Bärta felt more and more like she couldn't stand to live much longer as she was living. It had become more intolerable than ever, since one of Johan's countless foster brothers had begun to pay attention to her. Only a puppy—but completely impossible. She could neither wash nor dress in peace. Even when she went to the outhouse, he was after her, had managed to poke out a knothole.

Bärta came to Emelie and complained. But from her complaining, from the dirt, the clamor and the rutting, came the bright dream: a real home. Couldn't they find something together? Maybe a room and a kitchen to share, Emelie and Olof could take the room, Bärta and Gunnar the kitchen. And then there would be room for Johan, too, if he managed to get work in town and didn't have to live in some chimney sweep accommodations.

Emelie was doubtful, she hadn't thought of doing that. Of course, she liked Bärta. Still, she hardly wanted to share a home with her, even less with Johan. She had had experience. Bärta wasn't always so careful about paying for herself, not even if it was possible. And Johan could be downright mean sometimes.

Gunnar, Bärta's five-year-old boy, came running into the kitchen whimpering, he had gotten in the way of one of the women in Mom's house. Bärta dried his wet and dirty face with her apron and swore at all the hussies. And Emelie realized that for Gunnar's sake something had to be done. Gunnar forced her to look seriously for a solution. But even if it was difficult for Bärta and Gunnar as things were, she couldn't lose her head. There had to be a good solution—something better than moving in together.

Emelie began to take different routes home from work. She made her way through narrow streets off the main ones she usually took. She looked at the signs that enticed her with apartments available, went into the houses and inquired.

But it was on Söder that she began taking detours. The sight of Siberia had robbed her of all desire to think of any other part of the city. Water and plumbing were nice, but she didn't necessarily want to live in a barracks. She pushed on energetically up steep Glasbruksbacken, passed by the Lindska gunpowder store beneath the elevator's steel skeleton, looked down the alley that had stairs up toward Mariagränd, turned back and continued up the uneven cobblestones. Stora Glasbruksgatan and the stairs off it were too narrow and dark, the old stone houses seedy-looking and unfamiliar. This couldn't be good for Olof, nor appropriate for Gunnar. On Rutens Lane there were no signs for rooms available, and not on Lilla Glasbruksgatan either. She hurried quickly past the Dihlström workhouse, wrinkling her nose fiercely; there was a sour odor of poverty and old clothing surrrounding the whole establishment. And Högbergsgatan? She went all the way to Häckelfjällsgränden far out on the edge of the hill. There was nothing there either. One more day without any new ideas.

Deep in thought, she turned back from the dead end, taking Fjällgatan eastward. She had walked here several evenings without finding anything, but now she saw a white slip of paper fluttering from a gate in a fence.

The house facing the street, which was a modest wooden house with a mansard roof, appeared inhabited. She pushed open the gate and looked in at the yard. A stone house stood there, two stories high plus an attic.

Beyond the yard's fence, the hill dropped steeply down to the water at Stadsgården. The lights of the shoreline shone between the fence slats.

The house's owner, an old steamboat captain, lived in the attic. From the dormer windows, he had a view over the yard and toward the inlet. Before he took the trouble to show her the available rooms on the ground floor he interviewed Emelie to ascertain her ability to pay for them. The most recent tenants had lived there for four months without paying, and then moved in the middle of the night. Just disappeared. He didn't want to experience that again, he would rather leave the rooms unrented.

He had trouble walking, tottered down the stairs using the banister and a cane. In the entryway on the bottom floor, there were three doors. One led to a slightly larger apartment, which was rented out. The others led to two single rooms, both with fireplaces. The family that had run away had extravagantly rented both rooms.

This was just about what Emelie had been hoping for: close proximity to Bärta but still on her own. She followed the old man in and looked at the rooms. One had a view of the yard, and you could see a little of the drop off beyond, but to see a spot of water you probably had to lean out the window. The other room had a window in the gable. You could see a glimpse of city in the distance and water when you stood on your toes. If you sat down, the beautiful view disappeared behind the fence that stood there as protection against the precipice. The yearly rent was seventy kronor for each room. There was an outhouse and running water in the yard.

The rooms were dirty, one windowpane broken. It felt cold since no one had lighted a fire for several days. Still, Emelie felt like she would like it here, she could certainly make it look nice and the house was sturdy and retained heat well, according to the captain.

Could she come back in an hour? Could he hold onto the rooms until then?

That was fine. He hung the keys on a nail in the entryway. They could take them and look for themselves, then he wouldn't have to walk down the stairs unnecessarily.

They made up their minds that evening. Emelie had borrowed money from Matilda so she could pay the first month's rent for both of them. The captain was very happy and declared they were just the sort of tenants he wanted.

Emelie's decision meant increased expenses for Thumbs' family, but also some relief. Knutte and his girlfriend needed a cheap place to live—that was obvious now.

But it was a little difficult to part. Emelie and Olof had become children of the household. And inside Thumbs there was still an absurd thought that he tried to defend himself against: that he owed a debt to Emelie for what had happened with August. The girl had never really forgiven him, he felt. Maybe he had gone at August unnecessarily hard, gotten involved in something he should have stayed out of—for her sake. But he couldn't start asking to be excused, pride and class feeling got in the way. Still, he had thought that sometime he should say something that showed he understood her—explain that he hadn't wanted to drive August away. If he didn't get it said before she moved, he would never get around to it, he knew. Something unresolved would always stand between them.

Sometimes Thumbs felt like he wanted to go to Matilda and ask her to intervene. But at the same time, it irritated him that he had to capitulate in that way, it would be saying that Matilda had been right and he had been wrong. And he had handled it correctly; it was only the result of how he handled it that had turned out wrong.

The winter storms were howling through drafty windows and leaky joints of houses. The chains on the pontoon bridge at the Maria elevator were torn off, water flooded the bakeries down at Fiskarhamnen, a tree fell over in the yard outside Mom's house.

But Thumbs walked through the wind, pulling a cart. He had sacrificed half a day's work to struggle out to an auction at Liljeholmen. He came back with a dresser he had bid on for two kronor, and stayed in the shed a whole day planing and polishing it. The dresser was his and Matilda's farewell gift to Emelie and Olof, but it was Matilda who took

Emelie out to the work shed to show her the gift. Thumbs disappeared to Masis Knosis and sat grumbling over a tall drink and a piece of sausage. He didn't return until he was sure Emelie was asleep, was ashamed of himself—sentimental as a schoolteacher. But he was still content, it felt like the dresser filled a breach, settled a debt. Now he wouldn't have to say anything.

THE HIDING PLACE

Low houses, mostly of stone, edged the cobblestone-paved Fjällgatan. Gas lanterns stretched out arms of iron. The bakery in number 10 beckoned with two shiny golden pretzels. Sturdy trees raised their knotty black branches and twiggy tops like pen and ink drawings over roofs and fences.

One side of the street had stone sidewalks, and the inhabitants thought these gave the whole area a socially elevated appearance. On slushy days when mud ran down around the bend to Renstjärnasbacken, they could walk with almost dry shoes on the protective stones.

Down there, after the street followed a gentle curve along the edge of the hill, a wide vista of the water and the city suddenly opened up. There was only the kiosk at Söderberg's stairs—a gilded chicken coop that stood in the way.

But the idyll ended suddenly here, too. Right beside the low, red wooden house at number 12, a new apartment building rose up like an enormous giant over a band of dwarves. It was number 12 B and made of stone, the corner building for a wide street that was planned to replace the bumpy, crooked Renstjärnasbacken. The apartment building was a forerunner of new times, a messenger who brought the message that the idyll was doomed. But the messenger was far ahead of its time, and no new buildings would be connected to its expectant fireproof gables.

Bärta felt like she had stepped into a new world: clean, light and sheltered. She was so eager to move from Mom's cramped hovel that, after only two days, she showed up with her son and a mattress on a cart that she pulled herself. She moved in first and scrubbed it out later, even if the room was dirty, it was still cleaner than at Mom's.

Emelie wasn't in as much of a hurry. She began by cleaning. Olof helped her carry out trash that the previous tenants had left behind. Then she patched the wallpaper and went up to the White Hills and cut a hazel wand large enough for a curtain rod. They also bought a little paint and painted the doors and window mullions and whitewashed the fireplace.

On Sunday afternoon Bärta received guests. She had told her work-mates about her new home, and had lamented the fact that she didn't have any furniture. Now some of the brick carriers arrived pulling a large wagon laden with empty crates and pieces of fencing. They pulled out hammers and saws and some paper cones full of nails and set to work. One crate became a cupboard with wooden boards for shelves; they took apart other crates and made a table out of them. A pair of sawhorses with a plank across them—and Bärta had places to sit, too. In a few hours the whole room was furnished. It wasn't beautiful but Bärta was beside herself with joy.

Now they could set the table. A piece of smoked sausage, some herring, a loaf of bread. And schnapps, of course.

Bärta went into the room next door to get Emelie and Olof. Olof had already left. But Emelie, who had just given up working because of the darkness, and was hanging up cleaning rags to dry, went back with her.

Bärta's room lay beside the yard. It didn't have a fireplace, but had a ceramic stove instead. In it scraps of the brick carriers' crates now burned, over the fire hung the smoked sausage skewered on a steel wire. Since Bärta had only two plates, they had salvaged a few pieces of wood and placed them on the table, too. She had three cups and two glasses; they were set out.

Emelie was a little frightened by the scene at first: the dark room, three strange men in rough work clothes, the bottles of alcohol. But the men were friendly, exhilarated from the unusual work and by Bärta, who was in radiant good humor and tireless as far as joking and flirting went.

Emelie admired their work, a little amazed: so fast and so much. Now Bärta didn't need more than a bed, and it was furnished.

The men had been subdued a little by Emelie's wariness, now they thawed again, boasting and laughing. They became a little ceremonious: she should try out the new countertop, say what she thought, was it too high or too low? They served her bread and sausage, but when they

wanted to pour her a whole cup of aquavit, she protested: no, no she did-
n't want to get out of hand. But for the sake of keeping them company she
took a few drops.

Gunnar was called in from the street. He had begun getting to know
the kids on the block. He came against his will, a little afraid of the strange
men. Emelie asked him to get a stump of candle from her room. One of
the brick carriers lit the candle and stuck it to the tabletop with a few
drops of wax. The boy crawled up onto the counter, for safety he placed
himself beside Emelie. He received a bit of sausage on a piece of a board
they said was a plate. He ate quietly and quickly. He knew he should eat
while there was something to eat. It was unclear whether he would get to
hold onto it. The sooty sausage blackened his face, and the brick carriers
said that it sure showed that Gunnar was a real chimney sweep's boy. At
this, Bärta glanced quickly at Emelie—and then she laughed and said that
if anything, the boy should at least take after his own father. Emelie did-
n't really like that joke, but Gunnar sat silently and seemed to not hear
that they were talking about him. He stared into the flickering flames and
wondered if they were alive, they moved so, almost dancing. When he felt
sleepy after a moment, he slid down from the countertop and went and lay
on the mattress on the floor, where he fell asleep while the aquavit in the
bottles went down, and his mother and the strange men grew even nois-
ier. Just before he drifted off, he felt how someone tucked him in, felt a
hand stroke his hair. He realized it was Emelie, and felt safe knowing that
she would be so close by now. He snuggled down, let out a contented
fart—and slept.

The brick carriers were friendly and decent fellows, only boys really.
They already had hands that were as big and hard as clubs. They were used
to being plain-spoken, the ears of the mortar girls had had to grow used to
almost anything. Emelie, who lived in a somewhat more polished world,
was horrified at times, and was glad the room was dark. But she couldn't
dislike them—couldn't feel indignant. She thought from time to time, of
course, that maybe she'd better leave. Still, she stayed. It would be
unfriendly to leave already, seem like she didn't like the company. And

perhaps it wasn't so wise to leave Bärta alone with the three men who were beginning to act pretty drunk.

Sitting beside her on the bench was the one called "Twelve Shilling." He had placed his strong arm around her waist, taking hold of her tightly with his hand. Carefully but firmly she had removed his arm a few times— but finally given up. And it did feel good to have some support on the backless bench. But it didn't feel only like a support for her body. In some way, she got to be small—rely on somebody else's strength. The nearness of the strange man gave her a sense of security that she hadn't felt all the long, difficult time since her mother's death. She was always obligated to be the support herself, sometimes longed to give up the forced confidence and curl up against someone who was able to accept her. What she longed for no longer existed, not for her. This man was only a replacement, someone who reminded her of someone else.

He dug in his pants pockets, pulled out something that he held hidden in his hand. Did she want to see? He slowly opened his hand, as if for just a peek, letting the pale light from the lamp shine on a little brooch with glittering stones. A cheap thing, maybe he had taken it from one of the mortar girls, but it sparkled gaily.

He was going to give this to Emelie, just because she was pretty. He wanted to fasten it on her blouse, fumbling with his hands. Suddenly, she felt moved and grateful; hardly anyone had given her anything before, and, in any case, never for this reason. She turned toward him saying, put it on my cardigan. No, a brooch should be on a blouse. She unbuttoned a few of the buttons on the thick cardigan, blushed, felt like it was like getting undressed. She felt his hand over her breast, how it stopped and rested a moment. Still, she wasn't frightened, somehow his hand was safely big and awkward. He had difficulty fastening the pin, she had to help him. His hand was rough from brick dust, split and sore.

"Look at that," he said. "Look how it shines!"

She let her hand remain in his, not wanting to seem ungrateful by drawing it away, but when he wanted her to sit on his knee she said no, there was a limit. Then he satisfied himself with coming closer and taking hold of her waist again. She let it happen, sat quietly in the shadows and let him stay beside her. The closeness of the large, strange man: like a cave. Just to get to sit there, hidden, without responsibility and worry.

That was what she wished for right now, nothing else, nothing more. But for him, it wasn't enough. The man's eagerness and agitation grew, the hand that had held her by the waist wandered, searching for her breast. His agitation forced her to unwillingly pull away from her hiding place and return to her unprotected state. What had just been a sheltering embrace was turning into a dangerous trap; his hands were becoming hard, desperate. She sat caught, and struggled to get free. The hand on her breast gripped her like an iron vise, the other hand took hold of her thigh. He almost tipped her over and his hungry face, shining eyes, and drooling mouth came even closer.

She hadn't wanted to scream—but now she screamed.

"Take it easy," his friends said. "The girl doesn't want to."

Finally he released her, as if coming to. It was time to leave, his friends said. Tomorrow was another day and they had a long way home.

Emelie undid the pin of the little piece of jewelry he had given her. When Twelve Shilling reached out his hand to say good-bye she handed him the brooch. He backed up. No, she shouldn't do that. She shouldn't take it that way. Couldn't she be kind and keep it?

He asked so beseechingly that at last she gave in, perhaps out of fatigue, just to make him go. But this time he didn't get to fasten on the brooch, she did it herself and on the outside of her sweater.

Finally they left. Twelve Shilling stood waving at the gate while Emelie closed the door of the house.

"They're nice guys," Bärta said. "But they die young—it's not so strange if they want to have a little fun before the brick dust gets them."

Emelie waited a little while so the men would have time to disappear before she went out to the street. No Twelve Shilling was in sight, and she hurried down the hill, past number 12, and out onto the road toward Ersta and Åsöberget. Olof was asleep when she came home. She made sure his clothes were clean and tidy. She had to darn a little hole in his sock before she went to bed. When she undressed in the light, she pulled her camisole aside to look at her breast—large red marks. Tomorrow they would surely be blue.

Despite everything, she laughed a little to herself. She hadn't really been afraid, even when she screamed. Even when his hand had hurt, she had felt a strange safety. Then she recalled Bärta's words about the brick dust. Weakness and death inside the strong and the living. Danger in the midst of safety.

It was all so complicated and contradictory. So little one really understood. Was a grave the only safe hiding place? She lay awhile and thought in the darkness without finding any answer. Then she suddenly fell asleep, as if on a bed of rustling, unanswered questions.

A few days later Emelie and Olof moved into their new home. Thumbs and Matilda came along and helped them. Emelie had bought a table and some chairs at a junkshop. And she still had the wooden sofa and the bed—and Thumbs' dresser. That was enough to furnish with. She invited them all for coffee. Bärta and Gunnar joined them. They sat in the light of the kerosene lamp.

Olof had a hard time sitting still with the others. During the move, the paints and brushes he had received from Gullpippi had reappeared. Now he felt like trying to paint. He would have liked it if the guests had left so he could sit down at the table and start right away. He had never liked waiting. Time felt short to him, so many hours wasted working, so few left for living. And then Emelie would say they should go to sleep. He had no time to sleep, no time to sit and talk around the table over coffee. Something was hurrying him, he didn't know exactly what. When they were little, they played that they were riding under sealed secret orders. He was still doing that; the orders were secret, but he rode on, felt like he wanted to gallop so he would get there faster—but where?

Finally they left. In spite of Emelie's protests, he sat down with a paper and pencil, drew the kerosene lantern and the coffee cups and objected, annoyed, when Emelie cleared the table of his motifs. He stayed sitting where he was while she made the beds and lay down, muttering at her not to nag, he wasn't tired.

She turned her head to the wall, closed her eyes. She heard him coughing from time to time, was so used to it that she almost thought it was a part of him, missed it when he was out. Now, the first evening in their own home, she didn't want to let in any unsettling thoughts. She already liked the little room a lot; they had made it clean and light and pretty.

Safe, protected, it wasn't so easy to find what was hidden within the confines of their fence. Here, she could escape from the din and the clamor of the city. She didn't have to worry, she had done the best she could. Mama would have been pleased.

But Olof shouldn't be coughing like that—shouldn't sit up so late. Despite it going against her nature, she had to nag, really say it sharply this time. Then he finally gave up, crumpled the drawing angrily, and threw it into the fire.

He would continue, would learn to draw and paint. Even if he had to sit up all night long, every night. Emelie couldn't confine him in the long run. He was still the more stubborn of the two, that much he knew. Right now the orders were not completely sealed, instead they were open and clear: use the paints, make something real with them, but hurry, hurry.

He went out into the yard for a minute before he went to bed. While he stood there and took care of his needs, he saw the smouldering, glittering lights shining through the mist across the water, the matt, black shadows of the boat hulls sleeping along the shore, the barbed towers beneath the clouds' gray-blue downy puffs.

He would paint all of it. Exactly as it was, dark as hell, peppered with small angry splashes of light. Surely nobody had painted anything like this before.

ARTHUR WITH
THE HAIR

The winter had been mild, the snow disappeared early and all the imperfections of the city were revealed in the brilliant sunlight. The usual spring cleanup had begun. The wooden docks and stairs along Stadsgården were repaired. The old Dutch windmill on Ölandsgatan disappeared to reappear at Frösunda several miles out of town. The washhouses at Norrström below Rosenbad were torn down, and stones were being laid for the new quay.

The streets dried up, more and more bicyclists wobbled along between wagons and handcarts. Now even the delivery agencies had begun to send their packages via two-wheelers. The boys cycled lightning fast through the streets with bags of parcels dangling from their backs. Many were drunk on the thrill of speed; collisions and accidents with two wheelers happened every day. The authorities were worried by this new and dangerous haste, and forbade all bicycle riders on most streets with other traffic.

While everything was happening, while the city was teaming with life, Olof stood at the lamp factory and longed to get out. He had to force himself to stay and rub and polish the endless brass knobs. He knew how much a steady job was worth, how worried and unhappy he had been when he had been forced to go around like a beggar and beg for work. He repressed these wishes and stayed. He rubbed angrily and energetically, pretended not to see how the sunlight undulated on the wall in from of him.

Olof was an assistant. If he did well, he would get into the galvanizing division, it had been said. That was where they did nickel, copper, zinc, brass, silver, and gold plating. They disguised, corrupted and destroyed, he thought, feeling sick and tired of shiny surfaces. If he could have chosen he would have requested to be placed in the glass-painting atelier. But only women worked there, five girls from Dalarna under the direction of Miss Dragon. They sat there and painted views of the city, Nordic gods, and Swedish kings, and bards on shades and lamp bases. The apprentices, who would have liked to stop by and chat with the lively girls, claimed they were guarded by the dragon.

One evening, Olof had painted his own motif on the white shade of the kerosene lamp at home, a motif from the street outside. He had done at least fifty sketches first and was still not satisfied with the result; he didn't seem to have the right colors. Emelie insisted it was beautiful, but she didn't get it. He was going to wash off the whole mess.

As soon as his workday was finished, he hurried home, bolted some food, and took off. He had brushes and a bundle of small sheets of cheap paper he had bought in his pocket. He filled one page after another with quick sketches, but everything he did was wrong, he thought. And every evening he emptied his pockets of the failed drawings, burned them in the open fireplace. Some of the drawings he could still spare. There was, despite everything, a true line, a detail he could accept. These pictures went into the dresser drawer, were saved to be brought out again another evening—and rejected.

He saw in his head how it would look, should look. It was only a question of getting it down on paper—so simple. But on the way there the vision disappeared, the fantasy refused to become reality, there were only a few dead lines on the white surface of the paper.

And he who had been in such a hurry. A few evenings he was down at Norrbro, went behind the row of stalls in the bazaar, and saw how all the old dilapidated houses had disappeared. Only a long stable was left as an office for the city planner. People wandered around and rooted among the remains of the houses, as if they thought some treasure had been left behind. He tried to capture the lines of a young couple under a split, but still leafing, tree, and of the food stand that had been set up in the ruins. But nothing came of it, as usual—nothing. He returned to the bridge, hung over the railing, tried to draw the fisherman with a net and his boat, the snobbish dandies strolling about, the old blind man, Wiman, standing on the stairs to Strömparterren selling toys. Even though it was hopeless, even though nothing came to anything.

At the foot of the bridge by the square, a skinny youth with a large shock of wild hair stood selling small painted copies of well-known paintings. At first he felt a certain amount of contempt. He would never think of making copies. He looked for things nobody had seen. Maybe the motifs he chose were ordinary, but the impression given by the images would be completely different, something new.

But he had snuck a few glances at the light-haired fellow's copies, and could see, had to admit, that they were well executed, were real. That other artist knew something that Olof had not yet attained: technique, craftsmanship. He was probably a few years older.

One evening as Olof stood, as usual, sketching by the railing, someone clapped him on the shoulder. He quickly hid his drawing. It was the young man with the unruly hair standing there.

"Let's see, Man," he said. "What are you slaving away at?"

"Just junk, nothing really."

Unwillingly he showed him the sketch, was embarrassed. He could see himself how unsuccessful it was. The long-haired kid took his time before he said anything. He screwed up one eye, pretended to draw an erring line with his finger, looked again. "It's not quite there," he said, "but there's something in it. Let's go have a beer, I've sold a few pieces."

The beer hall lay in one of the alleys down by Skeppsbron, was mostly a haunt for the wage-slaves on the docks. They sat in clusters around brown stained tables teasing a monkey who hissed angrily at their fingers. The animal's owner, an Italian with an accordion, pretended not to notice anything, sat alone quietly huddled in a corner, and drank.

Olof knew that he really should have gone straight home. Now Emelie would get annoyed and nag because he came home late. But he had been caught off guard, gone along even though he had worried that he would be kicked out because he was only a kid. The fat woman serving had not even seen him; she had only put out the two drinks Arthur had ordered.

Olof's new friend told him he was called Arthur with the Hair. The surname was natural; nobody could avoid noticing his abundant locks. They were a grayish yellow and gone wild, neither cut nor combed.

Arthur supported himself by making painted copies of famous paintings. He had done this for many years, beginning when he was barely more than ten, though sometimes he ran errands for his father—the old man was a shoemaker. The copies, or cards as he called them, were only a means of livelihood. Sometimes he had sold drawings to the Sunday paper and other newspapers. That was what he would rather be doing.

While Arthur talked, his pencil glided across a piece of Olof's paper. The Italian with the accordion and the monkey appeared there, but everything as if seen in a mirror with wavy glass, so real and yet so changed.

Fascinated, Olof followed the pencil's movements, the marks it left behind. He would like to draw just like that, so confident, as if without any difficulties. What came from Arthur's pencil was complete, it existed and had life.

He pulled his own drawings out of his pocket, placed them out on the table, leafed through them until he found what he himself felt was the best one. What had he done wrong? Why didn't it turn out right? Arthur glanced at it quickly, changed a line, added another, and made the dead come to life.

"You're a little too hesitant," he said. "Just draw it. You have it in your fingers."

Olof tried to follow his advice. There was the fat lady lumbering along with a tray full of bottles. Arthur squinted at it again, lifted his pencil, drew a line on Olof's sketch, and then the old woman was an exact likeness, with the swelling backside she had. Olof shouted with the joy of recognition, and from the shock he received as the woman on his paper suddenly came to life.

He would never be as good as Arthur, not so self-assured. He looked admiringly at his new friend. Small and wiry. If it hadn't been for his hair you would hardly have noticed him. Arthur was seventeen, only two years older than himself. But for Olof he was already a wise master, a teacher. He had to meet with him again, learn more. But another day, now Olof didn't dare sit there any longer.

Together they walked to Söder, where they both lived. The gaslights flickered, shone from the dark of the alleys, and created a stripe of yellow light along the quay at Skeppsbron. When they reached Brunnsbacken, they could see the long rowing of glimmering windows in the Pelikan Restaurant; the veranda of the dining room hung like a large glowing lantern over the dark Järngraven. The night lay over the water like a blue mist, a feather-light down coverlet that as yet concealed the next day.

There, at Pelikan, they would sit someday and celebrate properly, said Arthur. When they became famous artists, like that guy Larsson who had an atelier on Stora Glasbruksgatan. They walked past number 15 where the great man lived and Arthur said they should pay homage to art by bowing deeply before the closed door. This they did—and the door swung open. A young woman stepped out, looked surprised at the two youths and burst into laughter. As they continued up the hill, Arthur said that must have been one of the great artist's models. They walked along silently and solemnly. The gaslights of the lane and the night sky, even all of life, had a red cast to it, a shimmer of a naked young woman, maybe the model of the great artist, maybe the goddess of the future and of success.

But in the room on Fjällgatan, Emelie waited, angry and worried. Of course, she was happy when Olof arrived, that nothing dangerous had happened. But furious, too, that he—just a boy—had sat and hung out in a beer hall half the night. Didn't he know how worried she had been? And how would he manage his work if he was so careless? Besides, he had to take care of himself, he understood that.

As long as she argued, he could handle it. It was worse when she grew silent and looked sad. He knew how well she meant, but he had to exercise his right to lead his own life. He tried to tell her about Arthur, hoped she would understand how important the meeting had been. From

Arthur, he could learn what he needed to know, maybe become an artist, like that.... But Emelie didn't want to hear: artist! What was he thinking? And was it any job you could live on? She had seem some strange-looking characters standing in the lanes painting—real ragamuffins.

He was going to paint. She could say what she wanted. And he had to meet Arthur again.

Emelie understood that a new era had begun. Olof wasn't a child any longer; she would have a harder time stopping him. Soon Olof would not allow her to carry out Mama's last wish.

It didn't turn out to be so calm and peaceful here in their new home, not as she had imagined. She understood that, now. And, evening after evening, she had to admit it. He took his time, was out with that new acquaintance, smelled like beer, was tired and crabby in the morning so that she almost had to pull him out of bed. And when she admonished and pleaded, he didn't listen, then she had to nag and argue, almost scream with despair and anger.

If it went on like this, they would become enemies in earnest, and he would move away from her. She had to resign herself, let him keep it up: make sure that he was neat and clean, try to get some food in him, wake him up on time for work. Everything became just routine and boring tasks, nothing gave joy or hope. And he went along with a guilty conscience because he took so much and gave so little in exchange. She toiled for him—and he couldn't even try to make her happy by coming home at a decent time in the evening. Because he knew it was a tug-of-war. If he gave in, she would haul in the rope—hold on to him even closer, tighter. With her care she tried to get him to give up some of the freedom he had taken for himself. He couldn't and wouldn't, no matter how ungrateful it seemed. He didn't intend to live a calm and quiet life behind the fence— sleep away his life.

A few times Arthur came home with him. Emelie fixed them a meal, and the two youths sat out in the yard afterward and looked down over the city. Emelie tried to be friendly toward Arthur, but couldn't really manage it. To her it seemed as if he had corrupted Olof. And she was irritated by his uncut and uncombed hair, by the enormous scarf Arthur had bought and thrown around his neck, by his gestures and expressions—even by the drawings he did. His people were ugly and deformed, she thought, disgusting and unhealthy. What he drew showed who he was: a dangerous and unsuitable companion for Olof.

Restlessness had arrived with Arthur. Frightened and at the same time fascinated, she noticed how this restlessness seemed to unleash something in Olof, something that agreed with the boy's way of thinking and being. Against her will, she had to admit that he had never seemed as happy as he was now. And so tireless. Evening after evening, he sat up at the table with his sketches, despite his coming home so late. She couldn't wait up for him anymore, and fell asleep, waking with the feeling that she had failed the impossible responsibility she had inherited. She wondered what Mama would have done, if she would have had the energy to put a check on Olof's happiness and ruin.

TWELVE SHILLING'S FATE

He had come to the city in the middle of the worst unemployment, when the city's own inhabitants were fighting by the thousands for any job. The slow and slightly shy country boy was pushed out of all the lines, shoved to the side by those who were quicker and more desperate.

But he was tenacious, didn't give up, just kept on coming back. Patient and hardy, sleeping out-of-doors or in barns on the outskirts of town, getting by on the food coupons he received when he sawed wood at the Salvation Army. At least once a week he went to the Salvation Army's bath and delousing facility. It cost fifteen öre to have his clothes "burned" and his body clean. And he had to keep on moving; once there, eighty bath guests had to be admitted during one hour.

Now he had turned twenty and gotten work as a brick carrier. The profession suited him, big and strong as he was. He had answered, "A twelve-shilling piece will do," when the boss had asked what wage he required per hour, and so he got his name.

Twelve Shilling had no relatives in the city and no other acquaintances other than his workmates. There weren't very many of them who had the time or desire to give the silent boy any of their free time. He ended up alone—if he wasn't satisfied with the companionship he got at the boardinghouse where he now lived. But he didn't go there before it was time to go to bed.

The boardinghouse was called Hotell Kalmar and lay on Ferkens Lane. It was one of the seedier ones, but Twelve Shilling had grown used to it and felt at home there. It was cheap, twenty-five öre a night, and as an old regular he had gotten one of the better sofas. He shared it with a bedmate, often a new one every night. The hotel owner was a beer bootlegger, selling different kinds of drinks down at the harbor.

The girl who did the cleaning was a whore who lived together with other drunken prostitutes in the apartment above the boardinghouse.

They seldom had to take the trouble to go out on the street, and got their customers from the hotel instead.

The women both attracted and scared Twelve Shilling. He was terrified that they were diseased, the other boarders talked about it often. They were insolent, and louse-ridden, and anything but beautiful. The one who swept away the worst of the dirt and changed the sheets from time to time was called "Magpie" because she tended to steal. She had to do the cleaning for free since the landlord figured it gave her many opportunities for income. But it was mostly new arrivals and temporary guests who jumped at the bait. The regulars thought she was too stingy and too quick, didn't even want to take the time to take her customers upstairs, preferring instead to fall onto the closest bed. She was in as much of a hurry as the Salvation Army's bath supervisors.

Twelve Shilling had pinched the prostitutes a little, felt each one, but then backed off. Even though he was alone and longed for women, the whores disgusted him. He held higher hopes for the mortar girls. At least some of them were young and cheerful. He could be a little forward in his shy clumsiness; he chuckled to himself, a little abashed. But the mortar girls had other favorites who were more fun than Twelve Shilling. One of them had given him a real horse kick in the crotch.

Then he had been invited to go along to Bärta's. He had had too much to drink there, more than he was used to. Maybe so he could talk to the girl who had come in. He had given her the brooch he bought. The other brick carriers fastened the sacks they slung over their shoulders with cheap jewelry they had pilfered from the mortar girls; he wanted to pretend that he too had had his conquests.

He had begun so well, had fastened the brooch on the girl's blouse, and felt her breast, had held her even though she had resisted at first. But then he had almost become crazed from having her so close—squeezed her much too tight. He shouldn't have drunk so much. She wasn't like the prostitutes or the mortar girls. She was more delicate, more refined—was everything he had dreamed of.

Eagerness and drunkenness had ruined it for him.

Eagerness was against his nature. He was slow and cautious when he was sober, but stubborn. Emelie had moved his hand away from her waist, but the hand had come back, time after time, slowly and discreetly, but tirelessly.

He could be pushed away. But he came back.

He still hadn't dared go visit her. He wanted her to forget first, not remember too clearly what had happened. He began by going past the house where she lived every evening in order to get used to the idea that he would dare walk up to it, that she might come out. He was lucky or unlucky—she wasn't visible, he was able to accustom himself in peace.

When summer arrived, he had worked for several months and been able to afford a used suit. Maybe a bit on the small side, but it was almost all the clothes he could get hold of. The jacket arms and trouser legs looked too short, his shoulders were really straining the fabric, and he could hardly button the waistband of the trousers. Still, he looked dressed up, looked at his reflection in all the darkened store windows, smoothed down his hair in front. Magpie, who sensed there was some capital to be had, was all over him, but he pushed her aside.

Twelve Shilling walked out into the summer light with confident and determined steps. Magpie's interest was probably a good sign, and for a moment, he was able to feel irresistible in his new suit. Glasbruksbacken's steep incline dampened some of his presumption, it was heavier going, his steps became somewhat less confident. But his suit gave him the courage to open the gate on Fjällgatan.

He looked in and found the yard empty. He slowly closed the gate behind him and walked across the yard and into the entryway. He could still avoid defeat, return to Magpie who would welcome him gratefully. But he summoned his nerve and knocked, as softly and carefully as he could, pulling a paper cone of candies from his jacket pocket.

Emelie started. Who could that be pounding on the door? Quickly, she picked up the socks she had been darning, stuffed them into a basket and placed her apron on top. She smoothed her hair. She didn't want to admit it, but she felt some hope and gladness—what if it was Rudolf? He usually knocked hard. Why had he come? Was something wrong with Gertrud? She opened the door so fast that Twelve Shilling jumped back. Surprised, she looked at him, as if she didn't recognize him at first.

He extended the candies and said these are for you. Emelie accepted them and thanked him. Didn't know exactly what she should say.

It was a beautiful evening, Twelve Shilling said, and stood there in the entryway. Wouldn't she like to take a walk?

Emelie, who wondered if she dared let him in, thought the suggestion was a good one. Then she wouldn't have to be unfriendly nor would she be acting incautiously. And the evening was truly beautiful and warm.

Perhaps he could wait in the yard while she freshened up?

She closed the door and stood still a moment, pondering. Would she regret this? But going out just one evening didn't mean that she would have to see him again—if she didn't want to.

She started to hurry. It was fun to have him show up, that somebody wanted her company. Twelve Shilling freed her, allowed her to slip away from all her duties, be young.

She pulled off her work dress, looked critically at her simple white camisole and everyday bloomers. It didn't really matter what she wore underneath, but still she wanted to be well dressed. He would have to wait a little, but he was comfortable where he was sitting. She half ran to the dresser, found a pair of light colored cotton stockings and changed everything. She was in a hurry to tuck in all the billowing white fabric, pull tight her corset strings, straighten the wide embroidered camisole straps over her shoulder, pull the lacy bloomers down over her knees, get the petticoats to sit well on top of each other. Then she put on the fine white blouse and her best skirt, combed her hair and fastened it with some hairpins. Lastly, she put the stiff, varnished hat with flowers on her head. Now she was as finely dressed as she could be.

She sailed out into the yard. Twelve Shilling, who was sitting on the stairs to the privy, got up quickly, gaping—wasn't sure at first that it was really

Emelie who came out. Was it true that he was going to get to go out with this fine lady?

Quiet and shy, he walked along beside her, with a feeling that he had made a mistake, met someone other than the one he had intended to meet.

So, where had he thought they should go?

He didn't know. She probably knew better than he did.

They continued along Fjällgatan to the vantage point from Söderberg's Stairs, stood a moment at the railing, and looked down over the city. The evening breeze gently puffed out the sleeves of Emelie's blouse, made the bows flutter. Twelve Shilling stood with his hands hanging heavily from his jacket sleeves, looked at her skirt flowing over her hips, the unbelievably small waist. He would have liked to hold her the way he did the other time. But then it had been dark, and he had drunk enough to gain courage.

Renstjärnsgatan was pot-holed and dusty. She held up her skirt with one hand and held onto his arm with the other for support. He liked that, it made him feel more confident. He helped her along, trying to avoid garbage heaps and thickets of nettles.

By the time the lane disappeared as they walked up into the White Hills, their restraint had vanished and they talked like friends. People were sitting here and there on the grassy slope, many with picnic baskets. Despite its beginning to grow late, they stayed, and children played and romped in the light dusk.

Should they sit down and rest a little while, he asked.

Emelie looked a little worriedly at the green grass, afraid of getting stains on her skirt. Then he pulled off his jacket, spread it out and invited her to sit. No, she didn't want to do that, it was a pity to ruin the jacket. He tried to insist, but, of course, was really glad when she sat on the grass. He folded up his jacket carefully and sat down beside her.

Wasn't he going to wear the jacket?

No, he wasn't cold.

If he didn't mind, maybe she could place it over her shoulders. It had grown a little cooler.

Delighted, he spread the jacket over her shoulders, tucking it around her carefully. She couldn't stop him from holding onto his own jacket? Pleased, he placed his hand on her waist.

She pretended not to notice anything, rustled around in the cone of candies she had received, offered him one. He chewed, noticed that the family sitting closest to them was packing up, and pulled her a little closer. She sighed, as if she was tired, and gave in to his stubbornness. Then she leaned against him, made herself a little more comfortable, closed her eyes. His hand wanted to slowly make its way up to her breast, but she took hold of it, pushed it back to her waist.

"We'll sit just like this," she said. "It's so nice to just sit."

And it was, of course. Just sit—and feel her so close. He stayed quiet and she didn't say anything, either. For a moment he wondered if she had maybe fallen asleep. It would be so nice if she slept here against him.

But right after that, she got up and said she had probably better go back, otherwise, her brother would come home and wonder where she had gone.

He followed her, said good-bye at the gate. Could he come another time?

Of course, he could. She was usually home in the evenings.

Twelve Shilling walked with a swinging, happy stride down Glasbruksgatan's steep slope; he stepped proudly into the boardinghouse. The stench of filth, urine and sweaty feet hit him. It seemed worse than usual. On the sofa beside his lay Magpie with a drunken smith. For once she didn't seem to have been in such a hurry. Instead she had fallen asleep in the middle of her duties. Apparently the smith had had plenty of aquavit. Her skirt lay like a ring around her waist, her white rear end shone in the light from the candle on the table. Twelve Shilling first thought of kicking her to waken her so he could get through, but then he spread the dirty blanket over her, hiding her shame. Tonight he could even feel sorry for Magpie.

He sat down on the edge of the sofa and undressed—until he was naked as was his usual habit—and wrapped up most of his clothing into a ball, which he placed next to himself, laying the jacket on top. Then he crawled under the covers and thought he could feel how the lice came walking across him. He blew out the candle, listened for the rats' gnawing and the tubercular boarder's coughing in the room next door.

The room was pitch black after he extinguished the light, a dark room without windows. But as he lay there he imagined he could see the light dusk again, feel the girl who leaned against him—the clean scent of her hair, her hand taking hold of his arm. He fell asleep happy, slept well in the squalor and stench of the boardinghouse.

THE JOURNEYMAN'S RETURN

As if in an invisible net, they were drawn toward the city: pale gray schooners loaded with wood, white steamboats, black sand barges with swollen bellies, tugboats pulling rows of small cargo boats with sails furled. The troughs in the whirling eddies were broken up by rapid steam launches and flat-bottomed ferries that glided along between the shorelines' quays and the token sellers' pointed roofs. Across the railroad trestle a train was chugging toward the tunnel on Söder; a moment later the bridge slid apart, swung outward and opened the way to the harbor.

Johan had been lucky, had been able to get on board a small cargo boat from Strängnäs. Now, once in the harbor, the boat was slowly guided alongside the quay with the help of oars. Johan stood up from the deck, looking hungrily at Kornhamn's bustling activity: the row of bent-over egg ladies, like brooding black hens, the street boys who whistled and yelled from where they were prowling about on the quay and in the squares. Housemaids out early in the morning were already flocking around the stalls to get the fresh produce from the country.

Home again. The years of roaming were over. He had been promised work, and, in addition, would not have to live at the chimney sweep lodgings. Everything had been decided rather hastily, he hadn't had time to notify Bärta. But if he surprised her with a man in her bed, she would have hell to pay. He had reckoned with that possibility, she was boy-crazy like all women. Besides, he didn't trust anybody. Only numbskulls believed the best of people.

As for himself, he was shrewd, a dangerous devil. Anybody who wasn't big and strong had to hold his own in other ways. He had learned the tricks.

He spat a stream of spit at the stone quay, lifted the sack with his goods to test its weight. It was a little heavy to carry. Luckily Bärta lived close by.

Suddenly, he regretted that he hadn't written, she could have come down and helped him carry things. Bärta had the strength of a horse—wasn't a mortar girl for pleasure's sake.

It felt good to come back to her, come home. He had been drinking quite heavily, especially during the time he had lived in the "blacksmith town." They had hung out together, a few journeymen, and drunk valiantly. Such as that night one of them, the Corporal as he was called, had dragged an angry horse into their bedroom. Washbasins and pitchers had flown over their heads, the hooves had left deep tracks in the walls and the bunks. Naturally, someone could have been kicked to death, it was a miracle really they had survived. But now the wild years were over, he was going to settle down. Bärta was a nice little horse, wouldn't kick. He could put a bridle on her, that much he knew.

He nodded his thanks and a farewell to the skipper, placed his sack on the railing, turned his back and hoisted the load over his shoulder. Was surprised at how light it felt, but he had barely made it over the west bridge of the locks before the sack weighed like lead. Sweaty and angry, he dragged it up to Södermalm Square. He knew one of the girls in a tavern on the small alley, Klotgränd, behind the bazaar buildings. She had been his "sweetheart" once upon a time. For old times' sake, he would be able to leave his sack there and fetch it later. He took a seat, and talked to the girl who was just as skinny and dirty as she had been once upon a time. He ordered food and drink; he'd been paid before he left. But the kronor quickly melted away, his old, worn out coin purse with the brass button already felt disturbingly thin. It would have been nice with something to start the new job with—something other than drunkenness and a hangover. Though Bärta would have to help him, of course, she had had work for several months and ought to have saved something.

He stayed at the Klotet tavern several hours, got tipsy, and the girl grew tired of him and drove him out. Angry, Johan stumbled home.

Emelie had to end work a few hours early. They were going to do repair work on the packaging room in the Melinder factory. Thankful and happy for the unexpected freedom, she made her way slowly through the city toward home. She looked in the shop windows and enjoyed the sunshine. But gradually her steps quickened, she began to feel a little uneasy. She wondered how Gunnar was; the boy was left on his own every day. Usually she couldn't do anything about that, but today she would be able to look after him. She felt it her duty.

Gunnar was nowhere to be seen, neither in the street nor in the yard. She knocked on Bärta's door, but nobody answered. When she entered her own room, she caught sight of the boy through the window; he was sitting hiding outside, in the narrow space between the fence and the wall of the house.

Emelie knocked on the pane, waved to him to come in. Gunnar looked up anxiously; tears had painted streaks in his dirty face. What had gotten hold of him? Why didn't he want to come? She hurried out. Unwillingly, he went back with her. When they came into the entryway, he tried to escape, but she held onto him tightly by the hand and got him inside.

What had happened?

There was a strange man in their room, he sniffled—a drunken and mean rowdy who had knocked over the table and lay sleeping on the bed with his boots on.

One of the brick carriers? Or someone else who knew that Bärta was out during the day? Emily felt the rage well up inside her, forced down any fear and caution.

She took the broom with her.

Pushing the handle down, she opened the door so quickly that it hit a chair with a crash. The whole room was a pigsty, the table tipped over, vomit on the floor. She took a step forward with the broom raised, ready to strike. Then she stopped.

"Johan!"

Her rage gave way for a moment to astonishment at his return. So, now he felt like coming back! He hadn't helped Bärta pay for the room. Instead, he had made a wreck of it, that was what he knew how to do!

She swatted at him with the broom, not too hard—Johan wasn't just any rowdy.

"Get up!"

He rolled over in bed, tried to sit up. At first he wondered where he was, then he remembered and recognized her. He burst out laughing, somewhat insolently but mostly embarrassed.

"This is a fine reception," he said. "People are supposed to be welcomed."

"You should be ashamed," she hissed, but lowered the broom. "The boy is scared out of his wits. And the way it looks in here..."

What boy? He hadn't seen anybody.

She took time with her answer, didn't want to say "yours."

"Gunnar, of course."

"Oh," he answered and burped. "He has probably seen drunk men here before. And he can't have been scared of his father?"

"Get up and I'll clean up the worst of it," she said. It can't look like this when Bärta comes home."

"Don't get mixed up in what doesn't...."

"You heard what I said." She raised the broom again, and he squinted at her worriedly, knew Emelie well enough to know that she just might hit him. Right now, when he was lying down, he was pretty defenseless, but he would show her who was head of the household here, teach her not to put on airs and meddle.

"Of course you can clean up if you like," he sneered and swung his legs over the side of the bed.

She got a scouring bucket and a rag. Johan sat on the bench and watched her while she got down on all fours and mopped up. He took a few steps forward to smack her on the bottom, but she heard him and whirled hastily around, putting up the stinking rag as a shield. Then he laughed again and ambled out to the yard.

Emelie satisfied herself with tidying up the worst of it. She was in a hurry to get back to her room, afraid that Johan would frighten Gunnar. But she would leave Johan alone now, best let Bärta, herself, take care of her returned man.

Together with Gunnar, she went out to the street in good time to warn Bärta. The leaves of the trees were dangling over brown and gray fences, glowing a sharp yellow and clear red in the light of the streetlamps. Some boys with an empty wheelbarrow scampered past. The iron-shod wheels clattered on the cobblestones. Olof came home from the lamp factory and received the news, his eyes darkening; he didn't like Johan. He coughed, spat and informed them that he was going to go meet Arthur.

Normally Emelie would have nagged him a little to come home early, but she was fully occupied with the problem of Johan and only nodded.

Finally Bärta arrived, carrying a bag of food. Gunnar ran to meet her, but he didn't tell her what had happened, just walked silently at her side over to Emelie who had to break the news.

Johan was drunk, was probably sleeping.

Of course, Bärta understood. He had surely been partying because he was so happy to come home. She didn't begrudge him that.

She laughed to herself. Thought Emelie was a little odd sometimes—to take offense at a guy drinking! Of course guys drank, they had always done that. Johan became bad-tempered sometimes when he drank—but he didn't scare Bärta. He wasn't that strong. Sure he had hit her. But she could take a lot, and if he went too far, she could bring him in line.

Bärta started to feel pressed for time. Would there be enough food? Could Emelie loan her something so she could run to the grocer and buy a little bit extra to celebrate his homecoming? Bärta couldn't put any more on her bill there until she had paid off the old one.

Johan had celebrated enough was what Emelie thought. Muttering and unwilling, she pulled out the money.

If Elsa came, could they tell her that Johan had returned, said Bärta. Elsa was one of Bärta's work colleagues, who had lived with Bärta for a few weeks. Emelie nodded, and stood there on the street with Gunnar while Bärta went off to shop.

The wind played in the trees, the leaves rustled in the dark gardens. At the bottom of the precipice the city lay hidden beneath a torn gray veil, light glittering through the holes.

From Bärta's room bellows and shouts could be heard. The journey-man was celebrating his return. The boy had been hit for not wanting to call the rowdy in the bed Father.

A few times Emelie had jumped up, wanted to rush in and get Gunnar, but that might have made it even worse for the boy. And Bärta was com-pletely on Johan's side this evening. Emelie had heard her shout at Johan to be quiet and obey his father.

She couldn't do anything—only sit and listen, wait for them to fall asleep. She wondered what the old captain up there on the top floor thought of his tenants. If he thought that Emelie was a part of it, too.

There was a rapping on the door; she recognized the signal: Twelve Shilling. She opened—and he stood there a little shy in the doorway, not used to being let in. Did she want to go for a little walk? It was gray and windy out, but it might still feel good. What did she think?

No, tonight she didn't want to go out.

She didn't give any reason, but she had to stay at home, know if any-thing happened to Gunnar. Even if she couldn't help, she had to know.

That was too bad.... Twelve Shilling stood there and looked unhappy. She invited him in. They could drink some coffee. But he couldn't stay long, it was a weekday evening, and she had some things to take care of.

Pleased, he walked in, placed his cap on the dresser and took a seat on the wooden sofa. Now she should come and sit beside him. But while the coffee was boiling, she took a seat on a chair at the table, keeping herself safely at a distance.

She set out cups and poured. He took a chair and moved even closer, wanted to hold her. But she was not in the mood, was unusually jumpy and out of sorts, and pushed him away. He didn't let himself be bothered by this, knew that she was a little difficult; he should take it easy. Gradually she had to give in to his persistence and let him sit with his arm around her waist. He had even been able to place his hand over her breast a few times with her pretending not to notice. Seducing her was a long-term plan. Twelve Shilling wasn't in any hurry, not when he was sober.

It had been peaceful for a while in the apartment next door; maybe they had fallen asleep in there. But then the shouting began again. Twelve Shilling looked up surprised, didn't know that Johan had come home. Emelie rushed over to the door, listening. No, she couldn't hear Gunnar's voice. Maybe they were letting the boy sleep.

She explained. Twelve Shilling offered to go in and punch the journeyman in the nose. But Emelie shook her head, that wasn't the thing to do. They had no right to get involved in what Bärta and her man were up to.

The noises died down but then they rose again. Emelie listened out in the entryway a few times. Twelve Shilling went out with her. Then he noticed how red and embarrassed she grew, she hurried back into her room ahead of him. Now he realized what they were up to in there.

Twelve Shilling understood that this evening it would be impossible to talk to Emelie, she was much too upset. At the same time, he was excited by the noisy lust at the neighbors'. He envied that journeyman who was celebrating with such violent lovemaking. He felt he could almost see Bärta right now, round and tasty, certainly something nice to take hold of, roll around with. Why did Emelie have to be so scared and cautious?

He had to go now, she said. But he wanted to stay and protect her. What if that crazy guy in the room next door came in?

She wasn't afraid of Bärta's man, she had the broom if necessary. Johan was a little weakling. And now she wanted Twelve Shilling to leave.

Finally he gave up. Left in a bad mood—excited and cooled down at the same time. He felt sick, the feelings stirring inside him didn't want to come together and settle down. He didn't dare stay, then he would only ruin things. And he felt like he didn't want to go either, that would be deserting her.

Still, he left, since she asked him to so stubbornly.

Emelie cleared the table. Everything felt a little better after Twelve Shilling was gone. Had she gotten so used to being alone that she was frightened of being close to people? No, that was only this evening, when all companionship seemed dirty and appalling.

But where had Elsa disappeared to? The girl who was boarding in Bärta's room couldn't willingly sleep in there? She had completely forgotten about Elsa. Of course, she had no responsibility for the girl, but still. Probably she had gone to a friend's.

Emelie pulled on a sweater and went out into the yard. On the way back to the house, she thought she heard something rustle in the woodshed. It was Elsa sitting in the open door of the shed. The girl was shivering with cold and fear, had been sitting in the yard for several hours, wrapped only in a shawl.

"I can't be in there," Elsa wept.

Emelie could understand that, but they had to arrange something, there had to be some corner where Elsa could sleep. It was best she came in now, before she caught pneumonia.

Emelie fixed more coffee; the girl had to drink something warm. It had grown quiet in the next room now. But it was unthinkable for Elsa to sleep there tonight.

Elsa had been a seamstress to begin with, but had become unemployed. Finally, she had been obliged to take whatever work she could get and step in as a mortar girl on the same construction site as Bärta. Now her fingers were ruined—she thought she would never be able to sew again.

Naturally Elsa wasn't at all suited for the hard job she had—small and thin, delicate and afraid. Once again, Emelie could almost feel responsibility weighing down on her. She tried to put up a defense, thinking: I don't have the strength, I can't. Still she had to think it out... plan. Was there any opening at the factory? The packer girls' work was considerably lighter than that of a mortar girl. And if they crowded together, Elsa could sleep in here while she looked for a new place to live. In any case, Elsa had to sleep here tonight. Emelie had shared the bed with Gertrud before; there would be room for her and Elsa. Olof might not like having a strange girl in the room, but he could stand it for a few nights. They had space, something to share, so there was nothing to think over.

For a moment Emelie almost felt happy and rich. But then there was

Gunnar, left out and frightened to death, yet so close. If Bärta would only go along with it, then Gunnar... no, they couldn't fill the whole little room with beds. But still, Emelie felt the desire to take care of the boy. Afraid of the burden and still so eager to take it on. As if she mistrusted everybody else, didn't think that anyone but herself could manage.

Elsa got to lie in Emelie's bed. Tired and miserable, the girl fell asleep quickly. Emelie was still sitting at the table when Olof arrived, and told him what had happened. He swore at Johan, but showed no irritation over Elsa moving in. He was preoccupied with other thoughts.

It was different in the morning when he woke up. A faint morning light streamed into the room over the high fence. On the table glowed the kerosene lantern Emelie had lit. His sister was already up, was in the process of putting wood on the open fire.

Olof lay still, was in no hurry yet, was the one whose job was most close by. He didn't indicate that he was awake, and watched through half-closed eyelids.

The girl who was their overnight guest sat on the bed. Her feet stuck out from under the long white nightgown. She was applying some liniment from a bottle onto some sores she had on her shoulders. While she rubbed it in with a cloth, her camisole slid down and one breast was exposed. The light from the kerosene lamp lent her skin a warm and soft glow, as if her face, shoulders and breast were shining in a circle of light.

Olof lay still, fascinated. His gaze burned in the image: the melancholy, the pain, the narrow shoulders, the ugly sore, the hair hanging down in her face, the hand moving the white cloth, the line of the arms, the breast—sweet and bitter. Life, the poor, beaten and tormented, and still, so soft and pure in the shimmer of the friendly light.

He wanted to paint it, nobody had done it, no one other than himself owned this image. The thought and the image engaged him so much that he almost forgot lust.

He moved, reached out his hand for a piece of paper and a pencil that he always had close by. The girl heard him, started, and pulled up her camisole. He pretended not to notice her, tried to capture with a few strokes the memory of the image he had just seen. As always, he was plagued by the gap between the vision and the possibility of capturing it. But he got something right, there was something there to continue with. A thousand sketches first, of course, he thought, then it would be time to take out Gullpippi's paints.

He turned his back to the room, his face toward the wall. It was best to let her get dressed in peace, he wouldn't disturb her. But he had to wake up in time while she lived here, recall the image, burn it into his memory enough so it could be reproduced.

Bärta knocked on the door, wondered if Elsa was ready. They usually kept each other company on the way to the construction site. Bärta was sleepy, with a day-after heaviness, yet proud and happy. It felt good to have her man back again. It had been a little noisy, they would have to be excused. But Johan hadn't been home for two years.

Was he going to begin work today? Emelie wondered.

No, not until tomorrow.

How was Gunnar doing?

He was managing, as usual.

Bärta and Elsa left. Emelie still had a few minutes left. She hurried to take out bread and milk, knocked carefully on the door of the room next door. Gunnar opened it, sleepy and red-eyed. She waved him out into the entryway.

He could eat in her room, could be in there as much as he liked. She would tell Olof to hang the key in the shed when he left so Gunnar could get it. He could fasten the door with the latch from the inside. He shouldn't say anything to his father; only Gunnar could be in Emelie's room during the day.

This was going behind Bärta and Johan's backs, but she had to give the boy the opportunity to get out of the way and get food if Johan didn't leave him anything. She was beset by worry while she walked through the city. The calm she had felt in their hidden-away house had disappeared.

Johan was home again, and had not gotten any better. How would Gunnar get by? How would Olof manage? Did she dare ask factory director Melinder if there was any work for Elsa? And how did she actually want to have things with Twelve Shilling?

She didn't know anything. Only that everything was black and heavy. And still it was she herself who had taken on the burdens, asked to carry them.

THE RUINED PICTURE

Elsa lived in their room for one week, slept in Emelie's bed. Olof tried hard to wake up on time, lay there quietly and watched her take care of her sores. But it was never again the way it had been that first morning, not that mood and not that image. Maybe it was because he now saw her with different eyes. Something of his devotion was gone—had been replaced by curiosity and attraction.

At the factory, one of the boys had brought in some copies of a periodical called "Easy Virtue." According to the text, the pamphlets would be "suitable reading for the boudoir and bedroom," but the boys read them in the outhouse. Sometimes Olof imagined Elsa resembled the girl on the cover. And when he saw her sitting there on the edge of the bed, the silly verses came to mind. They had fastened in his memory and he knew them by heart.

> *Her breast was heaving violently,*
> *Her glance was growing faint,*
> *Just as he began to dig*
> *In search of "pleasure's treasure"*
> *And finding tra-la-la.*

He swore quietly, rolled over on the wooden sofa, forced himself to lie with his face to the wall so he couldn't see Elsa. He closed his eyes and tried to recall the right image, but heard the pounding of his veins: tra-la-la, tra-la-la. He wondered what was actually meant by those meaningless words that came at the end of every verse. Though of course he could guess.

The pamphlets were repulsive, thumbed-through, filthy. Still, he couldn't get away from them, still, the odors and the images from them pervaded and got in the way of the vision he had that first morning when he had awoken, unprepared, with fresh eyes—when he could still see what was beautiful without sullying it with his gaze.

Now the picture was ruined. The rhyme pounded away, called up other images, brutal and ugly. But still he searched for the vision he had had. Hoped that a miracle would occur, that he would get to see her as he had seen her that morning.

Something had entered the house with Johan, a sickness, a pestilence. Everyone felt the change. They felt like they had to watch themselves and each other, trust and joy were gone. Olof was troubled by Elsa. Gunnar lived in terror, hid to avoid being hit. Twelve Shilling began to be impatient, never got anywhere with Emelie. Every time they met he had to start over at the beginning again. Bärta was jealous. Johan, who before had had no luck with the girls, swelled with pride at the reception she had given him, and now believed himself to be irresistible and began to flirt with Elsa and Emelie. Elsa was frightened by Johan's hand and Olof's gaze, Emelie was constantly on her guard—ready to slap Johan's fingers—and became more irritated than usual at Twelve Shilling's obstinate attentions. It was as if no one could feel safe and secure.

Bärta's love and the new journeyman status led to Johan's being almost unbearably self-satisfied. He tormented the small boys at the chimney sweep locale and hit Gunnar. He harassed Olof, a boy still wet behind the ears, who was always in the way and should learn to work. He could learn by cleaning up the yard and carrying in wood. And what was that clumsy brick carrier doing in this house? He couldn't be anyone for Emelie; couldn't Bärta get Twelve Shilling to realize this?

The girls were treated with contempt by Johan, even if it was well-intentioned. Silly women—they needed a man, wanted to change places with Bärta. If they asked really nicely, maybe he could help them a little on the side... although they were so timid and dumb, they ran away whenever he tried to encourage them.

Elsa had moved back in. Bärta wanted her, she provided rent money. Elsa had obeyed unwillingly, and Emelie kept quiet. In a way it was nice not to have anybody living with them, and it was up to Elsa to decide what she wanted.

But if Elsa had once been bothered by Olof's gaze, she now met with something harder to tolerate. Johan wouldn't leave her alone. As soon as Bärta left the room, he would try to approach her. She attempted to defend herself, but he only laughed. Girls' behaving like ninnies was part of the game. When a girl said no, she meant yes. Life had taught him that much.

One evening Elsa didn't make it out in time. Johan came into the room without her noticing, crept up to the window where she was standing. Before she had a chance to defend herself, he was upon her. At first, she tried to quietly push him off, didn't want anybody to come and see her here this way. She tried to scratch his hands—but almost all of her fingertips were bound in rags.

Then she lashed out in desperation, shrieking. He let her go, fell over. But he was after her again, perhaps to calm her down and quiet her. By this time she was scared out of her wits, and didn't care what anybody thought. She managed to get out to the entryway with Johan behind her.

Emelie, who had heard the shrieking, came out with the broom held high. Johan got it across his back when he tried to duck, blow after blow. He tried to defend himself, succeeded at last in wrenching the broom from Emelie's hand.

Then Twelve Shilling arrived. He had heard the girls complaining many times. Now he saw what it was like: Elsa crying desperately and Emelie, red with anger, trying to ward off Johan who stood with a broom in his hand.

Too late, Johan noticed the new arrival. Suddenly he was waving his arms and legs in the air, hit his arm against the door, and found himself out in the yard, still suspended, raised up by Twelve Shilling's strong arms. He wanted to beg and plead, but he understood that nothing helped. Then he was airborne. Twelve Shilling had thrown him. Johan crashed onto the garbage heap by the outhouse, lay still a moment, tried to feel around and see if he could get up. Nobody came and asked him how he was. Finally he sat up and staggered to his feet. Swearing, crying, and brushing himself off, he limped out to the street.

After that evening, it grew calmer in the house. Bärta complained a little, but allowed Elsa to move back to Emelie's room. Johan stayed out in the evenings in the chimney sweep locale and tyrannized the apprentices. It took almost a week before Bärta would let him back in her bed. By then he had lost most of his belief in his enormous manliness—whined about his injured leg and the world's cruelty and was comforted by Bärta. When he met the girls, he hurried quickly past as if he didn't see them. If he knew that Twelve Shilling was visiting, he hid in his room and didn't stick his nose out till he was sure that awful person was really gone for the evening.

The girls didn't want to tell Olof what had happened that evening, but he guessed. He felt some shame and guilt of his own. He had had his own fantasies about Elsa. Maybe he had wanted to do what Johan had done—whatever it was that had made them so upset.

As a penance, he worked on the picture he had seen that first morning. It shouldn't be too clear and revealing, shouldn't give the impression of peeking at nakedness. It should be beautiful, and, at the same time, tell a story about how difficult life was for people. He had shown it to Arthur, the way one shows a secret. For once, his friend had barely any objections or corrections to make. Olof had tried to explain his point of view, what he wanted to convey, and, Arthur had nodded solemnly. Olof was on the right track. Arthur might have done it differently himself, but that doesn't mean that he would have been right. He would have made it rawer, not made the girl so beautiful and the picture so full of light. But the picture was right for Olof.

They talked a long time that evening, about the true image, the right one. And Olof continued to look, made the first attempts at finding the right colors. For once he wasn't in a hurry, but instead had the stamina to search seriously. And he was happy while searching—for a while freed of everything that hounded and hindered him.

It was harder for Emelie. Peace wouldn't return despite Johan's staying away.

Of course, she had to admire Twelve Shilling's strength, been glad and grateful that he had arrived in time and stepped in so effectively. He had wanted to take care of Johan once and for all, continue what he had begun, but she had prevented it. She had explained that someone as strong as Twelve Shilling had to be generous, couldn't abuse his power. Johan would surely leave them alone now, he had been forewarned.

But Johan's attack on Elsa had made Emelie more sensitive to Twelve Shilling's nearness. He was certainly kind and good in every way, but she couldn't love him. The one who came after Rudolf, whoever it might be, would only be a replacement. But wasn't Twelve Shilling the best replacement she could get? Why did she hesitate? She felt false and miserable. Felt like she was treating him badly. Finally, she couldn't bear it anymore and had to speak out.

Of course he was unhappy. But still he seemed to take it better than she had dared hope. Then gradually she understood why.

Twelve Shilling and Elsa were workmates, had become good friends. The brick carrier had saved her from Johan, Elsa thought. She admired the strong fellow. She talked freely and easily with him when he came to visit Emelie, felt sorry for him at times when Emelie was cross and difficult. But out of loyalty to Emelie, Elsa would never have tried to pursue Twelve Shilling. Now it was different. Carefully, she inquired: did Emelie really mean that she didn't want to continue seeing him?

Emelie guessed the connection. And if Twelve Shilling and Elsa ended up happy together, then that would only be a good thing. Even if she felt set aside—abandoned once more.

Twelve Shilling had possibly given up hope on Emelie, even before she said the decisive words. He was looking for a girl, was no longer completely sure that Emelie was the right one. She was certainly exceptional and nice—but so strange, so impossible. Elsa was easier. Once he had begun going with her, he didn't have to start over, it was only a question of continuing. She let him hold her, even responded. At first, he was almost terrified, wondered if it was really respectable for a girl not to resist. But when she began to talk about the possibility of their getting married, he grew calmer. He was so happy that he almost smothered her.

Emelie saw how happy they were, how uncomplicated life could be. Could she have also been so happy if she had wanted, if she hadn't made it so difficult? No, she thought. Elsa had only herself to think of. As for Emelie, she had Olof and Gunnar. And then there was Rudolf, the memory and the dream that always came between, that stopped her.

Twelve Shilling got Elsa's sewing machine out of hock, and rented a room with an iron stove. Elsa moved out of Emelie's, sat in the new room and sewed. Twelve Shilling's stubbornness had finally won, he had gotten a wife and home, and Elsa had her sewing machine. Patient and persevering, he pushed onward, built up his world.

But Olof built the picture of the girl who disappeared. Time after time, he had put away the sketches and tried to work on something else as if, in spite of everything, he didn't really believe he could achieve anything. But once Elsa moved, it grew easier. The reality with its fluctuations and contradictions was no longer present. He could work completely from his memory.

He bought a fine sheet of paper, screwed up his courage, and sketched out the picture according to the drawing he had chosen. He took out his paints, added the glow from the kerosene lamp. Hours passed, he should have been tired but felt nothing. He was glad that Emelie was at Gertud's and would probably stay a while. Their sister was expecting another child. Now he could sit undisturbed and be spared any questions or comments. He stood up, coughed, stretched his back. He placed the picture far enough away to look at it. It was just about right: the mood, the pose, the expression, the daybreak from the window, and the lamplight. There was nothing that would bring to mind the drawings in those pamphlets.

He probably shouldn't do any more, he might ruin something. He let the picture remain on the table to dry, took off his clothes and crawled into bed. He would have liked to stay awake until Emelie came back to hear what she thought of it, but he fell asleep.

Emelie returned late after accompanying Gertrud to the lying-in hospital. She lighted the lamp on the table and saw Olof's work. At first, all she thought was that it was pretty good—it looked life-like. But then she grew horrified, saw that the girl was Elsa and that she was sitting with one breast bare. What had that boy been up to? Had he been spying on Elsa? And what would Elsa say if she caught sight of this? She would be beside herself. And Twelve Shilling would believe that Elsa had sat there being provocative in front of the boy, even that Elsa was some kind of model, like artists used.

And Olof... only a child and still he had drawn this. It must be Arthur's bad influence. Emelie felt responsible: for Olof, for Elsa's reputation, and Twelve Shilling's happiness. The painting was a threat to all of that. If he was going to draw and paint, he had to do houses or people with their clothes on. This could lead to unhappiness for everybody.

She crumpled up the picture, and burned it.

When Olof awoke in the morning, the first thing he asked after was the painting. A little annoyed, she was about to snap at him, but then noticed his agitation. Began to sense what it might have meant to him. She tried to explain why she had been obligated to do what she had done. It was best for everybody. Nobody should be portrayed against her will, least of all without clothes. He didn't want to make them all unhappy did he?

He cried—the big boy. She tried to console him; he would get a new piece of paper from her, more paints. He could have the whole table to work on in the evenings, but pictures like these he couldn't do, not before he was an adult, possibly. There were certain girls who let painters paint them naked. She couldn't understand it, but maybe they were different, she didn't know. On the other hand, it was for sure that you couldn't paint people without them knowing about it. You had to show consideration. She realized, now, that he hadn't meant any harm in it, but he had to understand that she was thinking only of what was best for him, and for Elsa.

He grieved for a long time, but didn't say anything to Arthur. Perhaps Olof understood Emelie's pain, and that despite everything she meant well. And, also, that neither Arthur nor anyone else would be able to understand it.

THE ROAD TOWARD
THE FUTURE

Garden plots and sheds were torn up, the sound of blasting thundered away. Dilapidated cottages clung to mangled rocky knolls as long as possible. The lines that the city planners had drawn with their long rulers began to take shape in the broad and straight avenues of reality. Construction had sped up once more, ever since the housing surplus had disappeared, and rents had begun to rise.

The economic cycle was turning around, people said. People were certainly complaining about the new tariffs on grain, and, of course, there was a risk of going to battle with the Norwegians who wouldn't be satisfied with the terms of the union. But everything would surely come out all right. These sorts of things couldn't be allowed to hinder progress. For every day that passed, the city increased in value, the prices of building sites demonstrated that. There was a lot of land that in the last fifteen years had gone up from one krona per square meter to one hundred. Wider streets allowed them to build higher buildings, and in the finest new buildings electric elevators were installed.

August Bodin stood at the window and looked down on Drottninggatan's snowy slush: brownish gray mud, water that sprayed around the wagon wheels and the horses' hooves. August had put on his new gray overcoat with the dark collar, he held his hat and cane in his hand. In the office in the next room, his employees worked industriously; there was a lot to do again. Still, he had difficulty feeling satisfied and secure. He felt like he'd learned how temporary success could be—how close disaster could be. If the firm had only continued for a few more months in the same way as before, this office would probably be standing silent and empty right now—bankruptcy a fact. Funds and reserves would never have been big enough. During times of crisis, even the most solid collapsed. Many were tempted to become liberal and wasteful as soon as good times came. He felt the temptation himself. It wasn't fun to be viewed as stingy and impossible. But not only did he have responsibility for himself and his own, but for his employees. Many probably believed that his reserves were larger than they really were. August had often felt the temptation to place all the papers on the table, show his employees why he couldn't fulfill their expectations for salary raises. That would be exposing his father completely.

Now, when rents were going up, he should have owned many properties. But Fredrik Bodin had frittered away a lot, and August had been obliged to sell during the reorganization. There were buildings that the firm had owned only while they were showing losses. Naturally, it was most important that the firm, despite all the difficulties, make it through the crisis. Still, August couldn't stop himself from wondering how much they would have earned if they still owned everything.

He would have liked to give Ida more and better things, anything she wished for. When he said something to that effect, she had really taken him to task; he shouldn't think this way. Everything was fine, much better that she ever could have hoped for. It was him and not luxury that she wanted. And he knew, by the way, how poor they had been at home during those years before her father got proper work again. Naturally, August was happy that she reacted that way. But the wish was still there—and fear that new abysses could open up.

I know what poverty means, he thought. The memory of the house on Söder came back, his parents, his siblings. He tried to comfort himself with the thought that Emelie said he would hear from her if she ever needed help. And when they had last bumped into each other, she had made it sound as if his siblings were managing all right. Apparently things were better for Bärta too. Naturally, they were living under completely different circumstances than he himself. In exchange, they didn't have the same heavy responsibility to carry.

A rented coach stopped beneath the window. The depressing thoughts quickly disappeared; the coach that waited was full of joy and hope. August hurried through the office, tried to look serious and adult even though he suddenly felt like a boy. He had already told the accountant he would be gone for a few hours, maybe the rest of the day. He guessed that his employees knew his errand, and he wondered as he ran down the stairs if they were perhaps standing with their noses pressed against the windowpane. Once out on the street, he had to force himself not to turn around and look up. He stepped carefully between the puddles, into the coach to Ida who waited.

From the stiff seriousness of the office to Ida's high spirits, the changeover was almost too sudden. It took a moment before he could shake off his formality. She laughed at him, kissed him so heartily that he just about lost his hat. When he looked around a little anxiously, she laughed again. The windows were fogged up, nobody could see them. Then he hugged her, though he had an unpleasant feeling that the accountant's sharp gaze could penetrate everything and that the always so solemn man now looked down on his young boss with utter distaste—such caresses during working hours and in the middle of Drottninggatan!

Ida was filled with excitement at what awaited. He wasn't in too much of a hurry to get back was he? There was so much she had to find out and take note of. He calmed her, they could stay as long as they liked. He wiped the windowpane with his glove to see a little. How far had they come? The coachman avoided the steep and slippery hills. Now they were crossing Gustav Adolfs torg. Some carriages had sought shelter from the wind against the statue; the remains of the old stable on Helgeandsholmen hid the pilings for the intended parliament building.

"Aren't you worried about being too far away?" he asked her. She shook her head. No, on the contrary. For her, it would be good.

It was true, he could take the Djurgården line to Norrmalmstorg, and then walk up Hamngatan to the office. If that car was running in the morning—he wasn't sure. And besides, they would have fresh air out on Östermalm, they would be almost by Djurgården. And what walks they would take!

But Strandvägen was not yet the fine street they had been talking about it becoming—it was still muddy and rutted, cluttered with carts and woodpiles. Countless gray cargo boats raised a wall of sails along the quay;

workshops and sheds lined the street's northern side. Rows of gray wooden troughs for draft horses lined up in procession between piles of sand and stacks of bricks. Beside Grevgatan the old smallpox innoculation center stood empty, and the stables were deserted. They were going to be torn down soon. The veterinary institute had been moved.

However, now a row of palatial buildings rose up, an alley of newly planted trees caught the eye. Everything would surely be beautiful here by summer.

Wouldn't she have preferred to live in one of those buildings, with a wide view of the water? Yet he couldn't offer her that.

They turned onto one of the cross streets. Here the buildings had a significantly simpler appearance. One of the corner buildings on Riddaregatan was owned by the Bodin firm. If they were to live in a refined style, they really should live on the second floor, or no higher than the third. But they had such good tenants in the building, and Ida had assured him that she had nothing at all against living on the fourth floor, the second floor from the top.

Like a child, Ida had to go and look at the nameplate on every door they passed. Then they arrived at the door that was still missing a nameplate and August took out the key. He opened the door, and smiling, looked at her. Should he carry her over the threshold even though they weren't married yet?

She smiled back and placed her arms around his neck. Carefully he carried her through the little hallway and into the corner room, placing her in the window with the view of the street that ran along the quay. Through the mist, they could see the built-up area on the heights of Söder outlined in black. Katarina's cupola rose high above the roofs of the houses surrounding it. Over there, next to the church was where he had once gone to school during his last years on Söder. Somewhere on the hill lived Emelie and Olof. And August had walked on the narrow streets below the church the day he moved away from home and was adopted by the Bodins. He could recall how afraid and, at the same time, proud he had felt as he walked away. Mama who had stood at the gate on Åsögatan and watched him with eyes red from crying. Mother who had welcomed him at Skeppsbron. And the city in the evening mist, gilded by the setting sun, enticing, inviting with all the promise of the future.

Now he would soon continue his journey, from the home he had shared with Father and Mother to his own with Ida. Dream and reality were not really the same, that golden mist couldn't be captured and held onto. Promise, transformed into reality, could be heavy with responsibility and gray with worry.

He wasn't a boy any longer.

But when he saw Ida standing at the window, he thought that the weak winter light on her face had a warm tone of spring and of new promise. She was still the girl from Friendship Point, the dream and the promise. The way toward the future went on from here, was only just beginning. Everything still remained to be sought and won. And now he wasn't doing it alone, now he had his friend for the journey.

Ida had pulled out a measuring tape, was getting ready to measure the windows.

After August got married and moved away from home, it was lonely for Annika Bodin. It was not as if August had been home much during recent years, the firm and his fiancée had taken up most of his time. Still, he had been there. She had, in any case, seen him at mealtimes, had him as a confidant. They had grown much closer during these years, closer than she had ever been to any other person, she thought.

Slightly jealous, she watched how he devoted every free moment to Ida: how they were almost silly, they were so in love. August was actually rather childish despite his twenty-seven years. And Ida, who was almost one year older, was no better.

The jealousy pricked her. He is ungrateful, it struck her. They had taken him in as their own, paid for his upbringing, given him the firm and a secure future, and then some young thing came along and took him from them. Of course, he came to visit sometimes, but usually he had Ida with him and the situation didn't invite the exchange of confidences between them as it had when it was just the two of them. She knew he had rescued the firm, but he shouldn't have gotten married so early. He could have stayed at home a few more years, and then at least settled in the same area and not so far out on distant Östermalm. While she and Fredrik had to go on living in the dreary and petit bourgeois quarter Fredrik had insisted on choosing.

Ungrateful—and still, of course, he wasn't. A person wasn't a housepet, not a lapdog. For most parents life led toward loneliness. Children grew up and grew away from them. And parents were left behind in the past, going over their memories, dying, deceived and abandoned.

It would have been different if she had had someone to share her loneliness with. She didn't count Fredrik. It was as if he had deceived her about life. He had once seemed so lively and nice—talked so big and promised so much. She had hurried to capture him, a little surprised that such a catch could be made so easily. It wasn't until later that she had understood why it had been so easy. Who would want him? Yes, he had some little girlfriend or other—poor, stupid girl. Annika could feel neither mad nor jealous of someone who let herself be fooled by Fredrik.

It might actually be fun to meet the one Fredrik went to... if only to free that poor person of her delusions. Annika would certainly like to set her mind straight. It would serve Fredrik right if even that one dumped him.

She watched her husband sitting heavy and dull in a corner, conversing with Ida's father. Fredrik had turned sixty; they had had to celebrate no matter how ridiculous it seemed. A few relatives and his so-called business friends with their wives had come to dinner: Fredrik's conceited sister-in-law with her eldest, unmarried daughter—who would want to have her, skinny as a rake? Accountant Forsberg with his little, roly-poly wife. Ida's parents—Henrik Wide did look haggard although he had made a surprisingly good comeback after bankruptcy and ulcers. And Signe— a little bit silly as the proud mother—but why not—lively and assured, refreshingly direct in manner and speech.

But still, it was mostly like a waxworks show, foolish, ugly and old people. Before, she had been able to view her guests in contrast to herself, thinking: nobody can avoid noticing that I am different. Now it didn't work as well to think this way. She still had one year left before she turned fifty, but she had lost her freshness and beauty. Had grown a little too stout, didn't feel like she had enough to compete for. Well, she did for August's sake, of course. But he saw her as his mother, wanted to actually think of her as a little round and amiable old lady.

Now it was August and Ida who got to be young and glittering, as if thrown into relief against the dismal background. Annika could be a little jealous and offended, but, of course, it was fun for the boy's sake. He certainly couldn't help comparing Ida to the dreary Birgitta Bodin. But didn't he also see his mother as the cheerful and clever hostess who thought of everything and everybody, and who could even turn the failed Fredrik's sixtieth birthday into a celebration?

She managed the maids, laughed with the gentlemen, invited the ladies into the drawing room, urged the poor Birgitta to sit down at the piano. Fredrik listened when he heard the chords at the piano. So, Annika had forced Margareta's daughter to play. He tried to arrange his seat to better survive the torment. So-called refined music was something he had never been able to comprehend.

And Fredrik felt lonely, missed August. His son had both been a connecting link and a barrier, had made it possible for him and Annika to live together somewhat tolerably and presentably. If they weren't talking to each other, they could talk to August, it hadn't become completely silent at the dinner table. When their son was home, they had to pretend they were decent and civilized people, they couldn't let the hate and disdain well over. It felt good to pretend sometimes, they could almost imagine they were living as they behaved. When August was away there was nobody to pretend for, nothing to talk about, nobody who stopped and checked them by his sheer presence.

Fredrik was afraid of the time that awaited, both because of the silence and because of the words that would come. There was no way out of the misery. Annika would surely not go along with a divorce, and he would-

n't demand one. There was no real reason and hardly any economic possibility either. And somehow Annika was his fate; without her life would
be even emptier. He had grown all too accustomed to her for all too long.

Finally Birgitta finished. Please, don't let Annika convince her to continue. Beautiful. Now he could go on talking with his friend, Henrik,
pretend that he was still enmeshed in his business. Naturally, his friend
knew otherwise—but he pretended so well and so congenially.

Margareta and her daughter made themselves heard. They had stood
and stamped their feet outside Central Station all afternoon, waiting for
the king to come home from Norway. The whole square outside the station had been filled with people who had greeted the king like a
hero—bands, hurrahs, jubilation. What an atmosphere. You could imagine the celebration could be heard all the way to Kristiania and make those
Norwegians settle down. There would probably still be a mobilization of
troops, weapons would have to do the talking now and the Norwegians
taught a thing or two. Both ladies were still filled with the experience and
tried to convey it to anyone who would listen.

Fredrik nodded, but tried to get away from his sister-in-law as quickly
as possible. The sight of Margareta always made him uneasy. She believed,
of course, that he had cheated her on both the firm and the properties and
she was partly right. But it was Annika's fault, Annika who constantly nagged
and thought he was too generous to his sister-in-law. And then he was
stuck with the shame, while Annika pretended that she and Margareta were
intimate friends. Though Annika hadn't really managed to dupe his sister-
in-law. Margareta Bodin was still rather reserved when she spoke to Annika.

He nodded, tired. They could go home now, there had been enough
celebrating. Now he wanted to sleep, but knew that he would lie awake the
whole night—lie and see a deserted, desolate road disappear into a future
without hope.

The carriage rolled along Strandvägen, catching a little in the wheel ruts.
Ida sat leaning against August, careful not to crush the enormous, almost
inflated leg-of-mutton sleeves of her dress. August held her, had

unbuttoned his coat so it would be big enough to go around her.

His thoughts were still back at his old home. He felt both discomfort and sorrow. His parents were unhappy; he had known that for a long time. But it was as if he noticed it more now that he came as a guest. Mother would manage in any case, she still had strength and willpower. But Father? So old, so falling apart. He couldn't hide that he was unhappy either, had sat melancholy and tired and obviously not wanted to be at the party that was being held in his honor.

August thawed a little hole in the ice on the window, looked out. They were almost there. Soon it would be a new working day, a lot to do, a meeting in the morning, a contract that had to be signed, and then.... The coach swung onto the side street and stopped.

Ida went ahead of him up the stairs, while he paid the coachman. The maid, who had heard her steps in the vestibule, hurried to open the door, helped her off with her coat, and went with her into the bedroom to help with the large and unwieldy dress that had to come off.

August walked through the darkened rooms, fetched soda water from the cold pantry and poured a glass, sat in the window seat in the darkness of the corner room and thought a minute while he waited for the girl to leave Ida. He wondered how things were for his siblings now, over on the hill, on the other side of the water. He should inquire and see if Emelie wanted to come visit them some evening. Even if they had grown apart and lived so differently, they were brother and sister. With Gertrud and Olof, it wasn't really the same thing. Gertrud was married to Rudolf, and Olof had been so little and gone his own way now, according to what he understood from Emelie. Emelie and Ida would be able to talk to each other, he thought—understand each other. But Emelie lived together with Bärta, of course. No, perhaps he should leave it alone. It would be as if some of Bärta came too.

Now the girl had left Ida. He knocked his little signal on the bedroom door. Ida sat in front of the mirror. She had swept herself in a long dressing gown, and under it she had that funny piece of clothing she had bought a little while ago, a combination of camisole and pantaloons. "Combination" it was called. A real little clown suit, he thought—loads of lace around the neck and arms and a long row of buttons all the way down the front. She had been a little shy to show herself in it at first, but what was all the lace for if no one other than herself was to see it, he had asked. Then she had laughingly shown off her elegance.

He put on the white nightshirt the maid had very properly laid out on the bed. He sat on the edge of the bed and waited.

"It's a pity about your old parents," Ida said suddenly.

"Yes, they're not really happy," he agreed.

She turned around quickly, looked at him. There was a trace of worry in her eyes and an appeal. "We must always be happy," she said. "And like each other."

"You know we will," he said. "You know that."

"You mustn't think too much about the firm, not so much that you don't have time to think about me."

"No," he answered, "I mustn't do that. You have to help me not do that."

He opened the door to the corner room, led Ida over to the window. Only a few windows were lit up in the buildings around them. Along the quay and up on the heights on the other side of the water glinted small flickers of light. A few coaches rolled along the edge of the water coming from Djurgården, their lantern light dancing quickly past. Soon the road down there would be a fine one, paved with stone—the main thoroughfare to the planned large exhibition. The exhibition: he had been asked to build one of the big pavilions. A fine and honorable commission.

He suddenly felt ashamed. Was he thinking about the firm even though he was standing there in the dark with Ida beside him, feeling her warm and soft body so close?

The snow on the roofs around them gleamed softly out of the darkness. How endlessly far away the stars were. Beautiful, huge—but cold. He felt some anxiety thinking of the infinite and the incomprehensible. He turned around, saw the faint light from inside the bedroom, the near and the comprehensible.

He pulled her to him, drew her back inside.

DREAMER, MADMAN

Black streams of people tramped toward Söder, a rumble of heavy, tired feet. A crowded steam-driven streetcar came chugging up Brunnsbacken, puffed out its cloud of smoke. Wagon wheels squealed and creaked on the difficult uphill climbs, horses' hooves clattered against the stones. A sinking sun painted Lortfjärden's waters a glaring pink.

Against the current, on their way down toward Slussen, two youths sauntered over the hump on Hornsgatan—jaunty caps, large red scarves that fluttered in the wind, billowing wide pantlegs. The working and laden swore at the two whippersnappers, who seemed to feel so insolently carefree. But a flaming redheaded girl, on her knees scrubbing the stone stairs outside a bread shop, smiled gaily. They took the time to stop a minute, laughing almost infuriatingly loudly until the woman keeping shop came out. Then they swung about on their way, with their hands in their pants pockets.

"I could have chatted up that bakery girl a little longer," said one.

"Watch out," warned the other. "She'll be trotting off for inspection soon."

The thought of the inspection bureau for prostitutes dampened his enthusiasm.

But Olof still couldn't forget the sight of the girl with the unnaturally red hair, how she had kneeled there scrubbing the gray stones while the reflections of the sun glittered in her hair.

"Do you have an extra smoke?" he asked.

Arthur handed him a cigarette, stopped to light it for his friend. Olof exhaled the smoke, coughed so hard he had to bend over double. He stood up and dried the tears from his eyes.

A fine hired coach rolled past. It was an open one; a fat, older gentleman sat leaning back comfortably. Olof took a few quick steps, as if he meant to run after the carriage.

"Caserio Santo," he hissed. He stopped and laughed. Santo, the anarchist who had murdered President Carnot with a dagger—the handle had been covered with red velvet. And he had cried "Long live anarchy!" while the police dragged him away. They had seen all of this at the waxworks. Everywhere, all over Europe, anarchists ran riot, throwing bombs and stabbing presidents and generals. But in backward Sweden there was only Hinke Berggen, and he was in prison on Långholmen.

The boys were not anarchists, yet at times, they played they were: the game of violent and exciting events, the bloody adventures of real life. To get to shout and scream and throw a bomb and stand in the middle of where it was all happening, finally get some attention. They felt like they needed to free themselves of all the suffocating grayness of everyday living.

But then another girl came along who diverted their thoughts. They were close on the heels of a lady's maid. She glared at them angrily and picked up her pace. They threw small teasing remarks in her direction. On the corner of Klotgränd, a fat policeman was standing there in a helmet and with a sword. She could feel safe there. They whistled a farewell and turned in the direction of the guard on Södermalmstorg. They started a little argument about the play of the sun on the water: was it beautiful and worth painting or a tasteless and cheap effect? Arthur contended you could make it even showier by putting a giant green sea monster in the middle of the red soup.

No, the girl with the red hair was a thousand times more showy, Olof replied. He would like to have her as a model, that would be something.

That's true, they needed to practice painting nudes, Arthur answered thoughtfully. You learned a lot from that, there was nothing harder than portraying the human body.

Naked... Olof hadn't exactly thought that far. He wanted to paint that girl while she was kneeling on the street scrubbing. But, of course, either way.

"We should get together with some other artists," Arthur said. "Rent a studio, get a place where we can really work."

Hopes and dreams began to flower. A studio—maybe a whole house—not too big but enough so they could both work and sleep there. Paint until they dropped, in the middle of canvasses and models. If they could only have peace and paint, they would probably get so far that their work would be recognized, even by their families. Now they heard only nagging at home. And it wasn't good if they were shut inside a factory all week long. They were so tired when Saturday arrived that all their desire and power to think had died away.

Olof tried to build up a self-defense. He had quit the lamp factory. Emelie couldn't accept it, she tried daily to convince him to get a new, steady job. But the thought of looking for odd jobs now and then was no longer as frightening. Now there was work available; you could take a week here and there and get by the rest of the time. If you didn't demand too much that is, and if you didn't attach too much importance to character references. But Olof was going to be an artist, of course. He chased away the thought of Emelie, the memory of all the evenings she tried to cajole him—while he sullenly sat at the kitchen table and drew. Once he had even promised to "try," but he barely wanted to admit it now.

Yes, a studio! That was what they needed. They could invite girls there too. There must be some who were up for cleaning and preparing food for a bunch of artists.

Every possibility glimmered from the pattern they wove, but then the thin fabric was blown away by the cool evening breeze. The sun had set behind the western hills; it was growing cold. In the immediate present there was only one girl who they could imagine would willingly take them in and offer them coffee.

"Let's go home," Olof suggested. "Emelie will surely give us a cup."

A little more subdued and feeling less sensational than before, they strolled up toward Glasbruksgatan. They took their time, as usual. Outside the entrance to the great artist's studio, they imagined one of his models might come along. They stood there shivering for a while until they gave up and continued up the hill. Emelie's coffee would have to warm them instead.

She received them a little sulkily, but made a place for them at the table where they could spread out their things. Olof wanted to show Arthur how he would like to do a picture of the girl on Hornsgatan. He would paint her in oil; he had bought a collection of brushes and paint in tubes with his last wages. Now he just sketched it out with a lead pencil, using a piece of colored chalk to emphasize the red hair. Unwillingly Emelie listened to them. She leaned forward to have a look when she filled their coffee cups. Apparently it was a girl they were talking about. She didn't really like the picture, it showed so clearly that Olof didn't look as innocently at the world as a boy as young as he was ought to. And she remembered the picture of Elsa.

But a moment later the boys had forgotten the red-haired girl. They were talking about hot air balloons instead. Had Emelie heard that you could steer those balloons really well now, and that some Swedes were even planning a journey to the North Pole in one?

That wasn't possible! People weren't meant to travel through the air that way. Something bad would certainly come of anyone's attempts to try.

Yes, it worked. They tried to convince her.

But she sat there quietly and thought of other things, remembering suddenly the first time she had gone up the Katarina elevator, what Mormor had once said when August had talked about the elevator. It seemed so terribly long ago when Mormor and Mama were alive and August still came to visit them—that happy time!

After Arthur left, Olof continued working on his sketch. He had brought out his watercolors, now he was going to experiment. He was still sitting at the kitchen table muttering when Emelie fell asleep. Now that he didn't have to get up early every morning, she seldom had the energy to wait until he went to bed.

When she woke up in the morning, he was asleep, of course. While Emelie drank her cup of coffee and ate a piece of bread, she looked at the picture that had been left out on the table. The hair was unnaturally red; some of the defiance of the girl in the drawing was still there. Still, Emelie liked it better now. There was something real and satisfying about it, too.

Not a lampoon, but a true picture—despite the hair.

For maybe the first time, she had to wonder if Olof wasn't right, if he in all his stubbornness was headed toward a real goal. It would have felt easier if she could have asked somebody's advice. But she didn't know anyone who would be able to understand it, who would be able to tell her if Olof was artist material or only a lazy and obstinate boy.

Gullpippi had painted hangings that were sold to the paint dealer. What if Olof could get work like that? Should Emelie ask old factory director Melinder for advice—didn't the factory sell its goods to the paint dealer as well?

She asked Olof cautiously one evening—but he didn't seem especially interested. And Emelie had something else to worry about. Things weren't going well between Bärta and Johan. The time of joy at reuniting was long since over. Johan didn't dare hit Bärta; she was able to hit back, so he took his anger out on Gunnar. During many evenings, Emelie had stood out in the entryway and suffered when she heard the blows and the boy's screams.

She talked with Bärta, asked her to do what she could. Earlier on Bärta had sided with Johan, thought the boy was impudent and had to be disciplined. Now Bärta, too, thought Johan was too hard on him, and she was grateful for Emelie's offer to take the boy sometimes. More and more Bärta managed to keep him out of the way. Johan didn't dare go into Emelie's room.

Bärta began to be in Emelie's room more often, too. She sat and complained. Sometimes she wasn't sober, she would stay at the construction site and drink. One evening she told Emelie she was expecting. She didn't know if it was Johan or one of the brick carriers who was the father. Emelie tried to get her to see reason. For Gunnar's sake—and for the baby she was expecting—Bärta had to manage to stick it out.

And Bärta promised. Though after another week or so it would be just as bad again. Bärta would come staggering home, Johan would swear and take it out on Gunnar. And the boy's howling would be heard all the way out to the street when Emelie arrived home.

Then it got to be too much for Emelie. She rushed into her neighbors', grabbed the screaming boy from Johan, and got some stinging lashes of the belt across her back herself. In the midst of the pain she still felt: with her body she shielded the child and Gunnar was spared the pain inflicted on her. She managed to get the boy into her room. From that day on Gunnar stayed in Emelie's room. He ate her food and slept in her bed.

Olof tried to draw the sleeping boy one evening, but he couldn't get a likeness. He was more successful with Johan, whom he did a portrait of sitting on the stairs to the privy, dead drunk. In that picture, Olof put together everything he felt about the chimneysweep journeyman. Nobody could mistake whose portrait it was. Emelie asked Olof to destroy the drawing or, at least, hide it.

He had sat for hours and carefully added detail after detail. Emelie had never counted on being able to convince him to destroy this work. "Now," he said, "We're going to burn that devil."

As carefully as he had done the drawing, he built a pyre of small pieces of wood, spread the drawing on top and lighted them. Then he laughed, satisfied with the result. Carnot's murder and Andrée with the hot air balloon had burned up in the conflagration at the waxworks the other day. This was a little private contribution to the fire.

ROWDY SPRING

Spring brought out the city dwellers, as the evenings grew warmer and lighter. They strolled around the streets and rediscovered their city. The imposing approach along the water on Söder Mälarstrand had been finished, gates and bridges at the locks by Slussen had been repaired, and the coalyard beneath Erstaberget's slope had been obliterated to leave space for the new harbor expansion. Over at Humlegården, the first electric train cars had been put into use. They ran all the way out to Djursholm. Another curious technical innovation was a tricycle that had a seat for a passenger in front. The city's usual multitude of cyclists was out on the streets once again—now that the kick-sleds had been put away for the season. With their careless weaving and wobbling there were a lot accidents and close calls.

People complained about the members of hooligan gangs: those idle and malicious young men who were more and more becoming a pest to the other citizens. At first, they stayed on the outskirts of the city, smashing windows and lamps and mugging decent folk. On Odengatan they had forced their way into a carriage, and the coachman had saved his passengers from being robbed by whipping his horses into a gallop. There were the Hornstull gang and the Kungsholmen gang and other unsavory alliances. Especially feared were those brutes who hung around Rackarbergen by Årstaviken, and made raids at night on Södermalm's grocers and beer vendors.

In the schools, some of the poorest children began to hope to spend part of the summer out in the country. A new philanthropic venture had been founded, the elementary school colonies. The children who had phlegm in their lungs or were severely undernourished were suddenly envied. Another authorized initiative that spring was the workers' garden at Sickla Zoo beside Hammarby Lake. Eight small cottages, each with its own plot of land, were to be rented out to workers' families at the cheap price of twenty kronor per year.

Despite everything that was done for the workers and their children, the socialists continued their propaganda with steadily increasing success. The First of May demonstration that spring was mainly a demonstration for peace with Norway. One of the speakers was a woman who had gone over from the liberals to the social democrats. Previously she had supervised a day-care center in the Katarina area, and her name was Kata Dahlström.

But Branting aroused the greatest enthusiasm. He warned that in the broad strata of society, there might be someone who, without orders but with a bullet, would want to prevent ten thousand bullets from being fired with orders, slaughtering friends and brothers. It was a threat directed at the king himself, many said. Branting was called an offender against his majesty and condemned to three months in prison for inciting violence. But the highest court lowered the sentence to a fine of five hundred crowns, and the money was collected by sympathizers with the criminal on both sides of the Kölen, the mountain chain between Sweden and Norway.

Arthur and Olof wandered around together, their red scarves waving madly in the spring wind. One Sunday they walked through the whole city out to Djurgården. The bridge to it was so bad that a policeman had to stand there and make sure that wagons slowed down on it; they couldn't drive faster than at a walking pace. But soon the bridge was going to be rebuilt. It would be ready in good time for the exposition.

Tivoli had opened for the season and attracted people with the magnificent view from the Café Bellevue on a plateau on top of the hill. The goal of the two youths was somewhere else: the panorama building on the point at Kaptensudden. There was an exhibition by an Italian artist of an enormous round painting of Mt. Vesuvius erupting in the year 79 when Pompeii was destroyed.

Silent, overwhelmed, the two budding artists leaned against the railing. So much canvas and so much paint that the Italian had at his disposal!

Would they have time to go through as much in their lifetimes?

Suddenly, Olof felt observed and carefully turned his head. He wasn't unused to people looking at him. His hair would soon be as long as Arthur's and his scarf naturally annoyed some people. Many probably believed he was one of those hooligan gang members, didn't understand that the scarf indicated something else.

There was a young, upper-class couple standing a little way from them. At first Olof was uninterested and, perhaps, a little disdainful and turned his back. But then he thought, didn't he recognize that well-groomed beard? He had to look again, half hidden behind Arthur's back. Could that be August? It had been so long since he last saw his brother that he wasn't sure. Six years ago Olof had only been ten. Would August really be able to recognize him now?

He was unsure. Maybe it wasn't August. In any case, he didn't feel like saying hello. He would only make a fool of himself, didn't even know how he should address them. He nudged Arthur, they could go on now.

August watched the boys as they jostled their way a little clumsily to the door, falling over each other getting out. He wasn't sure; the younger of the boys might be Olof. His brother should be about that age now. A hooligan? It probably wasn't easy for Emelie to raise a boy that age. But it was too late to try and help her now. They had gone their separate ways. And Emelie had said, when he had run into her once, that she was managing fine and that Olof was working. That was probably not Olof. Besides, he had to think mostly of Ida now. They were expecting their first child, although she wasn't showing yet. Sometime he would still invite Emelie over and really question her about how things were going with Olof.

Evening was falling, a light and melancholy blue. Inside the houses, people were beginning to light candles and lamps. But the lamplighters hadn't come out yet, and in a few weeks the street lamp lighting would cease for the summer. Coaches clattered quickly past, on their way from Djurgården toward town. The coachmen urged the horses on, the whips dancing lightly over their backs, the flames of the coach lanterns jumping and fluttering with the speed. Beside the wood-laden cargo boats, a few tattered gray figures were looking for bits of bark.

Arthur and Olof walked back toward Söder, first walking along the quays, then turning in among the lanes of the Old Town. From the windows along Österlånggatan, half-naked girls hung out and called to them. But the boys weren't interested. Those who were young and poor could only count on taunts from the whores.

At Slussen, the boys parted ways. Arthur was going to his home off Hornsgatan, where his father was a shoemaker. Olof met up with Thumbs' youngest son, Mikael, and they kept each other company. Mikael worked at the harbor, like his father. Things were brewing down there now; there was talk of a strike for higher wages. The time was right, sea traffic had picked up in earnest. Maybe they would start as early as tomorrow morning, Thumbs was at a meeting now. If Olof didn't have anything else to do, he could come and watch. Who knows, something exciting might happen.

A few harbor workers were meeting at Max's home. They were Eagle-Owl, Kalle Baker, Pork Nisse and Thumbs. Max had called the meeting. He took out some pieces of paper that he had tried to write on. The handwriting wasn't beautiful, but it was legible.

Today we don't give a damn about working. We are on strike.

That's what it said. Perhaps they could discuss the wording, but it was unnecessary since Max had already written it out. The meaning was clear and there was nothing to object to. The notices should be hung out around the harbor in highly visible places: one on the old customs house at Stadsgården and the other at Fiskarhamnen. But who would take the risk? If you were seen, it was as good as being fired.

Max had thought of that too. He called out to his old father who had gone to the neighbor's in the next room. Wooden-clog Anders was willing. He hadn't had the strength to work the past few years, he wasn't risking anything.

Perhaps no one would remember their real names. But their nicknames were etched in the memories of the harbor workers.

On Monday morning, when the foremen went to bring out their forces, the harbor workers who worked in other parts of the city also came to take part in the roll call. They clustered in front of the notices that had been hung up. Yes, someone said, that was right, they should strike. They couldn't live on promises, said someone else.

They grew more excited, everyone began talking at once. They should send someone to the waterfront at Värtahamnen and encourage the workers there to show solidarity with them. Someone with a bicycle took off for Värtahamnen.

More and more workers gathered. One of stevedore Lundström's sons came to the customs house and wanted to tear down the notice, but they refused to let him pass. This was none of his business. The stevedore's son hurried away. Maybe he was going to call the police. They couldn't stand and hold a meeting here at the harbor. It had happened before that those who had wanted to strike had been convicted of holding up traffic.

"Let's go to Lilljans!" someone began to shout. "Come together and come with us. To Lilljans!"

It was turning into a real demonstration with several hundred workers. They tried to form a line, falling over each other as they started off. Lundström's son came running again, now to try and convince the improvised demonstration parade to turn back. But they didn't listen to him, just kept on marching.

Thumbs and Max ran over to the streetcar on the other side of the square at Slussen. They were going to the editors of *The Social-Democrat* to try and find someone to keep order at the meeting. Thumbs, who had been a member of the party before, knew one of the old guys at the newspaper.

Olof had been standing at the harbor following what was happening. Now he hurried after the demonstrators. Large groups of work-clad men, unshaven and ragged, worn-out and marked by life. They thudded along resolutely in their heavy boots, frightening the refined dandies out promenading on Norrbro, causing the well-dressed children in Kungsträdgården to take refuge behind mothers and nannies.

At the cottages beside Lilljans, the harbor workers came to a halt, a little confused and unsure once they had reached their goal. What would happen now? When they heard that people had gone for help, they sat down on the hillside, offered each other snuff and grinned contentedly at the spring sunshine. Not until then could they take a breather. This was right to take a Monday off.

The stevedore's son had run with them all the way here, now he kept watch from a distance. And a young boy with a red scarf sat drawing. Were they going to make it into the newspaper? But the boy shook his head.

Two men jumped out of a carriage and hurried to the meeting place. A few recognized them: the bankteller Zeitnitz and a young journalist who had been a bricklayer earlier. His name was Tengdahl. They called to the gathering and the harbor workers slowly sat up. The two men began to speak; when one stopped the other began. Stay united and stick with it, they said. Put together the old union again, without organization you can't gain any lasting success.

There was a lot to ask about—some things to object to as well. The audience, unused to attending meetings, began to interject more and more. Finally, it was almost impossible for the speakers to make themselves heard. Some began to hiss, others to shout.

"Shut up you damned rowdies, when we're trying to do something for you!" It was Zeitnitz who, in a desperate outburst, had shouted at the top of his lungs.

That made them grow quiet, at last, perhaps a little abashed. Certainly, they were used to rough talk, but being addressed so scathingly was something they hadn't really expected to happen at their own strike meeting. A regular guy, the skinny little one. It was best to listen to him.

"Yes," they shouted, when he asked if they wanted to start to union again. And, at his suggestion, they decided to elect the journalist Tengdahl as chairman of the interim board.

Now they were to register as members. They were to set up a special column for nicknames; many were so used to them that they wouldn't answer if their real names were called. But, said the journalist, at all roll calls they would call out the real name, and if someone didn't answer then they would call their nickname. The goal would be to build a respected work force and eradicate the designation of rowdies. The first thing they would do would be to request that the stevedores provide near beer at the workplace, so the workers would avoid the excessive beer drinking. Heavy work made them sweaty and thirsty, and there were way too many sellers living off quenching the harbor workers' thirst.

Olof had been sitting under a tree drawing feverishly. He had focused especially on one of the men, a toothless old man in torn clothes. He was one of the ones too weak to participate any longer, and had to satisfy himself with doing odd jobs. He would never reap the benefits that a union could provide. The old man cupped his ear with his hand in order to hear as much as he could of what was being said. There was a lot of distrust, but also of hope, in his expression. But still he looked mostly tired. He had pushed himself to the limit in order to make it all the way to Lilljans.

Olof was proud of his work, felt like he had captured the mood and the intent, the destitution and the bewilderment that lay behind the protest, and the hope that the meeting inspired.

On the way home, he showed it to Thumbs and Mikael. But Thumbs shook his head angrily. It was inappropriate to use this occasion for lampooning honest old workers. They couldn't help it if they were toothless and ugly. It was toil and starvation that had made them that way. Olof shouldn't forget that his own father had been a harbor worker. Olof didn't believe they had been created this way? Hadn't he heard what Tengdahl had said: the harbor workers weren't going to be rowdies any longer. If Olof wanted to serve the working class and honor the memory of his father, if he wanted to draw in order to do something useful and help, then his drawings should be completely different. He should show how strong men stepped out from the depths of the people and waved the standard— how the rotten upper class society fell before their assembled strength.

"That would be lying," answered Olof. With his picture, he wanted to show how badly they had been mistreated. And how, in spite of everything, they continued living and had the strength to fight back.

Mikael agreed with him. Thumbs had a hard time defending himself, grumbled about the "spring chickens." What did they know, what had they ever accomplished?

Olof kept quiet. He didn't think it was worthwhile speaking; nobody wanted to understand him, Mikael was only pretending. Wasn't that always the way: those closest understood last. Thumbs and his friends were in the right in their struggle, and Olof wanted to be part of it, join in with them, but they pushed him away. They talked about how mistreated and oppressed they were, but wanted to be portrayed as victors. Olof wanted to show solidarity, but if they wanted him to paint pretty lies for them he would have to leave them, go his own way.

IV

THE NEW ERA

The world was young and new. It was true that a few years still remained of the old century, but it felt as if humanity had climbed the stairs to the twentieth century and managed to push the door ajar—and stood at the threshold and grew accustomed to the blinding light.

Boundaries and ties were being blown apart.

Andrée and his men prepared to sail a hot air balloon to the North Pole.

Hjalmar Branting had been voted into Parliament. In his maiden speech, he had said that the state that disarmed in order to raise its material and spiritual standards would overtake its neighboring states with a vengeance. Thus creating better protection than countless army regiments and instruments of murder could provide.

Perhaps the inventor of dynamite had had some of the same vision as Branting. Shortly before his death, Alfred Nobel had declared that he saw inherited wealth as a misfortune that only increased mankind's complacency. Instead, he wanted to further peaceful and literary advances and reward those who worked for understanding between peoples. His will was received with a mixture of joy and anxiety. Many were indignant that the Peace Prize was to be given out by the Norwegians. The inventor's brother's wife and children began legal proceedings to have the will declared invalid.

Perhaps more strongly than ever before, the dream of a better and happier world recurred. In the city then, this dream materialized along the shoreline of Djurgården. Out of the greenery grew a light and shimmering fantasy city with a whiff of the exoticism of eastern lands and the romanticism of the Nordic pine woods: minarets and onion spires, oriental palaces and red manor houses, Rhineland castles in miniature and medieval cities surrounding the Three Crowns Castle. An enormous candle in a giant candlestick, delivered from the factory out by Danviken's tollgate, stood as a flickering flame of enlightenment.

This was the large Nordic art and industrial exhibition that was being created, where manufacturers from Sweden, Norway, Denmark, and Russia together with Finland would exhibit their products. Vast halls were being filled. Over the piles of black iron goods in the Industrial Hall hung a white plaster image of the king; above stalls and bazaars rose the glistening balloon of the conqueror of the air; from the evening dark water flowed the fire fountain's gleaming cascades. Dreams of ancient times and times to come gave the heavy and material here-and-now a poetic shimmer.

Along with this exhibition, Oscar II also celebrated the Silver Anniversary of his union with his fellow men. He had now reigned for twenty-five years. When the exhibition opened on St. Sofia Day, the fifteenth of May, the entire city was in motion. Banners fluttered everywhere: from rooftops and boat masts, and from the high telephone tower in the city. Along the whole length of Strandvägen painted blue flag poles had been erected. When the royal entourage arrived, the street was black with people thronging between the slender, light green trees—plumes floating over the multitudes, drum rolls, shouts of command, cries of hurrah, rows of shining spiked helmets. The four-horse royal carriage rolled across Djurgården's new bridge with its depictions of "The Mythic Gods of Our Fathers," through the entrance to the exhibition and to the stairway leading to the Industrial Hall. Queen Sofia was carried in a sedan chair to the dais. Blue-uniformed princes and pink princesses followed the king in his general's uniform. The governor gave the signal. The royal orchestra and several hundred singers began performing Stenhammar's Inaugural Cantata with text by Count Snoilsky.

What Djurgården's catkins have concealed
We long await the glimpse revealed!

The introduction was cautious, the song groping its way toward certainty and light. But soon came rejoicing. It rose and burst into full bloom in the great cries of the chorus:

Pennants blend a symphony of color vast
Spring sings out that doubt and cold are past
Our chorus melds one great melody at last.

With bared heads the guests and subjects listened to the king's inaugural speech.

"While war dragged its bloody mantle across the classical world, crowned by high Olympus' many thousand-year-old silver diadem that spread from the minarets of the Hagia Sophia on the banks of the Bosphorus to Mount Acropolis with its magnificent columns beside the Aegean Sea, a completely different encounter was being prepared in Ultima Thule, the ancient mythical land," said the king.

"Here today, on St. Sophia Day, beneath the bright cupola of the Nordic spring sky's temple, a blow will be struck that will cause neither blood nor tears to be shed. Where once Svear and Goths made their peace and were united in ancient times, beside Lake Mälar whose praises have been sung by many, and whose far-reaching stream was carved out by Gefion according to the legend, all the way to the waves of Eystrasalt, there Sweden's capital was founded by the celebrated and magnanimous jarl who became the first protector not only of peace for the church, peace for women and peace for the home, but also of peace for the courts of law in the Nordic world. History itself has assigned a rightful place for the large, peaceful, all-conquering thing that is assembled at this time. Here the Swedish people have called a meeting with their brothers from the other side of the western mountains, with their friends from across the sound and along the Baltic beaches, and with their neighbors from the eastern edge of the Baltic Sea along the Neva and the Aura rivers for a peaceful competition on industry's playing field."

And the king declared the exhibition open, after which he wished everyone welcome in the name of the Swedish people.

Cries of hurrah and jubilation resounded, trumpet fanfares blared from the minarets. Skansen's cannons thundered, and church bells rang, the singers performed a new cantata. The moment was at hand. The door to the new era had been flung wide open.

THE PERFUME BOTTLE
AND
THE FAIRY GROTTO

The new era had also reached Melinder's cosmetics factory. Like Alfred Nobel, the old factory director had no closer relatives than his siblings and brother's children, but in contrast to Nobel, he believed that possessions should be inherited. There was a layer of society that had been selected and educated for the task of managing and increasing capital. Besides, it was through an inheritance that he had once been able to start his factory.

He had chosen his successor. For some years one of his brother's sons had been training under him, familiarizing himself with manufacturing and sales. The old man had been so finicky and admonishing that the young Konrad Melinder was now bursting with eagerness to get to do business himself and try out new ideas, The firm's products were good ones and well-liked, but too little known. To the old man's horror, Konrad had applied for an exhibit booth. Right beside the inlet at Djurgården's bridge, not far from the fairy grotto, he had had a little house built. It looked like a collection of large perfume bottles and contained two rooms, one for the exhibit and sales of his products and one where the work would be demonstrated. A "working exhibition" was considered by the experts to be of the greatest value from the viewpoint of the public. People quickly grew tired of looking at products, no matter how elegantly they were arranged, but they could stand endlessly watching an adroit girl wrap up soaps.

The girls had to be able to withstand being watched. Konrad really would have preferred to put some lovely ballerinas at the worktable, but annoying as it was, it wasn't so easy to take hold of bars of soap, polish them and wrap them up. It looked easy, but for it to happen quickly and neatly enough for people to be impressed, many years of training were required.

The old factory director had often expressed his satisfaction with "Little Emelie's" performance; she was one of the company's faithful employees and had been with them practically from the beginning. In Konrad's opinion, she was too old to be in the exhibit, she was probably approaching thirty. She looked a little worn and bitter—like women in the working class soon become. He stood secretly watching her, wondering what could be done to make her more attractive.

Besides, he already had made up his mind as to who should be included in the exhibit. For the sales room, he had found a delightful young lady who was in the process of learning all the facts about the manufacture of the different preparations. An assistant supervisor would stand beside a soap-making machine on display and work, looking handsome and inspiring confidence. A young packaging girl named Ingeborg was also an obvious choice—though he would have to send her to a dentist to fill in a gap. Otherwise, there was a pretty poor selection of beauties at the factory, but one didn't think of that when one hired people. Still, he would have to use that Emelie. It would at least make the old man happy. He had her sent for.

Curious and nervous, Emelie came to find out what he wanted. First she washed her hands and combed her hair, tried to make herself as neat as possible, but there wasn't much possibility—she was dressed for work. What if she got fired... how would they manage then? She had seen the young master standing and watching her, felt like he hadn't been really satisfied, even though she had done everything she could to work as effectively as possible. Things had felt more secure as long as old Melinder had been in charge of everything.

She knocked on the door and stepped into the office. One of the younger clerks gave the message that she had arrived, and politely held the door to the director's office open for her. Confused, she curtsied a thank you. Konrad Melinder stood at the window; the early spring sun shone through his light hair. He turned around, looked at her, frowned—so gray and simple. Emelie felt afraid: he was dissatisfied with her.

But he asked her to sit down. The old factory director had never done this. The employees had remained standing by his desk when they talked to him. Carefully, she sat down, hurriedly running her hand over her skirt to make sure that no paste or bits of paper were still there to get on the fine chair.

He presented his plan: she and Ingeborg and Persson would work at the big exhibition. In front of an audience, they would show how Melinder's soaps were created and packaged, but as she might understand... he searched for words, scratched the back of his neck, began again.

They wouldn't just show how the work was carried out, he explained. At the same time it would be like some sort of display window for the company. Since the firm manufactured soaps, perfumes and beauty products, this was extremely delicate. Even if there were capable old women down in the packaging room, he couldn't let any of them stand and represent a factory for beauty products. The visitors to the exhibition had to get the feeling that those who made the products had already been made beautiful. Emelie knew, perhaps, that he had sent Ingeborg to a dentist. This had been at the company's own expense. They did manufacture toothpaste as well. Emelie should take a few tubes home and use them diligently. How were her teeth, weren't they pretty good?

Yes, at least she didn't have any cavities that showed.

Face, hair and hands mattered as well. He had said to the stockroom manager that Emelie could have a complete set of whatever products she might need. At the company's expense both girls would go to a beauty expert and get help and advice, and then they would be given clothes. They had to be dressed identically, it would look best that way. He had a sister who would help them and take them to a seamstress.

Emelie felt her inadequacy—tried to object that she wasn't suitable— couldn't make herself pretty enough. He had to convince her that there was no one else who was capable. He grew very animated, the girl blushed, and then she wasn't so gray and dreary looking anymore. Now he almost believed what he said.

She gave in. You didn't say no to your superior if you were dependent on your job. Still red and afraid, she returned to the packaging room and had to tell her curious colleagues what the young factory director had said. They teased her. Emelie and Ingeborg would surely begin to smell like perfumed streetwalkers. Emelie kept quiet and continued working, afraid of what awaited. She didn't know what the young factory director would dream up next, he was certainly a real trickster.

The time before the exhibition opened was broken up and busy. Still, Emelie wasn't working very much, most of the time she was waiting around or was the object of other people's endeavors. Miss Melinder came in a carriage and drove Emelie and Ingeborg to the seamstress and the milliner. They got white work dresses with large aprons to cover them while they were in the Exhibition Hall. Ingeborg declared that they looked like brides. Each had her own suit and hat and umbrella to wear on the way to and from the hall. Their hair was cared for, and their nails filed and buffed and polished. Their faces and hands were rubbed with creams and cosmetics from the factory. They even learned to use lipstick, eyebrow coloring and powder. Miss Melinder and the beauty expert watched over them, corrected, checked the results.

Emelie was perhaps more horrified than delighted over the outward changes she underwent. It was surely a sin and a shame for an ordinary person to dress up that way. What would people think? Everybody must be able to see how artificial she was, and wonder what that smell was that wafted from her. For certain, they must think that she had become a fallen woman. She tried to hide in the shadow of the side streets when she walked back and forth to work. If she could have waited with all of this until the exhibition opened... but Miss Melinder said that it took a long time to become beautiful enough to be the subject of an exhibition.

Being together with Ingeborg made it a little easier. The young girl was so openly happy and proud, felt none of Emelie's anxiety. She did everything she could to persuade Emelie that all was as it should be. Emelie had become so pretty and refined; that was why people turned and looked at her. And her colleagues in the packaging room were jealous; that was the reason for their teasing her.

In some way, they had been excluded from their old circle. They had grown different—didn't belong to the packaging girls' hardened and worn out team anymore. If Emelie ever had time to make it to the packaging table she was met with taunts. So, she felt like working a little, wouldn't she ruin her fine hands?

It was really a relief when, one week before the opening, she got to go to the exhibition and get away from her colleagues. Emelie and Ingeborg had to help unpack and put out the goods that would be displayed in the exhibition hall. They tried out sitting in front of the fine and polished packaging table where they were to work. Brass posts with a rope between them were placed in front of the table. This arrangement would prevent onlookers from crowding too close.

During that week Emelie got to know some of the exhibition area. She came every day on the ferry that went from Slussen to Allmänna gränd, showed her pass, made her way among the construction and the piles of boards, and wondered if everything would be ready on time. She arrived to "her" part of the area near the canal at Djurgårdsbrunnsviken. Not so far from the Melinder pavilion stood the large, red fishery hall. Even closer, on the same block, were the sugar and vinegar factories' pavilions, a beer hall and the malt coffee company's café that looked like a giant coffee mill. Above them all towered the big candle. There were going to be exhibition and work spaces inside the candlestick and a powerful electric light would serve as a flame on top.

Melinder's pavilion looked like a collection of piled up perfume bottles in attractive pastel colors. At the back, there was an almost invisible door to a little closet where the girls would change. Persson, who was in charge of the soap machine, also had his clothes hanging in there.

Messrs. Melinder and some of the office workers came out the day before the inaugural ceremony. They inspected their working exhibit. The display employees had to pretend they were working in front of the public. This should go all right, thought Emelie. They wouldn't have time to think about the audience if the work was done quickly and well.

On the day of the inauguration, they stood on the gravel path outside the pavilion and looked over at the Industrial Hall while it grew black with people swarming. They couldn't see the royal entourage when it arrived, couldn't hear more than the distant noise of the orchestra and chorus. But when the cannons and the church bells broke loose, they hurried in and got in place. Now it was time, now people would begin streaming in this direction.

The Danish princesses Ingeborg and Thyra, with their attendants, honored the Melinder pavilion with a visit. They were among the first to arrive. The lovely Miss Berg humbly sprayed the princesses with perfume in the Exhibition Hall. They stayed a long time in the work hall, looking on with interest as the soaps came out of the machine, and then were caught and polished and magically wrapped in paper with the exhibition motif on it.

These soaps were for sale, were sold as souvenirs. But what if the princesses each wanted her own soap? Emelie was seized with anxiety; just work, don't look up, just be a part of the machine. Still, she thought it would be a great pity if they didn't each get their own soap. She summoned up her courage. Wasn't she suddenly being too presumptuous? She stood up and curtsied as gracefully as she could and handed them the soaps. The royal ladies nodded and thanked her and said some kind words that Emelie didn't understand. She curtsied again and said, thank you. Surely one could always say thank you? And the young factory director nodded, also, encouraging and concurring. He was even happier the next day, came and showed the girls what it said in one of the newspapers: the princesses had lingered a long time at the work exhibit in the "Perfume Bottle." They had been very impressed by the young working women's dexterity, and had each gladly received her own soap of the Melinder factory's manufacture.

This was good advertising and beyond all expectations. The young Melinder shone with delight, and invited the girls for coffee and pastries at Reinhold's Steam Bakery and Café located diagonally behind the large candle. He praised Emelie for her fortunate initiative. The old man had been right; this woman was good. Besides, she didn't look bad either, since she had been groomed and dressed up. Youth and beauty were not enough. The young Ingeborg would never have taken it into her head to offer those soaps. He should have thought of it himself—instructed them to do it. Now it had gone well, in any case. He could only thank the old man's "Little Emelie" for that. And he would remember to do that.

He ordered a photographer to come and take a picture of the personnel in the Exhibition Hall and at the worktable. They each received their own photo as a souvenir.

At first everything was so new that Emelie didn't have time to do much more than attend to her duties and try to get used to the new surroundings. Gradually it grew easier; it actually began to feel natural to go around finely dressed, perfumed and powdered. At the exhibition grounds this didn't arouse any attention. It was only on the simpler and poorer streets that people stared and wondered.

She began to feel at home at the exhibition, found her way around, formed habits. Every day she was over at the "Coffee Mill," brought bread with her, and drank a cup of coffee. She got to know the girls in the Mill and soon was sitting more often in the kitchen than at the tables.

Melinder's "Working Exhibition" wasn't open all day long. There were demonstrations at certain times in the morning, the afternoon and the evening. There were rather long periods that Emelie had free. She began to bring Gunnar with her in the daytime now that he had summer vacation from school. She knew the guards at the entrance and could bring the boy in with her for free. They may have thought he was her son. Gunnar couldn't stay inside the Perfume Bottle so he wandered around close to the Pavilion. He knew when Emelie was free and came and met her, went with her and got a glass of milk at the Mill. In the afternoons they went to the public cafeteria across from the funicular railway that went up to the Skansen Open Air Museum. It was often crowded, and on days when an extra number of trains offering cheap fares brought travelers to the capital city, it sometimes happened that they ran out of food. The poorer visitors to the exhibition gathered here, as well as the many workers who couldn't afford to eat at more expensive places. You could get a good and substantial meal for forty öre, and since Emelie was paid extra for the expenses that her unusual job might entail, she felt they could afford to split a portion and eat there.

Gunnar mostly stayed by the long dock at the Fairy Grotto, along the water behind the main restaurant. Sometimes he could make himself useful and earn a few öre running errands. He got to know the women from Dalarna who, with their short, wide oars, punted the boats through the grotto. He got to go along for free, mostly in the mornings when there were often empty seats. He felt like he could never see enough of the fantastic spectacle the grotto offered.

The boat glided in slowly, leaving daylight behind, met by the dusk inside the vault. Enormous stalactites hung from the ceiling. Sometimes the boat came so close, he wondered if they were going to run into one and he would get hit on the head by a stalactite. But then the rower would scull the boat a little and they would glide past unharmed in a shimmer of silver between glittering walls. And everywhere inside the narrow passage shone glittering precious stones. The boat glided on, into the golden vault, where an underground stream suddenly bubbled up—then on through the depths of the grotto—enormous columns seeming to float past in the twilight.

For a moment, it looked as if the ride was almost over, they came so close to the dock. But through a side opening in the mysterious rock, the boat slipped in under a high vault where the walls sparkled in every color imaginable. In the middle of this room, a pillar of water shot up to the ceiling and highest up was a fissure in the rock, and it let in flashes of lightning. By then the ride was almost over, and, overwhelmed by the impressions, the passengers climbed up onto the dock.

Much of what Gunnar experienced that summer he would forget, but never the Fairy Grotto. It was Emelie who took him there, who every day took him along to the exhibition's fairyland—Emelie who had become so fine and beautiful, that just walking beside her was treat. Since this fun exhibition had started, she was happier too, wasn't at all as strict as before.

Emelie was surprised herself over how calm she felt—at how she had grown younger not only in appearance but also inwardly. She had regained something—some of the joy of youth she hadn't really had time and energy for earlier. Olof had gotten work over the summer. It meant a lot to her that she didn't have to worry about him. She had Gunnar close to her all day long. Johan had been almost humbled by Emelie's new elegance. He admired her, she couldn't help noticing it. It didn't flatter her, but naturally it was nice that he stayed calm and showed her some respect.

Olof came to the exhibition one day. He especially wanted to see the art galleries. Emelie had never gone into any of them; there was so much besides paintings to see. Olof wasn't particularly pleased by them, she understood. He muttered something about "salon art," but she couldn't see what was wrong with that. It was nice when paintings were suitable for hanging in salons. But there was someone's paintings he wanted to see who wasn't included, a Norwegian. He tried to explain what they portrayed: a man who was running and screaming on a bridge, and a skinny and naked girl who was sitting on a bed with some kind of black cloud nearby. Emelie thought it sounded strange. She could well understand that such things weren't allowed to hang in the grand exhibition, but she didn't want to say this to Olof.

No, that Norwegian was worth more than everyone in the rooms here. He wanted to do that kind of thing himself—something that was real and provided something new about people.

He was never satisfied, never really happy. She couldn't comprehend him. But at least he was working this summer; it was a huge relief, and she had to be content with that.

One Sunday, when it was "general admission day" and cheaper tickets, she was together with Johan and Bärta at the exhibition. Bärta had been able to leave her little girl with a neighbor. She was having a hard time walking around—was expecting another child. This time there was no doubt that Johan was the father of the child, she had let Emelie know. He didn't seem especially proud, mostly embarrassed at his unwieldy wife who groaned as she walked and had to rest time and again. He pretended that it was Emelie he was out with and that Bärta was someone insignificant who happened to be walking in the same direction.

Johan offered to buy them dinner, but he didn't want to eat in the public cafeteria, so he led them to the Central Restaurant. It was certainly a good deal cheaper than eating at the Main Restaurant, but Emelie still thought it was a terrible luxury. They ate while the Rumanian gypsies played, and the tab was high, but Johan payed without trying to bargain. Emelie watched the money changing wallets, and couldn't help remembering that Johan and Bärta owed her a whole five kronor that she had been waiting to get back for a long time.

She met many people at the exhibition; everybody had to see it. One day she ran right into August and his wife. August called her name and she had to stop and say hello. They heard that she was working in the Perfume Bottle, and said they would come and watch her someday. August's wife seemed so easy to talk to—kind and nice. And August said that when the exhibition was over and Emelie had a little more free time, she absolutely had to come over to their place one evening.

She hurried on. Gunnar was probably waiting. August and Ida stood and watched the boy come running to her.

"Do you think that's her son?" wondered Ida.

August shook his head. No, that couldn't be. Maybe one of her workmates' sons. Gertrud only had girls as far as he knew, and Emelie definitely didn't have any children.

Emelie and Gunnar walked together among minarets and gazebos, beneath the green trees. It was time for a meal break; they were on their way to the public cafeteria. He was eager to tell her everything he had seen. She had to hear everything. For a moment she was solemn, couldn't escape from the thought that she had just left Gunnar's real father. But then, she couldn't do anything but laugh at the boy's chatter, enjoy herself again. Light-colored and erect, she walked with Gunnar holding her hand, the white dress cutting a swath around her.

It was a happy summer, a time that left a bright memory.

ROYAL JUBILEE

That summer was a party. Warm and beautiful, blessed with weather fit for a king. Trains with cheap fares rolled into Central Station completely filled. A huge public streamed to the exhibition. Princely guests were received with triumphal arches and salutes. King Chulangkorn of Siam, with his dark-skinned eastern entourage, received the most attention.

The heat held, but the evenings grew darker. The whole exhibition area glittered with thousands of small colored lanterns. Out in the city, too, decorations with lights were put up in preparation for the Royal Jubilee. The mood of excitement increased, people were working up for the finale.

Enormous lines formed at all the attractions of the exhibition. It was important to take advantage of it now; the party was almost over. Cinematographers recorded images of the latest events: Prince Carl and Princess Ingeborg leaving the church after their wedding in Copenhagen, their arrival to Stockholm. But the divers were still the biggest hit. People never got tired of watching the film backwards so that the divers flew up out of the spraying water, and after an elegant somersault, threw themselves up onto the diving platform.

Businesses and stands set out their Jubilee wares. Brooches and pins with his majesty's initials. Jubilee cards, Jubilee issues of newspapers and magazines, Jubilee history, flags, hats, scarves, candles. Even Jubilee bobbers for the use of royal sporting fishermen.

In Melinder's exhibition space, they changed paper and wrapped up Jubilee soaps instead of exhibition soaps. The young factory director smoked Jubilee cigars and offered the girls Jubilee candy.

The royal festivities lasted almost a week. As early as Tuesday evening, they had begun to light profile illuminations and obelisks on Norrbro, and the gas decorations on Arvfurstens Palace. On Wednesday evening, the large bicycle show was held in the Sport Park, preceded by a festive quadrille: driven by gentlemen in white shirts and black trousers, white-clad ladies carrying bouquets of flowers rested on the handlebars of their steel steeds. On Thursday, the garrison's guards appeared in parade dress. On Friday, the city's underprivileged were treated to coffee and rolls by Crown Princess Victoria, and then the official series of speeches in remembrance and in tribute began.

The foreign vessels began to arrive with their exalted guests. The German Kaiser's white *Hohenzollern* anchored outside of Fiskerhamnen, the black Russian Asia stopped a few hundred meters away. The Danish and Swedish vessels filled the water between Söder and the city. Cannon fire boomed without cease from Skeppsholmen. Windowpanes rattled. People staggered around, party drunk and half deaf. Bridges and quays were black with people. Boats and extra trains steadily pumped in new masses of them.

When the king arrived on Friday evening, traveling in his specially made Jubilee carriage with a crown on the roof, the whole city cheered. Then the large fireworks display was set off. But Sunday's illumination was still the high point, when the whole city glittered in the September darkness, and an arch of shining lights had been mounted over Norrbro. Only Söder had been neglected and lay dark and silent, emptied of people.

All the taverns were filled. People never grew tired of requesting the king's song, and the orchestras played while the public stood at attention. Waiters and waitresses bowed under their trays. Arak liqueur flowed.

Emelie's workmate, Ingeborg, had gotten a "fiancé" over the summer. There were many gentlemen who came and looked at the work going on in the Perfume Bottle, and there were those who lingered, hanging on the rope and talking to the girls. Emelie gave brief and somewhat curt replies. Ingeborg had another manner, she twittered away and didn't mind being flirted with.

Her fiancé wasn't from the city. He was one of the many who had come to display goods at the exhibition. A fine and elegant gentleman, he seemed to have plenty of money. Sometimes he would invite both Ingeborg and Emelie to the café next door.

Ingeborg hadn't dared say anything about her fiancé to her parents. They were old-fashioned and, in fact, didn't approve at all of Ingeborg working at the exhibition and going around painted like a harlot.

On Sunday afternoon, her fiancé came to get Ingeborg as soon as the last demonstration was over. They sailed off, beautiful and young, happy and laughing. He was going to take her to Bern's Café, where he had reserved a table.

Emelie stood there and watched them—maybe a touch envious. Ingeborg only had herself to think of. Her whole life lay bright and shining before her. But Emelie walked silent and determined through the crowds of people, had to go home and make sure everything was in order before the coming workweek.

All the lights glittered and danced in the September darkness, the orchestras played, the glasses tinkled, Ingeborg laughed. He said so many funny things, held her hand in his, ordered more to drink. Yes, the "Jubilee Day" was the culmination of this fantastic summer. Soon he would travel back to his city again—but he was coming back for her. He was never going to let her go, he had said. She pressed her knee against his, felt him press it back.

"Cheers," he said. And she toasted him and drank.

"Oh, my head's spinning," she whispered. But he just laughed, said they had to have one evening like this one. It should spin, the whole town was spinning tonight. It was nice when it was spinning, she thought. The week had been strenuous. Now she could just hope and dream and feel how nice it was to have him close to her.

But when they stood up to leave she was horrified. Her legs didn't want to. She sank back into the chair, sitting there helpless until he offered her his arm. She tried to hold her head high, nonetheless. People shouldn't see how badly off she was. But it didn't seem as if anyone had time to look, everybody had probably drunk too much tonight. She felt like everyone was reeling and pushing, but they were in such amazing good humor, they only smiled and said, "Upsy-daisy young lady!"

"Upsy-daisy," she said and took a few tottering steps across the gravel of the park. He led her to a carriage. She had to lean her head against his chest. She drooled a little on his lapel, closed her eyes, felt the carriage rocking, heard the horses' hooves clopping as if they were pounding on her head.

"I don't dare go home like this," she mumbled.

"You can rest a little first," he answered.

Quiet and grateful, she half-slept leaning against him. He would manage everything, she didn't have to worry. He led her up a stairway, she didn't know where but it didn't seem to matter now. As long as she got to rest a little, as long as the spinning slowed down.

"Where are we?" she asked.

"A hotel room," he said. "You can rest here a little."

Maybe she wanted to protest, it wasn't seemly, and they were probably wondering where she was at home, it was late. But she couldn't come home in this state either, she had to go somewhere. She didn't have the strength to think, she just wanted to sink down, go numb.

But he held her up, pressed hard against him. He kissed her. She tried to turn away her mouth, didn't want to be kissed when she didn't have any strength to resist. But he was so insistent and stubborn, just persisted.

"What are you doing?" she asked.

"Only helping you," he said quietly. "Your skirt will get wrinkled if you lie down in it."

And, of course, he was right, she couldn't lie in that fine skirt. The exhibition was continuing for two more weeks. What would the factory director say if the skirt was....

But she could leave her petticoats on, she thought hazily. How did she actually look? He mustn't see her like this. As if in a fog, she saw herself standing there in frilly white underclothes. A sense of terror welled up, but disappeared in tiredness. She closed her eyes, felt like she was sinking through endless emptiness. He knew best, he was kind. He lifted her up, carried her to the bed. The fine suit still lay on the floor. She didn't see it, only felt that at last she got to lie down.

She was asleep when he undid her underclothes. Then, from out of the darkness and drowsiness, she was awakened and tried to struggle, fight him off of her. But the stranger in the dark couldn't be checked, he was unrelenting. She screamed, but was immediately silenced—everywhere all over her was the unknown man in the darkness, his mouth over her mouth, his body pressing down and mercilessly tormenting her.

For a moment she thought she was going to die, that he meant to kill her. Then she understood what had just happened: what wasn't supposed to happen.

"Why, why?" she cried.

"I couldn't stop myself." He was panting when he spoke, sank down beside her.

"But why?"

"It will feel better soon," he consoled her.

She wept, but fell asleep, too completely drunk to hold onto the fear and pain.

Monday morning arrived with pouring rain. Ingeborg woke up, looked around horrified and wondered where she was—the dreary, cheap hotel room, the drunken man who lay snoring at her side—a stranger even though she thought of him as her fiancé.

She got dressed, left without waking him. She felt like she could never see him again. She searched for the excuses that would save her from her parents' wrath: it had been so hard to get across town, so many drunks, she had had to sleep at her workmate Emelie's, avoid making her way home alone.

Silent and feeling sick, she sat at the worktable at the exhibit. In the afternoon her fiancé came, followed her to one of the cafés. He was kind and friendly, wanted to see her again that evening. He was going home soon, didn't have many days left.

Of course she met him again. She was still ashamed and afraid, but tried to console herself with the fact that they were actually getting engaged according to what he said.

The day before the exhibition closed, he was gone. His job was finished. She never heard from him again, didn't even know his address.

The Saturday he left, the first real fall storm arrived. The Jubilee decorations and garlands that were still hanging were torn loose by the wind, whirled with the autumn leaves through the streets. The blast took hold of women by their skirts—carried them with open sails across the open spaces.

The summer with its games and pleasures was over. The Jubilee had been the great test of stamina, now nobody had the strength left to party any longer. It would almost feel good to return to order and everyday. Now only the closing day remained.

The first Sunday in October was sunny and rather warm. People streamed to Djurgården to take in the exhibit one last time. Once more the halls and restaurants were filled, but as the clock approached five, when the doors were to close, anxiety rose. Soon everything would be irrevocably over. Some little memory had to be taken home. More and more people began to hunt around to find souvenirs.

In the Perfume Bottle, the young factory director Melinder found that the otherwise refined visitors to the exhibit had been transformed. Elegant ladies tried to steal perfume bottles, showcases were opened without keys, a large gilt mirror disappeared from a wall.

From the larger restaurants, several hundred dozen glasses disappeared. At Godthem Restaurant they tried to appease the guests by handing out seven thousand plates as gifts—it didn't help. The most sought after were all the ten thousand small glass lanterns that glittered everywhere. Old gentlemen climbed like apple-snatching boys to get up into the trees and pull down the wires the lanterns were hanging from.

Gunnar had been allowed to accompany Emelie on the last day, to say good-bye to the women from Dalarna at the Fairy Grotto and to the nice ladies at the Coffee Mill. While he waited for Emelie, he played outside the Perfume Bottle. He saw the pretty lanterns being pulled down and rolling in the grass. One lantern had landed under a bush, and no one, besides him, knew that it lay there. He snuck over, took the lantern and stuffed it inside his shirt. Everybody else was taking lanterns. He thought he had a greater right to them, he had been here all summer.

Emelie finally came. Now the Perfume bottle was closed and locked, tomorrow the goods and machines inside would be fetched by transport wagons and the building torn down.

They walked toward the exit on Allmänna gränd to take the ferry to Slussen. A few visitors to the exhibition stood arguing with the guard. He had called for the police because they had taken too many souvenirs with them. The guard nodded at Emelie and Gunnar as they walked by.

While they waited for the ferry, Emelie saw that Gunnar's shirt was sticking out. She asked what he was hiding in there, and he pulled out the lantern and showed her. Everybody had taken them. This one had been lying under a bush.

That was stealing. The head guard, Major Olsson, had made a special announcement that all the lanterns were to be collected. They belonged to an Englishman who had loaned them for the exhibition. Gunnar had to go back and return the lantern. Then he cried and asked not to have to do it, he didn't want to end up at the police. Please, please, could he not do it, couldn't he just throw the lantern into the sea if he couldn't keep it?

No, it had to be returned. But she would go with him, everything would probably be all right.

She held him tightly by the hand, as if she were afraid he would run away from her. He did resist a little, wanted to put off the unpleasantness as long as possible.

"Excuse me," Emelie said to the guard. "The boy got a lantern from somebody. He didn't know he wasn't supposed to take it with him."

The guard looked up, smiled in a friendly way.

"Oh well," he said, "most have disappeared, naturally. But of course, it's good if some of them go back where they belong."

He accepted the lantern from Gunnar, who bowed nervously. Then the boy went right back to Emelie.

"Nice boy you have," the guard said.

"He isn't mine," Emelie hastily replied. "He's my brother's."

The words had come so quickly, they were said before she could stop herself. Now she had broken her promise to Bärta; nobody was supposed to know anything other than that Johan was Gunnar's father.

"Actually, that's not quite right," she said nervously. "He's a neighbor's son."

She blushed and felt confused and foolish. What would the man believe?

The guard watched them leave—a little thoughtfully. She seemed to be a genuine and nice person. He had really meant to talk to her sometime. But then he had decided she was married. Oh well, an unmarried mother was probably not what he was looking for either. Now she was leaving, now he would never see her again. A little irritated, he went over to inspect a group of noisy gentlemen.

When the unpleasant deed had been carried out, Gunnar walked safely and calmly back to the ferry holding Emelie's hand. Grown-ups were strange, he thought. Emelie, who was so particular, had lied to the guard. She said that someone had given Gunnar the lantern. It was to make it easier for him, he understood that much. But that, too, was lying. She had lied for his sake. Suddenly he felt happy and proud: she liked him a lot. He didn't miss the lantern now, felt like the little lie was a special confidence between them.

"You can have a souvenir bowl instead of the lantern," Emelie promised him. "I got two from the factory director."

TOO LATE, TOO LONG

The city was no longer a bright dream bathed in the strains of an orchestra. After the summer's ecstasy, only a dark and rather poor winter city was left with slushy streets and people burdened by everyday cares. For those who had experienced the party for just a few hectic days, it wasn't so hard to readjust to everyday life. It was different for those who, in the unreal world of the summer, had had time to find themselves in a new reality.

At Melinder's cosmetics factory, the young factory director sat leafing through the thick bundles of orders. The summer had been very lucrative. Still, he was irritated by success's uncertainty and people's ingratitude. The lovely Miss Berg, whom he had hired for the exhibition and to whom he had been so diligently attentive, had deserted both him and the company. The assistant supervisor who had been in charge of the soap machine had been lured away to a competing firm. And the girl, Ingeborg, had misbehaved and been fired.

Of the four who had been given the opportunity to work at the exhibition only Emelie was left—the old man's favorite. As if the old man had shown once again that the oldest know best. Emelie had returned as if nothing had happened, calmly and quietly resuming her place at the packaging table. She had come into the office and asked if she should return the clothes she had received. She didn't have to do that. Moreover, she had been the only one to do that; the others had taken it for granted that they would get to keep what they had received. She had been good, useful to the company. He should reward her in some way when the opportunity came. Though that would show that the old man had been right.

Even if outwardly Emelie appeared to be herself, she also had some trouble adjusting at first. She didn't feel exactly welcome among her old colleagues. It was clear that she no longer belonged with them in the same way. Since working in the bright Exhibition Hall, she noticed how bad the factory's packaging room was. The lighting wasn't good and all the corners were drafty. And she had to stand all day long. At the exhibition they had sat and packaged soaps, and no one could make the claim that the work went more slowly because of it.

She found herself longing to go back—imagined leaving the dark workroom and her taunting colleagues. She would have liked to find some work that was more like what she had had during the summer. Sometimes she dreamed of finding work in a perfume shop and standing behind a counter helping customers, finely dressed, without glue on her hands and clothes. But she wasn't good enough for that, it was best to get rid of all those foolish thoughts.

Quite often she thought of Ingeborg, wondered how things were going for the girl. Her fiancé had apparently disappeared. If Emelie understood correctly, Ingeborg had met someone else instead. Ingeborg had probably not been able to manage the big transition, hadn't been able to forget how much fun it had been to get dressed up and be admired. Emelie had put away all her cosmetics as soon as the exhibition was over, but Ingeborg had continued. That could never end well.

One evening Emelie found out what was going on with Ingeborg. The girl came looking for her. The fine dress she had received for the exhibition hung wrinkled and dirty on her, her boots were all streaked.

Ingeborg told her everything. It had been intoxicating: the exhibition, all the fine and merry gentlemen, and her fiancé, the whirlwind days before he left. He had promised so much. And then he was suddenly gone. And Ingeborg hadn't dared go home. She had lived in the room of an acquaintance for a few days. She had not dared nor had the strength to deny him when he, too, had wanted to sleep with her.

Two policemen had finally brought her home again. Since her parents had gotten a confession out of her as to what she had been up to, they had beaten her until they couldn't hit her anymore. Then she had been kicked out. She belonged on the street was what her father had said. She had slept in a shelter a few nights. Other nights she had walked the streets. But she couldn't continue this way, she would rather jump into the water at Strömmen. Now Emelie was her only hope.

Emelie listened silently, without questions or comments. Admonishments didn't help now. Ingeborg had gotten more than enough of these.

Could she let Ingeborg stay with her a few nights? What about Olof? Ingeborg was eighteen now, the same age as Olof. Emelie would have to keep an eye on them. She couldn't drive Ingeborg out.

Olof became very friendly when he found Ingeborg at home. He talked and listened interestedly, didn't do any drawing. Emelie observed him suspiciously, saw how he put on his best side for Ingeborg, and how the girl encouraged him.

Before Olof fell asleep, he chided himself a little. A whole evening had gone by without him doing anything useful. He could have at least taken advantage of the new face and done a little sketch. But then he came up with a good defense. Sometimes you couldn't find time to draw because you also had to live, sometimes you had to replenish your stores and just be on the receiving end.

He fell asleep expectant, close to life and to a dream—but in the morning when he awoke Ingeborg and his sister were gone.

He lay there a minute and stretched. He thought some of the smell of her perfume was left in the room as a greeting and a memento. He wondered what he would do with himself that day. Arthur was learning to be a lithographer now, was busy during the daytime. It was a good school he had said when he began. Olof had planned to get in there, too, as a student, but gradually he realized that it was hardly anything he could imagine doing. Arthur had refused to sign the contract they had put before him: a salary of forty kronor during his first year of training, sixty the next and one hundred the third. To enter this kind of training you had to be wealthy. Olof couldn't hope, as Arthur did, to not have to do the years as a trainee.

He went out and wandered from editor to editor looking for work.

But it was the same as always: full everywhere.

Fredrik Bodin had died after lying crippled for a time from a stroke. He had lain as if in a trance, couldn't talk. The doctors could not do anything. Maybe what had happened had been most humane. He had been worn out for a long time.

Emelie ran into August a week after the funeral. He told her about his father's dying, and reminded her that Emelie was to visit Ida and him one evening. They had agreed to this when they saw each other at the exhibition. Now he suggested next Sunday evening.

Emelie thought it would be fun to go see them, even if she was a little anxious about the meeting. She was afraid she would say something foolish or do something wrong and make August ashamed of her. And she would have to leave Olof and Ingeborg unsupervised the whole evening, but they would probably each go their separate ways. Olof would certainly meet up with Arthur as usual. Emelie thought about talking to Ingeborg, get the girl to promise not to encourage Olof to get too close. But that would be saying she didn't trust Ingeborg. For once, Emelie hoped Olof and Arthur would stay out late. She couldn't do more than hope.

August was happy that Emelie was coming. They had talked about it happening for so long. And in some way he would be freed of a burden— no longer feel like he was avoiding his siblings, behaving like he was ashamed of them.

Then something happened that irritated him so that he couldn't hide or control his anxiety and discomfort—so the meeting with Emelie maybe didn't turn out as well as he had hoped and imagined.

On Friday morning, a lady came to the office and asked to speak to him. He had never seen her before. Eventually, he realized that he had heard her voice once, her laugh. Now she wasn't laughing and her voiced sounded strained. She had come to see about her inheritance. Fredrik Bodin had promised to take care of her; they had been good friends for many years. There must be something written in the will. She was to receive a house.

There was no will, August answered. And his father didn't own any houses. The firm owned them.

Then she flared up. The firm—that was Fredrik Bodin, of course. Surely he had written a will. Maybe they had destroyed it to get out of it.

He repudiated her accusations. For several years, he had owned the main part of the company and borne all the responsibility. If Fredrik Bodin had set up a will, he would, without a doubt, have turned it over to the lawyer the company engaged. She could find out herself from the lawyer if she wanted. He would give her his name right now.

Then it was a plot. And she knew who he was, the young director: a poor boy that Fredrik Bodin had taken care of—one who apparently had managed to crowd his benefactor out of the company.

He didn't believe that Father had thought or said anything so dumb. But still the blow hit home. He suddenly felt like he didn't have any right— was only an adoptive child. Was it possible Father had loved this woman more than he had loved his family? But Father had never said anything about her inheriting anything. He himself had asked August to take care of the company and let the major part of the ownership be transferred to him.

She's lying, he thought. She was trying to use his grief and the fact that he wasn't Fredrik Bodin's real son. He didn't have to feel sorry for her; she had shown who she was.

If she could present some paper that supported her claims he would look into the matter. Otherwise there was nothing he could do. His reply was cold, a blow in return.

Then she began to cry. She had sacrificed everything for Fredrik. And Fredrik had promised, time after time, that she would get her reward.

Sin's reward was death, wasn't that what they said? He pondered it but wasn't sure about the formulation.

"I'm sorry," he said, "but I can't do anything. I am responsible for the company and have no right to give away the assets." If there had been some legal requirement, it naturally would have been different, but even a deed of gift from his father would hardly be enough since his father hadn't had any real resources of his own.

He wouldn't just make her leave? He had to respect his father's last wishes, didn't he? Even if it wasn't in written form? Hadn't his father said anything while he lay sick?

It was his mother and himself who represented the firm, now, he answered. She didn't expect him to go to the deceased's wife in this situation?

No. In which case she would have to go see a lawyer after all, and create a scandal, as well, if it was necessary.

She left. In spite of everything, he had to feel sorry for her. But he didn't intend to give her anything. The thorn stuck, the poison spread. It festered, made it hard for him to work.

Emelie noticed that August was preoccupied, different from when she had seen him last. Was it maybe the increased responsibility that weighed him down? He must be managing the whole firm since Bodin's death.

Or was he ashamed of her. Was that why he was so silent and strange? After much debating, Emelie had dug out the cosmetics she had hidden in a drawer. Now she regretted it. Maybe August thought she seemed frivolous and decked out. But Ida was so kind and friendly, had shown her the two children they had sleeping in the nursery, and absolutely wanted Emelie to address her in the familiar form. Emelie felt like Ida's friendliness was genuine. Ida, at least, didn't think there was anything vulgar about her. And Emelie had applied the cosmetics so carefully, just improved her looks very slightly.

They had invited her for dinner. Emelie tried to watch her hosts to avoid making any mistakes. Fear of embarrassing herself and thoughts of Ingeborg and Olof made her quieter than usual. And August didn't say much. The conversation went haltingly despite Ida's cheery efforts. Then Emelie didn't want to go home late, she had to get back to the young people, make sure that everything was in order.

The meeting between the siblings perhaps wasn't what had been hoped for: a reuniting. They were caught in their own worlds, couldn't really manage to reach each other.

Ida talked about the exhibition—how they had bumped into each other there. Who was that boy who had come running to Emelie? That couldn't have been Olof. He must be older than that?

No, that was Gunnar. Her neighbor's son.

Did Emelie take care of the boy?

She answered a little evasively. Not exactly... his mother was an old friend of hers and used to live with them, when Mama was still alive.

August listened silently. Bärta, he thought, but didn't say the name. Strange that he couldn't escape the memory. That might have been because of all the anxiety he had felt when he heard Bärta was expecting a child. Could that be the child she was expecting back then, Gunnar? He had never gotten around to telling Ida about Bärta, had felt like it was too shameful a memory. He almost regretted that he hadn't said anything when they met each other again.

Then maybe August knew the boy's mother? Ida asked.

He cleared his throat, wondered if he was turning red. Yes, he probably did. Did Emelie mean Bärta?

No more was said about Bärta and her child, but Ida had noticed August's discomfort. He was so torn up with everything that was happening in conjunction with his father's death and that woman appearing. Still, there was something about that Bärta as well. Some memory he didn't want to be reminded of?

When Emelie got home Ingeborg was already asleep and Olof was still out. She had worried without cause.

She lay and thought about the evening's company. Ida was kind and nice, and August obviously had his worries. But despite all the friendliness, she still felt that the meeting had taken place too late. The break that had occurred all those years ago had been definitive. Maybe it would have been like this anyway, even if there hadn't been a definite event to point to. Maybe it hadn't actually meant so much that Thumbs had scared August away. They would have drifted apart anyway, each to his or her own world. Time flows past and pulls people along with it. You can meet again but not return to the time when you separated. Those who do meet again are different people than they were when they separated. It was that hopeless.

Too long, too late.

But in time's stream, people floated along who, in spite of the distances between them, were bound to each other by invisible ties. She had noticed how unwillingly August had said Bärta's name, how intensely he had listened when Ida asked about Gunnar. Did August guess anything? And had she done the right thing when she withheld the truth?

SIMPLE PARADISE

The house was owned by a junk dealer. It was old and poorly cared for, blackened by damp and soot. It stood extremely close to the Katarina elevator's steel framework and could be reached both from Stadsgården and Stora Glasbruksgatan.

Up in the attic, with the view over Stadsgården, was space for an atelier. The painter Herman Feychting, who had retired there from his all too wild Bohemian life in "Chateau du Sud" on Åsöberget, had rented it for some years. Now Feychting had moved, but the many stories of him lived on in the house. This tradition created obligations. The young artists who took over the atelier intended to do their best, even if they lacked the resources of the former tenant. Feychting was from a wealthy family and had his own cutter anchored in the harbor below Ersta.

The newcomers dubbed the atelier Simple Paradise and the inside bedroom Little Sleeping Hell. They were young and unknown; everything remained to be conquered. Some of them had met as students at the Central Printers Lithography Institution. Their education there had been short; they hadn't had been able to afford to starve long enough to become trained lithographers. Now they were going to live as free artists instead, paint masterpieces and from time to time whip off a cartoon to earn their daily bread.

Arthur with the hair had been automatically included in the circle, was generally seen as the group's genius. The usual envy disappeared when it came to him. Everyone was prepared to admit that he had something that they perhaps lacked themselves. All except for that ill-tempered hooligan who accompanied him, and whom they would have hardly accepted had it not been for Arthur's sake.

It wasn't easy to like Olof. He was too self-involved, too irritatingly eager to assert himself and his individuality. Of course they could feel sorry for him, the guy was sickly and poor. And as far as he went, they could agree on the one thing they would have indignantly repudiated regarding themselves: he was sorely lacking in basic training. Certainly there was enough that was genuine in what he did, but it was so roughly hewn, so raw somehow. And he didn't want to listen to their advice, just the opposite: he criticized them back and declared that what they painted were copies of what had been created en masse before.

They called him Obstinate Olle. If Arthur hadn't so stubbornly insisted upon Olof's staying, they would have thrown him out. Now they had to accept him. And they had to admit that Obstinate Olle did his best, more than most of them, to meet their common expenses. He took heavier jobs than he had the strength for, went down to the harbor and labored when there was no other work.

In spite of Emelie's protests, he had moved. He was obliged to, he had said. He had to take the opportunity to learn. She tried as often as she could to give him a little money or a little food, but he was proud, had difficulty accepting anything.

In the long run she tried to persuade him to still sleep at home during the night, she suspected that things were pretty wild in the atelier. Then she could help him keep his clothes clean and mended and give him a meal.

He refused, couldn't afford to pay for himself in two places. If he was going to live at home he wanted to pay. She could take some girls as boarders now and manage better. Ingeborg was no longer living there.

She had to watch him leave. She sat there alone, could no longer hold onto the responsibility she had once received. What good was work if the result was failure? Nothing. Everything had been in vain. Emelie felt like she could see her mother's sorrowful and reproachful eyes. Why? She asked herself over and over. What could she have done to stop him? Why had Olof been captured by this dangerous passion? Was there something in the past that should have been different—that could have led him in another direction? Was it because of Gullpippi and her paints? Should Emelie have thrown them out when they moved? Should she have made Olof work harder, forbidden him to buy paper and paints, not let him go out with Arthur?

She understood that she would never have managed to prevent him. There was too much strength in his weak body—a stubbornness she would never have been able to subdue. I didn't have the strength, she said to herself. Please forgive me, Mama, I tried but didn't succeed.

But she felt that she would never be forgiven, because someone who is dead cannot forgive. The dead take the promise with them, hide it in the grave. No one can dig it up, it stays there, it calls, it demands. No one will have to promise me anything, she thought. And her aloneness gave her some kind of release.

And no one will have to give me anything, no one will have to take the responsibility for something I have done. Maybe I can, in spite of everything, help Olof sometimes. Maybe I can be of use to Gunnar. But they will never have to be responsible for me.

The first payday after Olof moved, she made a decision. From this payday on, she would always put away one krona, no matter how hard it might be. Krona after krona, finally they would be enough. If she got sick, if money was needed for her burial, she would take care of it herself. No one would have to help her.

In a few months she would turn twenty-eight. She already felt old—felt like it was time to prepare for death. Papa hadn't turned thirty-five. Mama had been just slightly over forty. The years weren't many.

And then she would have to look for some boarders. Two girls who could share the wooden sofa Olof had slept on. She herself lay in the bed together with Gunnar.

They painted models in Simple Paradise. The girl who stood naked on a packing crate froze in the gray winter light, her skin got goose bumps and she shivered sometimes. They pretended not to hear her complaints, but when she threatened to put on her clothes, something had to be done.

"Throw in a few more sticks," said Petter who was nicknamed Lankylimbs. Olof obeyed but muttered angrily, didn't like to interrupt his work. The fire rose up again, it crackled in the stovepipe. But it was uncertain if any warmth reached as far as the girl.

The day was short; the light disappeared early from the window of the atelier which faced north. The model looked as grubby to them as the dirty wall. In reality, they were tired of her. She was cheap but not interesting to paint, and they had used her much too long.

"Do you have anything to warm me up?" she whined. "A few drops, at least."

"Dry as a desert," Arthur answered. He sat wrapped in an old coat that was way too big for him. He threw down the brush, and went on: "Janne has probably arranged something."

They let her get down. It was getting too dark to work, and it was only the stubborn Olof who wanted to continue as usual. He stood there a minute after the girl disappeared into Little Sleeping Hell, but then he found that he had been unsuccessful again, and painted an angry red X across the canvas.

A minute later Janne arrived pulled some packages out of his pockets, and set out two one-liter bottles. They placed food and bottles on the crate and pulled it over to the wooden kitchen sofa. Janne shrugged off their praise; he really knew how to work magic. He had sold a painting to a half-drunk bigwig. Janne might have been the worst painter among them, but he had the best nose. Confidently and unsparingly he sniffed out people who he imagined would be able to buy. Catching flies was what he called it.

They got all worked up: what would the buyer say once he looked at Janne's painting with sober eyes? Janne swallowed all the epithets. They could say what they wanted. He was still the one who could treat them to food and drinks.

The model came in, a little revived now that she had some clothes on. She sat down on the sofa beside Olof who moved over so there would be room for her. She teased him—he wasn't shy was he? A little annoyed, he told her to keep her mouth shut, and she swore and turned away from him. He thought he had reacted stupidly, but was too proud to say he was sorry and drank instead. While the others sat there talking, he crawled off to Little Sleeping Hell where he had a pile of newspapers in a corner he usually slept on. He lay down on the rustling sheets, pulled up the quilt that Emelie had forced him to take with him, and fell asleep, despite the laughter and the shouting.

The next morning he was awakened by Petter walking around ringing a cowbell—clanging it like he was rousing a fire department.

"Up you scoundrels," cried Petter. "It's past eight o'clock."

They crawled out from Paradise's wooden sofa and Sleeping Hell's bundles of clothes and newspaper heaps.

Arthur sat in front of the crate, leaned his head in his hands to soothe his hangover. Olof went out to the attic and tried to wash away some of the headache with ice-cold water. He had slept in his jacket to not be too cold. Now he just remembered that he had forgotten to salvage the last cigarette from his pocket. He looked for it anxiously, pulled out the bent tube of paper that had almost lost its contents, and lighted it with shaking fingers. It flared up, the paper burned quickly and singed his lips. A few bits of tobacco were still there in any case. He inhaled, coughed until he thought his lungs would come loose. Everything was as usual. A new day had begun.

He went over to the window in Paradise and looked out over Stadsgården and Slussen. The elevator's large frame divided the view to the west, in the east, the sun shone weakly across the water. Before him lay Stadsgården and its workers. Steam winches lifted large bales and the contents of freight vessels, stevedores ran in circular paths with their heavy sacks of grain. A train engine released a cloud of steam from its smokestack and pushed away some rattling cars. On the open plaza below the house, the teamsters had assembled with their wagons.

The view was certainly good, toward work and activity. A lot that was worth portraying lay close by. Yet—it always caused Olof anxiety and a feeling of shame. The memories of the burdens he had carried—reminders of the burdens that waited during the lean days to come. But also thoughts of Fearsome, the old man he had liked so much and completely abandoned these last years. Now it was too late to make up for it. Fearsome was dead and gone.

Old friends, work—he had given up everything to paint. It was as if the sacrifice had not earned anything, as if he couldn't break through the prison bars of his incompetence. Yesterday nothing had gotten done, the only thing he had achieved was a failure, and today—the pounding in his head, feeling sick, feeling uninspired. The new day was already wasted, drowned in yesterday's liquor. He left his comrades. Couldn't bear to look at the dreary model one more day.

"Today Olle is really feeling obstinate," the others said.

He didn't hear them, went down the dark and foul-smelling stairs, out to the cold and the blast of the harbor. The wind tore at his coat, the chill crept inside his shirt. Listlessly he walked through the harbor, looking for something without knowing what.

Olof felt best when he and Arthur were alone. Sometimes they went to discussions in the socialist youth club. They were probably seen mostly as entertainment themselves, were too wildly radical and all around cheeky to really be taken seriously.

Some evenings they went to the dance halls on Söder, choosing the worst, most dilapidated wooden buildings where the hooligans and their girls hung out. Olof could, perhaps, be taken for a hooligan; he had his cap with a cord and the wide flapping pant legs. He pulled on his belt, swaggered over and asked one of the girls sitting on a long bench against the wall to dance.

Arthur preferred to stand concealed in a corner, drawing. It wasn't a question of idealizing them exactly, but in the characteristics of the swaggering hooligan, Olof recognized some of his own. Arthur had to laugh at the skinny figure with enormous hands that took a hold of his belt and hiked up his pants—and that beatific expression.

One evening in March as they walked homeward across Södermalmstorg, a girl came running. Olof recognized her immediately: Ingeborg. He hurried after her while Arthur, who didn't like to run, tried to watch which way they ran. He had to jump aside for a cop in eager pursuit, but did it in a way so he happened to trip the policeman. Of course,

Arthur would have been in the right to say that he was about to be run down, and he couldn't get his leg out of the way in time. But still, just to play it safe, he sneaked around the closest corner, into Klotgränd.

It took a moment before the policeman got to his feet and could decide which of the fleeing figures he should pursue. That gave enough time for Olof to take Ingeborg with him down into Järngraven, an old, dried up moat. They slipped inside the fence and slithered down the wall just beyond the Pelikan Restaurant's lit-up veranda. Down in the pit, rowboats were pulled up for the winter. They crawled in under one of them, lay quietly and tried to silence their panting. They heard footsteps running on the viaduct overhead, and didn't know if they had been seen. The footsteps disappeared. Now they only heard horses' hooves and the even thud of walking.

She had taken hold of him, as if she were trying to hide in him. When he felt her closeness, the fear and the cold receded. He forgot everything other than that she was there. He opened his jacket and tried to wrap her in it as well, putting his arms around her. For a moment she lay still, waiting. Then she pressed closer to him, working energetically until she was underneath him. She tucked up her skirts that were in the way, making herself ready to receive him. But he didn't dare come to her until her hands had opened his clothing.

Suddenly the ground began to sway. A train had rolled out from the tunnel under them, under Söder, passed under Pelikan, shot out toward the railroad bridge. He felt like they had become one with the ground, the earth itself shaking beneath them.

"Maybe you didn't want to," she said in a low voice. "I thought..."
He didn't answer.

"Besides," she said, her voice a little harder. "You probably know. Emelie has told you?"

"The cop was after you," he answered.

"Yes."

"You're not registered with the institution, you have to lay low."

"That's right. Let me go now."

"No," he said. "Where do you think you'll go?"

"Nowhere. Driven out again. There aren't many who want a whore living with them."

"You can live with us for a few nights," he said.

"No," she answered decidedly. "I don't want Emelie to see me like this. She wouldn't let me in anyway."

He explained. If she wanted to model for them, she would get more than her night lodging paid for.

Be a model! No, she had to set some limits! She didn't want to stand naked in front of a bunch of guys, anyway.

There wouldn't be more than five or six who were painting. Besides, it was an honorable profession, a lot of good girls did it.

But naked....

So what? Was she ashamed of her body?

She thought about it while she straightened her skirts.

"There's nothing wrong with my figure," she said, sounding vain.

Well then.

"Why not?" she burst out suddenly. "You might as well try everything. And I can't afford to reject anything anymore."

"Done," he said. "The guys will be delighted. We've had such boring models for a while."

"You don't have to worry about me being boring," she laughed. "What do you do when you model?"

"Just stand there," he answered. "Or sit or lie and be drawn or painted. No one touches you. Though it can be really hard to hold the same pose."

That sounded completely crazy, she thought, and wondered what her parents would say if they knew that their daughter was showing herself off naked in front of a gang of men. She couldn't get away from the idea that it was a very indecent proposal that the sweet and inexperienced Olof had come up with. But, of course, she followed him, even feeling a sense of anticipation faced with the novel experience. I am rather beautiful, she told herself. The young factory director wanted me to sit and be seen at the cosmetics exhibit.

She hung onto Olof's arm as he steered her over the uneven path under the arches of the railroad overpass, toward the harbor. They looked around before they crossed the square and went up the stairs. Arthur had gone ahead of them. Ingeborg settled herself comfortably among the company, hungrily biting into the slices of bread that were left and warming herself with a few nightcaps.

The next day was bright and sunny. Ingeborg fussed and giggled a little at first, but nobody teased her. Finally, she emerged from Sleeping Hell in Arthur's big coat, climbed up onto the crate and let the coat fall. They looked up, saw her and knew that that day they were going to work. They didn't know if it was the sun's or Ingeborg's doing. She wasn't a dirty gray smudge like the model they had had earlier. No, Ingeborg was life and woman, blooming vitality. She also had color—a must like new wine. They dug through their brushes and tubes of pigment—were in such a hurry, had to begin while the mood and hope of succeeding still existed. They readjusted her: like this, like that was how she should stand. Could she hold it even though she wasn't used to it?

She would try.

The insecurity she had felt was gone. Admiration and goodwill streamed toward her. If she helped the boys by standing here on the crate, she could certainly do that. But fatigue soon came on, she had to rest. They hurried to help her on with the coat and slippers she had borrowed. They wanted her to sit and warm herself by the stove, asked if she would soon have the strength to start again, they were in such unusually good working humor.

She stayed a week with them, and they competed with giving her their attention, and had seldom worked so assiduously. Though she tired of them rather soon. The boys were kind but odd, and it was still tiring to stand there. They also didn't have much money; she got food and drink but not much else. One day she went out on an errand. She didn't return. They wondered if the police had taken her, but a few days later someone said they had seen her with an older gentleman.

She had told Olof the very first evening that she was pregnant and was eating saffron to induce a miscarriage. She had given up she had said. Didn't have it in her to return to an orderly life.

There was certainly no hope. Olof had no dreams of meeting her under better circumstances. Still, he mourned her leaving. It was Ingeborg who had guided him into life, he thought. She was his first woman. He couldn't pass by Järngraven without leaning over and looking at the boats lying there and remembering how the earth shook one cold evening in March.

THE HOOLIGAN'S WALTZ

A melody had gotten stuck in Arthur's head. He couldn't get rid of it. It had come to him one evening at the dance hall, but not from the musicians' instruments. An acquaintance had hummed it. Songster-Johan had heard it somewhere at Erstaviken where the hooligans and their girls had organized a big dance one Saturday evening.

Melancholy and pride, soft, light steps and the elegant swaying, the sweep of the girls' light-colored cotton dresses and the fellows' strong grip on their belts, the butterfly-light and the clumsily heavy—everything was there in the melody, Arthur thought. When he whistled it, the atmosphere of the old, rickety wooden dancehall crept up on him. He could see the girls sitting along the walls giggling, see the hooligan stand in the doorway, pull his cap off his curly hair, stub out his cigarette and spit—a little abashed—before asking one to dance.

The last day Ingeborg had been a model and his comrades had painted so industriously, that tune had prevented Arthur from taking out his paints. It was there again in the lines of the girl—the high-pitched melody of the hooligans, The Hooligan's Waltz.

While the others painted, he tried to write, but he didn't get much down just then. Later, at dusk, the waltz returned with renewed vigor. He didn't hear the laughter and talk of his friends, just reached for his pen and paper and began to write feverishly. He didn't notice how they grew quiet and watched him curiously. He just hummed away, the words forming themselves while the couples whirled before his eyes. He saw them; the hooligans and their girls in the shabby old hall in the broken down building could hear them. And like a light streak in the midst of all that gray was the warm tone of Ingeborg's body.

"Hey listen to this, you guys!" he said.

He took a couple of quick, deep puffs on his cigarette, stubbed it out like a hooligan who was asking a girl to dance, and began to sing with his thin, anxious voice:

A hooligan enters the Söder hall
Ready to whirl and have a ball.
All the girls feel so light and carefree
A more stylish fellow they never did see.

They sat there silently, gripped by the mood. Arthur sang verse after verse, calling forth the scene. His unsure, half-singing voice gave an intense feeling of authenticity—an experience from another world.

It was a remarkable thing that Arthur had achieved. They agreed on that, but that it could also be used to cover their current pressing needs for survival was something they weren't as sure of. Somebody thought that the piece would become so popular everyone would be singing it, but others thought that it was probably too unusual. People wouldn't understand it.

Still, somehow it was surely to be published somewhere.

"Do a drawing to go with it and try *Strix*," advised Petter.

Arthur began to pull out his sketches. He had a number of half-finished ones from when he was out with Olof. The one where Olof was tugging on his belt, bathed in that blissful expression, was a beginning.

The following day Arthur went out with a roll of drawings and his waltz. His task was a difficult one. He was to find the *Strix* editor, Engström, who hardly ever showed up at his office.

They didn't hear from him again that day. They hid quietly in the recesses of Paradise and Sleeping Hell, anxious that the landlord, the junk dealer, would come. They were behind with the rent, had been threatened with eviction again.

Arthur had left in his dirty and shabby suit, in battered shoes and without anything on his head. Twenty-four hours later, he returned in a tailored black suit and gray vest, with new lace-up boots and an Italian hat. His friends emerged in amazement from their hiding places and took in his elegance.

Arthur had a hard time speaking, but an easy time falling. He tumbled down on the wooden sofa and tried to explain. In twenty-four hours time, he had partied with the great editor and his friends—drunk champagne even. Engström had personally guaranteed their rent; the junk dealer was satisfied. Both the waltz and the drawings were going to be published in *Strix*. And after all his extravagances, he had a whole twenty-five kronor left.

They had to celebrate.

First they had to be kind and undress him and put him to bed. He couldn't take one more step, drink one more glass.

Arthur fell asleep before they had time to get him into bed. While he slept they celebrated his waltz with beer and aquavit and beefsteaks. Paradise had been saved once more; the junk dealer with his unsheathed sword at the ready had been driven away.

Because of The Hooligan's Waltz being published in *Strix*, Arthur became a famous person. Visitors arrived at Paradise to buy his waltz for the revues. Emil Norlander wanted to include it in The Big Strike that was coming to the Söder Theater; the Folk Theater was also interested.

The huge hit had successors: The Söder March—*A gang of hooligans marches off, in Friesens park they'll get to fight.* And The Parade March of Kungsholmen—*On a starry night to Kungholm's gate we march, with accordion and sweetheart on our arm.* But The Hooligan's Waltz was the one people sang everywhere, the one everyone wanted to hear.

Arthur's fame meant that Olof spent more time alone than before. Now Arthur was drawn into a riotous Bacchanalian procession from tavern to tavern. There were so many who wanted to treat him and admire him, get a closer look at the strange little hooligan who had written the big hit, bask in his glory.

Falling down drunk, tired and miserable, Arthur came back to Paradise from time to time to throw up and sleep it off. He didn't have time for much more before his new friends came and got him for new parties. But still he took Olof over to *Strix* one day, wanted Olof to meet the quiet and gently disposed editor who managed the comic magazine's daily activities. The gloomy jokes they could take to put in the paper were hardly more than Forsberg himself came up with, he intimated with a smile that was friendly but sad. Still, he took two of Olof's drawings and didn't bargain him down when he paid. It would be all right if he came again, he said. But not too often.

"We should celebrate my business transaction," said Olof. He asked if Arthur remembered how they had walked through town one time and talked about sitting in Pelikan's rotunda once they were recognized artists. It was the same evening that they saw Carl Larsson's model in the doorway of Glasbruksgatan.

Yes, Arthur remembered. Reflecting on the memory of their boyhood hopes and golden dreams, they stood there and looked at the roof of the rotunda where the gilded mother pelican fed her young—with her heart's blood, of course.

Arthur, who was most used to restaurants, went into the dining room first. Musicians played The Hooligan's Waltz when he walked in, a few drunken guests applauded his entrance.

Olof didn't get the opportunity to talk very much to Arthur; it didn't end up being their private celebration. So many people came over and asked to sit at their table for a moment. When the dining room closed, they were invited to continue on in the private party room where a group of successful artists and businessmen was gathered. From the private party room they were to go for a late night supper in an atelier. Everybody wanted to be with Arthur; naturally his young friend should come along too. But Olof gave up, had already drunk too much a long while back. And he didn't want to meet these people. It was Arthur he wanted to sit with in peace and quiet. But the two of them couldn't anymore.

Olof walked alone from Pelikan while the carriages whirled off into town with the jolly party. He stood there a minute, hanging over the railing above Järngraven, looking down on the rails and ties that lay there now that the boats had been put in the water. Everybody was gone; he was alone. And time was short. He didn't have a lot of time to make new friends and find new love.

Downhearted, he descended Brunnsbacken unsteadily, and continued on toward Stadsgården. He returned to Simple Paradise and his pile of newspapers, tried to fall asleep to escape his disenchantment and disappointment. His head pounded. When he fell asleep he thought he could hear The Hooligan's Waltz still playing in his ears.

A MEETING WITH MEMORIES

The small gardens on Fjällgatan were turning green. It was mostly the land-lords themselves who cultivated their plots. But Emelie's landlord, the old captain, didn't have the strength for such endeavors; he had let his tenants take over the gardening.

Emelie had gotten a pair of gooseberry bushes. In addition, she had a potato patch. Gunnar had helped her put in the potatoes in the spring. She remembered how he had tried to act big and grown-up, even though he was only nine years old. He was going to take such big shovelfuls with the spade, but he was thin and not especially big, his weight wasn't really quite enough. His father had stood and hacked with the spade just like him. August had been about Gunnar's age when he had helped Papa dig on Åsöberget.

Her memory was hazy, but she still remembered how her father had said: you should cut up the potatoes in the same number of pieces as they have eyes. Each piece should have its own eye to see with so it could aim true and send its shoot up toward the light. She told Gunnar this last spring. Now he could really be assured that each eye had been able to send its shoot straight through the dark earth. The tops were standing high.

That day they picked gooseberries. Emelie had a milk pail and Gunnar a cup. He had to empty it into the milk pail when it was filled. They weren't in any hurry. Emelie had a couple of days off. The factory director wanted to reorganize a lot of things down at the factory, and was doing it during the summer when there was the least work. There was only one factory director now that old Melinder had completely retired.

This reorganization would mean a lot for Emelie personally. It was something she could be both happy and nervous about, now, while she was waiting. She had been called into the office. The factory director had told her that in the future, packaging would be its own department, while packing larger quantities would be taken care of separately. Emelie would be the supervisor for packaging, he had thought. The new responsibility would mean a larger salary.

The factory director had even asked if Emelie had any views regarding the workspace and the work. Was there anything she wanted to change? Naturally, it would have been easiest if she could have just answered no—been able to say that everything would be fine just as the director thought. But her conscience didn't allow her to do this. She had opinions—and even disclosed them to some of her work colleagues. So she had to say what she thought, even if it made him angry.

She thought they would work better if the lighting were stronger, she began carefully. He nodded at this, almost encouragingly—maybe he had actually thought of that himself? Some of the older ones, also, had quite a bit of trouble with the cold and the drafts during the winter. It affected their hands, they said. They grew clumsy and worked poorly.

They only had to tighten up the insulation in the room and keep the doors and windows closed, he said. There would be less running in and out of the doors now that the packing of larger boxes was to be relocated. And what else?

Well, she had a few more suggestions. They could maybe divide up the jobs so that each worker had her own assigned task. And she also had ideas about how to position the boxes and utilize the space.

He thought this was too detailed for him to listen to. These kinds of things she could organize on her own in the future as she thought best. What else?

Then she came to the hard part, the part that could be easily misunderstood. He would surely think that they were lazy and indolent.

Yes, well... at the exhibition they had sat and wrapped soaps. The factory director had perhaps seen that the work didn't go any slower? She had nothing against standing, but she believed that the hard stone floor gradually caused cramps. Many of them had aching legs and the pain impeded their work. She had been looking down at the floor, really feeling quite ashamed.

And the question that followed didn't make it any easier: was she thinking of padded armchairs? He laughed when he asked, but she didn't dare assume he was joking.

Oh no, she really stumbled over the words: a few simple wooden stools, ideally very high, so that they could sit and stand interchangeably.

He said he'd think about it. And she knew: if he went and asked the old factory director for his advice, there would never be any stools. It probably wasn't good that she said that part about sitting. She should have understood that you weren't supposed to be comfortable while you worked. That issue with the stools made her almost more anxious than the increased responsibility that waited.

Gunnar came to empty the cup.

"You can take some berries now," she said. "It's getting to be time to stop for today."

He plucked off the little stem, pressed the downy berry against his mouth, let it explode in his mouth, and carefully sucked in all the juice before he chewed up the skin.

The gate in the fence opened.

Emelie didn't have to turn her head to see who it was, could read it in the boy's face. The calm happiness that so recently had been there was gone, a shadow of fear crossed over him. Like the small birds who grew silent, huddled up and made themselves smaller when one of the gulls from Strömmen soared above the hillside. The shadow glided past. She heard how the door to the house opened and shut.

As she often did, Emelie had to wonder if Johan guessed that Gunnar wasn't his. Why was he so hard on the boy otherwise? What joy could Johan get from creating fear and hate around himself? He himself must have been so afraid as a child, he should know how it feels.

They said that people learned from experience, but she thought that many learned wrong. The experiences became whiplashes that drove them into darkness, and they lacked eyes that might lead them back to the light again.

Still, things had gotten much better during recent years. Now Johan didn't have as many chances to get angry at Gunnar since the boy lived with Emelie. But Johan wasn't as loud as before. He had calmed down a bit, become a little puffed up, with an almost ridiculous sense of self worth that didn't allow him to fight as much as he wanted.

To some degree this depended on the fact that the chimney sweeps had become organized, one of the last working groups to form its own "union." They had had a hard time getting started, they lacked a leader, and most of them were almost illiterate. Many had joined the profession at the age of seven or eight, and hadn't had much in the way of schooling, tired out as they were with long hours of heavy work. The system for expenses and lodging had turned them into prisoners of the workplace. Many felt like slaves and had taken the attitude of slaves toward life. But during the past several years, changes had arrived. Now only the apprentice boys still lived in the chimney sweep quarters. Working hours had been regulated to sixty hours per week, and a fully trained journeyman could get eighteen kronor per week with an additional five-öre piece for every sooty chimney. They had become free men, and this spring they had proudly celebrated it with a party in Oxtorgskällan's party room. Dressed in their Sunday suits, they had eaten and swung their girls and wives around, and chaired their leaders around the room.

Emelie lifted up the pail of gooseberries, was going to carry it in. Gunnar went to the shed to put back the box he had been standing on. While Emelie was on her way in, Johan came out again. She halted and asked him if he and Bärta felt like stopping in for a cup of coffee the following evening. Gertrud was coming over to visit them with her family, it didn't happen very often. Gunnar stood in the woodshed and peeped through a crack in the door, didn't come out until his father was gone.

The visitors from far away came by streetcar to Slussen. From there they were going to take the Katarina elevator. Rudolf had finally given in to his wife's and children's insistent begging.

They stood below and looked up at the giant steel structure. The oldest girl, who went to school, spelled her way through the lettering on the painted signs up there: *Wiman's stoves and Halda pocket watches.*

Rudolf had the day off, was going to work on Sunday instead. Calmly but firmly, he herded his wife and two daughters into the elevator, then stepped in himself with his three-year-old son on his arm. He seemed mostly uninterested as the elevator began to move, pretended not to notice Gertrud pinch him in the arm, shushed the girls who shrieked with excitement. He didn't like to attract attention. Gertrud could irritate him at times with her childishness. Adults shouldn't create so much commotion. If you didn't have anything of importance to say, you should say nothing at all. But Gertrud preferred to chatter. It was as if it bubbled out of her.

When they got to the footbridge that led from the elevator to firm ground, the girls hurried over to the railing—but stopped and backed away when they saw the enormous drop off beneath them. Then they returned cautiously to the edge. In spite of everything they had to see what was down there under them. They caught sight of the steam-powered streetcar and asked how it could move all by itself, where were the horses? Rudolf tried to explain, though he didn't really like to deal with the cars of the southern streetcar line. They could boast about their steam-powered cars, but their business was poor, much worse than the northern line where Rudolf worked.

He didn't believe that streetcars without horses had any future. It was only a fad. There was talk of something called automobiles, they had even organized competitions for such things abroad. But everyone could understand that those machines would never be able to seriously compete with horses. There was nothing safer, stronger nor more beautiful than a pair of stately horses. He was proud to drive them.

They walked across the footbridge and Mosebacketorg, and passed the new water tower that stood so high it could pump water to the highest houses on Söder. But in the little hovels surrounding it, there were no water pipes—it wasn't as well organized here as in Siberia.

"Söder has lovely views," said Gertrud. "We don't have that."

"We don't have the steep hills either," answered Rudolf curtly. He didn't like the fact that Gertrud missed their old home. Those who moved should forget the old places, at least not speak well of them. It was the same as devaluing what one had now, could sound as if one felt regret. They had moved to make life better. It was better, otherwise they would have made a mistake. But he didn't make any mistakes, he planned carefully. Still, he didn't really like coming back to Söder, despite the fact that he should walk around and be glad to have been spared the life here.

Gunnar lay on the outhouse roof, keeping an eye on the street. When he saw the guests arriving he wriggled down from the roof and hurried in to notify Emelie.

She ran out to the street to welcome them. And then it wasn't long before they were sitting around the table drinking coffee in Emelie's room. Johan and Bärta had been ready to come in as soon as the travelers arrived. But Olof, who after much pleading had promised to come and see his relatives, was as yet nowhere to be seen. He lived close by and certainly had the most time. Emelie guessed that he didn't want to come earlier than necessary. When he had heard that Johan was going to be there, he wanted to be released from his promise.

Gertrud and Bärta sat a little aside on their own; they had a lot to confide in each other. They had always been such good friends, much closer than Emelie and Bärta. Now they also had children and homes to talk about.

Rudolf talked with Johan. They didn't know each other especially well, but could always discuss working conditions and salaries. Johan tried to take the same tone as Rudolf: calm and assured, clarifying, decisive. Big, sturdy Rudolf and little, but no longer so thin, Johan didn't seem as essentially different as Emelie might have believed, they went quite well together. And both were a touch afraid of Emelie, preferred not to be alone with her. Rudolf had memories from when he had courted her and a vague but absolutely forbidden sense that he had chosen wrong at the time—Emelie was smarter than Gertrud, not so silly. Johan remembered all the times Emelie had argued with him, and how he had once hit her with a belt. Everything would be fine from now on, of course, but he still wasn't perfectly sure of her. He preferred to stay out of her way. She was a little odd, he thought.

Emelie found that her guests were so caught up with each other that she hardly had the opportunity to talk to them. But her duties as hostess and the children kept her completely occupied.

Olof came at last, when everybody was taking a second cup. He threw his cap on the dresser and walked over to the table. He had had a few drinks. Not too many, just enough to be able to bear the company.

He stood a moment in their midst, bombarded with questions. Rudolf wanted to know how artists like him could support themselves. Was it a profession you could live off of?

As they could see, he wasn't dead yet.

No, but thin, was Gertrud's opinion. Olof looked at her quickly, thought how she had grown a little round instead. Or was she expecting more children? Her streetcar coachman was an industrious breeder.

Rudolf asked if painting pictures actually had any justification. What was it good for? Did paintings do anything useful?

"They could be beautiful to look at," said Gertrud.

But Olof answered curtly that he didn't paint any beautiful paintings.

Emelie looked at her brother anxiously, realized that he had been drinking. She knew how easy it was for him to get mad—explode. Though now he just looked satisfied, as if he had gotten confirmation as to how stupid they were, and liked being misunderstood in their company.

He drank a cup of coffee with them, then went out to the yard and played with the children. Kids were, in any case, better than pig-headed adults.

While Olof was outside, Gertrud took the opportunity to ask Emelie how things were with their brother. Wasn't he neglecting himself? That cap and scarf, he looked a little like he was a member of a hooligan gang, didn't he? And he was so contrary.

Suddenly Emelie found that she had to defend her brother against the same criticism that she herself usually came out with. She told about the artists he was living with, gave them real praise. Surely Gertrud and the others had heard of The Hooligan's Waltz—it had been written by one of Olof's best friends. And another of them drew for the *Sunday-Nisse* paper on a regular basis, and another sold a lot of paintings. Olof had sold some drawings to *Strix*, though they hadn't been published yet. And he learned so much by living and working together with his friends. Of course, she had resisted and wanted him to have a steady job. But all his thoughts were of being an artist. Gradually she had come to believe that, in spite of everything, he was on the right path.

"Boys should hold a regular job," Rudolf said. Emelie must not have been strict enough with Olof.

Yes, he probably should have had a normal job, said Gertrud. And Emelie should forbid him to dress like that.

"Scoundrels do best when they have a hard time of it, and find out how to mind their manners," said Johan. Besides, it was certainly only hooligan gang members and such scoundrels who sang The Hooligan's Waltz.

Emelie reddened with anger. The attack on Olof included her as well. He was old enough to decide for himself, she said. She couldn't prevent him any longer, nor choose his clothes or the company he kept either. Besides, he didn't have the strength for just any work, as they well knew.

But she must be supporting him? asked Gertrud.

No. Emelie kept quiet about the help she sometimes gave him. Anyway, Olof largely managed his own expenses.

One could only guess how his cronies lived, said Johan—wild living and naked models.

Johan sounded envious, snorted Gertrud. Rudolf looked sternly at his wife, and Johan gave an irritated grunt.

Then Gertrud began to talk about August. It was, in spite of everything, more exciting to be related to a rich company director than a poor artist. Gertrud and Bärta couldn't hear enough about how fine and large and nice it was inside August's home. They wanted to know everything about his wife and children. They sighed, envious and delighted: imagine having it so good!

Rudolf and Johan sat silent and a little bitter, didn't like the subject of conversation as much. In any case, they had heard it all before.

Then it didn't take long before the visitors from afar had to start for home. Rudolf was going to begin work early in the morning and the children had already been up way too long. But they had had fun, gotten to ride around the yard on Olof's shoulders and been treated to gooseberries.

The inhabitants of the house waved them off from the open gate. Johan and Bärta went into their room and Olof went inside with Emelie to talk a little while before returning to Paradise.

He criticized bitterly those who had just left. Rudolf had grown more and more hardened—a philistine and a tyrant at home—you could see that. Gertrud sat closed in her narrow world with kids, washing clothes and dishes, lacking all interest in life outside. And Rudolf's condescending tone when he talked to Gertrud.... He treated her like a domestic animal, and she really wasn't much more than that.

Emelie had to protest once more, but it was a dutiful protest. In truth she had to admit that Olof was probably right. Rudolf's manner with Gertrud had not really been nice. Now it was noticeable in another way from before that what Rudolf said was rather stupid and self-satisfied. When he was young the harsh words could have given the impression of a fresh and healthy toughness. It was no longer so. Now he often sounded whining and a bit simple-minded.

After Olof left, Emelie stayed sitting at the table and pondered things: a youthful dream that no longer existed, an illusion that had burst. Had Rudolf changed so much? Or was he actually the same and the changes had occurred inside her? Did she see him with different and clearer eyes now?

If things had gone as she had once hoped, she and Rudolf would have now been married, would have a home and children together. Maybe Rudolf would have treated her the way he treated Gertrud. She could guess that she wouldn't have accepted such behavior. But she wasn't Gertrud; he could not have behaved that way toward her.

But Rudolf was Rudolf, his manner was what it was, and his home a little kingdom where he ruled unchallenged. If Rudolf had wanted to have it that way, they could never have been happy together. Emelie knew that she couldn't obliterate herself the way Gertrud did. She would have resisted. They would surely have quarreled often. They perhaps wouldn't have lived together the way Gertrud and Rudolf now did. Probably worse, more unhappily.

As if she had suddenly been freed from an old, foolish dream, now she couldn't understand why she had been bound up with Rudolf for so many years. Of course she still had beautiful images in her memory to recall: how they had walked together through the city, how handsome he had been in his new streetcar driver uniform, how young and gay and happy she had felt.

It was youth she missed more than Rudolf—those years before responsibility arrived, when she still could be young and be herself. Now she could smile at everything: young and silly, young and irresponsible. Finally she was free, from memories and dreams. She could think: Gertrud can keep him. I'm no longer sore at Gertrud because she took him from me. I can even feel sorry for Gertrud for getting him. Emelie had to smile. But also feel tears and pain. To be freed of something was also to lose it, even if it was nothing more than a foolish dream.

She had freed herself of Rudolf. But getting away from Olof and the thoughts of him didn't happen as easily, not even when he tried to flee from her. She had seen that he wasn't completely sober, and thought about Gertrud's words about how thin the boy was. They might be right to think that Emelie hadn't fulfilled her promise to Mama.

What could she do, now when everything seemed too late, now that he had freed himself?

She looked for a piece of paper and a pen, tried to write a few words that would make him understand that she always wanted to help him, unconditionally, and without ulterior motives. *I really want to help you, if only I can, with whatever you want. I won't ask questions or argue. Don't forget that I am here and I am prepared to help.*

That was what she wanted to say.

She tried to find the right words, printed them carefully. She found a paper bag she could cut up and use as an envelope. She would place the letter in the mailbox at the atelier the next morning.

Gunnar often wondered: was last summer's dream completely gone, was there nothing at all left of the exhibition?

Emelie had promised him that they would go out sometime and look at it. They went one Sunday morning.

The boy woke up early, was dressed and ready before Emelie had time to get out of bed. He sat in the doorway to the yard and waited for her. For a minute she thought he looked like Olof when he sat in the sunlight, remembering her brother from the time when they lived down on Nytorget, and Olof often sat on the stairs and talked to old Fearsome.

But when the boy turned around and looked at her, he didn't look as much like Olof any longer. Gunnar had stronger and more irregular features. Perhaps Emelie was calmed by the dissimilarities. Gunnar would probably not become an artist in any case. He seemed to have some of Olof's stubbornness, but his strength was of another kind, she believed. More practical you could say. The boy was hard and tough. He hadn't been broken by Johan's treatment. But he had hardened, she guessed that he would hit back someday.

He jumped up. Was it time to go?

They looked for memories on Djurgården, sometimes found some building that was left from the exhibition that they recognized, despite the change in the surroundings. The Hunting Lodge was there, Godthem and Reinholds, and the Mining Building from Skåne. Then they went up to Skansen.

This was a big luxury, but Emelie thought that, for once, they could indulge themselves in the expense. Of course, it wouldn't be until next month that she would get her raise in salary, but the promise made her light-hearted. Now she had borrowed a whole three kronor from the money she had set aside for sickness and a funeral. Their encounter with the past summer shouldn't be too shabby; she and Gunnar should have a really fine day together.

They got in line at the big entrance behind Hasselbacken. The man at the gate was an old acquaintance; he had stood at the entrance to the exhibition. Now he let Gunnar in for free and scared Emelie by saying her brother was a good boy. She looked at Gunnar nervously, hoped he hadn't heard the dangerous words. But she didn't say anything to the guard, there was no reason to try and explain.

They walked up the hill toward the small birds' house and the doghouses. Soon they were in the teeming crowd around the inn from Bollnäs. The whole open space outside was filled with horses pulling carts and donkeys and teams of dogs. It was even livelier at the marketplace where the farmer comedian Jödde stood perched on his stone and sang songs and told stories. Sometimes he changed the snuff in his lip and carefully stroked his beard around his mouth with his jacket sleeve; sometimes he took up his accordion and played a peasant polka.

Close by stood a dense wood, and in among the greenery was a lot to explore: caves with birds of prey, the bear cave, wolf dens. And on Renberget, the Lapps lived in their tent. The family from Frostviken was celebrating its seventh summer at Skansen.

There was a lot to experience—a lot that could make a boy happy. Gunnar opened his mouth wide and swallowed everything he could come across. Emelie followed him—found pleasure in the surroundings, in the coolness beneath the trees. Didn't really understand how yesterday's meeting with the past could have had such an effect—that she could now find herself so agreeably freed, so much lighter. Had she ever been able to be herself before, like she was now?

Gradually evening arrived and they traveled back over the darkening water.

She sat in the tidied room, didn't really know what to do with herself. Everything was washed and put away; she didn't have so much to think about since Olof had moved away from home, and in addition she had just had a few days off. The girls who rented from her were out as usual. Gunnar was asleep. Siblings and friends, everybody had somebody. She sat alone. She was glad that she had Gunnar to take care of. They had had a fine day, seen a lot. His happiness made her happy. Next time she was paid she would buy him a pair of boots.

She wondered if Olof was reading the letter now, if he had understood her correctly. He wasn't to think that she was trying to force herself upon him. To her he was still a boy—a persecuted boy, driven by his anxiety. How did he have the strength?

She thought of their father, who year after year toiled in the harbor, coughing and staggering but persevering. Until he collapsed. Did Olof have the same mindset, a will that exceeded his capacity? She watched and felt how Olof wore away at himself unsparingly.

THE SÖDER GIRL

The days were short and gray; the eternal sleet whirled outside the windows. The harbor lay winter empty, and the waters were without life. Through the open and windy streets of slush struggled small, black figures.

Olof was alone in the studio. He stood there listlessly and saw how the shorelines were obliterated by the increasingly heavy snowfall. He should have been working but the darkness oppressed him. It was impossible to paint when each new day was equally gray. It was pointless when no one wanted to buy.

Simple Paradise's other inhabitants had vanished. They had frozen and starved, hardly had anything to drink. They were waiting for the junk dealer, were behind with the rent again. They hadn't even had kerosene for the lamp.

Finally they had moved, as they usually did when things got too tough. Some friends of Arthur had come to get him. The rest had moved to a female rescuer who had promised to give them room and board when things were at their worst. Olof certainly could have gone with them. But he didn't want to give up, had to try and work anyway.

And so he had gone for the whole day without being able to do anything. It was too cold to hold a brush. He had gone out and found a few sticks, been frozen through while looking for them, and had to sit up against the stove to get a little warmth. Now it was too dark.

That was how his days disappeared, amounted to nothing.

Soon it was evening, and he couldn't stay there any longer, had to get away. But he needed a few öre to avoid wandering the streets in the cold.

He took the route past Emelie's. He wouldn't stay with her, didn't have the energy to sit and listen to how worried she was about him. Though he would drink a cup of coffee if she offered one.

While he drank the coffee Emelie tried to mend the frayed edges of his jacket sleeves. She would have preferred to fix his pants too, but he didn't have the patience to sit any longer. He borrowed a krona and left. He hadn't said much, but he sensed her anxiety and caring and knew how weak he was now, how easily he could be captured by her. That drove him away from her, out into the darkness and cold where there was no help.

There was going to be an "entertainment" at a workers' vaudeville on Brännkyrkagatan. There were various scenes and duets on the program: farmers' songs and conscripts' stories, guardsmen's monologues and hooligans' songs. All for the entrance fee of thirty-five öre. Olof had seen shows like this earlier and had no hopes of being amused. But he had taken it into his head that he might get some salable drawings. He could depict "a gala variety show in Hornskrokan" in a few burlesque scenes.

The show had already begun when Olof got there. About fifty people, mostly workingmen, sat on the long benches in the little hall. One corner of the room served as the stage; a few gaslights shone there, and against a backdrop of hideously painted white birches and red cottages, sat the farmer comedian and played accordion. Worn, aging, working desperately to make himself ridiculous and squeeze out the laughs:

They complain about us farmers on every blooming day
And never can a farmhand please a slicker in any way.
When someone tries to make 'em laugh and plays the silly goose
You can be sure he's just a poor ass from the farm let loose...

The flickering lights. Wooden boards laid across sawhorses, flecks of snuff on the wooden floor. The audience, half in darkness, heavy, tired and dressed in work clothes, some of them drunk. The listening faces, one and another contented grin.

Olof's pencil flew across the paper, finally he could work again. Now he no longer wondered if it was something he could sell. Food, wood and candles weren't what mattered now. Here was life as he wanted to show it—what he knew and believed he could tell about.

The comedian's song was over. He was applauded good-naturedly; some stamped their feet in approval. They talked and shouted, put snuff in their lips and blew their noses while they waited for more.

A livelier song was squeezed out of the bellows of the accordion—one that Olof had heard countless times but still not tired of: Arthur's waltz.

A dark, middle-aged man stepped forward, dressed in the hooligan's youthful, stylish rig. He took a hold of his belt, pulled up the wide trousers, struck up a song: *A hooligan…*

And then the Söder girl came dancing in. She wasn't dressed like the many young girls at the dance halls. Her dress was blazing red, cut liberally low, and so short that it fluttered up and showed her legs halfway to her knees. Beneath a large straw hat, her hair stood out like a cloud when she flew around with the singer, who had a hard time combining catching his breath with singing. He let go of her and she whirled away while he sang.

The girl was young, a blonde and, despite her make-up, pale—more high-spirited and lively than pretty. She was the one they meant by "and others" on the posters, the show's walk-on. The singer was included in "the famed duettists."

Olof drew her in quick, sweeping lines, drew her large mouth even closer to her ears, her skirt up to her knees. He wrote "The Söder Girl" under his drawing, and began to look for the lines of "The Hooligan."

But the little shiny-clean duettist's features couldn't really catch his interest; the girl was undeniably a lot more interesting. He tried to concentrate on her face—that deliriously happy and at the same time lost expression, something helpless about it in the midst of an air of confidence. But she never gave him enough time. She changed expressions, fooled him.

He worked on it up to the last minute. Sat there in his corner while the audience began to troop off. Suddenly the girl was standing before him, laughing. "Can I see? It's of me, right?"

He was so surprised that he dumbly handed her the pad of paper. She leafed through the pages, giggling a little: "Do I have a mouth like that?"

"No, well... of course, it's exaggerated."

"Are you walking down into town?" she asked.

He looked up, got an unaccustomed feeling of finding a kindred spirit.

"Yes," he answered. "Let's go."

Brännkyrkagatan wound, narrow, dark and hilly, among the tumble-down houses. Old wooden stairs bordered by a simple wooden fence climbed the hill on the Lake Mälar side. Gas lanterns, few and far between, spread their yellow glow across the dirty snow.

The girl glittered, laughed, chattered on. And Olof felt as if he had been woken up from a trance. How she pulled him along with her. Nothing was as gray and insignificant as before.

She almost slid in the slush, grabbed his hand, put her arm under his. "You have to hold me up," she said.

But then he slipped and she held him up.

"If only as a support," she said. "We seem to have to help each other."

He wanted to find a deeper meaning in the words, a promise. "I would like it if you helped me," he said and looked at her.

He caught her gaze, a flirtatious and uncertain question.

"I want to paint you," he said. "As you appeared this evening, as a Söder girl."

He told her that he had been there when The Hooligan's Waltz was created, that it was his friend who had written it. But then he almost regretted telling her. It was like borrowing some of Arthur's glamour, maybe fooling her into believing that he himself wasn't so unsuccessful.

She seemed interested, though hardly impressed. Maybe she had to appear a little blasé. She herself worked with the two popular duettists and the hilariously funny farmer comedian was her uncle.

It was Uncle who had trained her to appear on stage and gotten her the engagement, she told him. She was still a beginner and had to be sat-isfied with small roles. But she was going to continue in her new profession. It was a lot more fun than being a nursery maid as she had been before.

While they were talking, they had come to Besvärsbacken: an enormous hill that dropped away to the hovels down on Guldgränd. Some boys from a hooligan gang had stolen a sled for hauling and were riding down the hill on it, shrieking and shouting. Far below shone the lights on Södermalmstorg and beyond them lay the waters of Strömmen.

"Oh, I want to ride on that!" she cried.

After paying the boys five öre, they got to borrow the sled. The girl held on tightly. He sat behind her, and tried to get a good grip so they wouldn't slide off. With a few forceful shoves, the boys gave them so much speed that Olof thought the sled would leave the ground and fly straight up into the sky. She screamed with fright and joy; lanterns and doorways flew by. He held onto her tightly, ready to throw them both out of the sled if it looked like it was taking a dangerous course. Suddenly it tipped, and they were hurled out, rolled over a few times and lay panting in the snow and slush. Far below them the sled rushed on, finally crashing into a lamppost.

He felt stiff and bruised all over, but at the same time happy—the adventure, the speed, that giddy feeling, and the girl.

"How are you doing? Did you get hurt?" she asked.

"I'm okay. How about you?"

"Just great," she laughed, and sat up. When he stood up she reached out her hands, wanting to be pulled to her feet. They tumbled down the rest of the hill, sliding on parts of it, taking many opportunities to grab hold of each other and not fall anymore. They came to a stop at the foot of the hill and laughed.

He led her to Brunnsbacken, past Pelikan, wanted to show her where the atelier was. He pointed, up there was where he hung out and painted.

She couldn't do it this evening she said. She lived with her aunt and uncle on Tyska brinken, a lane in the Old Town. They would wonder where she was. But if Olof wanted, she could come tomorrow morning. She didn't have anything special going on the next day. In the afternoon she and the others were going to Södertälje to perform.

That would be good, he said. They could hope for a little light in the morning.

Olof woke up earlier than he usually did—while it was still dark out. He got out of bed in the dim, early light of Little Sleeping Hell, took the large broom and tried to sweep up the paper and trash.

Something had to be done about the cold. He had fifty öre left of what he had borrowed from Emelie. If he could get a hectogram of coffee on credit from the grocer, then he would be able to buy half a bag of wood. There were a few lumps of sugar in a box, and such luxuries as cream and bread weren't even to be considered. He would have to manage without.

Even though he understood that she wouldn't come for a while, he put a note on the door explaining he would be back soon.

He got the coffee after reproaches and promises, then he got the wood and returned to Paradise and made a fire in the stove till it glowed red. He set the paints out and borrowed Petter's easel, arranged the cloth he got to appropriate after Arthur and which he had scraped as free of paint as possible. He was ready, now she could come.

She's not coming, he thought. It was only something she had said, an idea. Otherwise it was an unusually fine day for working, not nearly as gray as it usually was. But gray enough for his friends to continue to stay away, he hoped. If only she were to come now....

Then there was knock on the door and he recognized the rhythm: someone was rapping The Hooligan's Waltz on the door with his or her knuckles.

A little abashed, she stepped in, as if the daylight made them less familiar.

"It's so nice and warm here," she said and looked around. She sat down on the wooden sofa and picked up the string bag she had with her.

"Do you have a mirror?" she asked. "I have to make myself up if I'm going to look like I'm on stage."

There was a piece of mirror tacked to the wall in Sleeping Hell. He fetched it for her. When he came back she had taken off her coat and thrown it over the arm of the sofa. Now he understood why she looked so pale despite the red mouth and the painted bloom on her cheeks. Her slender arms were so white, like the skin that had shone at the open neck of her dress. She was a pale child, thin and fair-haired. But her face was different. Especially now that she had painted her large mouth a gaudy red.

"If you like I can paint it all the way up to my ears," she said. "But then I will be more like Pelle Jöns the clown than the Söder girl."

He wondered how she should best stand, wanted to have her in the middle of a dance in a whirl of colors and wide, sweeping skirts. He leafed through his pad of sketches.

"Look," he said, "that's how I want you."

She came closer to him. And he couldn't avoid seeing what he saw of her breasts when she bent forward.

She tried to strike the pose he wanted. Gradually they managed to figure out how she could stand. And he squeezed out the brightest red there was in the tubes.

She was maybe not the ideal model, had a hard time standing still, talked without cease, and was curious as to how it was turning out. Still it was easy work, he liked being with her so much that he didn't get irritated. And then she was so rewarding to paint, in bold, clashing colors. She was like part of the gray, everyday reality suddenly poured into a package bursting with color. The red sheen of the mouth and the dress made the gray so gray, so pathetic. The girl in his painting was obviously *dressed up,* but it showed, also, that she was aware of it and thought it was fun to be dressed up.

The portrait of the Söder girl didn't get finished that day, but he thought it was shaping up, could turn out well.

"When can you come again?" he asked.

She had washed off her make-up and was putting on her coat and hat. "Tomorrow at the same time," she said. "If you like. I don't have to be on stage in the evening either, so we don't have to be in a hurry."

She had opened the door. When he reached out his hand to say good-bye, she didn't take it. Mischief shone in her eyes and suddenly he felt her large mouth close over his own, then she puckered up to make a really loud smacking kiss.

She ran off before he regained his senses. He heard her quick steps, the clicking of her heels on the endless stairs. He stood there a long time at the door, and thought he could hear the small echo of a laugh up the spiral staircase long after the door below had slammed shut.

Then he walked over to the painting and looked at the dancing Söder girl for a long time. He took the paintbrush and drew the large mouth a little wider. He stuck his tongue in the corners of his mouth, as if he was trying to measure how big her mouth had been.

"Just wait," he thought. "You run away now, but you'll be back."

Her name was Jenny.

Muttering over his lack of initiative—simply letting her run off after taking him by surprise!—he began to work on the background of the red Söder girl. Hunger made him weak. But now he was able to work, now he didn't have to destroy the mood by thinking of food.

OUTSIDE

Jenny was on tour with her uncle. Olof received letters, small pieces of paper on which she had scribbled down whatever came into her head, experiences and words of love indiscriminately. Her outspoken style took him aback at times; they hadn't been that intimate. The words she was writing she would never have said to him directly. Who was she, really? He looked at the painting of the Söder girl: you dress up, pretend so much, sometimes it's hard to find you.

They were friends and certainly a little more than that. They hadn't had time to go farther before she left. Beneath the liberated artistic demeanor there had been so much shyness and uncertainty. Now distance gave them a feeling of security that brought out what had been concealed and unsaid before. The letters brought them closer to each other; one word drew out another. He felt a little worried at the thought of how it would be when they met again. Things were heating up now.

In her last letters he thought he had detected a change. There was anguish and desperation. She had gone through something that made her alternately push him away and cling to him.

Be happy with someone else, she wrote. And on another of the scraps of paper: you must never let me travel away from you again.

The words that he interpreted as desperate cries were in the middle of the whirling current, amidst the jokes and the flirting and the descriptions of their shows in theater barns and Good Templar lodges.

"I long to come home," she wrote. "I pretend that you're holding me, so hard that I grow calm."

And a few lines further down: "You can never forgive me."

What should he forgive her for? Was there someone else? More and more impatiently he waited for her write back. Now he couldn't write to her anymore, she hadn't given him any more addresses. He had to wait and try to drive away the time with work.

Then the last letter arrived. She asked if he could meet her at the train. Not inside Central Station where the whole theater troupe was arriving, but in the railway park, she suggested. If it was raining they could meet in the third class hall. It lay at a reasonable distance from arriving passengers.

He went there early. It was cloudy but it wasn't raining, so they would meet in the park. For once he had money. He had been lucky enough to sell a few drawings to *Strix*. He sat down on a bench so he could see the tracks and the lineman's cottage beside Klara strand. The train was almost on time, rolled in thundering and puffing steam between the lowered crossing gates and in under the glass roof of the arrival hall.

Some open carriages and a baggage wagon from the Hotel Rydberg drove over the deserted central square. A cattle handler came along pulling an ornery cow. The newly painted urinals on both sides of the large entrance shone a summery green.

Olof had never been past the city's closest surroundings. Jenny had become a real traveler. Though from her letters, it had been evident that she could hardly tell one town from another. She mostly saw the halls where she performed and hotel rooms.

He walked out through the bushes in the park to better see when she arrived. Maybe she had some luggage to carry. But she had expressly instructed him not to come too close and be seen by her traveling companions. He didn't believe she was ashamed of him, he was more afraid there was someone else.

He saw her coming—thin and pale, an overgrown girl in a light blue summer dress. When she came closer he saw the harried expression on her face.

"Let's go," she said urgently. "I have a suitcase on the baggage car that's arriving—but the others are there now. I can get it tomorrow."

Olof followed her without asking questions. She walked toward the small walkway on the railroad bridge. Out on the bridge, she slowed her pace, as if she felt safer where no carriages could go. She leaned over the railing, looked out across the water that was lapping against Strömbadet baths' yellow walls. Suddenly, he noticed that she was crying. "I'm just so happy to be home again. Home with you."

"Don't go away anymore," he said.

"No, I won't. Nobody will ask me to do it again, either. Now I know I can't do anything. I'll never be a real artist."

He should have protested, said that he thought she was good. But he kept quiet. Because he wanted her to stay with him? And what did he have to offer? Could he do anything himself? Would he ever be a real artist in his field?

They could hear noise and splashing from inside the baths. There were apparently many people who were taking the opportunity to take a dip during the warm summer evening.

"I would like to rinse off," she said. "The trip and everything...."

If it's nice weather, we can rent a boat at Björkman's by the dock at Barnängen early tomorrow morning," he answered. "Tonight it's too late and everything is rented out already."

She was hungry, and she also had something that she didn't usually have: money. She had been paid and put aside part of it. Their last difficult days, when their tour had been close to falling apart, she had lied and said that she didn't have any money left. The others had probably come home more broke than before but she, who didn't have an öre when she had left, had a whole ten kronor with her coming home. She had saved the money just so they could celebrate when they saw each other again.

It felt easier to continue; their spirits had brightened. They went across Riddarhusbron to the square where the statue of Gustav Vasa stood in front of a low, pointed balustrade flanked by four lampposts standing at attention. They walked on across the square at Munkbron. The white flags on the many stalls fluttered in the evening wind, the handcarts stood in rows with their shafts up in the air. Alongside Kornhamn the small cargo boats lay densely moored, and around Slussen the waters of Lake Mälar and the Baltic had merged in the blue dusk.

They ate on Pelikan's open summer veranda in the greenery above Järngraven. The new proprietor, Miss Uddelius, came and talked to them.

She knew that Olof belonged to the group of artists at Stadsgården. Olof was a little unused to such flattering attentions and answered monosyllabically, but Jenny liked it. Restaurant keepers usually came over and talked to the stage artists this way when they stayed in the municipal hotels. Especially with her uncle, he was best friends with all the restaurant keepers.

But the thought of her uncle dampened the mood.

I have to get away, she thought. Can't go back. But she knew she had to return there, for at least a while, for her aunt's sake. What would her aunt think otherwise?

"What are you brooding about?" asked Olof. He was starting to feel full and contented even though he hadn't eaten a lot. He was unused to a lot of food; he usually had a piece of bread and a cup of coffee, a bit of herring and a drink of aquavit.

"I want us to get married," she said suddenly.

Astonished, he stared at her. It wasn't a very good joke.

"That was exactly what I expected," she said calmly. "That you'd think I was crazy if I said it."

She went on eating, didn't offer an explanation.

Afterward he walked with her to her uncle's on Tyska brinken. As they walked through the silent and pale evening, he had to bring up the question again.

"Did you really mean that about us getting married?"

"Yes. Otherwise I wouldn't have said it. But you don't have to if you don't want to."

"But I do want to. If I could only figure out how. We don't even have work. And neither a room nor furniture."

She laughed and suddenly began to dance around like the Söder girl had done.

"You really are a philistine. If people want to they can get married anyway. But you don't have to I already said."

He wanted to talk about it more, discuss how they could make it happen.

But she was tired from her journey and the meal. They had arrived at her uncle's now. She didn't want anybody to see them from the window.

"We'll talk about it tomorrow," she said.

He had to be satisfied with that, returning to Simple Paradise feeling giddy. It was only himself and Janne sleeping there now. The others had moved out.

"What do you think about marriage?" asked Olof.

"You've been drinking. Go to sleep now," muttered Janne and turned toward the wall.

Olof didn't say any more. But he had a hard time falling asleep. He lay and wondered what could have happened to Jenny. He hadn't really gotten an answer.

The next morning, he waited for her at the gunpowder shop beneath the elevator bridge. He stood there with his easel and paintbox. They walked up the steep street, where gas lanterns jutted out and washing hung out from the crumbling gray houses. Up by the Dihlström workhouse, hand-carts rattled over the cobblestones; the old fellows were on their way to fetch the milk for breakfast. The large, empty bleach bottles rumbled on the platforms on the carts.

At the butcher's on Nytorgsgatan, Amilon, the butcher, stood in the doorway and gave a friendly nod to passing customers. The houses grew smaller and lower—here and there were only low sheds where the flies buzzed in clouds over the half-tainted pieces of meat. At Nytorget, Olof showed her the house where he had lived for so many years. Fearsome and Johanna were dead now, and Ludde and his family had moved a long time ago. The dog man was still there. He had his stall and his boiling pot of dogfood outside the old firehouse that had been turned into a market hall. The school was empty for the summer and closed. On Värmdögatan the dust whirled. But at the end of the street, Hammarby Lake glittered and the rowboats lay close together tied to the dock.

Olof left the one krona deposit for a boat and looked until he found a good skiff. Jenny sat in the stern and he punted them out through the opaque water. Then he had room to turn it around and could take longer strokes with the oars. They glided out into the shimmering sunlight, on water with a surface smooth as oil. She trailed her hand in the water, examined her fingers. Could you really swim here?

You couldn't have too high expectations, he said. It was somewhat better closer to Lång Lake, farther from the sewage outlets. He turned around, looked toward the shore at Hammarby farm and Mormors holme. But he didn't want to look in the direction of the candle factory. That's where it had happened with Mama. He would prefer not to row over there.

The trip across the lake took almost half an hour. They didn't say much. It was taxing for Olof to row and he was afraid of another fit of coughing. He let the boat glide in, gave Jenny his hand and helped her out. She lifted her long skirt. Her chalked white cloth shoes shone as white as her cotton stockings. And he was almost frightened by the fact that they were alone on the island. She was so unreserved and incautious.

"Let's swim first," she said. "Can I go in here where there's a sandy bottom? You can go behind the bushes over there."

He jumped in, swam out a bit. It had been a long time. During his childhood, he and Ludde had often swum in the lake even though they had been forbidden to do so. He remembered how sometimes Mama would check if he had obeyed by looking at his neck: those who swam close to the warm stream got a black ring around their throats since oil was released there. Close to the stream, they were careful to put their heads underwater.

Now it felt lovely and refreshing in the water, despite his being aware that it was anything but clean. But he had overexerted himself, had difficulty breathing. He grew worried about a coughing attack and began to swim back. He saw Jenny standing by the boat. Her body shone unnaturally white against the greenery. Unembarrassed, she waved to him, but he didn't have the strength to wave back.

He arrived at the shore, threw himself heaving in the grass. The coughing took hold; everything grew black before his eyes.

When he could see again, he saw her. She was standing there anxiously staring at him.

"How are you?" she asked. "Are you sick?"

"It's over now," he said.

"You did too much."

"Nah...."

"Have you been to a doctor?"

"A long time ago, but it feels better now. Go swim. I'll be alright."

I shouldn't let her stay with me, he thought. I should tell her to find someone else, someone who can help and protect her, someone who is strong and healthy. Still, he knew that he wouldn't be capable of doing that—that he would ask her to stay and be his.

Jenny turned away from him when she told him. She had been born out of wedlock, and had grown up with her mother's sister and her sister's husband, the comedian.

It was her uncle who had insisted on Jenny becoming a stage artist. He had worked out small scenes with her, taught her to dance. It had taken a while before she understood that his interest wasn't so selfless. But after realizing this, it had been hard to endure. She felt like his eyes and his hands were always glued to her. His interest became a persecution and a seduction. And now, during their long tour, she had no longer been able to protect herself from him. Now that Olof had heard how things really were, maybe he didn't want anything to do with her anymore.

He understood. He knew that nothing could get in their way now. She could not return to her uncle. He pulled her to him, hid her from the sun and the wind, kissed her passionately. She started to laugh and then to cry. And he cried with her.

When they had calmed down a little, they sat in the shadow of the bushes—just held each other and finally felt some kind of safety. However things were they belonged to each other now.

"You understand that I'm sick," he said in a low voice.

"Yes."

"I may not have much time left."

He shouldn't say that. There must be some cure.

He shook his head. No, he knew well that it was hopeless when you had this sickness. She must know that. And he wouldn't blame her if she left him.

She took his hand and held it to her chest, pressing it tightly. He felt how his hand was filled with life and warmth and how he loved life and wouldn't be able to force her to leave him.

"You don't want to change your mind? You really want to?" He had to ask though it was too late to ask now.

It was evening before they returned to the lake. He rowed slowly.

"You can't go back to your uncle's now," he said.

"Where shall I go?" she asked without any anxiety in her voice.

He was silent a long time.

"We'll have to go to Emelie, my sister," he said finally. "She's the only one I know who can help us."

Once he had said that, made his decision, it felt easier. He took slightly more powerful strokes with the oars and landed at the dock.

AUTUMN'S CHANGES

When Emelie walked back and forth to work, she saw the brilliant red clusters of barberries in the hedge around Adolf Fredrik's churchyard. They shone in the gray morning light and in the evenings' lantern light.

She arrived early and left late. Being supervisor didn't only include an increase in salary. She had to make sure everything was ready for the day's work, and when evening came she had to fill in the accounts with the work results.

The packers had gotten their high stools, the work area had better lighting and was freer of drafts. Conditions had improved, but they didn't seem especially grateful. At least they didn't thank Emelie. Some complained instead. It had been nicer before, when the packing men had been in the same room and so many people were running in and out. In those days you could stand and talk a little, disappear for a few minutes without anyone noticing it. Now everything was so controlled. There weren't more people than before, but they had time for the increase in orders. These innovations only improved things for the factory director. Emelie played up to him, naturally, wanted to look good. It was certainly no coincidence that she was the one taken out to the exhibition a year or so ago and then got to be supervisor.

But there was no reason for her to put on airs. They could manage themselves, and if anyone was going to be their superior it should be a man.

Gradually they got used to it, some of the dissatisfied ones quit. The new ones took it as natural that Emelie was supervisor. And of course it was nice to sit while working—which they were all in agreement upon.

The clerk who received Emelie's accounts, and who took charge of the stockroom accounts, couldn't resist letting the factory director know about the improved results. Yes, the factory director had probably noticed it. And when old Melinder came to visit he also got to hear about it. The old man listened with interest, smiled contentedly. "Little Emelie" was one of those he had had his eye on and counted upon. It made him happy that Konrad had proven himself to be such a good judge of people that he had made her supervisor.

Before the old man left the factory, he took a look in on the packaging room, may not have appeared completely happy about the changes. They were sitting and working! Somehow he thought it was immoral. But the improved result couldn't be ignored. If production went up it couldn't be helped that morals were lowered.

He stood and watched a little while. Emelie had gotten involved in the work and was nimbly placing perfume bottles in excelsior and boxes. He could remember how he had stood there and watched her when she was a child. She had been in the factory's employ for many years, a loyal employee. A feeling of thankfulness, almost tenderness, gripped him. He shuffled over, supported by his cane. Before he had time to change his mind, he had quickly patted her hand: congratulations, he had heard that things were going so well for Emelie.

She curtsied and thanked him.

Then he turned and left. It was the last time he visited the factory. A few weeks later he was bedridden.

Of course Emelie had thought that he was difficult at times, demanding and strict. But she had a lot to thank him for, and as long as he had been with the firm she had felt a security that she maybe found lacking now. When she saw him hobble away she still felt mostly compassion. He was so old and tired—had no one who really took care of him. The young factory director thought mostly of himself, had no time left over for the old man. Now that his money no longer meant anything, he was put aside and had only death left to wait for.

Through the window she saw him walk across the yard: a little, crooked figure against a gray background of sheds and smoke.

Once more she reached for the perfume bottles. One hadn't been properly filled. She lifted it to the light, shook her head. It shouldn't contain so little. She looked a moment at the colorful label: a woman in a red dress gracefully leaning toward her dressing table mirror.

The red dress drew her thoughts to Jenny. Although Jenny didn't use her red dress any longer—had only used it on stage before. One evening she had put it on and danced and sung to Gunnar's great amusement.

Jenny could be uproariously funny.... Sometimes she scared Emelie with her easy-going ways, but at heart she was certainly a good person. Olof had been lucky. Though truthfully, she wasn't beautiful with her angular figure and her enormous mouth. It was good that Olof was an artist and didn't think like other people; he never got tired of painting Jenny.

Jenny had gotten an extra job, stood behind the counter in a sewing goods store on Hornsgatan in the afternoons. She had to work late into the evenings. In exchange, she had her mornings free.

In the beginning Jenny's arrival had resulted in certain problems, it grew crowded in the little room. When Emelie realized that Jenny was going to be a long-term guest, she had given the two girls who were living there, their notice. It was not to her advantage from an economic stand-point, but she felt she should try to afford it. She had received an increase in salary after all.

Jenny was kind and willing, took on her share of the household chores, tried to pay her way. She didn't make enemies with anyone either. Even Johan had really come to like her—he who otherwise got annoyed by any-thing that had to do with Olof.

No, with Jenny it wasn't hard. It was Olof there were problems with. Now there was no question of a steady job. It was too late. He didn't have the strength for a real job anymore. And there was something more diffi-cult: to get him to go to a doctor. Emelie had tried to persuade him but it hadn't helped much. Now she placed her hope in Jenny.

She had managed to convince Jenny to wait a little with getting mar-ried. As long as they weren't expecting a child there was no hurry. Emelie didn't know exactly what papers would be necessary if Olof and Jenny were to get married before he was of age. Surely it would be complicated.

Next year Olof would turn twenty-one, then it should be much simpler.

Emelie also seemed to think that it was rather strange that they wanted to get married when they weren't even going to live together. For people to move in together without getting married was nothing unusual. But to get married without moving in together was something she had never heard of. It must be one of those "artistic" ideas.

The barberry hedge's green leaves began to turn red. Soon it stood like a glowing wall along the gray street but Emelie hardly noticed it, she was too preoccupied with the threat that was aimed at her world.

Johan and Bärta were going to move. They had a hard time managing in the little room where there wasn't even a stove for preparing food. They had three more children now, besides Gunnar: two girls and now, since a few months back, a son.

Their moving in itself was no tragedy, quite the opposite. It meant some relief for Emelie. They had not always been such good neighbors— shouting and screaming, borrowing money and food and seldom paying anything back. But Johan had let Emelie know that Gunnar was moving with them. The boy was to begin working as soon as possible; kids got spoiled from just going to school. Johan wanted to place him in a chimney sweep apprenticeship. That would be a real education. The boy needed to be brought under control if they were going to get him into shape.

Emelie had not answered Johan. She knew she had to calm down first. If Johan found out who Gunnar's father was, he might begin to harass August and try to squeeze money out of him.

She understood that, knew Johan too well. She had to try other alternatives.

When she got home that evening, she invited Bärta over for a cup of coffee. Her plan wasn't formulated. She just knew that Bärta was the only possibility.

So now they were going to move, Emelie began. And Johan had said that Gunnar should move with them.

Yes, Johan wanted that. And it was certainly the right thing to do. Now they could thank Emelie for taking care of the boy for so long. He was a little troublesome and willful.

Emelie didn't think so. But didn't Bärta believe that Johan realized he wasn't Gunnar's father? Wasn't that why he was so hard on the boy?

No, Bärta didn't want to think that.

But if the boy came under Johan's care again, he would be completely destroyed. For Gunnar's sake, they had to do something. Emelie understood that Bärta wanted to have her child with her, but still....

Bärta began to cry. Johan was so unreasonable. Despite everything, she could usually manage him, but when it came to Gunnar she had failed. What could she do?

Bärta had to stand up to him, get Johan to allow the boy to stay with Emelie.

He would surely not want to go along with that. Now he had resolved that Gunnar would move with them.

Emelie delayed a moment—she stopped, faced with the obstacle she had to make herself get past.

In that case, Emelie would be forced to tell Johan who the father of the boy was. Yes, she had to tell August so he would step in and prevent Gunnar from being destroyed for life.

No, no. Emelie mustn't do that. Bärta was crying, distraught.

For Gunnar's sake, it was necessary.

Then Bärta would rather convince Johan. Anything, as long as Emelie said nothing. Bärta understood that Gunnar was best off with Emelie. It was Johan, not Bärta who wanted to bring the boy along. Of course Bärta was attached to Gunnar, but she herself knew that she really didn't have time for him. The younger children demanded all her time. And if she tried to take care of Gunnar, Johan did everything he could to prevent it and spoil it. For her part, she would feel happy and calm if Gunnar could stay here. She would tell Johan that he wasn't the boy's father, and he probably suspected it the whole time, by the way. But she never wanted to say it was August. It would be better to let Johan believe that she had had so many men that she didn't know who the father was.

Emelie met Johan in the hallway the next morning. He was surly and bitter.

"You can have it your way," he said. "Take the bastard. But don't come begging me for help if you can't manage. He's never coming into my house again."

She could have easily answered. Asked if she had ever asked Johan for anything. But all that was meaningless now. The only big and important thing was that Gunnar got to stay.

That morning Emelie saw how the hedge glowed. She surreptitiously broke off a sprig and fastened it to her blouse. In the evening she took out the box with the kronor she had saved, the funeral money. She wondered if she shouldn't go ahead and buy those boots she had thought of giving Gunnar for so long. There would always be money for a burial. Now she was needed and had to live a long time.

IN GRAY AND RED

Emelie had gone to work, Gunnar to school. It was quiet and still in the room, only the fire crackling in the chimney could be heard and when the pine logs gave a snap from time to time.

Jenny was awake, but still lay on the wooden sofa. She had worked late the previous evening. There was a lot to do in the shop so close to Christmas. She seldom could leave before twelve every night.

She shifted to be more comfortable, lay with her head resting on her hand and stared into the fire Gunnar had lighted. It was still dark out, and dark in the room except for the light from the fire. She liked it here, the darkness was also safe. She felt that for the first time in her life, she had found a place where she was at home. It was so easy to live together with Emelie and Gunnar. They had all formed a good relationship, and she had grown into it without any resistance.

But Olof stood outside.

She knew that Emelie had asked him to move back home many times. But Olof had refused. He was afraid of being pulled into their everyday life, couldn't deal with anything that was like an idyll. It scared him he saw only the ties that bound him.

Still, he came by almost every day. But only when he knew that Emelie and Gunnar weren't home, and unwillingly, furtively. Ashamed and bad-tempered at the same time, always ready to defend his freedom. It was as if he didn't really like Jenny being so happy there; maybe he thought that Emelie pulled Jenny away from him.

Still he knew that nothing in life could keep them apart any longer. He was attached that way anyway. She dared to believe: he wanted to be attached.

But he demanded nothing that was possible, only the impossible. He wanted to live with his comrades in the atelier, but Jenny couldn't come there. He was jealous, and she could smile at that. It was so unnecessary.

If they had had their own home, she would probably have been left sitting alone there. He wouldn't have been calm enough to stay there for very long periods. Jenny would tease him: he wanted her to be so small that he could carry her around in his pants pocket, always available and never any trouble.

No one knocked, but she heard the door open, carefully and slowly. He had come.

Anxiously she looked at him, hurried out of bed.

What had happened?

It was nothing. Probably a toothache had ruptured overnight, one that had been broken for a long time. But he didn't intend to be forced into going to any dentist. It would have to do the way it was.

"Come," she said, and took hold of him. "Come to me."

He followed her to the wooden sofa, a little unwillingly. He certainly didn't want to ask anyone for anything, not even Jenny. The toothache made him feel even more of a failure, even less worth loving. The whole day before he had failed, painted one canvas more frightful than the next. But there was something he wanted to achieve, an image he still hadn't seen and thus was unable to capture. It evaded him.

Now he was destroying Jenny as well, maybe infecting her with his sickness, maybe he had created a sick child inside her unfit for living. Why did he struggle against life any longer? Why didn't he accept the unavoidable end?

The other day a boy, younger than himself, had jumped from the Katarina elevator. Olof had heard the scream, the thud—had hurried to the window of the atelier and seen the body, the blood that ran in the snow. The unknown boy had dared to jump, whereas he sat dangling on the edge, clinging fast to life, lacking the courage required to relinquish his hold. Desperate, he reached out for Jenny. This impossible desire that remained in his sick body.

She stood before him, her camisole lit by the red fireglow. She brought his hands to her breasts, asked him to hold her tightly, live a little longer. And suddenly, it was as if pain and fear melted away. He felt like he ate and drank her, his hunger was insatiable. And the fever that burned inside him couldn't be extinguished, it could only devour.

Exhausted and heaving, he sank down beside her. He heard her soothing voice, saw her shining white body through the blood-colored gleam of his eyelids.

They had arranged it now, she said low and beseechingly. August was going to talk to a doctor who could get him a place in the hospital. No, he mustn't protest, he had already promised. He had to think about the fact that they were going to have a child together. Surely he wanted to see that child? Surely he wanted to go on living with her?

He didn't have the strength to protest any longer. He felt how they tied him with their love and their care, pulled him in even though he was meant to live outside. Doctors and hospital beds, not to get to paint, not to get to be with Jenny, not to get to be himself. Life without living.

But he had promised, they had conquered him in the end. Now there was even money, August had come to their aid. They were going to kill the little inside him that was capable of living and worth keeping alive.

Empty and tired, he lay there on the wooden sofa while she got up. It would soon be time for her to go, time for him to return to the atelier. He still must have a few weeks left of freedom. He had persuaded them to put off the decision for so long: had to try and clear things up a little, sell some drawings and pay his debts, pack up his possessions.

Silently he followed Jenny down the hill on Glasbruksgatan. She walked so lightly. Her large mouth smiling, her skinny body so close to him. But now in the wind and in the cold, gray light of day, he could only feel that he was soon going to lose her. He felt like the distance between them was growing, the cold and their clothing and the looks of other people separated them. Jenny was on her way to the shop, would talk and smile, sell and wrap things. He would stand at his canvas, and feel how everything he undertook was a failure. And he would go over to the window and look out at where the dead body had lain.

She stopped. This was where their ways parted.

If they could have stayed on the wooden sofa, if she could have gone with him up to the atelier, if life had still remained....

He felt like he couldn't let her leave him. He had to hold onto her, hold her really tightly against him. Finally she pulled herself free and ran toward Brunnsbacken. But time after time she turned around and waved.

When Jenny got home late in the evening Emelie sat up waiting for her. August had spoken with the doctor. Since Olof had absolutely wanted a few more weeks, they had gotten an appointment for one of the first days in January. August would go along, to discuss what could best be done. Hospital or rest home, it depended on how badly off Olof was.

It seemed as if Emelie was seeking Jenny's forgiveness. She knew this should have happened much earlier, could only hope that it wasn't too late now. She had not managed to persuade Olof herself; it was Jenny who had succeeded. Maybe she hadn't wanted it enough to trouble August either. Whenever he asked how things were going for them she usually answered that they were managing, even if Olof was frail, like he always was. They were so used to his being frail and sickly, hadn't believed there was anything they could do about it. They had hoped he would grow out of it. It was Jenny who had understood how serious it was and forced them to take care of it.

The doctor had asked about Olof's parents, wanted to know if any of them had suffered from the same sickness. August had told them about his father. Now doctors knew why the children of consumptives also got the disease. They didn't inherit it, they got it from the infection that was spread by coughing.

That would make Olof happy, said Jenny. Then he wouldn't have to be so worried about the child. Jenny was pretty sure now. There most likely would be a child, she was three weeks late. They had said the whole time that they wanted to have a child. The only thing that scared them was the thought that the sickness was inherited.

Emelie picked up the money she had gotten from August, twenty one-krona bills. The doctor had said it was very important for the sick person to eat properly, and take care of himself. Somehow Jenny had to get Olof to accept the money and use it for food.

It wouldn't amount to much food if Olof took care of it himself. It was better if they bought the food for him themselves.

When Olof arrived the next morning the table was set: porridge and milk, white bread and two boiled eggs. And Jenny refused to go to bed with him before he had eaten well. It was doctor's orders she said.

The time was so short. As if everyone wanted to get in his way, make it even shorter. It was Christmas and Gunnar had time off from school. The boy was out a lot. But he could come in at any time.

Olof preferred to avoid the food, didn't have the energy to eat. Now when he couldn't be with Jenny undisturbed he stayed at the atelier, blamed it on having a lot to do.

He met her outside the shop in the evenings instead. They walked through the streets in the cold, sat in a café sometimes. The longing to lie with her screamed inside him. Soon everything would be over, soon there would only be the sickbed and death. The fear of what was to come, the feeling of time running out—he grew desperate.

He pulled her into the woodshed one evening. She resisted a little, but then gave in. He fell down on top of her, felt the warmth of her body but also the cold that made them both shake.

So poor and dirty, so cold and dark.

He cried over his misery. It didn't help that she tried to console him, that she assured him she was happy in spite of everything.

When he woke up one morning and saw spots of blood after his coughing attacks, it called up a memory. It reached back in time like a thread—past the man who bled to death beneath Katarina elevator, past the terror of blood in what he coughed up, back to his childhood. There was an image he had fled from and was drawn to in fascination. Could that be what his brush had sensed, and what had evaded him?

He was nine years old again. Was out walking with Ludde. Gray winter, then like now. Animals that screamed in agony before death, who stomped and fell in their blood. The man lifting up the pig stomach, pulling it out of the still living animal.

There it was, life's red blood spilled and the black giants. Everything that had been clubbed down. The man who had plunged from Katarina elevator, the blood he himself was coughing up. The life that was being pulled out of his body—agony, blood and excrement.

He didn't know how he would find the time, how he would capture the vision: the red colors and the gray mist, the giant-like black men—black against all the red, black rather than blue.

He didn't hear his friends, they were going out. Someone had money of course. In the evening, when they returned, he had placed the canvas out, and sat frozen next to the stove. They stopped and looked.

Now it was getting too damned awful. It made you want to throw up to look at it. So brutal—did he believe anyone could bear to have that sight hanging on the wall?

He didn't have the strength to answer, left to go meet Jenny.

When he came back they had taken down the painting and turned it to the wall. He couldn't hang it up; they couldn't bear to see it.

Arthur, who would have understood, was gone. Olof didn't know where.

The rain poured down; the city was hidden behind a gray curtain.

It was a sad farewell the old century gave. But for those who were going to celebrate the evening indoors, it turned out well enough. His friends had reserved a table at Pelikan.

Olof had intended to go with them and celebrate his departure, so he had said to Jenny that she shouldn't count on him coming home. New Years Eve was going to be his last evening with his friends.

But then he got into an argument with them. They had turned his painting around again. They could go without him. He didn't want to go along. He stayed in the atelier to pack up his belongings.

He saw his work: the few paintings, the large bundles of sketches. The stove was burning warm and friendly; they had splurged on a sack of wood on this day of celebration.

Everything seemed so bad—poorly drawn, coarse, cheap effects. He couldn't die leaving this. It was enough that a person was made a laughingstock during his lifetime. They wouldn't have to feel sick from his paintings afterward. He took the bundles of sketches and shoved them into the stove. He broke the stretchers and rolled up the canvasses.

He had a bottle of aquavit. Actually he had meant to leave it, it was going to remain as his greeting to his friends. But he could take a few swigs to be able to look at all the wretched work he had accomplished. And burn it up.

Nobody liked what he did. Arthur had said some encouraging words sometimes. But maybe only out of decency. Jenny was too close to judge.

Though the scene from the slaughterhouse was probably the best he had done, whatever they might say. And then Jenny as the Söder girl. He placed the two paintings beside each other.

Strange, he hadn't thought of it before. They used the same palette: red, gray and black. The red Söder girl and the red blood, the gray sky and the gray mist, the black hooligan that he had hinted at in the background of the girl, and the giants who stood black and large as if enclosed in a red hell.

Now he, himself, didn't feel he could bear to look at that slaughter-house any longer, tore it out of its frame, threw it in the stove. The fire dizzily took hold of it.

He took a swig from the bottle. There wasn't much left to burn up. It was just as well to throw in the last. There, everything was gone, except for the Söder girl.

Take that too—did he dare? Did he dare jump from the elevator or did they have to throw him off? He wanted, of course, to have a little hand-hold left to cling to, hoped that someone sometime would see his Söder girl and say: he wasn't such a bad painter, that strange Obstinate Olle.

No, don't try to fool yourself. They will laugh at your Söder girl, think that you were a bungler. And worse: laugh at Jenny.

They weren't going to come with their insolent remarks; he was going to free her from all that. That much, at least, he could do.

Everything was gone. Even the picture of Jenny.

He heard how the bells began to ring. Their thundering clamor rose over the whole city.

CHILDREN
OF
THEIR CITY

The church bells tolled.

The rain that had poured down on the city all day long had ceased. The air still felt heavy with humidity, a premonition of spring.

All the churches and all the restaurants had been filled to their last seat. Enormous crowds of people roamed the streets, defying the seemingly bottomless slush. Not since the "Jubilee Day" had so many people been set in motion.

It felt as if not only the old century, but also a whole era was now stepping into the grave. Mankind was going toward a brighter and better world. Everything was there for them within the walls of the new century.

Settlements that had sprung up on the edges of town were beginning to spread beyond the old tollgates as well. The city had gotten a railway, steamboats and horse-drawn streetcars; they were already planning for electric streetcars, and automobile omnibuses. New bridges were under construction; streets were being blasted through what had once been impassable rock.

And all these new things were still only in preparation—signs of what was to come. The world was young and new.

When the bells began to ring, they hurried out into the garden.

The air was filled with the thunder of the bells, it felt like heaven and earth shook. When the bells had quieted down, shouts and cries of hurrah rose from the dark night. Jenny joined in and got the others to join in too. They gave three cheers for the new century. They hollered till the old captain on the second floor opened the window and looked out. Apparently he thought they were paying homage to the landlord. He bowed politely, "Thank you, thank you and the same to you."

After Gunnar had fallen asleep, Emelie and Jenny sat at the table in the light of the kerosene lamp. Emelie had read some words in a newspaper and tried to recall them now. They conveyed a thought that made more sense than this outburst of joy over having the date change.

All the hopes of the people would be fulfilled only if the fruits sown of their labor were those that would ripen in due time. That's what it had said. Emelie thought the words lent meaning to much that had seemed meaningless before. She had often felt that hard work and doing without were in vain. But what if one dared to believe that one day it would yield a harvest?

A fruit that had been sown.

Jenny couldn't help thinking of the child she was expecting. It would be the same age as the new century. If only the child could grow up in a real home! What was weak needed support. Jenny didn't think that she herself had enough strength. She flitted off so easily, got caught up in her dreams. Didn't believe she could create a home. And felt like she had never had a home before this one.

"If Olof has to remain in the hospital—can I stay with you?"

"I'm happy as long as you want to stay," answered Emelie.

"It's the first time I have felt at home anywhere, truly safe."

Emelie looked at the tall and angular girl. Jenny was perhaps impractical, a little sloppy, unsettlingly outspoken and open-minded. Emelie's own ideal looked different. Still Emelie liked her so much.

Maybe all the work and worry over Olof was not without meaning. He had had confidence in her, brought Jenny here—Jenny and the child they were expecting.

Her brothers' children.

Gunnar slept soundly in Emelie's bed. Of course, he had been marked by Johan's treatment. He could be bitter beyond his years sometimes. Still she believed the wounds would heal, that she hadn't come too late.

She didn't dare give way to dreams that were all too bright. Such good things as one wanted to imagine on an evening like this were not what the new century would actually bring. It would surely not be as bad as the old one either, not as hard as the one that had so quickly and mercilessly consumed her parents.

It was time to go to bed. She turned down the lamp.

"Perhaps we can dare hope for a better life for the children of this new century," she said.

Hidden behind the high fence, the city's many small lights shone through the mist.

THE STOCKHOLM CITY MUSEUM

The Stockholm City Museum tells the stories of the city—the buildings, the people and their dreams. It examines the past, the present and the future. The Stockholm City Museum's function is to preserve the city's cultural heritage, bring it to life, and convey it to Stockholm residents, visitors, and future generations. The museum's mission is to deepen your understanding of Stockholm.

The Stockholm City Museum is situated in a 17th century palace next to Slussen, strategically located on Södermalm, the Southern Island of Stockholm. Today, the Stockholm City Museum is Sweden's largest municipal museum and preserves the collections and treasures of the city. Visit the museum's website at: www.stadsmuseum.stockholm.se.

Visit www.stockholmskällan.se to view photographs and illustrations from the times and locations of Per Anders Fogelström's novels in the Stockholm Series. Stockholmskällan is a website where you can access historical and current factual sources that provide information about Stockholm and its populace over the years. On the website you will find photographs, architectural plans and drawings, films and original documents. The website also gives hints about additional reading matter and links to other sources of information.